# Thomas Holland

## in the Realm of the Ogres

by

# K. M. Doherty

Wizard's Mark Press

ISBN-13   978-0-9915720-5-2

LCCN: 2016942435

First Edition: Aug 2016

The Thomas Holland Series
Book 2

Visit the website: www.ThomasHollandBooks.com
Visit us on Facebook: www.Facebook.com/KMDoherty.author
Tweet with the author on Twitter: @authorKMDoherty

Printed in the USA

Cover art by: Daniel Johnson of Squared Motion
www.squaredmotion.com

Map Graphic, Layout & Cover Design by: K. M. Doherty

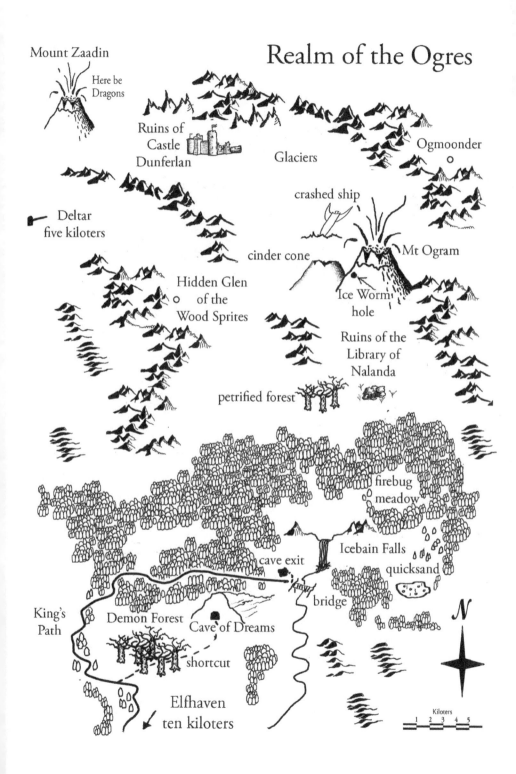

## **** About the author ****

No matter what Bellchar the troll says, K. M. Doherty is the real author of the Thomas Holland series.

KM is a software engineer who has raced sailboats, skied, flew hang gliders, studied martial arts, ridden motorcycles, been a professional musician, and acted in theater. He loves to write, hike, practice Tai Chi, attend plays, and watch way too many movies. KM is a professional public speaker giving presentations at schools, businesses and civic organizations across the country.

He also donates books to children in need.

KM's love of science and technology began in his childhood and continues to this day. He believes that for writing fantasy and magic anything goes, however, for science fiction, the physics must be correct or if more advanced, follow current scientific theories.

Finally, and most important, please remember K. M. Doherty is the true author. Don't listen to Bellchar. As Avani, Goban, and Devraj remind us in this book: HE'S A TROLL!

# Acknowledgements

A huge thanks to everyone who helped make this book possible. First off, to my partner Lin. Without her encouragement and support, and most importantly not saying I was crazy to be an author, I could not have finished this book. Thanks to my close friends and family for taking the time to read an early draft and who gave me important and thoughtful feedback: Lin, Jan, George Callis, and my grandson Travis Marshall who's creative ideas and honest feedback helped a lot. And thanks definitely go to my writer's group consisting of authors Mary Ellen Humphrey and Elliott Baker. They are two excellent writers in their own right, and I'd like to thank them for the countless hours they spent critiquing various versions of my novel. Lastly and most importantly, to my granddaughter Mackenzie Lipe who read several drafts and answered all my questions along with patiently explaining to me the correct usage of kid phrases such as "That's messed up!"

Oh, and I'd like to congratulate the winner of my "Dragon Naming Contest" Charlotte Gauthier for her wonderful dragon name Ninosh. Perhaps you'll even meet Ninosh later in this book? Who can say?

# Contents

One      Treachery, so it begins...      1

Two      Proof, that's the ticket!      9

Three      Misfits in hot water      17

Four      Friend or foe?      21

Five      Playing with mist wraiths      26

Six      Now what?      32

Seven      This is amazing!      34

Eight      The adults have a plan      40

Nine      Busted!      44

Ten      Give us a break      47

Eleven      Running on fumes      49

Twelve      Their own plan      53

Thirteen      The games a foot      59

Fourteen      A trail of two cities      62

Fifteen      So far so bad...      65

Sixteen      The trap is set      71

Seventeen      A fairy springs eternal      73

Eighteen      One step forward, two steps back      78

Nineteen      The cave of nightmares...      83

Twenty      Avani      85

| Twenty-one | Devraj | 88 |
| Twenty-two | Tom | 91 |
| Twenty-three | Goban | 94 |
| Twenty-four | A dream come true? | 96 |
| Twenty-five | The trap's about to be sprung | 101 |
| Twenty-six | You call this a bridge? | 107 |
| Twenty-seven | Just ropes and planks | 112 |
| Twenty-eight | Gone but not forgotten | 116 |
| Twenty-nine | Unlikely allies | 119 |
| Thirty | Here crystal, crystal, crystal | 122 |
| Thirty-one | We're being followed | 128 |
| Thirty-two | The Library of Nalanda | 135 |
| Thirty-three | The hills are alive... | 142 |
| Thirty-four | The end is nigh! | 147 |
| Thirty-five | Mom in hot pursuit | 151 |
| Thirty-six | Déjà vu all over again | 154 |
| Thirty-seven | How soon they forget | 166 |
| Thirty-eight | Avani gets a makeover | 174 |
| Thirty-nine | Play it again, Tom | 180 |
| Forty | Lava, geysers, and ice-worms? | 188 |
| Forty-one | And things were going so well... | 198 |

| | | |
|---|---|---|
| Forty-two | Frozen waterslide from Hades | 202 |
| Forty-three | Ogre hospitality – somewhat lacking… | 213 |
| Forty-four | Trolls honor? | 221 |
| Forty-five | Find Naagesh, we find… | 228 |
| Forty-six | Go now, or feel our wrath! | 237 |
| Forty-seven | Dinosaurs and giant serpents | 244 |
| Forty-eight | A Battle of Titans | 251 |
| Forty-nine | Ready, fire, aim | 256 |
| Fifty | Wisdom in silence | 262 |
| Fifty-one | Open the gates! | 266 |
| Fifty-two | Home, home, yet lost | 273 |
| Fifty-three | A turn for the worse | 278 |
| Fifty-four | All for nothing! | 281 |
| Fifty-five | Shades of Aladdin | 287 |
| Fifty-six | Out of time | 293 |
| Fifty-seven | Never too late | 296 |
| Fifty-eight | A universe apart | 302 |
| Fifty-nine | The Prophecy's over? | 306 |
| Sixty | A few goodbyes | 311 |
| Sixty-one | Time's a wasting! | 318 |
| Epilogue | Library books, long overdue… | 325 |

# Chapter 1: Treachery, so it begins...

Tom ducked as a book magically floated by, narrowly missing his head. "Anything you wanna look for while we're in the library?" he asked Avani.

The Elfhaven library had the usual dry musty smell of old parchment and leather, but an unusual chill surrounded them.

Tom rubbed his hands together vigorously, then placed them into the pocket of his Chicago Cubs hoodie. He gazed at the ceiling high above them. For the hundredth time he stared in awe at the massive crisscross wooden beams that capped the warehouse sized room. The dark ceiling stood in stark contrast to the gigantic windows whose light cast eerie shadows everywhere.

Statues of monsters and strange beasts adorned alcoves along the walls, each looking poised to leap from their pedestals.

"Shush," whispered Avani, brushing a lock of her long golden hair from her face, exposing a tall pointed elven ear. "I want to find a book of maps so we can trace the route the king's expedition is taking."

"The Guardian of the Citadel could show us a 3-D holographic map," suggested Tom.

"I want a book of real maps. One you can touch, feel the roughness of the parchment, hear the crackle as you turn the pages."

Tom shrugged.

A few people sat quietly here and there, though it was late and the library was mostly deserted. Rows of bookshelves towered high above them, but posed no problem for library patrons. All they had to do was ask the librarian for a book and it magically floated to their desk, opened to wherever they'd left off, and even turned the pages for them.

Avani carefully scanned the elvish runes at the head of each aisle. "Where's Goban?"

"He went to the castle to talk to Prince Devraj." Tom still marveled at the fact that just two weeks ago, he'd been in his room in the suburbs of Chicago, putting the final touches on his robot Chloe. He'd always been a nerd and he definitely didn't believe in magic. Well, at least until he went through the portal at Mom's lab and ended up in Elfhaven. Now, only two weeks later, his best friends were Goban, the bright twelve year old son of King Abban, the leader of the dwarf nation, and Avani, an equally bright, magically gifted thirteen-year-old elven girl. Avani was not only the last Keeper of the Light, but also The Chosen One by the Magic Crystals. This would have been totally unbelievable two weeks ago. Now it seemed normal. "Amazing!" he said out loud.

"What?" asked Avani.

"Oh, nothing. Just thinking."

As they turned down a narrow aisle between two tall rows of shelves, a book floated off the stack right in front of Tom. Stopping abruptly, he leaned back doing his best to avoid getting hit. Still, as it passed by the book brushed his nose then pivoted sideways in mid-air and smacked his ear. It was headed in the direction of the librarian's desk. Tom spun around and glared at the ghost who called himself *"The Librarian."* The spirit's gaze immediately dropped to his desk, busying himself with his work. *Did the apparition just smirk?* Tom's frown deepened.

"Come on," said Avani. "What are you waiting for?"

Tom watched the ghost suspiciously for a moment longer, then followed her. "We should've waited for your little brother. He likes the library."

"Kiran isn't interested in maps. He'd much rather be with the adults, searching for the lost magical artifact," she replied.

"So would I," muttered Tom. He paused, then added, "Technically it's not lost. And it's not magic, for that matter. We know where the power source is."

"Yeah, deep in the Realm of the Ogres."

"Hmmm. So where's Kiran, anyway?" asked Tom.

"At home, playing with your pet."

"Kiran and Max sure have taken a liking to each other."

As they strode down the dark aisle, the bookshelves towering above them, Tom reached out and let his fingers flap across the spines of several ancient leather-bound books embossed with ornate gold lettering. The leather felt dry and gave off a faint musty smell.

"I can't read these titles," said Tom. "Isn't the magic supposed to translate the words?"

"Just spoken languages. Many old elvish scripts and runes exist, plus all the dwarvish dialects. I can read five or six. Grandfather claims he can read twelve, but I think he's lying."

"Nadda, lie?" said Tom. "No way."

Avani shrugged.

Tom paused. "So where is this book of maps? I thought you said you could read these signs."

"I can," she said, craning her neck to see down the aisle.

"Why don't you just ask The Librarian?"

"I can find it myself," she said sharply. "Besides, you know how tiresome that ghost can be. Oh, there it is." Avani headed briskly down the row. Tom watched her go.

Two more books flew off the shelves in rapid fire, one on each side of Tom. This time he managed to miss getting slapped in the face by both of them. Tom glanced over his shoulder at The Librarian, but he was talking with someone, looking the other way.

As Tom turned to follow Avani he heard voices in the next aisle. Normally, he would have ignored them, but he thought he heard one of the voices whisper *'the artifact.'* Tom stopped and looked around. No one was watching, so he slid a book off the shelf, leaned casually against the bookcase and pretended to read.

"Did they leave?" said a sinister voice.

"Yes."

"When?"

"This afternoon."

Two voices were speaking, but Tom could barely hear them. A small gap between two large books stood off to his left. Tom scooted over.

"Has *He* been notified?"

"Yes."

"Then the trap is set."

By now Avani was down at the far end of the aisle holding a book and gazing at it intently. Tom tried to catch her attention. *"Pssst,"* he said, waving his own book frantically. She didn't respond. Tom frowned, then leaned against the bookshelf and pretended to read once more.

"We're to meet *Him* tonight," the sinister voice continued.

"Where?"

"The old granary."

"When?"

"Half past midnight."

Tom waved both hands at Avani. *"Pssst,"* he said, a little louder this time. She still didn't notice.

"Did you hear something?" the voice hissed.

"No."

Someone moved in the other aisle. Books were thrown. Suddenly a huge eye peeked through the bookshelf. Tom whipped around, his back to the bookcase. A giant hand thrust through the shelf right beside Tom's head. A ring in the shape of a skull adorned one of the fingers. The skull's eyes began to glow a deep blood red. Books crashed to the floor as the hand thrashed around beside him. Another hand burst through the bookshelf on Tom's other side, scattering still more books. Grabbing Tom's hood in its fist the hand jerked back, slamming Tom hard against the cabinet.

"I've got him!" cried the voice.

"Avani," hissed Tom, his hoodie now tight about his throat. He couldn't breathe. Tom got a glimpse of her but she was still intently studying her book.

The sound of fabric tearing filled his ears. Glancing up in horror, Tom's hoodie tore as the out-thrust fist pulled harder. Raising the book he still held, Tom struck the fist as hard as he could. There was a shriek of pain and the hand lost its grip. Tom dropped to the floor, crawled frantically a few feet then jumped up and rushed down the aisle. Still clutching the book firmly in his right hand he grabbed Avani's arm with his left.

"What?" she said, scowling at him.

Tom gasped for breath, unable to speak. He pulled her quickly behind the bookcase at the end of the row.

"What's going on?" she said.

"Shhhh!" Tom moved over to the edge of the bookshelf. He heard voices arguing down the same aisle they'd just been in, then feet running toward them. Tom glanced around frantically.

"Come on!" Still holding Avani by the arm he ran to some tall potted plants and pulled her down behind them.

"What's—" she began. Tom clamped his palm over her mouth. Slowly rising above the pot he pushed aside a large orange and red stripped frond and cautiously peered out. Two men sprinted around the corner and stopped. Tom got a quick glimpse of them as he released the leaf and hid from view.

They were tall and wore short grey cloaks. Their hoods were up, obscuring their faces, though on one of them a long crooked nose, as if it had been broken, protruded from his dark hood. That same person wore a skull ring. Slowly, one step 'creak,' then another 'creak.' The footsteps grew louder. Then suddenly stopped.

"May I help you?" asked a familiar sing-songy voice.

"Ahhhh—no. We were—just leaving," replied a deep voice.

"That's right. Just leaving," added the other.

Footsteps receded into the distance. The heavy library door echoed as it closed.

The pots in front of Tom and Avani rose from the floor and floated away. The ghost of the library hovered directly in front of them, his arms crossed, his brow furrowed.

As usual, Tom could see right through him. The spirit gave off a faint white glow and the objects behind him warped slightly as The Librarian moved, as if looking through a magnifying glass. Rigid cheek bones and brow framed his face accented by his long elven ears. Adding to his persona were the small round glasses perched far out on his sharp hawk nose. His clothing had the look of an aged college professor's badly wrinkled graduation gown.

"Thanks," said Tom, awkwardly rising to his feet. Avani stood up beside him.

"For what?" asked the Librarian, gruffly.

"For saving our lives," said Tom.

Avani faced him. "What?"

"Um—it's a long story."

The spirit turned and floated down the aisle they'd just come from. Avani and Tom followed behind.

As they walked, Avani's eyes dropped to the cover of the book Tom still carried. "*Mating Habits of the Wild Zhanderbeast?*" She raised an eyebrow.

Tom turned red, then inhaled a deep breath. "No—I. Come on." Tom hurried to catch up with the spirit.

As the ghost neared the spot where Tom had been attacked, he shook his head. A pile of books lay strewn across the floor.

"And what, may I ask, is all this?" The Librarian's scowl deepened.

"It wasn't me," said Tom. "It was them. They reached through the bookshelf, scattering books everywhere. They tried to strangle me. They tore my hoodie."

The ghost glared at him. Tom glanced sidelong at Avani. Her eyes showed concern.

Still glaring at Tom, The Librarian casually flicked his wrist. The books launched up into the air, some flying around the ghost, some through him. For several seconds the books flew around in a flurry colliding with one another till they found their correct slots on the shelf.

The spirit resumed floating down the aisle coming to a hovering rest behind his desk.

Tom sighed, then followed.

"Did you see who those two were?" Tom asked.

"Which two?" said the spirit flatly.

"You know very well which two," yelled Tom. A library patron shushed him.

Tom whispered. "You know very well which two."

The ghost crossed his arms, raised his nose, and tipped his head. "Oh, you mean the two that had you cowering behind a potted plant?"

"Yes! Those two," said Tom. The same patron scowled at him.

"No. To me, all *living* creatures look alike. Besides—" The ghost raised his hand. A book on his desk opened and The Librarian pretended to read. "It's not my job to memorize each and every one of my patrons." The book turned to the next page.

"Why, what's wrong?" Avani asked Tom.

"I overheard two people talking. I'm not sure, I didn't hear the whole conversation, but it sounded like they'd betrayed the king's mission."

"What?" she said.

"At some point they must have figured out I was listening. One of them knocked all those books down." Tom glanced at The Librarian, who glowered at him. Tom added, "And nearly strangled me."

"Come on," said Avani. "We've got to find Goban."

"What about your map?"

# Chapter One

"Never mind the map!" Avani grabbed Tom's hand and pulled him after her.

As they sprinted from the library Tom glanced back. The ghost seemed lost in thought.

## Chapter 2: Proof, that's the ticket!

"So what exactly did you hear?" Goban asked Tom. The three sat on a hard wooden bench in Bandipur Park. Water gurgled from the park's magic fountain. It rose up a few feet then morphed into the liquid filled head of a long dead elven king. The king's mouth moved but he made no sound.

"They spoke of a group that left this afternoon," said Tom. "Then one said he'd spoken to someone else."

Goban's huge bushy eyebrows squished skeptically together into a unibrow as he glanced from Tom to Avani. "That could describe anything. What else did they say?"

"They said—" Tom paused, trying to remember exactly, "The trap is set."

The portly dwarf squinted, his eyes flicking back and forth, considering.

"What's more, they said they'd meet tonight at the old granary at half-past midnight." Tom stared intently at Goban, but when he didn't respond, Tom rushed on, "We've got to warn the palace guards!"

Tom turned to Avani, hoping for support.

She hesitated. "I—I didn't actually hear them."

"You saw the books on the floor. You heard the voices when we hid behind the plants."

Avani glanced at Goban.

The dwarf sighed. "I think we need proof before anyone'll take us seriously."

"But there's no time. The king's expedition is walking into a trap," pleaded Tom.

"How 'bout we drop by the old granary at—say, midnight, a half oort before they arrive," reasoned Goban. "We can hide and find out exactly what's going on."

"If I'm right, that'll be too late." Tom's eyes flashed from one friend to the other.

Goban and Avani didn't respond.

"Fine," said Tom, crossing his arms. "We'll do it your way."

They had time and Goban was hungry, so they went to Avani's grandparents' house to find something to eat. Flickering candles, scattered around the tiny living room, dimly lit the space.

Tom refused the slithertoad pastry that Avani offered him and instead accepted a slice of a dark gray pie which leaned to one side ominously. As Tom cut off a slice it oozed a slimy, green-brown liquid that assailed his nostrils with the smell of rotten eggs. He scrunched up his face, pinched his nose and took a tiny bite.

His face lit up. "Hey, not half bad. Tastes kinda sweet and nutty, with a hint of cinnamon."

He stuffed a large forkful into his mouth. "Wher's Kirn and yer granparnts, eneewaee?"

"Don't talk with your mouth full," said Avani.

"Dat's rit!" added Goban, swallowing a huge mouthful himself. "Say, can I have a slice of that?" Tom slid the pie toward his friend.

Avani glared disgustedly at them both. "I don't know. It's not like them to be out so late."

"Speaking of late," said Tom, glancing at his watch. "Come on. We're running out of time." He gulped down the last bite, then hastily wiped a slimy brown glob from his chin. "It's almost midnight. We've got to get there ahead of them."

Goban and Avani threw on their cloaks. Tom did the same with his hoodie, but the hood drooped to one side.

"Oh, yeah," Tom said. "My hood's torn. Avani, does Nadda or Nanni have a needle and thread?" He twisted his neck and pointed to the tear.

She walked into the kitchen and returned a moment later with a small curved bone needle with a tiny hole in it and a loop of animal gut '*thread.*'

"Sweet!" Tom took the items and stashed them in a pocket on his adventures belt.

Goban watched. "Got your belt with you, I see."

"Course."

Goban placed two fingers to his cheek and looked thoughtfully at Tom. "Let's see. Night vision goggles?"

"Check," said Tom.

"Sky beacon?"

"My flare gun, check."

"Magic light?"

"Electric headlamp, check."

"Folding dagger?"

"Swiss army knife, check."

"Magical talking devices?"

"No. I lent my walkie-talkies to the king."

Goban scratched his head. "Ah—anything else?"

"High tensile strength wire. Mini tool kit, smoke bomb and lighter, and now a needle and thread."

Goban appeared impressed.

Avani glared at them both. "I thought you were worried about being late? Come on." But as she reached for the door knob, the door swung open and in walked her grandmother Nanni, and her grandfather Nadda followed swiftly by her younger brother Kiran and Tom's dog, Max. Nadda took his wife's cloak. He shook it off, causing a small cloud of rain drops to fly in all directions, then placed it on a wildly-curving beast's horn coat rack that stood by the door.

"You're home late," said Avani, quickly lowering her outstretched hand.

11

"Before the king left on his quest," began Nadda, placing his own coat on the rack, "he setup a meeting for the townsfolk. Tonight they instructed us, in the event of an ogre uprising whilst the king's away, the guards will blow three blasts of a blandaloo horn. We're to rush to the castle and leave our belongings behind." Nadda studied Nanni intently, a concerned look in his eyes. Nanni shuddered.

"Ah—I'm sure there's nothing to worry about," said Avani, glancing nervously at Tom.

"Where are you going, child?" asked Nanni, apparently noticing Avani's cloak for the first time.

"To the old granary," blurted Tom.

"Can I go?" Kiran asked, excitedly. Max barked.

Avani glared at Tom. "No. We'll just be a moment. We're—ah—going to make sure everything was put away properly after our last magic class."

Kiran's brow narrowed as he studied his sister suspiciously.

"Oh, child," said Nanni. "It's starting to rain, and it's well past your bedtime. Can't it wait till morning?"

"Larraj forgot to check," Avani lied. "When the wizard left he asked us to make sure all the potions were locked up. We won't be long."

Avani pulled Tom though the door before Nanni could object. Goban hurriedly followed.

"Bye," Avani called over her shoulder, slamming the door behind Goban.

They rushed down the poorly lit street as a gentle rain fell. Dim light reflected off the uneven cobblestones underfoot. Their shoes clacked, echoing eerily off of the magic-infused homes, which expanded and contracted slightly, as they breathed. This gave Tom the creeps, reminding him how alien Elfhaven was compared to Earth.

Goban and Avani's cloaks were long with large hoods that covered their heads. Tom flipped up his own hood and it once again fell sideways, so he held it in place as he ran.

By the time they reached the old granary the temperature had plummeted and the rain was now pouring down. Tom was soaked. What's more, lightning flashed, making the decrepit building look even spookier than usual. Tom shivered.

"I don't remember it being this creepy during magic class," said Tom.

Goban unslung the battle axe that he lovingly called 'Aileen,' from his shoulder and carried it snuggly against his wide belly. "I do."

"Quiet, you two," scolded Avani.

As they approached the granary, lightning flashed and a sudden gust of wind smacked a loose board against the building with a loud 'whack.' The three of them jumped. Tom let out a long, slow breath.

Ahead, the granary door hung slightly ajar. Beside the door stood a stone gargoyle guarding the entryway. The statue's gnarled hands covered its eyes.

Tom kept his gaze fixed on the statue as he walked past, then pushed open the door. It creaked loudly.

"Guys, the gargoyle is covering its eyes," said Tom. He shivered, only partly from of the cold. The others chuckled.

"No, really." Tom glanced back. A flash of lightning illuminated the doorway. The statue had moved. It was now looking directly at him, only its hands covered its ears, its eyes wide, its mouth in a tight circle. Worse—far worse, as the light faded into total darkness, Tom got a glimpse of a hooded figure hunched beside a monstrously shaggy beast.

"Guys." Tom pulled urgently on the back of Goban's cloak.

"Let me guess, the statue moved." Goban pulled away from Tom's grip.

Avani glanced at Goban.

"Yes—No—YES!" Tom gave a muffled scream. "Yes, the statue moved, but there's also someone else out there, and whoever it is has a monster with him."

"We're early. They won't arrive for half an oort. It's probably just the lightning playing tricks with your mind," Avani assured him.

Tom fumbled for the correct pocket on his adventurer's belt. Pulling out his LED headlamp, he placed the strap around his head, flipped it on high, and faced the doorway. A beam of blue-white light illuminated the statue which now had its hands over its mouth. But there was no sign of the hooded figure, or the beast.

Tom addressed the statue, "I get it. See no evil. Hear no evil. Speak no evil. Very funny."

"What?" said Avani.

"Still seeing your ghost?" added Goban.

"It wasn't a ghost," Tom paused. "At least, I don't think so." Tom crept to the door and cautiously peered out into the dark downpour. The rain made loud popping noises as it splattered off the cobblestones. Glancing side to side, the light beam illuminated only vertical slashes of pouring rain.

The other two ignored him and kept moving.

As Tom rushed to catch up with his friends the light from his headlamp slowly faded. "Darn. Batteries must be dead." He pulled it off and slapped it against his palm. "Yup, dead alright." Tom put it away.

Avani conjured up a magical light and sent it floating before them. They couldn't see anyone on the ground floor. Avani, Tom and Goban began climbing the rickety stairs which wound around the cylindrical outer wall of the granary. The floor creaked underfoot. The noise echoed throughout the large open space. They slowly crept upward.

Finally they reached a small platform at the top of the stairs. Tom heard a noise below and peered over the rail. Lightning flashed. Thunder boomed. The silhouette of the hooded figure and his massive beast stood momentarily illuminated on the ground floor.

"Guys!" whispered Tom, swallowing hard. "I'm not kidding. We're not alone."

"We've already been through this," replied Goban. "They won't be here for several myntars."

Tom looked back but the room lay cloaked in darkness once more.

The three hurried across the narrow landing. A tiny room with a plain wooden door stood before them. Avani opened the door a crack. Three heads stacked one on top of the other, peered cautiously inside. Just two weeks ago they'd been studying magic here taught by the evil wizard Naagesh, posing as Professor Snehal, and then, up until a few days ago, from the wizard Larraj. As before in magic class, the room was far larger on the inside than on the outside. Auditorium size, in fact.

Though dark, it appeared outwardly the same, but the room had a new stale moldy smell. Magic made the walls and ceiling transparent and they could just make out the faint silhouettes of tall trees blowing in the violent storm outside. Momentarily a few flickering lights shone from Elfhaven castle off in the distance, then once again the rain and clouds engulfed the horizon. Across the hall the wide stage with its tall podium stood mostly in shadow.

"Come on," said Avani. "Nobody's here. Let's find a place to hide."

She led them down the gently sloping center aisle between rows of wooden chairs. Halfway to the stage she scooched sideways down a row and over to one of the benches they'd used for their magic experiments during class. Several empty cages and large wooden crates lay scattered about.

"Let's stack these boxes and hide behind them," she said. The three quickly rearranged the heavy crates until they had constructed a small barricade.

Avani and Goban sat down behind their makeshift fort.

"Douse your light," said Tom. Avani mumbled a cancellation incantation and flicked her wrist.

Tom glanced back at the door. As the light from Avani's magic slowly faded, a hand reached through the partially open door. The room went completely black.

"They're here," whispered Tom.

Goban exhaled heavily. "Tom, for the last time—" The door creaked. Goban fell silent.

They heard footsteps.

The footsteps grew louder.

The footsteps suddenly stopped.

Avani jumped to her feet as another magic light sprang to life. Goban leapt beside her, his axe at the ready. In the row directly behind them stood the hooded figure, dressed in black, the same figure Tom had seen outside and on the ground floor. The figure slowly reached up, grabbed his hood, and threw it back.

# Chapter 3: Misfits in hot water

"Slow down!" Malak, a mischievous elven boy, hurried to catch up with his best friend Chatur. "The king's soldiers will hear us."

"They won't hear us if you'd stop shouting at me." Chatur hid behind a tree then whirled around to face Malak.

Malak glared at Chatur.

Chatur turned back and peered cautiously around the tree. Up ahead the king's party had stopped near a bend in the road. A heated discussion raged, but the boys were too far away to make out what was being said. Chatur dashed to a closer tree, then peeked around it. A moment later Malak knelt beside him.

"First I tell you we're too close," Malak said. "But instead of moving farther away like a sane elf would do, you get even closer. Are you trying to get us caught?"

Chatur's jaw flexed angrily.

"If we get caught," warned Malak, "they'll send us back to Elfhaven for sure."

"We're too far into ogre territory. They'd have to take us with them now." Chatur frowned. "Why are we even out here in the first place?"

"We're out here because you wanted to see the crashed sky ship, remember?"

"Yeah, but I thought we'd just volunteer for the mission."

Malak laughed. "The king would never let a couple of screw-ups like us, tag along. He wouldn't even let his son Prince Devraj come. No, our only chance is to follow them."

"Devraj is a spoiled brat."

"Yeah, so?"

"So that's probably why the king left him home."

"Because he's a spoiled brat?" Malak snickered.

"Sure, why else?"

"I've heard Devraj sometimes loses it in tense situations."

"What?"

"Yeah, he shuts down. Gets all mopey-like."

"Go on!" Chatur sneered at his friend. "Well, in any case." Chatur puffed out his chest and adopted a regal pose. "If I was king I'd have left Devraj home, too."

"You? King?" Malak snorted, then completely lost it.

Chatur put Malak in a headlock and threw him to the ground where the two rolled around, kicking and snarling. Malak squirmed, trying desperately to break Chatur's choke hold on him.

"Shh!" gasped Malak. "Listen."

"Listen to what?"

Malak tried to speak but only raspy guttural noises came out. Chatur loosened his grip slightly.

Malak inhaled a large breath. "Listen," he repeated. "Tappus is talking with the king."

Keeping his grip tight around Malak's neck, Chatur rolled on top of his friend to get a better view of the king's party.

"I can't breathe," wheezed Malak.

"Shush! I'm trying to listen." Chatur peered through the dense underbrush.

Tappus was bedecked in the garb of a senior ranking palace guard wearing a rich green tunic with a double row of gold buttons. His wide belt held a sword whose ornately carved hilt glistened in a ray of sunlight that somehow managed to penetrate the dense forest. A tattered parchment map crackled as Tappus unrolled it and pointed to a spot near the lower left. "We're halfway to the bridge at Icebain Falls."

"We are making good time, despite our caution," replied King Dakshi, looking questioningly at his lieutenant.

"Yes, but from here on, we must be even more cautious. We're sure to come across ogres soon, and there'll be more and more of the beasts as long as we stay on this road."

"Once we cross the bridge we will leave the road behind and follow little known trails from there. Besides," continued the king, "the wizard Larraj cast a spell to focus unwanted attention elsewhere."

"Speaking of Larraj, where is he?" said Tappus.

"Hmmm, I haven't seen him or his curious monk friend in several myntars."

"That monk is often silent, my lord. I don't like him. And when he does speak he's insolent."

"I agree," said the king, "but I'd give a hundred of my elven warriors for another sword master like Zhang."

Tappus stared off into the forest, then slowly nodded.

Still holding Malak by the throat, Chatur smiled down at him. "Sounds like they don't suspect they're being followed. I told you we could fool them." Before Malak could respond one strong hand grabbed Chatur's shoulder as another clamped down on Malak's. The two were jerked violently to their feet.

"Wizard!" exclaimed Malak.

"Zhang!" chimed in Chatur. Chatur's gaze dropped to a throwing star which hung loosely from the monk's belt. The weapon gave off a yellow glow and pulsed with energy.

The martial arts master followed Chatur's gaze to the star. "Larraj added *magic* to increase the weapon's potency." Zhang Wu adjusted his full-length leather cloak, hiding the object.

Chatur glanced uneasily at Malak. "Ah—we were just wondering if you needed our help."

"Yeah," agreed Malak, swallowing hard. "Need our help."

# Chapter Three

The wizard half frowned, half smiled. "Is that so? Well perhaps we'll let the king decide, see how he feels about you two delinquents *helping* us, shall we?"

# Chapter 4: Friend or foe?

"Kiran!" cried Avani, as he threw back his hood. "I told you to stay home! You nearly scared us to death."

Kiran grinned. "I wasn't going to let you guys have an adventure without me." Max walked up beside him. Kiran bent down and petted Tom's dog. Max shook the rain off himself, drenching everyone.

"That was you and Max outside the granary?" said Tom. Kiran nodded.

"Get over here this myntar and hide with us," commanded his sister. "They'll be here any sectar."

"Who'll be here?" asked Kiran, but before Avani could answer footsteps echoed on the stairway outside.

"Dowse the light," Tom said. The classroom grew dark once more.

"Kiran?" whispered Avani. No answer.

"Kiran?" she repeated.

The door creaked. Two sets of footsteps sounded. Someone carried a flickering torch, its dim light causing an army of distorted, possessed chairs to come alive and traipse across the walls heading toward the center of the hall. A hooked nose protruded from one of the figures hoods and his hand was adorned with a ring in the shape of a skull. The skull's eyes glowed a deep blood red.

"*He's* not here," whispered a deep voice.

"*He'll* be here."

"Why did *he* pick this awful place?"

"Don't know. Don't care."

"If they find out—If they catch us—"

"They won't. Just shut up and wait for *him*."

From his vantage point, the figures were too dark and far away for Tom to make out their faces. He leaned forward, putting his weight precariously on the edge of the crate below, lifting his head so he could see better.

"Who are they talking about?" Tom whispered.

"No idea," replied Goban.

"Shush," said Avani.

Just then the door creaked a third time. The temperature dropped. The torch flickered. Tom couldn't hear any footsteps yet somehow he sensed the person's progression down the aisle. The hairs on the back of Tom's neck stood on end.

The pair of traitors removed their hoods and bowed low. They were elven.

"What did you learn?" hissed the newcomer in a high raspy voice.

"Lord, we did as you asked. We alerted the ogres of the king's mission," said the one with the deep voice.

"They're walking into a trap," added his partner.

"Good. When will the ambush occur?"

"Tomorrow, at dusk."

"Excellent! Where?"

"Near the bridge at Icebain Falls, as you suggested, my lord."

Suddenly the crate Tom was leaning on cracked loudly. Tom lowered his head and rocked back taking his weight off the box. The room went deathly silent. Tom heard whispers. Then silence.

"I'll make sure you two are justly rewarded for your efforts," resumed the high pitched voice. "Once this war is over, you shall be declared heroes, those who helped overthrow a monarchy grown bloated and lazy with—"

Two huge goons kicked the crates aside and grabbed Tom, Goban and Avani. Goban reached for his axe but he was too late. The traitors wrestled the weapon from his hands.

"Well, what do we have here?" said one of the goons.

"Bring them to me. Now!" commanded their leader.

The three were dragged forcefully toward the stage.

Avani struggled against her captor's iron grip. "Let us go," she screamed. "I told my brother if we weren't home in half an oort to send help," she yelled.

Neither captor spoke.

"You'll all rot in the dungeon where the spider-rats will eat your eyes out," said Avani. The nearest goon's stride faltered. He glanced nervously at his partner, but remained silent.

"And if you harm me, or any of my friends, you'll have the entire dwarf nation to contend with." Goban fought to free himself but his hands were pinned to his sides.

"And my uncle Carlos," chimed in Tom. Goban and Avani stared at him.

Tom defended his statement, "You don't want to piss off Carlos."

"Your uncle's on Earth," whispered Goban. "There's nothing he can do."

Tom whispered back, "Yeah, but they don't know that."

As the procession neared the stage the raspy-voiced leader threw back his large billowy cowl from his head.

Avani spat. "Naagesh! You're supposed to be dead."

"As you will soon be," replied the evil wizard coldly. Naagesh studied them one-by-one. "How much did you hear?"

"Enough to know you three will hang for treason," replied Goban.

Avani's eyes flashed to the back of the hall.

One of the thugs threw Goban's axe to the floor, making a loud thump, then pointed at Tom. "That's the one who spied on us in the library."

"What?" yelled the wizard. "Why didn't you seize him?"

The thug cleared his throat nervously. "Ah, we tried but the ghost interfered."

"A ghost? You were afraid of a ghost?" Naagesh glared at his henchmen, his face turning a deep crimson. "What were you afraid The Librarian would do to you? Read you to death?" The wizard fumed. "Why didn't you seize the boy outside the library then?" The two thugs didn't answer.

Avani broke the silence. "When we left the library we informed the palace guards," she said. "They'll be here any myntar."

The evil wizard's eyes scanned the hall. "Will they now? I thought you said your brother would go for help if you were late."

Avani gritted her teeth.

"Perhaps, instead of informing the guards as you should have, you foolishly decided to take matters into your own hands." The wizard gave them a sick smile.

One of Naagesh's lackeys shook Goban violently. "Shall I kill them, my lord?"

The wizard paused. "Not here. Not now. Lock them in the storage cabinet on the back wall."

"But they can identify—" began the henchman.

Before the goon could finish, brilliant emerald green bands of magical energy leapt from Naagesh's hands and encircled the henchman. Tighter and tighter the bands wrapped, until the goon was bound head to foot in sparkling green energy that pulsed and surged. Naagesh whipped his wrist back and the man shot toward him stopping only when his face was a mere inch away from Naagesh's.

"Never—question—my orders—again," hissed the wizard through clenched teeth. "Do I make myself clear?"

The magical strands arced and popped and began to give off a foul smelling smoke where they touched the elf's bare skin.

The goon shook his head emphatically. "Yes, Lord Naagesh."

The wizard glared at him a moment longer, then his hand shot up, releasing the magic. The bright glow faded and the man crumpled to the floor, still smoking.

"If you'd have let me finish, I was about to say—after we're done here, take them out beyond the barrier. Tie them up and cut them up a little. Just a touch of blood, mind you. The scent will attract mist wraiths. They will do our work for us." Naagesh sneered coldly.

Avani glanced toward the back of the hall again.

"What is it?" said the wizard, studying her. "Expecting someone?"

"Yes," she said defiantly. "I already told you. I'm expecting the king's guards to burst through the door any myntar."

Naagesh's steely eyes bored into hers for several long seconds. "Lock them up," he commanded. "Then search the premises. Make sure no one else is hiding about."

## Chapter 5: Playing with mist wraiths

Tom strained to listen in the dark, cramped cabinet. Naagesh was having a heated discussion with his lackeys, but they were too far away for him to hear everything. Tom just got bits and pieces of their conversation: King Dakshi, the wizard Larraj, the barrier, the artifact, ogres, his mom, Tom himself.

Things suddenly went quiet.

"I think they've finished talking," whispered Tom.

"What shall we do?" asked Goban. "They took Aileen."

"It's OK. I'm sure Kiran understood and went for help," said Avani. "He won't fail us, you'll see. The guards will be here soon."

Before they could discuss it further, a loud commotion in the hall caught their attention.

"See," she said. A moment later footsteps strode purposefully toward the cabinet. A chain rattled. A metal bar clattered on the hardwood floor.

Tom, Avani and Goban huddled together in the dark. Tom realized the thugs hadn't taken his adventurer's belt. Frantically, he searched for the pocket that contained his Swiss army knife. Before he could find it, though, the door swung outward. The three squinted against the unaccustomed torchlight.

"Kiran," cried Avani. "You did it. You brought help!"

Kiran stood before them, a deep frown on his face. One of Naagesh's henchmen stepped from behind the door, a tight grip on Kiran's arm.

"Thought you might like some company," said the traitor. He shoved Kiran forcefully into the cabinet and slammed the door. The chain rattled as they were locked in once more.

"Kiran," said Avani, disappointment in her voice. Her brother lowered his head and turned away.

"What happened?" asked Tom.

Kiran spoke softly, "They left the door ajar. I'd almost made it when they grabbed me from behind." Kiran didn't meet his sister's gaze.

Resting his hand on Kiran's shoulder, Tom said, "It's OK. We'll find a way out."

Tom pushed on the cabinet doors. They flexed outward slightly, opening a small gap between them. He peered through the gap.

"There's a chain. It's been threaded through the two door handles, and a long bar stuck between two links of the chain. That's how they locked us in." Taking out his knife Tom opened the saw blade. Pushing the blade through the gap he caught the chain and pulled it slowly toward the cabinet.

"Just a tad more." The chain slipped, swinging out then back in. It hit the cabinet door with a '*bang.*' Tom held his breath. Hearing no footsteps he relaxed and tried again. This time he brought the chain quietly up to the doors.

"Now if I can just—" he said, twisting the saw blade sideways. "If I can spread the links far enough apart, maybe the bar will slip out of one side."

"It's starting to move! Almost there." One side of the chain slipped free. The bar dangled precariously.

"So far so good." Tom pushed on the door and it opened enough so he could reach through and grab the chain.

"Got it!" Pulling in the chain it made a soft clacking noise as the links passed over the door handles. Tom carefully reached for the bar. As his finger brushed it, the rod slipped and fell to the floor making a loud clatter. Footsteps headed their way. Tom hissed, then hastily folded up his knife and stashed it away. The door flew open.

"What's going on in here?" said a henchman. No one spoke.

"No matter." He grabbed Kiran and Goban and yanked them out of the cabinet. The second goon did the same with Tom and Avani. "Time to play with mist wraiths."

From the stage, Naagesh regarded Tom and his friends smugly.

"Proud of your minions, are you?" said Tom.

Before the wizard could respond someone banged loudly at the hall's main door. A second later the door burst inward, shards of broken wood flying in all directions. Max charged in, leading several palace guards. The dog bolted straight for the henchman. Leaping into the air he landed square on the closest goon, knocking him to the floor. Max bared his teeth, growled and slobbered.

Two guards grabbed for the second henchman. He sidestepped them, punched one in the stomach, causing the guard to double over, then the traitor stuck out his foot as he pivoted, tripping the second guard. The henchman took the opportunity to run for the side door. But as he neared the exit the door burst open and half a dozen more guards stormed in. The goon struck out at the nearest one, but several guards tackled him, pinning him to the ground. He struggled for a moment then lay still.

Max stepped back as two guards grabbed the first henchman and jerked him to his feet. Dog slobber covered the traitor's face.

"Max?" said Tom, wonder in his voice. Max barked then walked over and raised his paw. Tom laughed, took his paw and shook it vigorously. "Good boy, Max! I forgot all about you."

Kiran knelt down and hugged the dog.

One of the king's head palace guards marched up holding a flaming torch.

"Sanuu. How did you find us?" asked Tom.

"Your beast. He wouldn't stop bellowing until we followed him."

Suddenly remembering, Tom twisted around to face the stage. "Where's Naagesh?"

"What?" cried Sanuu, drawing his sword.

"He was right there." Tom pointed to the now empty stage. "These henchmen were just the evil wizard's puppets."

Avani and Goban looked around nervously.

Sanuu signaled his men. Several of them dashed around the hall searching. A few minutes later they returned. They faced Sanuu, then shook their heads, no.

"Sanuu," said Goban, hurriedly. "Someone's got to warn the king. These traitors told the ogres about the expedition. The king's walking into a trap. It's set for tomorrow, at dusk."

Sanuu turned to his men. "Take these traitors to the dungeon. Lock them up, then find Prince Devraj. Tell him to meet me in the castle's great hall. I'll awaken the troops." His men dragged the traitors toward the door.

Sanuu stormed after them, then stopped, "Are you four OK? Do you require assistance?"

"No, we're good," said Tom.

Sanuu nodded, then pivoted smartly on his heel and strode up the aisle.

"Wait," cried Tom. Sanuu stopped and turned back.

"Can we come with you? We want to help."

"Do you have more information for us?"

"Well, not exactly."

Sanuu regarded them. "Then no, this is a military matter now. You children were a great help. Now leave this to the adults."

"But—" began Avani.

"That's an order!" snapped Sanuu. He turned on his heel and hurried from the hall.

They stared at his retreating form till he exited the hall.

Goban bent down and picked up Aileen, "They didn't hurt you did they, girl?" Goban kissed the flat side of his axe. Tom glanced sidelong at Avani. She looked as if she might throw up.

Replacing Aileen on his shoulder Goban said, "Come on."

They started walking toward the exit.

"Kiran, would you take Max back to Nadda and Nanni's house and get him some food and water?" said Avani. "He deserves it after rescuing us." Avani faced Tom. Tom nodded.

Kiran's eyes lit up. "Come on Max." The two of them dashed from the hall.

After they'd gone, Tom said, "You wanted to lose your brother, huh?" Avani gave him a wry grin and nodded, then the three headed toward the exit.

As they passed the stage, Tom saw a large painting encased in an ornate gold frame hanging on the wall. In all the excitement before, he hadn't noticed it. Tom squinted at the painting. It was a dark portrait of someone. The face, though mostly in shadow, gazed outward with a haunting look. The painter's heavy use of shadow with only a hint of light reminded Tom of pictures he'd seen of Rembrandt paintings back on Earth. But this one lacked the same rich warm glow that Rembrandt paintings had. This light felt cold and harsh. Oddly, the person in the painting looked vaguely familiar. But the canvas appeared stained and badly in need of cleaning. *It must be at least a hundred years old. No way I could recognize who it is.*

"That's odd," said Tom.

"What?" asked Goban, as they continued on their way.

Tom shrugged. "Nothing." Striding past the stage, Tom kept staring at the painting. Something about it gave him the creeps. When they neared the exit, he glanced back one more time. *Had the eyes moved?* He shook his head, then followed his friends onto the landing and down the stairs.

\* \* \*

Once the echoes of everyone's footsteps had faded into total silence, the painting shook for a moment. The face in the picture flexed the canvas outward as if trying to break free. Then suddenly the whole picture, frame and all, dissolved into a thick, greasy black swirling cloud. The cloud rotated slowly as it floated off the platform, up the main aisle and through the doorway.

# Chapter 6: Now what?

"You heard Sanuu," said Tom. "They don't want us here."

"We've never done what the adults told us before. Why start now?" Avani replied. Goban snorted.

When they arrived at the castle's main gate, the courtyard was in total chaos. Soldiers dashed everywhere. Weapons clanked and leather creaked as sword belts and quivers of arrows were hastily lashed tight. Aides hurried to pass out swords, long bows, and crossbows. Horses whinnied and steam drifted from their nostrils as the beasts pawed the ground, eager to be off.

Tom struggled to keep up with Avani as she wove her way through the crowded square, then hurried up the steps to the castle's main hall. Two palace guards stood at attention on either side of the massive doors. As Avani, Goban, and Tom approached the doorway, the guards stepped in front of them.

Avani cleared her voice. "Let us pass."

"I'm sorry, but a traitorous plot has been discovered. An emergency military tribunal is about to begin. Only authorized personnel are allowed in."

"We know. We're the ones that discovered the plot," Avani replied.

The guard didn't flinch. "I'm sorry miss, orders."

Goban stepped forward. "I'm Prince Goban, King Abban's son. In case you are unaware, he's the supreme leader of the dwarf nation."

"We know who you are, Prince Goban," the Guard gave a slight nod.

Goban continued, "As Avani said, we uncovered the plot, and we've got valuable information that may help."

The guard glanced at his partner, shifting his weight uncomfortably. "I'm sorry your highness. If you care to wait, I'll inform Sanuu that you wish to speak with him—after their meeting."

"But—" began Goban. Avani placed her hand on his shoulder and gently pulled him back.

"Come on," she said. "They obviously don't want our help."

Goban glared at the guards a moment longer, then whipped around and stormed down the steps. The others followed.

"Why are you smiling?" Tom asked Avani.

Glancing back she whispered, "I used to live in the castle, remember? There are—" she winked at them, "—secret passageways."

# Chapter 7: This is amazing!

By now the storm had passed and starlight dimly illuminated the way ahead. Avani led them through a narrow alley that circled behind the castle. She stopped before a stone gateway with an ornate arched top. A tall, lush green hedge grew in a courtyard just beyond the gateway. Carved into the rock archway was a triangular wedge with squiggly lines rising above it.

"What's that symbol?" asked Tom.

"Not sure." Avani gazed up at the arch. "Maybe a hot tart fresh from the oven? The curvy lines could be steam." She sounded uncertain.

"But why above the gateway?"

Avani shrugged, then led them under the arch and into the courtyard. It was warm and humid in here and the dense green shrubs smelled faintly of vanilla, reminding Tom of a Ponderosa Pine forest back on the west coast of the United States. A two-foot wide opening in the hedge lay just ahead.

"Come on," Avani said, hurrying into the opening. Once through, another thick green wall of leaves blocked their path. This one had three openings, equally spaced, ten feet apart.

"This is amazing!" said Tom. "Get it? A-maze-ing."

"We got it," she said, sighing. Goban shook his head. Avani turned right, walked to the third opening and stepped through. Tom followed.

"You know the difference between a maze and a labyrinth, don't cha?" asked Tom. Goban gave him an inquisitive look.

"With a maze, like this one, there's lots of dead ends and false paths, with only one correct way through."

"Yeah, so?" said Goban.

"With a labyrinth there's only one path. You can't get lost. It's not trying to trick you."

"What's the fun in that?"

"A labyrinth isn't for fun. It's meant to be relaxing, calming. Gives you time to think. Sort of a meditation."

"Sounds boring," said Avani, pausing for a moment at the branch of two paths that veered off in different directions. A sharp pointed stone jutted up from the ground in front of them.

"Avani, how do you know where to go?" asked Goban.

"When we were kids, Kiran and I spent hours exploring the maze. Once we figured it out I memorized the pattern. I just count the number of openings that make up the sequence."

Five openings stood on the left, four on the right. Avani turned left at the rock then briskly strode to the first opening and entered. There she turned right, walked down the aisle, counting out-loud as she went. When she reached the fourth opening she once again stepped through.

"Hmmmm," said Tom, lightly touching Avani's arm, stopping her. "So, starting off, you took the third opening. Then at the pointed rock you took the first opening. Last time you took the fourth opening." She nodded. A broad smile crossed his face. Suddenly he bolted through the first opening, the others hurried after. Without hesitating, Tom raced down the row and into the fifth branch then he sprinted clear to the end and took the last, the ninth pathway.

Avani and Goban rushed through the final opening and abruptly stopped beside Tom. A dark green, broad-leafed climbing plant with tree-frog style suckers griped the building, covering most of the back wall of the castle. One of the suckers released, reached up and reattached itself a half-inch farther up the wall, pulling the leaf with it.

Water splashed in a pool to their left. Droplets flew everywhere. When they landed on Tom's hands or face they felt cool and moist. A giant statue of a white unicorn rearing up on its two hind legs stood before them. Water gushed from its open mouth, falling into a miniature sculpture of Elfhaven castle, then flowed from the castle's main gate into the pool below. A few flowering water plants, in blues and pinks, floated here and there and several two headed purple salamanders and bug-eyed orange and red striped fish swam in the crystal clear pool.

Tom bent down and touched one of the flowers. Its petals felt soft and fuzzy and the flower smelled of Jasmine. The place reminded him of a greenhouse, damp and peaceful. Tom inhaled deeply.

"How did you know where to go?" asked Avani, looking astonished.

"It's simple as Pi." Tom's lip curled up into the hint of a smile.

"What?"

"That wasn't a tart on the archway. It was a slice of pie. Someone had a sense of humor."

Avani and Goban stared blankly at each other.

"3.14159 is an important mathematical number. It's represented by the Greek letter Pi." The others remained silent. Tom picked up a stick and scribed a circle on the ground. Then he drew a straight line through the circle. "If you multiply the diameter," Tom tapped the stick on the line, "by Pi—3.14159—you get the circumference of the circle. He traced the outline of the circle with his stick. Of course Pi has an infinite number of digits after the decimal point, but that doesn't really matter here. Pi is used in tons of mathematical formulas." Tom scanned their blank faces. "Probably more evidence of the crosstalk between our universes that the Guardian mentioned before," Tom dropped the stick and rubbed his hands together. "So, anyway, we're here. What now?"

Avani glanced at Goban, then stepped forward. Placing her hand firmly on the upraised hoof of the unicorn, she pushed hard. Slowly, the leg pivoted backward from the knee down. A deep grinding noise emanated from a small section of the wall as it swiveled inward. Now it was Tom and Goban's turn to look astonished. Avani beamed happily at them.

"Watch your head," she said, pushing aside some of the frog ivy. The suckers popped softly as they released from the wall. She stepped through the foliage, disappearing into the darkness beyond.

Barely visible in the dim light coming from outside, several pitch-covered torches lay scattered on the dusty floor. Total darkness lay beyond. Avani picked up one and muttered an incantation. Instantly flames shot up a foot above the torch. The flickering yellow glow illuminated a narrow passage, but only extended far enough to see a few feet ahead.

"That's awesome," said Tom. "Can you teach me?"

"What?" she said.

"Teach me to use magic to make flames." Tom looked expectantly at her.

She peered over at Goban and paused. "Sure." She bent down, picked up two more firebrands and handed them to Tom and Goban.

"First," she said. "Speak these words slowly, with total focus, just like professor Schnel—errr—Naagesh, taught you. Then say the following words in this exact order: mea infantem venit ad lucem ignis."

Tom looked down, concentrating hard, repeating the unfamiliar words over and over in his mind. Finally, he raised his head, looked straight at the firebrand and boomed the words, "Mea infantem venit ad lucem ignis." Instantly both his and Goban's torches burst into brilliant flames, two feet high. At the same time several smaller flames ignited on the floor around them. Goban and Tom danced around like possessed break-dancers, madly stomping on the flames until those on the floor went out.

Avani stared at Tom.

"Sorry," he said, looking sheepishly first at Avani, then at Goban.

Avani continued to stare at him. Goban's brow rose.

"What?" said Tom. Neither of the others spoke.

Finally Avani faced Goban. "You want to try?"

He laughed. "No, I'm good." Then he changed the subject, "How did you ever find this place?"

"Kiran and I were playing. He pushed me and I fell backward against the single horned beast."

"The unicorn," said Tom.

"Un-i-corn," repeated Avani.

"You don't have unicorns here? Ahhh—beasts like that?"

Avani shook her head.

Tom responded, "Yet you've got a statue of one. Weird."

"Do you have—Unicorn's, back on Earth?"

"Well, no. At least, not anymore."

"The topic of mythical beasts," began Goban, "fascinating as it may be, isn't getting us any closer to hearing the guards' plans."

Avani nodded, then led them down a long, narrow passageway. As they treaded lightly onward, their torches cast elongated shadows that bobbed along beside them. Stones and rough wooden beams crisscrossed their path, causing them to crawl under some and over others. Avani brushed aside a mass of dust covered cobwebs. Several huge hairy spiders, with armored spikes on each leg joint, scurried up into the rafters and across the floor. Ignoring the creatures, she turned a corner to her right. One of the spiders crawled up her back, headed for her neck.

"Ahhh—Avani," said Tom. He reached out, but couldn't bring himself to touch it. "Avani!"

Goban reached over and flicked the spider off her back. Goban grinned, then followed Avani.

Tom swallowed hard, glanced around nervously, then stepped right into a massive cobweb.

"Get them off me," he screamed, frantically trying to pull the sticky web off his face and hair.

A second later Avani pulled off the web and brushed off several spiders. "They won't hurt you," but she added, "Unless of course you startle them."

Moving on, Avani stepped under a rough wooden crossbeam, her torch flames momentarily engulfing the beam above her.

"Aren't you worried these flames will start a fire?" asked Tom.

Avani faced him and pushed the torch toward his face. Instinctively, Tom raised his hand and turned away. The flames surrounded his hand and—nothing happened. No pain, no burning. It wasn't even warm.

"They're magical flames," she said. "They give off light but no heat." She continued on.

Soon they came to an intersection. Passageways branched off to their right and left. As they stepped into the junction a high-pitched screech stopped them cold. Tom looked down. Avani stood on the tail of one of those rat-from-hades creatures, the ones with mangy clumps of spiky blue hair.

"Sorry," she said, raising her foot. The animal bared his teeth and hissed at her, then scampered off into the darkness to their right. As it scurried away, the echoes of its tiny claws scratching the floorboards faded.

"Where do we go now?" asked Tom. "Not right, I hope."

Avani pointed over her head. "Up." Tom and Goban's heads fell back in unison. The flickering torchlight exposed a rickety wooden ladder that disappeared into the blackness above. Tom began to sweat.

# Chapter 8: The adults have a plan

Tom reached slowly upward, carefully feeling for the next rung of the ladder in the near total darkness. *We must have climbed up at least three stories by now.* It was hard holding the torch in one hand, leaving only the other hand to reach upward. *At least it's too dark to see down. It's not as scary if I can't see down.* Goban stood directly above him. Suddenly, the rung Goban was standing on cracked ominously. An instant later the rung broke and Goban's heavy foot slammed down on Tom's hand.

"Aaahhhh!" screamed Tom.

"Quiet," scolded Avani.

"But Goban's standing on my hand!"

The dwarf shifted his weight and removed his foot. Tom shook his hand vigorously.

"Sorry," whispered Goban.

Avani groaned. "You two are as bad as Malak and Chatur."

"No one's that bad," replied Goban, sounding insulted.

"Come on," she said, "we're almost there."

Mindful of the broken step, Tom eased his way up the last ten feet, then pulled himself onto a wide platform. Above them the cold stone roof of the castle sloped off behind them. Massive wooden rafters, a few feet apart, supported the heavy structure above. Light filtered in from tiny cracks in the inner wall. A cold draft wafted around them. The draft, combined with their footsteps, stirred up dust which danced in the stark light. The faint sound of voices emanated from just beyond the wall ahead.

"I think I can hear Sanuu's voice," whispered Goban.

"And Prince Devraj's," added Avani.

"What now?" asked Tom.

"This way." Avani strode briskly to the right. The castle roof, now low

40

and directly above them, forced them to walk hunched over. After climbing through several more rafters they rounded a corner and entered a small alcove. The voices grew louder. Avani flipped four latches then carefully pulled on a section of wallboard and lifted it free. She set the panel aside then muttered an incantation. The three torches extinguished. They set them down.

"How did you ever find—" began Tom. Avani touched her finger to his lips, hushing him. She motioned for Tom and Goban to scooch up beside her. The back side of a huge statue of a multi-horned beast stood directly in front of them, blocking their view. Avani slipped out behind the statue, then crawled a foot or so to a short railing at the edge of a narrow balcony. Tom followed her, but Goban struggled hard to squeeze his wide girth past the statue. A moment later, slowly and in unison, three heads rose up above the railing and peered down into the great hall. Several massive candelabras lit the wide space.

"We should send a legion of troops on horseback," said one of the king's chief advisors. He sat directly below them at a small table across from Sanuu and Prince Devraj.

"The trail they're on is not passable by horse," argued Sanuu.

"The path they took is long and winding," countered the advisor. "A legion of elven warriors on foot will never reach them in time."

Prince Devraj cleared his throat. "There is a quicker route."

Sanuu stammered, "You don't mean…"

"Through Demon Forest," finished Devraj.

"Sire," began Sanuu, looking alarmed. "With all due respect—you can't be serious."

The prince paused, glancing from one to the other. "It halves the distance."

"Yes my lord, but—"

"I will take a small contingent of soldiers," the prince rushed on. "We'll be at the bridge by mid-day."

The advisor drew a deep breath. "A small contingent may not be enough. We don't know how many ogres we're up against."

"Besides," added Sanuu. "No one has ever survived that accursed Demon Forest without the protection of a wizard, and the only wizard we have is currently with the king."

"But—" began Devraj.

Sanuu cut him off. "No, I will take a legion of our finest via the same path the king took, but we will go with all due haste. The king's party is moving slowly, stealthily. If we hurry we may yet catch them before they reach the bridge."

"May yet catch them?" spat Devraj. "May yet catch them is not good enough. We *must* catch them!" The prince sat rigid, his eyes locked in battle with his father's men. The others calmly held his gaze. After a tense moment Devraj spoke, "Fine, but I will lead the expedition."

Sanuu paused, fidgeting slightly.

The prince continued, "My father placed me in charge of Elfhaven castle in his absence."

"And he put me in charge of his army," countered Sanuu. "This is a military matter. It's my decision."

The prince leapt to his feet. "I am Prince Devraj and heir to the throne."

"You are." Sanuu sighed. "Prince Devraj, ahhh—sire." Sanuu bowed, glancing sidelong at the advisor for support.

"What Sanuu is trying to say," chimed in the advisor, "and there's no tactful way to put this—is that your father feels you are not yet ready to lead."

Devraj turned a dark shade of crimson.

"And," broke in Sanuu, "he feels it most important that you remain safely in Elfhaven. After all, if something were to happen to his majesty, the gods forbid, the kingdom must have a ruler. But if you should both be captured—or worse…"

The prince glared at them both for a moment then jumped to his feet and stormed from the room. The great hall door slammed behind him.

In the balcony above, three small heads slowly sank back down below the railing. Goban, Tom and Avani scooted over near the wall.

Goban leaned back against the statue. "Well, what shall we do now?" Under the dwarf's ample girth, the horned beast tipped precariously. Tom and Avani grabbed the statue, straining desperately to keep it from falling. It tipped still farther. Goban swiveled round, realized what was happening and grasped it too. The three struggled for several long seconds. Finally, the statue thumped back into place, rocked a couple of times, then stopped.

"Whew, that was close," said Tom.

Avani nodded.

Goban grinned sheepishly at the others. "Sorry. Hey, at least no one heard us."

"What was that noise?" said a voice from below.

"It came from the balcony." The hall erupted with the sound of swords being drawn and guards thundering up the staircase.

# Chapter 9: Busted!

"I must send you back to Elfhaven." King Dakshi looked angrily at Chatur and Malak. The pair stood before him, held firmly by the Wizard Larraj and the sword master monk Zhang. "You two have endangered our mission. If ogres heard you following us they would have been alerted to our presence. If our mission fails, all of Elfhaven is lost."

"We didn't mean any harm." Chatur shifted his weight uneasily.

"Yeah, we just wanted to see the star craft," added Malak. "Besides—"

Chatur cut him off, "Besides, you might need our help."

"Yeah, our help," agreed Malak, glaring at Chatur for cutting him off.

"Help? From you two?" Tappus laughed. "What could you two delinquents possibly do to help us?"

"Ahhh—we're small, and—" Chatur looked to Malak for support.

"Light weight—" continued Malak tentatively.

"And—well—maybe the entrance to the star craft is tiny."

"Right," agreed Malak. "Maybe the aliens are miniature bug-eyed monsters. We'd be just the pair to get into a tight spot."

"You're already in a tight spot," said Tappus.

"We could do the cooking," said Malak.

"And carry supplies," added Chatur. The two friend's heads bobbed in unison, as they stared expectantly at the king.

A hint of a smile flicked across King Dakshi's face, and disappeared just as quickly. He took a deep breath. "No. For your own safety, and to insure you two do not unwittingly jeopardize our mission, I am sending you back to Elfhaven." The king faced Tappus. "Choose two men to escort these troublemakers back home. Make sure they don't elude your men and try to follow us again."

"Sire," said Tappus. "With all due respect, we can't afford the loss of two men, not this deep into ogre territory."

"What do you suggest?"

Tappus twisted so that only the king could see him. He grinned and winked. The smile dropped as he faced the children. "We could tie them to a tree, your highness. We would then untie them on our way back from retrieving the artifact."

The king adopted a serious look. "But what if ogres find them first?"

"Hmmmm, they'd torture them into revealing our plans."

Chatur and Malak's eyes popped open.

"Exactly." The king rubbed his chin, considering.

"We could cut out their tongues," suggested Tappus.

"A bit drastic, don't you think?"

Sweat dripped off Malak and Chatur's faces.

Tappus tipped his head sideways and shrugged.

A similar grin dropped from Larraj's face as the wizard stepped from behind the two boys. The wizard cleared his throat. "Might I make a suggestion."

"Please," said the king.

"I could turn them into toads. That way they couldn't tell the ogres our plans. Once we retrieve the artifact, I can change them back. If, of course—" the wizard bent toward the two, knowingly. "The ogres haven't roasted them and eaten them as a delicacy."

"Good idea," agreed the king.

The two friends turned white, gulped air, and started shaking. Larraj raised his staff. The golden owl atop it rotated toward the pair and blinked. Blue lightning raced around the staff, glowing brighter and brighter.

"No, wait!" cried Malak and Chatur in unison.

Malak blurted out, "We won't be any trouble. We promise! We'll be quiet as linterbat pups."

"Yeah, linterbat pups," agreed Chatur, nodding vigorously.

The king paused, then signaled the wizard to stop. Larraj lowered his staff. The magic slowly faded.

"All right. You may stay with us, but you must remain totally silent the whole way," said the king, earnestly. "And you will do exactly as commanded. Agreed?"

The two nodded. "We promise."

The king glanced at his lieutenant. Tappus rolled his eyes.

# Chapter 10: Give us a break

The great hall boomed as several guards raced across the narrow balcony. A moment later the sound stopped.

"There's no one here," said a voice.

A faint scraping noise sounded from the far end of the balcony.

"Over there!" yelled a guard. The footfalls grew louder.

"Quick!" whispered Tom.

Avani hurriedly slid the secret panel back in place then she and Goban reached over and latched it.

"Got it." Avani secured her second latch and leaned back, wearing a smug grin.

Tom nodded to her.

Goban however, looked horrified. Extending his fist he turned his hand over. Slowly opening his fingers his palm held a broken latch.

"It came from over here," said a voice, just outside. A loud scrapping sound signaled the statue outside being moved.

Avani looked at Goban and mouthed the words, "Which one?" He pointed to the upper right-side latch. As one, the three leaned forward and pushed on the upper corner. But at the same time someone on the other side began pushing in. Even with the combined strength of all three friends the panel slowly began to flex inward.

"Over here," yelled a guard's strained voice. "Help me."

Tom began to panic. Making matters worse, one of the spikey blue haired rats scampered up beside them.

Sweat dripped from Tom's forehead. "What a nice ugly rat," whispered Tom, to the critter. "That's a good boy." The rat from hades hissed, exposing long razor-sharp teeth, then charged straight for him. Tom, kneeling by the wall awkwardly tried to kick the creature away. The rat opened its mouth wide then bit down hard on the outstretched sole of Tom's Converse sneaker. Tom shook his foot vigorously but the creature just flailed about, not letting go.

"Goban, get him off me," Tom mouthed.

"Who, me?" mouthed back the dwarf. Goban didn't move, he just stared at the ugly creature. All-the-while the pressure kept increasing on the panel they struggled to hold shut.

"Boys," whispered Avani. In one quick move she let go of the panel, grabbed the rat behind its neck while simultaneously pulling its tail. The critter immediately released its death-grip on Tom's sneaker and hissed loudly, bearing its teeth at her. By this time, without her help, the panel had flexed inward three inches. Avani tossed the creature out the opening then once again helped her friends push.

Several things happened at once: immediately the pressure released from the panel, slamming it back in place. Curses and stomping feet sounded just beyond the wall, accompanied by a loud chittering noise.

"The noise was just a devil-rat," yelled a voice.

"So get it," called someone else.

"You get it," cried yet another. The sound of footsteps madly chasing the hissing creature around the balcony, then down the staircase, slowly died away. A few minutes later the main door slammed shut as everyone exited the hall. All was quiet.

Tom, Avani and Goban leaned back, let out a collective sigh, then simultaneously burst into a fit of uncontrollable laughter.

# Chapter 11: Running on fumes

"Avani, do you have your key with you?" Tom asked, as they walked down a narrow back alley. By now the asteroid belt the locals called the Ring of Turin had risen. At night it reflected sunlight, just like the Earth's moon does. But the many different sized asteroids, rotating at various speeds, twinkled like diamonds and easily provided enough light to make out the outlines of buildings nearby.

"The key to the Citadel?" Avani looked over at Goban.

Tom nodded.

She reached inside her tunic and pulled out a blacker-than-black star shaped object. "Why?"

"I've got some questions for The Guardian."

After a ten-minute hike past the Elfhaven homes that seemed to be constantly watching them, past the odd clock tower that showed the exact time in three different universes, and Bandipur park, they arrived at the Citadel. Avani placed the key in its matching star-shaped indentation in the entryway wall. A deep hum sounded beneath their feet. The ground vibrated in time with the hum. Suddenly the wall before them vanished.

Stating their names as they entered, to avoid what Tom called the "Indiana Jones style trap junk," Goban, Tom and Avani treaded down the long dimly lit corridor leading to the Citadel's main chamber.

They walked the last few feet to the Citadel's control room with only the echo of their footsteps to mark their passage.

The central console stood in the middle of the large round chamber with its brightly lit panels, displays, blinking lights and tall crystals that jutted out at odd angles. There was no sign of The Guardian.

"Guardian," called Tom. "We've got some questions for you."

# Chapter Eleven

A door creaked then slammed followed by footsteps that grew steadily louder. A moment later The Guardian appeared. This time he was dressed as a wizard, complete with pointy hat and tall gnarled staff. As always, they could see through his 3-D holographic image. Tom was pretty sure the door and footstep sounds were just for show.

The Guardian scanned their faces. "I did not expect to see you three here again so soon."

"The king wouldn't let us go with him," replied Tom.

"Ah, then what can I do for you?"

"Show us that map again," began Tom. "The hologram you showed us before. The one with the crash site."

The fake *'wizard'* waved his staff and a 3-D map of Elfhaven and its surrounds filled the space in front of them. Tom rolled his eyes at The Guardian's theatrics then walked through the picture of Elfhaven castle and up to the middle of the scene. Tom pointed to a red *'X'* which floated in the air before him.

"Is this it?" Tom asked.

"Yes,"

"The crashed space ship?"

"Correct," said The Guardian.

Goban stepped up beside Tom and pushed his finger through the picture. The red *'X'* warped across the hairy backs of the dwarf's stout hands. Goban grinned as he waved his hand back and forth through the three dimensional image.

"In the Realm of the Ogres," said Avani softly, as if to herself. The wizard's visage shifted to regard her.

"You of all people should know where it is, Avani Dutta, last of The Keepers of the Light."

Avani's eyes narrowed. "I was talking to myself, and you don't need to be so formal. We all know my title."

The figure flickered, then stabilized. "Ah, but I live for formality."

"Technically, you don't live at all," said Tom, as he walked around inside the map. "You're just a snippet of AI code, an artificial intelligence '*bot*' with a quirky human interface program."

"Depends on your definition of '*living*,' I suppose," huffed The Guardian.

"What's that just ahead of the crash site on the trail," asked Tom. The view zoomed in.

"The ship crashed on the side of a volcano. Due to the high degree of volcanic activity in the area, the ground is littered with cracks that became vents, which in turn produced geysers, mud-pots, and super-heated pools. It will not be easy going for the king's expedition."

"How long will it take them to reach the crash site?" asked Goban. "If they reach it that is…"

"What do you mean, if they reach it?" asked The Guardian.

"We discovered a plot," said Tom. "Naagesh got word to the ogres. They're going to ambush the king's expedition near the bridge at Icebain Falls."

The Guardian waved his hand and the '*map*' shifted, then zoomed in on the bridge. A brilliant glowing orange arrow hovered above the bridge. The scene slowly rotated. "There?"

"That must be it." Tom studied the map. "So let's say someone is able to warn them before the attack, how long would it take for them to reach the crash site?"

The map zoomed out to its original viewpoint.

"Assuming they take this route—" The fake wizard's staff rose once more and a neon blue winding line lit up around them. The path appeared to go in one of Tom's ears and out the other. Avani giggled. Tom shook his head and stepped out of the holographic line's path.

The Guardian's voice sped up, "—Calculating an average walking speed of 3.2745 kiloter's per oort, taking into consideration breaks for organic needs, and figuring they will be able to maintain an aggressive twelve kiloter's per day, I anticipate they will arrive at the crash site in 5.27893 days, give or take."

"So, that's good, right?" Tom smiled. "They should be back in ten or eleven days." Plenty of time to replace your power source before you run out of juice."

"I'm afraid not. At the present rate of consumption, my *'juice'* as you so quaintly put it, will run dry before they even reach the crash site."

"What?" cried Tom. "But you said you had over a month's worth of power when we gave you the jump from Chloe's battery."

"That was two weeks ago, remember? It took time to put together the expedition. Plus the power drains on my system during the reboot, and henceforth, took far more resources than I initially estimated."

Tom took a step toward the Guardian. "You miscalculated."

"I wouldn't put it quite that way," The Guardian scowled at him. "There were factors that I could not foresee. For instance, the power consumption of launching all those trolls and ogres into the air when the barrier reactivated. Do you know how much the average troll weights? Plus there was assisting your uncle in his feeble attempt to open a portal."

"So now you're blaming Uncle Carlos for your miscalculation."

"Boys," said Avani, stepping between them. "No one's to blame. But what do we do now? Does the king know how little time we've got left?"

"He does," stated The Guardian. "And I've already shut down all unnecessary subroutines and services to minimize current drain. If Elfhaven should come under attack before they retrieve the new power source, I'll redirect most of my energy toward the part of the barrier being attacked, and shut down the barrier elsewhere."

"What if the ogres attack in more than one place?" Goban asked. The Guardian didn't respond.

"Come on then, let's stop wasting the Guardian's precious energy," said Tom.

# Chapter 12: Their own plan

"The library?" asked Avani, sounding puzzled. The three had left the Citadel and were headed back toward the castle.

"I'm working on a plan. I just need more info," Tom said.

"Info?" said Goban.

"Information," Tom explained. "Without more information, we don't stand a ghost of a chance." Tom snapped his fingers, the hint of a smile crossing his face. "A ghost of a chance! Ha, The Librarian, get it?" Avani rolled her eyes and took off at a fast pace.

"We get it." Goban followed her without saying another word.

"Come on. It was a good joke! Hey, wait up."

As they shuffled along, Tom asked Goban, "How 'bout contacting your father, King Abban? Maybe he could send the dwarf army to help."

"The dwarf city of Deltar, though closer to the crashed ship, is even farther away from the ambush site than we are. Anyway, a runner couldn't reach the dwarves in time." Goban's eyes lit up. "What about your sky beacon? Could you signal the king that way?"

"My flare gun? They're probably already too far away, and in the forest under all that tree cover, they'd never be able to see the flare." Besides, Tom continued, "I've only got one flare left. I don't want to waste it."

Rounding the last corner, the library stood directly ahead, its massive stone columns with the murals of heroic elven deeds wrapping around the pillars, towered above them. The windows were dark. They stopped below the wide row of steps leading to the library's entryway, then twirled around at the sound of running feet.

"Kiran," said Tom. "How did you find us?"

Kiran skidded to a stop beside them. "When you didn't come home, I first checked the castle, then the Citadel. The library was next on my list."

"Where's Max?"

"Still eating back at Nadda's."

Goban scratched his bushy eyebrow as he stared up at the dark stone building. "Looks like the library's closed."

"Of course it's closed, it's the middle of the night," replied Avani.

Tom's gaze rose above the steps to the massive red door beyond. "Kiran, give it a try."

Kiran grinned, then raced up the steps taking them two at a time, dangerous in the dim light. When he reached the top he lifted the huge brass door knocker. The building thundered as he brought the knocker down hard against the door. No response.

"Well, I guess The Librarian's not here," said Goban, turning to leave.

"Goban, you're the bravest person I know. You're not afraid of ghosts, are you?"

"Course not!" Goban said, a little too loudly. "Dwarves are never afraid."

"'Cept when they're low on food," said Kiran, as he sprinted back down beside them.

"What?" said Goban.

Kiran grinned. "Just kidding."

Before the dwarf could defend his honor the massive door creaked open an inch.

Tom sprinted up the steps, followed quickly by the others. "Librarian?" he called. "Librarian, it's Tom Holland. We need your help."

The door opened halfway. The ghost floated out a foot and stopped. He was dressed in a glowing white full-length nightshirt with pink bug-eyed baby frog creatures embroidered on it. What's more, The Librarian wore a matching night cap topped with a long fluffy pink tassel that flopped over to one side.

Tom scrutinized the spirit's nightgown. "That's messed up."

"The library is closed," snapped the spirit. "Come back at a respectable hour." The apparition pivoted smoothly then floated back inside. The door began to shut. Tom shoved his foot in the doorway, blocking it. The Librarian scowled at him from inside.

"It's an emergency." Tom once again studied The Librarian's nightclothes. "Say, you mean to tell me you sleep?"

"I rest," huffed the spirit, crossing his arms and frowning. "What business is it of yours?"

"Just curious. Look, it really is an emergency. Remember me talking earlier about those two guys in the library? Turns out they're traitors and they've sent word to the ogres. The king's party is walking into a trap, we've got to—"

"All right, all right, slow down. Come in, it's getting drafty with the door open." The Librarian pretended to hold the door for them.

As they entered, Tom whispered to Goban, "The ghost feels a draft?"

"I heard that!" said The Librarian.

Tom gave the spirit his best innocent look.

"Just listen to us," pleaded Avani, stepping forward. "Tom has a plan."

After explaining what happened and confirming their need for urgency, they stared expectantly at the ghost.

The spirit waved his hand. A large book floated down from a tall bookcase, wafted over to his desk and stopped, hovering a few inches above it. The Librarian flicked his wrist. Flames leapt from large candles suspended above his desk. He flicked his wrist again and dust flew in all directions as the book opened to a map showing the narrow winding path to Icebain Falls.

Tom squinted, waving his hand to keep the dust away from his face.

"There," said the ghost, pointing to a section with two parallel lines near the falls. As his transparent finger touched the parchment it went through the page. "There's the bridge where you say the ambush is set to occur. And there," His finger, still protruding through the page, traced a long curvy line from Elfhaven, ending at the bridge. "That is the trail the king is taking." The path wound around a large section outlined in red.

"Yes. The Guardian already showed us," said Tom, studying the book intently. "What's that?" He pointed at the red highlighted area.

"Demon Forest," replied the ghost, solemnly.

A black dotted line led through the haunted forest straight toward the bridge.

"Hmmmm, Devraj was right. The trail through Demon Forest cuts off half the distance," Tom said thoughtfully. His eyes met the others. "That's the only way to reach them in time."

"Devraj suggested that, but Sanuu chose to go the same way the king went," said Avani.

"I'm not talking about Sanuu," said Tom. The others stared at him in shock.

"No one has attempted that trail in yaras," said Goban.

"Yaras?" Tom looked up from the map. "Oh, years. Why's that?"

"Those who tried," said Avani, in a hushed voice, "never returned."

Tom rubbed his chin. "We've got no choice. We have to try."

"What?" said Avani, Goban, and The Librarian in unison.

Avani and Goban glanced at The Librarian.

The ghost shrugged.

"Look," said Tom, ignoring the spirit, "it's true we don't have a wizard, but we've got Avani's magic and Goban's axe, and my knife," he patted a pocket on his belt.

The others looked skeptical. Kiran pulled Tom's sleeve.

"Oh, and Kiran's—ah, bravery." Avani's jaw muscles tightened.

"And?" said Kiran.

"And Kiran's magic," added Tom. The corners of Kiran's mouth sprang up as Avani's dropped.

"Only fools would attempt to go through Demon Forest," said The Librarian. "Besides, wizard magic hid the entrance long ago. It would take a wizard to see through the illusion."

"But you know where the entrance is, don't you?" Tom asked.

"Yes, of course but—" began the spirit, looking suddenly uncomfortable.

Tom stared at him.

"I don't leave the library. You know that."

"Yes, I know. You're agoraphobic," replied Tom.

The others looked confused.

"He's afraid of crowded public places." Tom explained. Facing The Librarian once more, he continued, "But we'll be in the forest. There won't be any crowds of people there, right?"

The ghost leaned forward and narrowed his eyes at Tom. "Agoraphobia also means a fear of places or situations which might cause panic or feelings of being trapped, helpless or embarrassed. Besides," the spirit continued, "I never leave this building."

"I saw you at the awards banquet," Tom challenged.

"That was different. I was—"

Tom cut him off, "Are we agreed, then?"

Kiran beamed. Avani and Goban nodded nervously.

"Fine," said Tom. "Goban, go to the castle and get any supplies you think we'll need. Avani tell Prince Devraj to meet us at the East gate. Kiran, leave a note for your grandparents. Oh, and bring Max."

"Kiran's not going," said Avani firmly.

"Oh yes I am."

"You know he's coming whether you say so or not," said Tom.

Avani glared at him, her hands on her hips.

Tom ignored her. "Goban, while you're at it, find Chatur and Malak. Ask them if they'd like to go on an adventure."

"Are you crazy?" said Avani. "Those two are idiots! They fight constantly and cause more problems than they solve."

"They helped you rescue me from the dungeon," reasoned Tom.

Goban grinned.

Avani frowned.

"Besides, we need more help. Let's meet outside the east gate in—" Tom checked his watch. "In half an hour, er—half an oort. That includes you, Librarian."

The ghost folded his arms firmly across his nightgown covered chest, causing the nightcap's tassel to fall in front of his face. He blew at the tassel. It didn't move. "No! I'm not going. You can wait a thousand lifetimes and I still won't show!"

# Chapter 13: The game's a foot

"Where's the prince, and Malak and Chatur?" asked Tom, standing in the dark outside the East gate of Elfhaven's outer shield wall.

"The prince'll be here," Avani said.

"I searched everywhere, but I couldn't find Malak and Chatur," said Goban.

Tom noticed a coil of rope slung loosely across one of Goban's shoulders. His battle axe, Aileen, lay firmly strapped across his other shoulder. A small knapsack hung from his massive belt. "What's in the pouch, Goban?"

Goban chewed, then swallowed. "Just some extra snacks in case we get hungry."

"In case *you* get hungry, you mean," said Kiran.

"What?" mumbled the dwarf, crumbs falling from his chin.

"Nothing."

Max pawed Tom's leg. "I know, we'll get going soon, boy. Once Devraj arrives."

A moment later the bushes rustled and out stepped the prince.

"What kept you?" asked Tom.

"Official business."

Tom nodded. "So, are we ready?"

"I haven't yet agreed to accompany you on this fool's errand," said Devraj.

"It was your idea."

The prince's eyes narrowed. "How did you know that?"

"Ahhhh," began Tom, glancing nervously at Avani.

Avani blurted out, "We hid in the balcony."

"You were spying on us adults."

"You're fifteen, just two yaras older than me!" Avani responded sharply.

The prince ignored her and addressed Tom, "I was just pointing out all the options."

"No, you were right," said Tom. "This is the only option."

The prince regarded him coolly. When Devraj didn't respond, Tom continued, "OK, stay here in Elfhaven, where it's safe, just as Sannu told you to. The rest of us will go save my mom and your dad. We don't need your help anyway. Come on," he said to the others. "I guess Devraj is too scared to help." Tom turned and took a step.

"I am not afraid!" yelled the prince, as he jerked Tom around to face him.

For a moment Tom thought his goading plan might have worked a little too well, but after a tense few seconds the prince released him saying, "Fine Avani, my future bride, needs my protection, so I will accompany her. You know you would not survive without my help."

"I don't need your help." Avani's eyes shot daggers. "If you're waiting for me to thank you for protecting your—*weak and future bride*, you'll be waiting a long time!"

Goban cleared his throat. "Children, please. Can we just play nice and get going? The sand in our oort-glass is nearly drained."

Avani and Devraj glared at each other.

"We're waiting for someone else," Tom said.

"Who?" asked the prince.

"Librarian?" called Tom. "I know you're out there."

A shimmer appeared before them as the ghost of the library slowly materialized, thankfully dressed in his usual librarian garb instead of his bizarre night-clothes.

"How did you know I would come?"

"I just knew."

"I will take you as far as the entrance to Demon Forest," said the spirit, frowning as his gaze met each of their eyes. "And not a kilotar farther."

"What are you scared of?" Tom asked. "Nothing can kill you. You're already dead."

Kiran snickered.

The apparition glowered at them. "Little do you know. Demons can do far worse things than kill you."

Goban glanced at Tom.

"Fine," said Tom. "Then we'll just have to get through the haunted forest before the demons even know we're there. Let's go."

"If I am to accompany you," said Devraj. "I give the orders."

Tom stepped back and threw out his arm sideways, gesturing for Devraj to lead.

The prince stormed past, followed quickly by Avani.

"I thought I was leading," huffed the ghost, as he floated after them. "After all I'm the one who knows the way."

Lastly, Goban and Kiran passed by. Goban gave Tom a knowing wink.

Bending down, Tom scratched his dog behind the ears. "This is going to be a long trip, Max."

Max whined in response.

# Chapter 14: A trail of two cities

Juanita, Tom's mom, pulled nervously on her plain brown knee-length skirt. *Why do elven women put up with these things? This skirt's material is as scratchy as burlap and it keeps riding up. I can barely walk in it. How am I supposed to handle my sword if there's trouble?* The king's tailors made her the clothes, but the proportions were all wrong. The curves might have worked for an Elven woman, but they were in all the wrong places for a woman from Earth. She squirmed, trying furtively to tug the rouge skirt into place. *I'd give anything to have my old jeans back, or even my Wushu martial arts outfit.*

As she walked beside King Dakshi, down the primitive forest road, a spooky croaking sounded nearby. *A bird, an insect, a frog?*

Not wishing to insult the king or his tailors, Juanita tried hard to hide her displeasure with the skirt. She glanced at King Dakshi and forced a smile, then cleared her throat. "Once we have the replacement power source, how much time do you think we'll have to get it to Elfhaven? Before the barrier collapses, I mean."

"Not enough, I fear. On our way to retrieve the artifact we are heading straight through ogre territory and thus, we must use stealth. That requires extra time, but we have no other option. We do not have enough soldiers with us to fight our way there and back. Once we have the device, however, the time for stealth will have passed and we will make all haste for Elfhaven." The king smiled back, his eyes scanning her face intently.

He continued, "I have asked King Abban to lend any support the dwarf nation can afford us in our flight back home. He is discussing the matter with the dwarf high council as we speak." The king's eyes sparkled as he watched her. His gaze lingered.

Their hands brushed by each other, momentarily touching. Juanita's heart raced and her face felt hot. She looked away. *What's going on? How can this guy, this king, make me blush? He didn't you idiot! You made yourself blush. I'm a scientist, for gosh sakes. I'm not some school girl easily smitten with royalty or a handsome man in a well-tailored uniform.* She shook her head to clear it.

Juanita was slender and fit, owing more to her hobby of teaching Wu-Shu than to her day job leading a team of scientists trying to prove the existence of parallel universes. *Well, I guess we proved that much, anyway.* A bitter-sweet smile crossed her face as she remembered that fateful night when the portal first, unexpectedly opened, and the second time, when her son chased his dog Max through the portal.

*I wonder what my brother Carlos and the team are doing right now? Probably just sitting around.* She groaned. *That's not fair. I'll bet they're agonizing over the data we collected when the portal first opened, looking for a pattern, looking for anything that might explain what happened.*

Juanita ducked as a branch nearly slapped her in the face. *Better watch where I'm going.*

*Where was I? Oh yeah, I'm sure Carlos and the others are quite concerned and hoping I'll find a way to open a portal back home to Earth. They probably wish there was something they could do, but what can they do? Nothing. It's up to me. I've got to find the replacement power source, bring it to Elfhaven and get the Citadel back up to full power. Carlos will just have to wait patiently for me to solve the problem.* Juanita smiled at the thought of her brother waiting patiently.

\* \* \*

Carlos visualized himself as a tiny particle being accelerated to velocities approaching the speed of light. No matter how many times he visited Fermilab's nuclear accelerator, it always thrilled him.

"Do we have power yet?" Carlos asked, zipping up his parka. It felt colder than he remembered in here. To be expected, he guessed, working near superconducting magnets that had to be kept within a few degrees of absolute zero. His eyes followed the path of the huge tube of the accelerator as it gently curved to the right, eventually disappearing into the massive tunnel that housed it.

"The connections are complete," replied Cheng, tightening the last nut on a power cable the size of his leg.

Inhaling deeply, Carlos noticed the faint odor of oil and ozone in the air. "What about the modifications to the detection grid?"

The other scientists looked nervously at one another. Sashi absently straightened her bright orange sari, then cleared her throat. "We've nearly finished the upgrades to allow it to handle the increased power."

Carlos knew he was lucky to be leading this amazing team of scientists. But who was he kidding? It's his sis, Juanita. She's the brains behind this operation. He wouldn't be leading these guys if she hadn't gone through the portal, hadn't chased his nephew Tom to a bizarre planet in a bizarre parallel universe.

Carlos scanned the detection grid, carefully looking for any flaws, for anything they'd missed, anything that might spell disaster. He still couldn't believe that Cheng had talked the director of the accelerator complex into letting his team use the main injector loop's power supply while the accelerator was down for an upgrade, even acknowledging the fact that Cheng's sister is engaged to the director.

Carlos checked his watch. "This power supply can deliver a thousand times more energy than our old system. Will the modifications withstand that kind of power?"

"It better," said Cheng. "If there's another explosion, like last time." He paused, "—if we damage anything over here in the accelerator complex, we'll lose our jobs."

Carlos' expression hardened. "With a thousand times the power, if there's an explosion—we won't have to worry about losing our jobs…"

# Chapter 15: So far so bad...

"There it is," said The Librarian. The sun had risen, yet the trees were still cloaked in shadow. The ghost's transparent arm shook slightly as he pointed to a dark section of the forest ahead.

"Where?" Tom squinted, trying to see where the ghost was pointing. There was something odd about the trees around them, but he couldn't put his finger on it.

"Avani, can you see anything?" Tom asked.

She relaxed her shoulders and tipped her head forward. Beneath her breath Avani quoted an ancient incantation. The forest shifted, the colors brightened and shimmered momentarily, then darkened again, but that was all.

Avani stared at the trees before her, pursing her lips. "The magic is too strong. I don't have the power without my crystals."

"You're sure this is the entrance to Demon Forest, spirit?" said Devraj. "Have you forgotten where it is and are attempting to cover up your faulty memory?"

The Librarian floated over until his face stood a mere inch from the prince's. "I—never—forget." The two stood frozen in a battle of wills.

"So—" said Tom, trying to ease the tension. "How do we get through this magical gateway, then?"

The ghost slowly shifted his gaze from Devraj to Tom.

"You just run through the trees as if they were not even there."

"Ah, like track nine and three quarters," said Tom.

"What?" said the spirit.

"It's from a book, back home. Ah—never mind." Tom studied the trees ahead. He took a deep breath, then squatted down preparing to run.

"Stop!" cried Devraj. Everyone stared expectantly at him. He adjusted his tunic then spoke, "I am the leader and the bravest. I will go first.

Where exactly did you say the hidden entrance lies, spirit?"

A slow smile crossed the apparition's face.

"There," said the ghost, pointing to his right without looking.

Devraj focused on the spot, rocked back, then shot forward. When he reached the tree-line, the forest gave way, flexing inward for a moment, then flung the prince back violently. He landed hard on his bottom. Kiran snickered. Tom fought the urge to do the same. Devraj scrambled to his feet and glared at the ghost as he dusted himself off.

"Ah, you must be correct," began the spirit. "Perhaps my memory is faulty after all. Oh, now I remember." While still looking at Devraj the spirit pointed off to his left. "There's the entrance."

Tom faced the prince.

"Go ahead," said Devraj, smiling. "You will receive the same fate."

Tom hunkered down, glanced at Avani, who nodded reassuringly. He sprang off charging full speed toward the spot. When Tom neared the trees he closed his eyes. As before, the forest gave way for a moment. It appeared he'd be tossed back just like the prince, but the area around him began to sparkle. It appeared as if he was slowly running through bubblegum. The area shimmered gold for an instant then a faint *'pop'* sounded and he was gone. Everyone stood in silence.

"It's OK," came Tom's voice, sounding muffled and far away. "I made it. Come on you guys."

Tom checked out his surroundings uneasily. It was dark. Far darker than on the other side of the gateway. It wasn't so much a physical sensation of cold, as a mental one. What's more, on the other side there'd been vibrant colors of greens and reds and yellows, plus spicy smells and the sound of birds chirping. Here the colors were drab, dingy grays and browns, and the place smelled dank, like a musty dirt floor cellar. Humming, clicking, and clacking calls of unfamiliar insects sounded, along with deep croaks and a chill moaning off in the distance. A narrow trail led into the dark woods to his right.

Tom waited.

"Any time now," he called. No answer. He stepped back. Another moaning sounded, this time closer.

"Guys?"

At that moment Goban appeared right in front of Tom, running full out. They collided and ended up in a heap.

"Quick, get up," said the dwarf. "The others are right behind me."

"Look out!" cried Goban as Kiran and Max popped through.

Tom jumped sideways barely missing them but Kiran crashed into Goban. This time the dwarf remained standing but Kiran fell over backwards. Max barked.

"Over here," called Tom, moving to the side. The others followed him just as Devraj bolted past, narrowly missing them. They all waited, but Avani didn't come.

"Avani?" called Devraj. He glanced at Goban. "Avani?" Suddenly she appeared.

"What kept you?" asked Tom.

"I tried to convince The Librarian to come with us."

"And?" said Tom. She shook her head.

"Oh well." Tom ran his fingers through his thick hair and said, "Welcome to Demon Forest. May all your nightmares come true." The others stared at him in horror.

"It was a joke," he said. Everyone, including Max, turned and walked down the dark windy trail that quickly closed in upon them.

"Seriously? It was just a joke."

* * *

A rasping noise sounded off to Tom's left. *A bird?* He hoped so. Glancing in that direction Tom thought he saw something. Something big. Something dark. Tom blinked and looked again. There was nothing there.

Sounds of buzzing insects and small skittering creatures surrounded him. The bitter stench of decay had gotten stronger.

*How long've we been walking in Demon Forest?* Tom stared at his watch. *Only an hour? Seems like days.*

At that moment Tom brushed up against one of the magic-infused trees in this accursed forest. Instantly the long thin twigs, resembling fingers, reached out, wrapped around his arm and tightened their grip.

*I hate these creepy things.* Tom shuddered, then reached for the pouch on his adventurer's belt that contained his Swiss army knife. He flipped open the long blade and slowly hacked through the tough twigs. He'd had to do this several times and the repeated effort exhausted him.

Tom could see his breath. *Why is it so cold all of a sudden? It was warmer just a minute ago.* Tom shivered, pulling the elastic strap on his Chicago Cubs hoodie's waistband tight. He listened. The forest had suddenly gone deathly silent.

Slowing his pace, Tom waited for Goban to catch up. He sniffed the chill afternoon air. His eyes began to water. A new smell mixed with that of decay. The pungent odor of skunk or fox or—something worse.

"I don't like these woods," Tom said quietly, as Goban walked up.

Max whined beside him.

"Me neither," whispered Goban, his eyes scanning their surroundings.

"I think we're being watched. I just heard a noise and I thought I saw something."

"Yeah, I heard it too. Hope we're out of Demon Forest soon. Of course—" Goban patted his axe handle and smiled knowingly. "If a demon gets close enough, Aileen gets to come out and play."

"I'm not sure a battle axe will do much good against demons," muttered Tom.

"What?"

"Nothing."

At that moment they heard footsteps behind them. The two spun around.

"Oh, Devraj. It's you," said Goban, releasing his death grip on his axe handle.

"Who did you think it was, Malak and Chatur? As if those two were brave enough to be outside the safety of the barrier."

Tom looked at Goban. "Actually, we thought you might be a demon. Goban and I heard something a moment ago."

"I sense them too. But they must be afraid of us. Else why have they not attacked by now?" Devraj's hand repeatedly flexed and released his sword's hilt. "Sanuu already left Elfhaven to warn the king," the prince pointed out. "Remind me again—why we are in this demon infested forest, Thomas?"

*Hmmmmm, Thomas is it? The prince never called me Thomas before. He must be scared.* Tom sighed. "As I said the last five times you asked, this was originally your idea. It makes sense, since it cuts the distance in half."

"Sanuu will reach my father in time."

"And if he doesn't? Are you willing to risk his life, and my mom's?"

The prince glanced sidelong at Tom. Neither of them spoke further.

Goban changed the subject. "If we don't get out of the woods soon, we may have to break for lunch." As if on cue Goban's portly belly rumbled.

Kiran overheard him and spoke up loudly, "Lunch sounds good to me."

"Quiet Kiran!" hissed Avani. "You're making enough noise to attract every demon for kiloters around."

It was mid-day, but the forest was dark, too dark. Tom fumbled for the right pouch on his adventurer's belt then pulled out his infrared night goggles. Slipping them on, he flicked a switch on the side and heard the familiar, satisfying hum as the forest around him burst into various shades of green.

Apparently having the same thought, Kiran recited an incantation and a dim light appeared, floating before him. Kiran grinned.

"Great! As if making noise weren't enough, Kiran adds light to guide the demons to us." Avani frowned.

Kiran sneered at his sister, but he cupped his hands around the light forcing it to shine down at his feet.

Another noise. It was a deep moaning sound, and close by. Turning toward the noise, Tom scanned the forest with his infrared goggles. There was nothing. No, wait! One of the trees had a faint green glow surrounding its trunk, as if someone, or something, was hiding behind it. The hairs on the back of Tom's neck stood on end. Max growled.

"You smell it, boy?" whispered Tom. Glancing down he absently petted his dog. He blew on his hands, his breath clearly visible, then slid them into his hoodie's pockets. Tom glanced back to where he's seen the green glow. A figure stepped out from behind the tree. No two figures. No three. The creatures stood hunched over. Three long clawed fingers hung from arms covered with thin, ropey muscles. Each had a single large eye in the center of their forehead. Quickly glancing to the other side of the trail Tom saw four more creatures, and they were closing fast.

"Run!" yelled Tom.

# Chapter 16: The trap is set

"Da scout back soon," said Lardas, Supreme Commander of the ogre forces to his first lieutenant, Dumerre. Lardas flexed his powerful arm muscles, causing ripples to cross his generous, round green-tinged belly. Dressed in typical ogre leather with bone leggings and forearm battle armor, he also wore a necklace of razor-sharp Zhanderbeast claws that clinked as he spoke. In his right hand he grasped a massive tree trunk with jagged, gnarly roots protruding from its top.

"Why you send troll scout, 'stead of ogre?" asked Dumerre.

"Da troll commander insist a troll come with. Probly to spy on us. I ask for Bellchar." Lardas's deeply set beady eyes flicked from side to side.

Dumerre growled, "Why Bellchar? Bellchar an idiot."

Lardas smiled, exposing several missing teeth. "Exactly!"

Dumerre frowned then slowly smiled with understanding.

A commotion sounded just down the hill, as if someone tripped, followed by a stack of spears crashing to the ground. Lardas winced.

As the massive troll neared the clearing he brushed against a tree. Immediately finger thin twigs reached out and wrapped around his massive forearm, then tightened their grip. The beast causally jerked his arm, uprooting the tree.

The ogre commander exhaled heavily. "Bellchar! I thought dat ruckus be you."

"Not Bellchar's fault," said the troll, stepping forward. The long scar above his right eye rippled as he spoke. "Ogres move weapons."

Lardas gave him a flat smile. "Dat OK. What you find?"

Bellchar grunted, "I stay hidden, like you say. I kill no elves, like you say. I just watch, like you say."

"Yes, yes, you do good. But what you see? How far away are dey?" Lardas clenched his teeth.

Bellchar glanced from Lardas to Dumerre. "Bellchar see plenty. Dey almost here. Twenty elves, one huu-man da boy's mother. Plus wizard and monk."

"The wizard Larraj? And his sword twirling friend, Zhang," Lardas spat, his bloodshot eyes seething with anger.

"Ders more." Bellchar paused, then grinned.

"What is it?" snapped the ogre.

"Da elven king wid dem." Bellchar beamed proudly.

Lardas's eyes sprang fully open. "King Dakshi? Here?" The ogre's eyes sparkled as he rubbed his hands together.

"Dumerre, ready da troops. Have dem hide. Await my signal. Tell dem I want da elven king alive!"

* * *

They'd been racing full out for several minutes. Each time Tom looked back the things grew closer. Worse, now there were over a dozen of them.

It was also getting darker and colder. The forest itself seemed to be closing in on them. More and more enchanted trees grabbed at them, slowing them down, as if the trees were in league with the foul creatures that pursued them.

"We're not going to make it," yelled Avani.

# Chapter 17: A fairy springs eternal

Rounding a bend they entered a small clearing. Tom glanced over his shoulder. The creatures were gone. Frantically searching all around, the demons, if that's what they were, had disappeared.

"Stop," shouted Tom. "I think we lost them." The others stopped and looked around nervously. Max panted nearby.

"I could see the demons with my night goggles," said Tom excitedly. "My goggles only register infrared, ahhhh—heat. If they give off heat the creatures must be alive, at least partly." The others stared at Tom as if he was an alien. Which, technically he was.

Shafts of light and shadow cast from the tall trees above, illuminating the space around them like a warped chess board. At the center of the clearing stood a bubbling, gurgling spring shrouded in mist. A small stream meandered from it into the forest beyond. Tom slid his goggles up onto his forehead.

*It should feel warm in the sunlight,* thought Tom. *But it still feels cold. Icy cold.* Tom exhaled. He could see his breath.

"All right!" exclaimed Kiran. Running to the spring he made a cup with his hands, dipped them in the water and raised them toward his lips.

Max barked urgently.

"No," yelled Avani. Rushing to her brother she knocked his hands away, sending water flying in all directions. An eerie, bitter-smelling steam rose from wherever the droplets fell. Tom's eyes began to water.

Kiran blinked. Avani let out a deep sigh. Kiran frantically wiped his hands on his cloak.

"I must agree with your sister," said a high pitched voice.

"Who said that?" cried Goban. Deftly swinging his battle axe off his shoulder he stepped into the center of the clearing.

A moment later, rising from the mist, a disembodied visage of a fairy materialized before them.

Max growled. Kiran grabbed his collar, hushing him.

Prince Devraj drew his sword and stepped beside Goban. Avani touched her satchel, but her Magic Crystals weren't there.

"Who are you?" asked Devraj.

"Your weapons are of no use, but lay your fears to rest. You are in no danger here as demons will not approach this spring."

"Why not?" asked Avani. "Who are you? Why are you here?"

"I was once a carefree wood sprite, a queen of wood sprites, actually." The image of a mirror appeared and the fairy smiled, admiring her reflection. The mirror vanished with a 'pop.' "That was long ago, however. Back before demons inhabited this forest. Back when we wood sprites ruled these lands."

"What happened?" asked Avani.

"Ah, you must be Avani Dutta, Keeper of the Light and The Chosen One, chosen by the Magic Crystals themselves." The fairy's eyes darted around Avani, searching. "Where are your crystals, dearie? May I see them? I haven't seen Magic Crystals in—"

"How do you know my name?"

"Come now child, I wouldn't be much of an oracle if I couldn't divine people's names, now would I?" The fairy gave her a broad grin.

"My crystals ran out of magic during the war with the trolls, so I discarded them."

The fairy frowned. "Oh, a pity. I would love to see their brilliant colors—to hear their haunting melody, once more..." The sprite seemed lost in thought.

Avani cocked her head, studying the misty apparition intently. "Go on. How did you get here, like this I mean?"

"Long ago, an evil wizard demanded I do his bidding. When I refused, he turned me into a spirit and magically bound me to this fountain. He said, 'Henceforth, you shall be known as The Oracle of Demon Forest.'

Then the wizard laughed."

Avani stepped closer. "What was this wizard's name? The one who imprisoned you?"

"Naagesh. I never forget a name. Being an oracle, it would be bad for business, don't you think? Yes, that's it, Naagesh! Definitely Naagesh," the sprite nodded enthusiastically.

They all stared at one another, uneasily.

"I know why you're here." The oracle's misty head grew larger as she leaned toward them. "You're trying to warn your friends. Trying to reach them before it's too late." The mists swirled, changing from the oracle's visage into that of the elven king.

"Father," said Devraj, taking a step forward. "Where is he? What have you done with him?"

The visage returned to that of the oracle. "I have not—*done*—anything with him. But your enemies, the ogres, are converging on him as we speak."

"I'm afraid your current path, though quicker than the one the others took, will still not get you there in time." The oracle's misty eyes focused on each of them in turn. "There is another route, however, one that will allow you to arrive ahead of your foes."

Tom asked, "Where? How?"

The oracle's gaze shifted to him.

"Ah, the boy from the prophecy. The famous Thomas Holland from another world, am I right?" The sprite giggled. "Of course I'm right. I'm always right." Squinting, the visage leaned toward Tom. "Hmmm, you don't look much like a hero."

Kiran chuckled.

"Anyway," began Tom, glaring at Kiran. "Will you help us? Will you tell us how to reach them in time?"

"I will. But the journey's not without peril." The fairy adopted a concerned look.

"Go on," said Tom.

"I'll tell you. But are you sure you want to know?" The fairy's eyes suddenly glowed bright yellow. She seemed to be staring at all of them simultaneously. They slowly nodded.

"Very well then," began the visage. "A hundred paces up ahead on the path you're following, you will find a fork in the trail. Go right at the fork. Soon you will come to a cave. The cave is hidden, guarded if you will, by a stand of razor-bush, or so it seems. But the bush is only an illusion spell. By using a counter spell to reveal truth, you may gain access."

"I know that spell," piped up Avani.

The oracle's eyes sparkled as she faced Avani. "Oh, I'm sure you do, child. I'm sure you do. But be forewarned, once you enter the Cave of Dreams there can be no turning back. You are committed and there's only one true path through, though many false ones. Some may cost you time. Some may cost you your life."

"How will we know the true path?" asked Tom.

"It's a puzzle, one that even I don't know the answer to. But you're a bright bunch. I have complete confidence in you." The sprite smiled cheerfully.

"Where will this cave lead us? How long will it take?" asked Devraj.

"If you make no wrong choices it will take only three oorts and you will emerge near the bridge at Icebain Falls, with plenty of time to spare."

Tom leaned over to Goban and whispered, "I don't know. Something doesn't feel right." He paused, then to all said, "I think we should stick to our original plan."

Tom glanced from one to the other of his friends. "Let's put it to a vote. All in favor of following the fairy's path say aye."

Prince Devraj didn't hesitate. "Aye."

Goban scrunched up his face and said, "Nay?" It sounded more like a question than an answer.

"Nay," said Avani, with a little more certainty.

Tom noted that Kiran was petting Max and not listening.

"One aye, Devraj. Three nay's: myself, Goban and Avani, and one abstention: Kiran. The nays have it. We go around."

"I'm the leader," said Devraj. "What I say goes. We go through the Cave of Dreams." The prince shot them a fierce look, then stormed off down the trail.

As the others hurried to catch up, Avani shouted over her shoulder to the fairy, "Thanks."

The fairy smiled back. "Good luck, dearie!"

Tom walked next to Goban. "I love working with Devraj," said Tom. Goban snorted.

Once their footsteps had receded into the distance the misty spring swirled once more, resolving itself into a different visage. Its face had a single blood red eye in the center of its massive jutting forehead and a long twisted nose with a wart on one side. It was the face of a demon. In a deep guttural tone the creature rasped, "Yes, good luck indeed. You'll need it!" The demon laughed, then the spring exploded and everywhere the droplets fell the ground hissed and steamed, yet the laughter continued.

# Chapter 18: One step forward, two steps back

"I don't know Goban. It still doesn't feel right. There's something odd about that fairy," said Tom.

"So, you're an expert on fairies now, are you?"

Tom grinned. "No, but—"

Goban pulled a morsel out of his satchel and shoved it near Tom's face. "Care for a slither-toad pastry?"

The smell of vinegar and liver that was way past its sell-by date filled Tom's nostrils. He scrunched up his face and turned away. "Ah—no thanks. Knock yourself out."

Goban shrugged, then took a huge bite. Tom shuddered.

"Did you pass on my snowboard designs to the dwarf master smiths?"

Goban struggled to swallow. "Yes. They were excited. Might give us an edge, if there's ever fighting in the mountains during the winter months. They're experimenting with different materials, hardwoods and metal, to get the right stiffness."

"Course they'll need to learn how to ride. It's harder than it looks," warned Tom.

"We're talkin' dwarves, here," said Goban. "Dwarves can do anything."

Tom gave his friend a wry smile. "I think dwarves'll be natural boarders. You're compact, and have a low center of gravity."

Goban gazed down at his portly belly, then grinned. Tom gave him a thumbs up.

"What's that mean?" said Goban

"The thumbs up? Ah—it means, it's great, or I'm good, or you're good, or everything's fine."

Goban nodded.

"But back to my original topic. Don't you think that fairy seemed a bit too—helpful? And that ear-to-ear grin of hers reminded me of the Cheshire Cat."

Goban raised his brow. "A Cheshire what?" He took another bite. A slither toad tail hung from his mouth. Goban slurped and the tail disappeared.

Tom's face went pale, "Never mind. I think I'll wait for Avani."

The color in Tom's face slowly returned as he waited for her at the fork in the trail.

"What did you think of that fairy?" asked Tom.

"What do you mean?" she replied, but before Tom could answer they heard a shout from up ahead.

"It's here. I found the razor-bushes!" Kiran shouted.

"How do we get through these things?" asked Tom. The stand of razor-bush was so dense he couldn't see beyond it. The plants glistened with dew and had dark flat leaves armed with tiny spikes on the edges. They were woody stemmed and covered with thorns. But instead of being long sharp points the thorns were fan shaped, as if curved razorblades had been super-glued to their stems. The shrub swayed slightly in the breeze. Except, there was no breeze.

Tom reached out his hand. When it came within a few inches of the plant the bush slashed out violently. Tom jumped back in pain and grasped his wrist. Turning his hand over, blood oozed from three neat parallel slashes. Tom gaped at Avani in horror.

"It's only an illusion," she said.

"Some illusion." Tom wiped his hand on his pants. A dark red stain spread across his jeans.

Avani chanted an incantation, "Veritatem revelare." Tom recognized it from the Citadel, the same spell she'd used to reveal truth. Nothing happened. Absently, she touched her satchel. Closing her eyes she spoke the ancient incantation once more, but louder and with more force. "Veritatem revelare, veritatem revelare, veritatem revelare." For a moment, still nothing. Then the bushes began to vibrate. Next the shrubs became transparent and suddenly made a soft *'pop.'* The razor-bushes vanished.

Tom turned his hand over. The cuts were gone, and the blood stain on his pants had vanished too.

"Sweet," said Kiran, dashing toward a small cave entrance ahead. Max loped after him, barking.

"Stop!" yelled his sister. Surprisingly both Kiran and Max froze. The pair turned and stared at her, Kiran frowning, Max Drooling.

"What do you make of those runes above the cave entrance," Tom asked.

Avani's eyes scanned the markings. "They look ancient, possibly Wood Spite runes? What do you think, Goban?"

The dwarf stepped forward and squinted. Dirt fell as he brushed off the deeply etched markings. Slowly he traced his hand across the characters. "Doesn't look like any form of Dwarvish script I've ever seen."

Tom scratched his head. "Can anyone read these?"

"What?" began Devraj. "You cannot read simple runes? Too hard for an Earth boy?"

"Can you?" Tom asked.

The prince glared at him. "Of course I can."

Tom stared at him.

Devraj cleared his throat and shifted his weight from foot to foot. "It says—" he glanced at Goban. "It says—that—it is a short cut to Icebain Falls."

"Does not!" challenged Tom.

"Does too!"

Avani broke in. "Boys, boys. Let me think." Her face brightened. "I've got it! Yaras ago dad taught me a spell he used when he came across troll or ogre scribbles, carved in wood or stone. Maybe it'll work here." Relaxing once more she muttered the words, "Adiuva me, ut intelligerem." The ground shook accompanied by a loud grating sound, as if the stone was screaming. Slowly and incredibly, the marks began to shift. Within moments the runes had stopped moving and the sound faded.

"I still can't read them," said Tom.

Goban squinted at the new runes. "They're elvish. I think."

"It's a riddle," began Avani, clearing her throat.

> "Once you enter, no way back.
> A maze of dreams, on the wrong track.
> Insanity greets those baseless fools,
> who didn't study and learn the rules.
> But if you've got a mathematical bent,
> You might survive before you're spent.
> Just add one and you may find,
> the way out, and save your mind."

"What does that mean?" Avani asked.

"That first line sounds like we're committed, if we go in," replied Goban.

"The oracle told us that much," said Devraj. "What do we care what it means?"

Max barked at the cave.

"Not now Max," said Tom. Max barked again. "Just a minute Max."

"But the oracle also said this was the only way we'd get there in time," Avani said anxiously. "What do you think Tom?"

"I think we should turn around and go—"

"Hey guys. When I went in, flames flared up on the walls," cried Kiran, from inside the cave.

"Kiran, you come out here this instant!" yelled his sister. No response. "Kiran? Kiran!" She turned toward the others. "My brother never listens to me!" Avani screamed in frustration then stormed into the cave.

Goban smiled at Tom. "Well, I guess that makes up our minds for us." Devraj and Goban ran after Avani.

Tom glanced around uneasily, then followed them into the Cave of Dreams.

# Chapter 19: The cave of nightmares...

Every fifteen feet or so, torch-less flames burst forth atop small stone outcroppings in the cave walls, just as Kiran had said. The flames, though far apart, cast eerie shadows on the walls that were monstrous caricatures of themselves. It felt cold and damp and the air smelled stale. Tom blew into his cupped hands then rubbed them together vigorously. Five tunnels led off from the main cavern. In the dim flickering light he could just make out several more branching off from each of those, farther down the tunnels.

"Kiran? Kiran?" called Avani, a panicked look in her eyes.

"Guys," cried Goban. "You'd better have a look at this."

Goban stood back where they'd entered the cave, only—the cave entrance had vanished. Everything appeared to be solid rock. Deftly, Goban swung his battle ax off his shoulder and in one smooth motion slammed the handle against the spot where the entrance had been. A loud *'boom'* rang out, echoing for several long seconds.

"Avani, try your magic. You know, that spell you did outside, to show truth," said Tom.

Avani repeated the same incantation but nothing happened. "It's no good. This is real." Her worried look returned. "We've got to find Kiran."

"Let's split up," said Devraj. "We can cover more ground that way."

"Are you crazy?" said Tom. Devraj's familiar scowl deepened.

"There's no time. We have to split up," agreed Avani.

Tom wasn't convinced.

Devraj continued, "Avani, you take the left tunnel. Goban, take the second one. I will take the one next to yours. Tom, you take the branch beyond."

Goban unslung his battle axe then shifted the coil of rope from one shoulder to the other.

"There are five tunnels," said Tom. "What about the one on the far right?"

Devraj paused. "First one back takes the last branch. Yell if you find Kiran. If not, meet back here in approximately ten myntars. Any questions?" No one spoke. "Then let us be off."

Avani bolted down the first tunnel yelling, "Kiran!" More flaming torches roared to life on the cave walls as she neared them.

Goban held his axe loosely across his chest and disappeared into the next branch.

Devraj's sword rang out as he drew it from its scabbard, echoing down the passageways. He sprinted off.

Tom sighed, then headed toward his cave but stopped abruptly when he noticed a combination of squares and vertical line symbols roughly chiseled above his passageway.

*Looks like the letter I and the letter O.* Tom paused, then read them aloud, "II, *hmmmmm.*" He wandered over to Goban's branch. The markings above it read IIO. Avani's read IOI. Devraj's IOO, and the last tunnel O.

*They're all different. Wonder what they mean?*

Max whined, then licked Tom's hand. Tom absently scratched him behind the ears. "Come on boy. Our tunnel awaits."

# Chapter 20: Avani

"Kiran? Kiran? If you can hear me, please answer!" Avani's forlorn plea echoed off the cold stone walls, slowly dying away in the distance. The cave floor had become rocky and slick with moisture, forcing her to slow to a walk. A damp chill, accompanied by the sound of dripping water came from somewhere up ahead. Every twenty steps or so another flame erupted above her, casting more eerie shadows. Soon the tunnel narrowed so she had to turn sideways to continue. Next the roof gradually sloped down, forcing her to bend over. Before long she had to crawl on her hands and knees, then on her belly on the cold damp rock. Inching forward, her satchel got stuck. She struggled in the cramped, confined space, finally managing to swivel her belt, letting the satchel rest on her back.

*If this gets any narrower I'll be in trouble. I'm glad there aren't any animals in here. At least, I hope there aren't.* She shivered. The light from the last torch was no longer visible and none had appeared ahead. The walls of her tunnel closed in about her, wedging her in tight.

*Kiran's smaller than I am, and he loves a challenge, but he'd never keep going once it got this narrow.* She tried to crawl backwards but a rock behind her foot prevented her from moving.

*Uh-oh. I'm in trouble.* She began to panic, then tried to calm herself. *Relax. Come on. You're a girl, after all. You can do it! Just think of something.* Twisting her body so that her left shoulder lifted up slightly relieved some of the pressure on her arm. Slowly, pushing with her toes while pulling with her fingers, she managed to inch forward into the darkness. Sharp rocks kept scraping her exposed hands, arms and legs.

After crawling for several myntars, she noticed a faint glow up ahead where the tunnel widened slightly. A moment later the cave opened into a large cavern. A torch ignited above her.

Standing, she took a deep breath, then dusted herself off and stretched her sore muscles. Her knees, knuckles, and elbows burned from multiple cuts and scrapes. She slowly turned around. Flickering light reflected off orange, ropey stalactites that hung from the ceiling far above. Equally massive stalagmites grew from the floor, straining to reach their brethren above. A few had made it, had grown together with their stalactite brothers forming a narrow waist, as if a giant had grabbed a huge lump of sweet-gum then slowly pulled. In fact, the smooth, gracefully folded orange-brown rocks looked a lot like Nanni's sweet-gum taffy, much more so than solid rock. Reaching out she touched one of the many folds beside her. Cold and wet and impossibly smooth, she smiled, momentarily forgetting her lost brother.

Avani walked around a corner and passed through a narrow stone archway, then abruptly stopped. A huge cavern stood before her, much larger than the one she'd just passed through. The echo of water dripping somewhere nearby grew louder, and even though another flame erupted above her, the room was so large the torch's illumination was swallowed up by the caverns immense size. Focusing her mind on her outstretched hands she conjured up two handfuls of magic lights and cast them forth. Slowly, the softly twinkling lights spread out, floating across the cavern, revealing an amazing sight.

Avani gasped. At her feet a crystal clear lake lay before her. In the cave, no breeze disturbed the water's surface. Completely still, it created a perfect mirror for what lay beyond. Across the lake several spots on the walls had bright yellow splotches, as if thrown from a painter's pail. Other areas sported deep, rich oranges with here and there a splash of red. Blazingly white squarish structures, similar to white sand castles that a child might have made, littered the floor and spread up a gently sloping area to the right. From the ceiling hung hundreds of pencil thin, crystal clear tubes. The lake formed such a perfect mirror it was difficult to tell where the cave wall ended and the water began.

*This is so beautiful. I wish Kiran could see it.* With that thought footfalls echoed from across the lake. From an alcove on the far wall, behind some of the taller white structures, out stepped Kiran, heading for the lake.

"Kiran! I'm over here." Avani took a step forward and waved, the toe of her moccasin barely touched the edge of the water. A hissing sound filled the cavern, accompanied by the tangy smell of burning leather. Looking down, smoke rose from her shoe. Quickly pulling off the moccasin she slapped it against a rock until the smoking stopped.

Her eyes snapped up. Kiran had reached the water. "Kiran stop! The water's not safe!" To her horror her brother stepped calmly into the lake. "Kiran no!" Her scream echoed around the cavern. But her brother continued calmly onward. Deeper and deeper he went until he disappeared completely beneath the surface. But the surface remained still. No ripples. "Kiran." she sobbed.

"Yes?" said a voice behind her. Avani whirled around. Standing a few paces from her stood her brother, completely unharmed. She started toward him.

"Kiran! But—how?"

"Why did you abandon me?"

Avani stopped, then blinked. "What?"

"I'd have been fine, if you hadn't abandoned me."

"I don't understand. What's wrong with you?" Arms outstretched, she took a tentative step toward him. Kiran vanished.

"You promised Dad you'd always protect me," said her brother's voice, off to her left. She turned.

"Kiran why are you doing this?" Walking briskly toward him, he disappeared again.

"Dad would be ashamed of you," boomed her brother's voice. Then he began to cry. Avani whirled all around, searching for Kiran, but he wasn't there. The crying grew louder and louder.

"No!!!" she screamed, slapping her hands over her ears.

# Chapter 21: Devraj

Devraj heard water dripping somewhere nearby. This section of cave was dimly lit, and the floor was littered with hundreds of sharp rock shards. The prince had to tread carefully. With each step the shards underfoot tinkled together softly like a glass wind chime. Suddenly a flame erupted above him. He scowled, turning away from the burst of light and heat.

*Where is that accursed child? I should never have allowed Kiran to accompany us. He is too young and always getting into trouble.*

The cave angled down and to the left. A pungent, spicy smell of well-aged cheese filled the area. It became stronger the farther he went.

*This is absurd. How can there be food here?*

A rich yellow glow spilled from an opening up ahead. Drawing his sword and holding it firmly before him, Devraj cautiously entered the cavern. The small space was better lit than the outside tunnel, but he could not make out the source of the light. Creeping slowly around a narrow passage, behind a huge stalagmite, another section of the cavern became visible. Before him stood a stone table piled high with cheeses. Across the make-shift counter sat a plump woman with a sweet smile. Clothed in a rich royal blue velvet dress with deep pleats and many gold buttons cascading down the bodice, she sat skillfully slicing cheese. Once cut, she stacked the slices neatly on an ornately inlaid golden platter.

"Mother?" said Devraj, stopping in his tracks.

The woman smiled but didn't look up. "Devraj, my son." She patted the seat beside her. "Come help me, won't you?"

"Mother, what are you doing? We have servants for such menial tasks." The prince surveyed the chamber around him warily.

Just then a small boy of four or five years of age crossed the room and sat beside her. The child bore a striking resemblance to the prince.

"Devraj, my sweet," said his mother. "Place these slices on the platter, like so." She arranged two slices neatly then handed two more to the boy. He placed them haphazardly on the tray."

"What is this?" said the prince. Sheathing his sword he took a step forward. His mother and his younger self ignored him. Taking another step he slammed smack into an invisible barrier. He cursed, then banged his fist against the obstruction. It didn't give, so he felt around for a way through.

His mother gave the boy a mock frown. "Not like that, Devraj, my son. Like this." Gently guiding his tiny hands, she placed the slices in a star pattern on the plate, then handed him more slices. He followed her example. She smiled and kissed him on the top of his head. "Well done, my little prince."

"Honey, could you get me another cheese round from the pantry?" The boy grinned up at his mother, then stood and walked across the cavern and out of sight to the right.

At that moment a figure stepped from the shadows. The glint of steel reflected off something mostly concealed beneath his cloak.

"No!" cried Devraj, drawing his sword he slammed the hilt against the invisible barrier. A boom echoed in the chamber, but he could not get through. This time he tried swinging the blade hard at the obstruction. It too, bounced off. *"Zing."* The blade vibrated violently in his hand.

"What do you want?" demanded his mother. Leaping to her feet she knocked the cheese platter to the floor scattering slices everywhere. The knife clanked as it spun across the room.

Off to the right the boy emerged carrying a huge round of cheese that threatened to topple him. When he realized what was happening the boy hid behind a pickle barrel. The young Devraj's gaze darted to the cheese knife lying directly beside him.

Devraj's mother's eyes locked with the assassin.

"Guards," she yelled.

"They can't hear you," he said, taking a menacing step forward. "I've made sure of that."

Devraj slammed his sword hilt against the obstruction once more. "Let me in!" he screamed. He looked directly at the boy. The boy looked at him.

"Pick up the knife," yelled the prince to his younger self. "Protect our mother or run for help. But do something!" The boy's hand shook as he started to reach for the knife, froze, then pulled back in fear.

The assailant drew his dagger.

"No!" screamed the prince. The light in the cavern went out. In total darkness, Devraj collapsed, sobbing.

# Chapter 22: Tom

Tom's tunnel rose gently as it curved for a time then abruptly angled back. The air grew colder and had the pungent odor of ripe gym socks. Several stalactites hung from the ceiling, some close enough together that he had to turn sideways to walk between them. Carefully stepping over shards from a stalactite that had crashed to the floor eons ago, Tom saw faint flickers of green light up ahead. The cave curved right. The green light grew brighter. Stepping over some slick rocks, a narrow cavern stretched off to his left. The wet cavern walls were covered with thousands of half-inch long tubes that glowed a rich emerald green. Walking over, Tom reached out and touched one. Instantly the thing curled around his finger and wriggled vigorously. Tom flung it away.

*Ugh, phosphorescent cave worms.* Where the worm had touched him, his finger now glowed green. He wiped it on his jeans, but his finger continued to glow.

*Hope this wears off.*

Max pawed the fallen worm, sniffed it, then gobbled it down.

"No Max!" Tom scrunched up his face, then grabbed Max's collar and pulled him away. "Don't eat those things. That's gross." Max's tongue hung out. It glowed green.

"Yuck!" Imagining himself covered in wriggling, glowing worms, Tom shivered. Continuing, he stayed in the center of the tunnel, keeping as far away from the walls as he could.

The tunnel curved again and another torch loudly burst into flames ahead of him. *That's odd, the worms seemed to be inching away from the flame. Too much light? Or maybe it's the heat.*

Suddenly the tunnel opened into a large cavern. Thousands of wriggling tube worms cast their eerie green light on everything. On one side stood dozens of stalactites and stalagmites. On the other side, various sized smooth, round silver-grey rock columns completely covered the massive wall. They towered above him. The image of a petrified pipe organ sprang into his mind. Tom visualized a ghoul, seated at the stone organ, playing a haunting melody.

He chuckled to himself. *A ghoul playing a 'haunting' melody. Very funny.*

The sound of a rock-slide clattered nearby. Tom spun around in a circle, noticing for the first time that Max was no longer with him.

"Max?" called Tom. "Max? Come here boy." No answer.

Continuing on, Tom heard the sound again only this time he could tell it came from ahead. Across the cavern stood a small opening in the cave wall five feet up. Someone was lowering themselves down backwards out of the hole, onto a ledge covered with loose rock shards. Tom scrambled down a small embankment and hurried over.

"Kiran?"

As Tom neared the wall the boy dropped to the ground, brushed his hands off, then turned around.

"Josh? Josh Mallory, from Leman Middle School in West Chicago?" Tom blinked, in disbelief. "How did you get here?"

"Same as you," said Josh, stepping nose-to-nose with Tom.

"What? Through the lab? Through the portal in the detection grid?"

"There you go again. Using those big fancy-shmancy words. You think you're better'n us, don't cha'?"

"Us?" said Tom, taking a step backwards, right into someone else. Tom twirled around. A tall fat boy smiled down at him.

"Tyler?" Tom couldn't believe his eyes.

"How's the school nerd today?" Tyler said. The two bullies snickered.

"I—I'm fine."

"Still the useless wimp, I see," said Josh.

"What?"

"Yeah," agreed Tyler. "You know what we mean. Lousy at sports.

Afraid of heights. Head up your behind. A loser."

"Ahhh—I've been helping my friends. We're trying to find the power source. Get it back to—"

"Sure you are," said Tyler. He grinned, exposing multicolored braces, a wad of old gum stuck on one side.

"Um—nice braces," said Tom awkwardly. The smile immediately dropped from Tyler's face. Tyler shoved Tom hard, slamming him into Josh. Josh grabbed Tom's shoulders and whipped him around violently.

"So, we come to visit, all friendly like, and the first thing you do is insult my best friend!" Josh glowered.

Tom gulped. "I didn't mean to insult him. I think the braces look cute, er—sick," said Tom, wincing.

This time Tyler whipped Tom around. "Cute! You think I look cute?"

"I didn't mean—. Look, you guys aren't even real. You can't be. You're just a figment of—" Tyler punched Tom hard in the stomach. Tom doubled over, wheezing.

"Not real? I'll give you real." Josh kicked Tom on his backside, sending him sprawling onto the cold rock floor. Something warm dripped from Tom's nose into his mouth. *Blood.*

# Chapter 23: Goban

The sides of Goban's tunnel reminded him of sand patterns he'd seen at the beach on Lupus Lake. Distinct ripple patterns lay cast in the sand by countless waves rushing up onto the shore. But these patterns were on the cave walls, as if a sandy beach had been turned to solid stone then tipped up to form the walls.

Goban ducked as a large, charcoal gray spiky-haired cave bat flew by, narrowly missing his head.

The tunnel meandered left, then right, then finally ended in a small chamber. Several sharp stalactites hung from the ceiling in a semi-circle with corresponding stalagmites below, giving the impression of a giant creature's wide open mouth, teeth and all. Beyond the teeth, in the center of what would have been the creature's throat, a hole opened into the blackness below. A large stalactite hung from the ceiling directly above the opening in the cave floor. Goban walked to the edge and peered in.

"Holla dog? You down there Kiran?"

*Was that an echo or did I just hear something?*

"Kiran? Yell if you're down there." Nothing. Goban idly scratched his chin. Re-slinging his battle axe, he uncoiled his rope. He next tied a bowline knot firmly around a sturdy looking stalagmite, then tossed the other end into the hole.

*Caves were meant to be explored.* Goban grabbed the rope and leapt into the abyss, swinging back and forth, he continued down, hand-over-hand in the pitch black. Suddenly his foot touched down on solid rock. A flame erupted loudly on the wall across from him.

*Those magic torches give me the creeps. Just give me a good old wooden firebrand soaked in plantar pitch, and a shard of fire-rock any day.*

He stood in a small cavern with a low ceiling. No problem for a dwarf lad. To his right the area opened up and got brighter. Smells of hot seasoned meats and warm fresh baked bread filled the space. Following his nose, he rounded a corner and stopped. Before him stood a glorious sight. To his right, a flat stone slab was piled high with steaming cooked meats. To his left, another rock table lay covered with hot baked breads slathered with squamberry jam. Directly before him, on a tall slab, stood flagons of juices and ale.

One of those furry cave bats fluttered in above him, flipped upside down in midair, and grabbed the ceiling. As it folded its wings tightly around itself it shook side-to-side for a moment, then stopped. It blinked, staring straight at Goban.

"Hope you don't mind if I help myself," said Goban to the bat.

Reaching out Goban grabbed a huge cooked bird's leg. Savory juices oozed from the meat. The scent of butter, nuts and exotic spices filled the cavern. Still warm to the touch, he raised the leg to his mouth. Licking his lips he took a huge bite. Instantly the leg turned to dust, sifting through his fingers it covered his stout leather boots and part of the floor. Goban spat. Then spat again. Grabbing a succulent thickly sliced meat he moved it cautiously toward his mouth then stuck out his tongue, slowly licking it. The meat disintegrated. Frantically he raced over to the bread, lifted a warm moist slice slathered in jam to his mouth. Dust drifted through his outstretched fingers.

The bat squeaked as if laughing.

"No!!!" screamed Goban.

# Chapter 24: A dream come true?

A scream echoed through the cavern. Lying on the cold wet stone, Tom looked up, still short of breath. He was alone. Shakily he rose to his feet. Touching his nose, he glanced at his hand. No blood. He whirled around. And no sign of the bullies.

\* \* \*

Racing into the main cavern, where they'd first entered the cave, Tom stopped. Devraj screeched to a halt beside him, then Avani. A moment later Goban sprinted in, dragging his rope behind him. He began coiling it up.

"What happened?" said Tom, panting. "Who screamed?"

"I did," said Avani, Goban and Devraj in unison. Tom studied each of their faces.

"Anyone find Kiran?" Tom asked.

"Well, sort of—" Avani's lip quivered and a tear trickled down her cheek. "—Only—it wasn't really him."

Each of them hastily recounted their experiences. Devraj left out the part about his cowardly behavior as a child.

"I tried to get through the barrier, but it was too strong." yelled Devraj, tears streaming down his face. "It wasn't my fault."

"No one said it was," Tom said awkwardly. "It was just a dream."

"I—I couldn't reach the knife. It was too far away."

Tom tipped his head sideways. "Knife?"

The prince collapsed to the ground. Tears mixed with the dampness of the cave floor.

No one moved. No one said a word. Finally Avani walked over, knelt beside Devraj and softly placed her hand on his back. After a time, his crying subsided, though he shook silently for a few moments longer.

Tom glanced at Goban, then cleared his throat. "These experiences are our deepest fears. This is the cave of nightmares, not the cave of dreams."

He paused. "Once, at a party, I overheard Mom talking with one of her psychiatrist friends. The woman said that dreams come from our unconscious. Dreams are one of the only ways we ever get a glimpse of what's going on deep within our minds. What we want—and what we fear the most."

Tom's eyes scanned the cavern. "We've got to find a way out of here, and fast. If this continues, we'll all go insane." Before any of the others could respond, a noise came from the last tunnel, the one that none of the others had taken. A moment later Max followed by Kiran walked in. Kiran acted as if nothing had happened.

"Kiran!" yelled Avani. She ran over and hugged her brother bone-crushingly tight. So tight in fact, Tom feared Kiran's eyes might pop from his head.

"I'm fine," he rasped. "You can let go now." Avani held him close a moment longer, then thrust him out at arm's length and studied him. Her jaw clenched tight but a tear dripped down her cheek.

"You scared me to death. Don't ever do that again."

"I won't," said Kiran, glancing sheepishly at Goban. "I promise."

Goban snorted. Tom grinned. Avani looked angrily at the three of them.

"Did you have any weird dreams?" Tom asked Kiran, changing the subject.

Kiran peered blankly at each of them in turn. He shook his head, no.

Tom's eyes scanned the room then stopped at the markings above the cave that Kiran had just come from. Tom read aloud. "O."

"What?" the others said.

"Kiran went down the tunnel marked by the symbol O." Tom pointed above the cave entrance. Since he was the only one who didn't have nightmares, I bet it's safe to say that's the correct tunnel; the tunnel that will lead us out of here.

"I turned around when I came to a junction of several more tunnels," said Kiran.

"Did you see different symbols above each tunnel?" asked Tom, a hint of a smile crossing his face.

Kiran paused, squinting. "Ah—I think so."

"These symbols must be some kind of code. If we break the code, we find the way out. If we don't break the code…" The smile fell from Tom's face. His friends looked at each other.

"Ideas?" Tom asked. Nobody spoke. "Goban?"

Taking a small step forward Goban peered up at the symbols. "Ummmm, if they're words, they're not in any dwarvish language I've ever seen."

"Nor any elven or wood sprite script," added Avani. Devraj nodded.

"Maybe they're not words? Maybe they're numbers?" said Goban, scrunching up his face.

Tom slapped his friend hard on the back. "Bingo!" yelled Tom. Goban looked at the others, then back at Tom.

"Go on," Tom urged.

"Let's see—" continued the dwarf. "If they're numbers, there may be a pattern to them." Goban's eyes scanned the symbols.

"Exac-a-lacal!" Tom strode quickly to the tunnel that Kiran just emerged from. "I thought these were the letters O and I. What if they're really zeros and ones? Have you guys studied bases in math?" No one responded.

"O—KAY. How do you guys count up? Start from 0," said Tom.

Goban inhaled deeply then started counting, "Zero, one, two, three, four, five, six—"

"No, I mean, how do you represent them as numbers?"

Goban scratched his head, then picked up a stick and drew in the dirt covered rock floor: 1, 2, 3, 10, 11, 12, 13, 20, 21, 22, 23, 30—

"That's plenty," said Tom.

"Do the elves use the same system?" he asked. Avani and Devraj nodded.

"Then you guys use base four." The others stared blankly at him.

Tom exhaled in frustration, then grabbed a rock and began making marks on the cave wall. As he did so, sparks flew from the stone. Tom studied the rock in his hand.

"Fire-rock," stated Goban.

"Oh, like flint, only better." Tom rolled the stone around in his palm, then placed it in a pouch on his belt, saying, "Just in case." Then picked up another stone and continued.

"1, 2, 3, that's normal for any base above three. Next you drew 10. That's a one followed by a zero. In base ten, the most common base back on Earth, that would mean one group of ten and no units or 10, see? Likewise on Earth eleven would be one group of ten and one unit written as 11, and twelve would be one group of ten and two units written as 12. But in base four, like you guys use, 10 would mean one group of four and no units or just plain four. Each time you counted up to another multiple of four, you added one to the next higher group."

"I get it!" said Goban, "I think." Avani squinted, then slowly nodded. Kiran just did his zombie imitation.

"Look. I believe these symbols are numbers in base two, or binary, as we say on Earth. Digital computers are based on binary." Now all four of them looked like zombies.

Tom tossed the rock up in the air and caught it, then scratched more markings on the wall. "In binary you've only got the numbers 0 and 1 to work with, so you'd count to up like this: 0, 1, 10 which is one group of two and no units, since two plus zero is two, three would be 11 which means one group of two and one unit, 'cause two plus one is three. Got it?"

"I think so," said Goban.

"Good! Anyway, if we count to five in binary, zero, one, two, three, four, five, it would look like this: 0, 1, 10, 11, 100, 101. Simple, huh?"

Goban's eyes lit up. "So, 110 would be six."

Avani quickly added. "And 111 would be seven."

All eyes focused upon Devraj. The prince shifted his weight nervously. Sweat began to trickle down his forehead. He swallowed hard. "Ah, would 1000 be eight?" His brow rose inquisitively.

"Perfect!" Tom grinned and punched the prince in the shoulder. Devraj leaned toward Tom, glaring as he clenched his fist. The smile dropped from Tom's face.

"Ah, exactly right!" Tom stepped back and hurried on, "The important thing is—if we go down the tunnel marked 0 to the junction where Kiran turned around. Then take the tunnel marked 1, assuming there is one, we should be on the right track. If that works, we just keep adding one to the previous number until we exit the cave."

Avani chimed in excitedly, "That's what the riddle above the cave entrance said:

But if you've got a mathematical bent,
You might survive before you're spent.
Just add one and you may find,
the way out, and save your mind."

"Wow, that's right," called Tom as he tore off into cave 0.

# Chapter 25: The trap's about to be sprung

"Elves almost here," whispered Dumerre. "Da ogre troops await your signal. I tell dem 'capture king, not kill.'"

"Good," replied Lardas. "You and Bellchar cross bridge and hide. We let a couple elves escape. Dey lead us to magic talisman. You two follow. Without dem knowing you there." The ogre stared pointedly at Bellchar.

Bellchar and Dumerre nodded, then headed off into the woods.

Lardas drew his rusty bone handled dagger and smiled, exposing several missing teeth. "Some days it good to be an ogre."

\* \* \*

A tall figure walked up beside Juanita and the king, a hint of a white beard poking out beneath the hood of his long gray cloak. A golden owl stood perched atop his tall white staff. The metallic owl occasionally rotated its head toward the man and blinked. Beside him strode a shorter man with spiky orange hair, bright yellow eyes, and two ornate silver sword handles poking out from under his long, well-worn leather cloak.

"Larraj," the king acknowledged the wizard. Then to the sword master monk, "Zhang."

King Dakshi addressed the wizard, "What do you think, Larraj? We are nearing the bridge. Do you sense any—obstacles?"

The wizard gazed outward. "The psychic probes I sent forth haven't revealed anything, yet something doesn't feel right. It's as if someone, or something, has cloaked the magical realm." Larraj faced the king. "I think it would be prudent for you to send scouts ahead, just in case." King Dakshi nodded then to his guards called, "Tappus."

"Your majesty," replied his lieutenant, stepping forward.

"Take two men and scout up ahead. We are not expecting trouble this soon into ogre territory. Still, make sure there are no surprises."

"Yes, sire."

\* \* \*

Running from the cave, Tom stopped in a small clearing. He squinted, unaccustomed to the bright daylight. It was warm outside the cave. Sunlight glistened off the mist covered shrubs and trees. The roar of a nearby waterfall filled the glade.

"Yes!" cried Tom. He closed his eyes, raised his left arm, leaned back and gave a brilliant air guitar solo.

Without taking her eyes off Tom, Avani leaned toward Goban and said, "I think he gets it from your side of the family."

Goban snorted.

The trees surrounding the clearing had thick vines hanging from them. Tom, excited to be free of the cave, grabbed a nearby vine and swung across the clearing like Tarzan, letting out the appropriate yell. Then he bowed dramatically. Avani and Goban clapped. Devraj scowled. Kiran grabbed a vine and swung over beside Tom. Max barked.

A single narrow path led off though the dense vine covered forest. The thundering waterfall sound came from that direction.

"What time is it?" asked Goban.

Tom glanced at his watch. "We were in the cave about—ten hours, er—nine oorts." His jaw dropped. "Our dreams must've lasted hours, not minutes."

"Nine oorts!" cried the prince. "We're too late!"

Drawing his sword, Devraj raced down the path.

The prince sprinted from the forest onto the road and stopped, the others right behind him. A narrow gorge lay to the left of the road. At the bottom of the gorge the Icebain River raged by. Just upstream, a waterfall thundered, dumping its savage flood into the river below. A cold mist rose from the flood swollen waters and enveloped them. Tom covered his ears to dampen the roar.

To their right a steep, tree-covered hillside towered above them. On the river side and just ahead, a flimsy bridge swung lightly in the breeze, its rough-cut planks haphazardly lashed together. Each log lay a foot apart. Moss and vines covered the rickety structure. As far as Tom could see, before the bridge vanished into the mist, several large gaps existed where planks had rotted and fallen away. The bridge creaked as it swayed. What's more there were no rope handholds on either side, though here and there strands of rope dangled below.

The mist parted for an instant exposing the far side of the gorge, thirty feet away. Then the mist returned swallowing the far bank once more.

Prince Devraj raised his sword and called to the others, "Come on, there may yet be time." At that he stormed off down the road, Goban right behind him, followed swiftly by Avani, Kiran and Max.

Tom walked across the road and carefully peered over the edge. Rushing water thundered below. He squinted, trying to see through the mist, but the chasm was too deep, he could only see maybe ten feet down. The mist swirled giving a brief glimpse of a few gnarly trees, the ones he hated, the ones that grabbed you with their finger-like twigs. The trees had stubbornly rooted themselves in crevices on the cliff face.

Tom's gaze rose to the bridge once more. *At least we don't have to cross that thing.* Tom shuddered. Slowly easing himself back from the brink, he let out a long held breath.

Tom caught up with the others as they rounded the first bend. The noise from the river and the falls quieted somewhat, allowing him to hear the faint sound of voices from up ahead. A moment later Tappus and two elven guards strode into view.

"Tappus! It's a trap!" yelled Devraj, his chest heaving from the effort of running. "They're walking into an ambush!"

Tappus winced. Immediately he and the two guards drew their swords and rushed back the way they'd come, Devraj close behind.

Goban, Avani, Kiran, Tom, and Max tried to keep up but the guards ran too fast. As the road wound around another bend, shouts, screams and grunts sounded, along with the twang of crossbows firing and the whir of arrows.

Tom felt a tingling sensation all over. He slowed down. *Someone's using magic.* Glancing down at his hands, blue sparks danced playfully around his fingers. Tom blinked, his jaw slack. *But why's that affecting me?* He hurried to catch up.

A few moments later they crested a small rise and stopped. Tom couldn't believe his eyes. *We're too late. We were supposed to warn them but we failed.*

Tappus and Devraj and the two guards had just joined the fight. Tom stared in horror at the unbelievable scene. The wizard Larraj's odd friend Zhang, the Cimoan monk sword master, launched himself into the air. He seemed to float effortlessly, yet his two silver handled swords hummed as they sliced through the air, too fast to see. Zhang's eyes glowed yellow. His swords glowed red. Ogres fell before him.

The wizard spread his arms apart, his staff on his right, his open palm on his left. In front of him white lightning arced, popped and crackled between his hand and the staff. The lightning grew in brilliance. Suddenly, a powerful magical blast leapt out smashing down trees like matchsticks and sending ogres flying. The elven guards stood beside their king, battling the ogres courageously. King Dakshi himself took out two ogres with a single sword swing. The king and Tappus appeared to be having a heated discussion, even as they fought. Tappus glanced in Tom's direction.

Suddenly, Tom noticed his mom, Juanita. Her own expert sword work kept the ogres at bay. He knew she taught martial arts back home, but he'd never seen anything like this.

Tom bit his lip as he stood transfixed. He wanted desperately to call out to her. To let her know he was here. That he was all right. But if he distracted her, even for a moment…

Goban swung Aileen off his shoulder in a well-practiced arc, slapping his axe handle into his left palm. Yelling a dwarvish battle cry, he charged ahead.

At the same time, Tappus sprinted toward them, followed by Devraj and two other elven boys. As they drew near, Tom could see the other two clearly.

"It's Chatur and Malak," said Tom.

Avani shook her head. "Why would the king bring them along? They're nothing but trouble." Max whined as Kiran held his collar firmly.

Tappus stopped Goban. Prince Devraj, Tappus and Goban were having a heated argument, but with the river and the battle noise Tom couldn't hear what they were arguing about. A moment later they all sprinted up.

Devraj was red in the face. His nostrils flared, his jaw muscles taught.

"My father wants us to cross the bridge and wait for them there. Like a bunch of sniveling children!" The prince's voice quaked with anger.

Tappus glanced back at the battle. "Prince Devraj, the king is only concerned for your safety, and that of your friends. Please lead them across the bridge. We will join you shortly." Tappus glanced back once more, the muscles on his sword hand flexed anxiously.

"Father needs our help! Goban and I—"

"King Dakshi ordered you to lead your friends to safety!" broke in Tappus. "Will you follow the king's orders, so I may go back and help fight?" The two glared at each other, their faces frozen inches apart. Mist, mixed with sweat, dripped off of their rigid noses and chins. Finally Devraj's blade rang out *'zing'* as he slammed it into its sheath. Whipping around he stormed off up the road.

Goban didn't look much happier. The dwarf nodded to Tom as he and the others followed Devraj. Glancing over his shoulder Tom saw Tappus racing back toward the fight. The fierce battle raged stronger than before.

Tom could no longer spot his mom amidst all the action. *I wish I could've talked to her. Told her not to worry. She thought I was safe back in Elfhaven. Which I would've been, if we hadn't learned of the plot to ambush her expedition.* Tom frowned. Then he remembered what Devraj had said. *'Father wants us to cross the bridge.'* Even with the chilly mist, Tom's palms began to sweat.

# Chapter 26: You call this a bridge?

As they neared the bridge, Tom's heart raced, his palms continued to sweat, and he thought he might throw up. Once while on vacation in New Hampshire, Tom's uncle had convinced him to try a ropes course up at Gunstock resort. The course ranged from easy, solid walkways only a few feet off the ground (level 1) to high up in the trees with extremely unstable footings (level 5.) Tom hadn't even gotten past level 1 before a worker had to come rescue him. And back then he had the security of a safety harness. Here he had no such harness, let alone anything to hang on to.

To take his mind off the bridge he ran up beside Malak.

"What are you two doing here?" asked Tom, squinting as he tipped his head sideways. "King Dakshi asked you to come along?"

"Not exactly," began Malak, grinning sheepishly. "Chatur and I wanted to see the crashed ship from an alien world. We thought if we followed the king's men, they'd lead us to the ship. But they caught us."

"Malak couldn't stay quiet," said Chatur.

"Nice. Blame it on me." Malak bared his teeth. "It was Chatur who gave us away."

Tom shook his head. *I see these two haven't changed.*

When they reached the bridge, it creaked as it swung slightly in the breeze. The ropes dangling below swayed even more. Mist from the raging river coated the moss covered logs giving them an icy sheen. Tom could see his breath. He shivered, and not just from the cold.

"I'll go first," said Goban. He stepped out onto the first plank. The whole bridge sagged, creaking loudly. It swung side to side for a couple of seconds, then slowly stabilized. Stepping to the second log his foot slipped on the slick moss. The log shifted to the left and tipped precariously. Goban waved his arms frantically, then caught himself.

Goban looked back. "Now I got it!" He grinned, then stepped to the next log, this time placing his foot in the exact center of the plank. The bridge bounced slightly, but didn't tip or shift. As he released his back foot the logs ahead swayed out and back in a zig-zag pattern as far as they could see before the mist engulfed the bridge.

With each step, the logs moved less and less. Goban seemed to have gotten the hang of it. But a broken log lay ahead. It hung straight down from the right side. Goban stopped, squatted down, then sprang up into the air. Tom held his breath. The dwarf made it across, landing hard causing the bridge to swing violently. Goban lost his balance and fell.

Tom covered his eyes. Hearing Avani gasp he cautiously peeked out from between two fingers. The bridge swayed slightly and it was hard to see with all the mist, but Tom could just make out someone hanging by an axe handle, the axe wedged firmly into the log.

"I'll go help," cried Kiran, running onto the bridge.

"No!" yelled his sister, reaching for him. But she was too late, he was already a third of the way there. Kiran's light weight and sure-footedness barely caused the bridge to sway at all. Jumping easily across the broken gap he knelt beside Goban and gave him his hand. Within moments Goban lay across two logs, his chest heaving.

Tom gasped, realizing he'd been holding his breath.

Avani shivered, then studied Tom's face intently.

Tom returned her gaze. Then he yelled to Kiran, "Kiran, call Max."

"What?" Kiran yelled back, straining to hear over the rapids below.

Tom pointed down at his dog, "Call—Max!"

Kiran nodded. "Here boy. Come here." He waved his hand toward himself.

Max looked up at Tom and whimpered.

"We've got no choice, boy. I'll be right behind you. It's OK." Max pawed the first plank, then his big brown eyes stared at Tom.

"That's it. Go on." Max faced forward and stepped onto the first log. The bridge barely moved. Max whimpered again.

"You're doing fine, boy. Keep going."

Kiran yelled encouragement too. Max took another step. Then another. Soon he'd made it half way across and it wasn't long till he'd reached Kiran. By now Goban had continued on. Kiran waved to Tom then he and Max followed Goban. The mist was so thick they disappeared before Tom could see if they'd made it to the other side.

The prince stepped up to the bridge. "I'll go next," he said, then faced Avani. "You be careful." He tipped his head toward her awkwardly.

Avani seemed surprised, but quickly recovered. "Ah, thanks. You too." Her lip curled up into a weak smile.

Tom squirmed nervously. *Why does that make me sick? I'm not jealous, am I? After all, they're engaged. It's been planned since birth. Once Avani comes of age, they'll be wed, uniting the royal house with the last Keeper of the Light—Avani. So why do I care?* Tom paused. *Because Avani's my friend and Devraj is a jerk, that's why.*

The prince stepped onto the first log, then to the second. The bridge swayed only slightly. Continuing, he quickly vanished into the mist. Avani watched him go.

"Why don't you go next," said Chatur to Malak.

"No, I think the dumber one should go first," Malak replied.

"That's what I said. You first." Chatur grinned wide. Malak sneered at him but stepped out onto the bridge. It shimmied for a bit then stopped. He sighed, then continued. Within moments he, followed by Chatur, was enveloped by the mist.

"I know you're afraid of heights," began Avani. "You go first and I'll be right behind you."

"Afraid of heights!" yelled Tom. "Afraid of heights! This is a theme park ride from Hades!"

Avani blinked. "Hades? What's a theme park?"

Tom sighed. "Never mind." He stepped to the edge of the chasm and let out another long, slow breath. Swallowing hard he stepped onto the first log. The bridge sagged and swung violently. *You've got to be kidding!*

Stepping back he said, "I can't do this." His voice cracked slightly.

"Yes, you can. I'll be right behind you."

He inhaled deeply, then stepped out again, this time directly in the center of the log, like Goban had done. The log barely moved. Tom swallowed once more.

*Don't look down. Whatever you do, don't look down.*

*What do you mean don't look down? I have to look down, you idiot!* Tom shook his head to clear the warring voices that threatened to immobilize him. For an instant he got a glimpse of the river violently churning a couple hundred feet below. Plumes of water shot thirty feet in the air where the intense torrent struck a submerged boulder. Even this high up he felt a cold spray on his face. Far below, scraggly trees clung tenaciously to the cliff face. Thankfully, the mist returned, obscuring his view.

*Are those the same accursed trees I struggled with this morning in Demon Forest? Was it only this morning? Seems like weeks ago.* Tom took another step. His foot slipped. His arms flailed. The bridge swayed violently. Slowly, after a couple of seconds the swaying stopped.

"That's it. You've got it," said Avani.

"Yeah. Piece of cake," he called over his shoulder.

"You want desert? Now?"

Tom sighed, then took another step. Focusing his mind on the exact center of the next log, he stepped again. As he released his foot from the log behind, the log he now stood on shook slightly. Tom held his breath. Sweat dripped off his forehead into his eyes and mouth. He could taste the tang of salt and his eyes burned. It was getting hard to see. He took another step.

*I just need to treat this like a video game. Like Halo or something. I need to quiet my mind. As Mom used to tell me "Live in the moment. Halt the mind's chatter. Give it your complete attention. "*

Tom took a deep breath then let it out slowly, as she'd taught him. That helped. Time seemed to alter and before he knew it he was to the halfway point. Ahead lay the broken plank, the one Goban had almost died trying to cross. It presented a three foot gap with ropes on either side. On the right, and barely attached, the broken log dangled below the bridge, its lower end gently swaying in the breeze.

*Now what do I do? It's too far to jump.* Tom eyed the ropes. *I guess I could try walking a tightrope, like in the circus. It's only three feet.* Tom slowly inched over to the one side of the log he was standing on. As he did, the other side of the bridge rose slightly.

Tom put his arms out sideways and tentatively placed his foot on the rope. The rope vibrated for a second then stopped. Tom gulped and moved his back foot from the log behind, stepping directly on top of the end of the broken log, hanging below the bridge.

Suddenly, the log popped loose and fell causing the rope to hum as it vibrated violently side-to-side. Tom flailed wildly, but just before he fell he jumped for the other side with all he had. Clawing desperately at the log ahead, he managed to catch hold, though his body hung below.

The bridge swung wildly like a rodeo bucking bronco.

# Chapter 27: Just ropes and planks

"Take my hand," urged Avani, reaching down.

"Avani? How?" Tom grabbed her arm, but he wasn't strong enough to pull himself up.

"Come on you wimp! Help me," cried Avani, her face turning blue from the effort.

"That's what Josh said." Tom stared up at her.

"What? Never mind. Just help me."

Shook up, Tom marshaled himself and pulled hard at the same time Avani leaned back, struggling to pull him up. Slowly, they managed to get him up safely lying face down across two logs. Avani lay beside him, both too exhausted to speak.

"You called me a wimp, just like Josh," wheezed Tom.

"Who?"

"A bully from the cave of dreams."

Avani hissed. "Sorry. I didn't mean it."

"Then why?" Tears streamed down his cheek. He couldn't help it.

She winced. "I knew you could do it. I just wanted to shock you, to make you try, that's all."

"That's OK. I am a wimp." Tom wiped off a tear. She stared at him.

"You're not a wimp," she said. "You're the bravest boy I know."

Tom blushed. "Human boy, you mean."

"Human or otherwise." she said.

"How did you—" Tom changed the subject, "—get here so fast?"

Avani smiled. "I am an elf, ya know."

After resting a few minutes, Tom continued on. Avani stayed behind, in case he needed her help. It wasn't long before he stepped onto solid ground on the far side.

Falling to his knees Tom couldn't stop shaking. But, concerned for Avani, he looked back over his shoulder. The sound of the wild river below seemed to fade as, like a painting of an angel, the mists parted and there she was. A ray of sunshine momentarily highlighted her features. She seemed radiant. In fact, her moccasins glowed a rich golden color and each time she stepped the bridge didn't sway at all. It was as if she weren't really walking on it.

Hopping off she said something beneath her breath and the glow faded. She seemed to just settle to the ground.

"You used magic. That's cheating!" said Tom. But curiosity got the best of him. "Were you flying?"

"Last week, in magic class, Larraj taught us how to float, remember? I can't quite fly—yet, but I'm getting there." She broke into a broad grin.

"After that," piped up Kiran, "the wizard showed us how to take a piece of heavy cloth and turn it into a flying rug. I stood on mine and it lifted me up and flew me around the room."

"Flying carpet," corrected his sister, "and you immediately crashed into Malak. You both ended up in a heap."

Kiran sneered at his sister. All the others laughed, except Devraj, who stood rigid, his eyes flicking from Tom to Avani.

Tom collapsed completely.

Sounds of whizzing arrows, ringing swords and thudding clubs grew louder.

"I'm going back to help," said Devraj, taking a step toward the bridge.

"Your father ordered you," Goban reminded him coolly. "You told Tappus you'd wait for them here."

"I said no such thing! My father told me to lead you to safety. Well I have done that. Now I am going back."

At that moment the mist parted. Thirty feet away, on the other side of the bridge, the elven guard's swords slashed tirelessly yet the ogres kept pressing forward. Somehow, each time the guards seemed overwhelmed, Zhang would appear, his blades humming, driving the stunned beasts back once more. Even so, several times a spear flew through their ranks, straight for the king. And each time a brilliant white blast from the wizard's staff turned the spear to ash.

As the king's desperate party neared the bridge, the ogres pressed in harder, forcing the king's men to huddle close.

Zhang pulled out a magic infused throwing star. It glowed bright yellow, pulsing with magical energy. Instead of throwing it at an individual ogre, he hurled the star at the feet of the advancing enemy. The ground erupted in a violent explosion. Ogres were launched up and over the heads of their startled comrades behind them.

"Now is our chance!" yelled the king. "Cross the bridge!"

Juanita was the closest so she started across.

"Mom!" cried Tom, before he could stop himself. Miraculously, over the sound of fighting and the raging torrent below, she must've heard him because she looked straight at him and froze. Time slowed. Tom watched in horror as two ogres jumped from the steep hillside above landing just behind his mom, cutting her off from the king's men. Time sped up.

Hearing the ogres, Juanita spun, swinging her sword in a wide arc. Too late. The first ogre thrust his lance forward. She leapt sideway, barely parrying his thrust. The spear missed her stomach by less than an inch. However, this put her heels over the edge of the bridge, throwing her off balance. Her arms flailed wildly for a second, then she fell.

"Mom!" cried Tom, stepping forward. At the last moment Juanita reached out and grabbed a rope that hung from the bridge and swung beneath it. The ogres, however, heard Tom's cry and stormed across the bridge. One of the logs snapped sending one ogre screaming into the mist below. But the other ogre charged on. His weight caused the bridge to bounce wildly, tossing Juanita around like a puppet on a string below. As the ogre neared Tom and his friends, the beast raised its spear, took aim at Tom and let out a fierce cry.

The ogre's battle cry faltered as a loud 'snap' sounded and the whole right side of the bridge gave way. The beasts arms flailed, then he fell. Tom saw his mom still dangling below the bridge. Her sword's momentum carried it several feet downward before she managed to stop it. It was clear Juanita had cut one of the two bridge supports. She'd cut it to save Tom's life.

Tom heard a grunt nearby. Searching frantically for the noise's source, he quickly spotted it. The bridge logs creaked and bobbed as they hung straight down from the one remaining rope. Like his mom, the ogre had managed to catch hold of a dangling rope. Holding the rope in his left hand the ogre raised the spear with his right and again took aim at Tom. But as he started to throw, the bridge collapsed entirely, taking the ogre with it. Tom ducked as the spear flew over his head. Tom's eyes darted back to his mom. As before, her sword hand scribed an arc downward having just cut the final bridge support. As the bridge fell, the side she hung from slammed hard into the chasm's rock wall, ten feet below the top. Desperately hanging on, her gaze met Tom's. Time seemed to stop. Neither of them blinked. She slowly shook her head, a tear flowing down her cheek. Then she fell.

"Nooooo!" screamed Tom, bolting to the cliff edge. Goban grabbed him, Tom's right foot suspended over the edge.

Tom's mom disappeared into the mist below.

## Chapter 28: Gone but not forgotten

King Dakshi froze staring over the cliff in disbelief, his shoulders slumped, his gaze distant. "Juanita sacrificed herself to save her son, to save my son, to save them all."

"Without the bridge our mission has failed," replied Tappus.

Absently, King Dakshi raised his hand and wiped off an unaccustomed tear, then stared at his wet hand.

"Sire?" said Tappus.

The king's gaze rose across the chasm. The mist once again obscured the other side.

Tappus glanced nervously at the battle around them.

"Sire, we cannot hold out much longer. There're too many ogres. The wizard and monk are exhausted, as are our troops."

The king had a look of resigned failure in his eyes. "I know Tappus. I know."

\* \* \*

A brilliant golden blast erupted from Larraj's staff. The ground shook from the powerful magic, knocking the nearest ogres over. One tried to get up, twirled around drunkenly, then fell back down. Another row of ogres, however, immediately took their places. The wizard watched his friend. The monk leapt into the air, his two swords hummed from their speed, though not quite as fast as before.

The wizard's look hardened. *Even you are tiring, my friend.* Glancing back, the king's guards had formed a protective ring around their liege, but the ring was steadily being driven back, tighter and tighter, closer and closer to the cliff at the river's edge. With the bridge gone, they had nowhere to go.

The wizard let out a long, slow breath, then raised his staff once more.

* * *

"We failed. We were too late. All this was for nothing!" Devraj stabbed his sword hard into a tree.

"Devraj is right," admitted Avani. "The king and his men are trapped on the wrong side of Icebain Gorge. Even if they survive the ambush, they'll have to backtrack kiloters to get around. They will never be able to find the crash site, get the talisman, and bring it back to Elfhaven before the barrier collapses.

Goban nodded, looking down at his feet. Tom lay on the ground, sobbing. Chatur and Malak looked on sadly. Max licked Tom's hand. Avani walked over to him, knelt down and placed her arm around Tom. Seeing this, Devraj fumed. He jerked at his sword but it remained firmly embedded in the tree. He jerked again.

"We'll just have to get the magic talisman ourselves," said Kiran.

All eyes turned his way.

Kiran stepped forward. "What? We're on the correct side of the gorge. It's not that far. We can do this," He looked at Tom for support. "Tom. Tell them we can do this."

Tom slowly raised his head, his bloodshot eyes gazed mournfully up at Kiran. "I'm not going. I just lost my mom. I have no reason to go on. I have no reason to go anywhere. Don't you get it? Mom's dead! If I'd got here sooner, she'd be alive. If I hadn't called out to her, hadn't distracted her— It's my fault she's dead. It's all my fault." Tom dropped his head and wept. Avani tightened her grip around him, then laid her head against his back.

Devraj pulled ferociously on his sword.

"Tom, you've got to go with us. We can't do this without you. We don't even know what this magic talisman looks like," pleaded Kiran.

Tom raised his head and yelled, "It's not a magic talisman. It's a power source. And anyway, you don't get it, do you? I just lost my mom, for God sakes!" Everyone fell silent.

Kiran stared at him, then spoke softly, "I do too understand. I never knew my Mom. But Dad died last year in the first troll uprising. Dad went on when he lost Mom. I went on when I lost Dad." A tear dripped down Kiran's cheek and his lip quivered. He swallowed hard, then continued, his voice a little stronger now, "We are Elfhaven's only hope. If we do nothing the barrier will fail. Thousands will die at the hands of blood thirsty ogres. Maybe we are just a bunch of sniveling kids, like Devraj said. But what if we aren't? What if we can do this? What if we can save Elfhaven? But we can't do it without you. Without your knowledge." Kiran paused. "Besides, you still want to go home, don't you? Go back to Earth? You'll need the power source for that." Kiran stood still, his eyes intently scanning Tom's face.

Glancing at Avani, Tom rose shakily to his feet.

"I'm sorry Kiran. Of course you know how I feel." Tom's lip quivered, as well. He gazed sadly at each one of them in turn. "Mom would want me to go on—" Tom sighed. "Count me in."

Avani jumped up beside Tom, a tear running down her cheek. She threw her arms around him and squeezed hard. Tom's eyes ballooned as he tried to pull away.

Devraj jerked and jerked on the sword's hilt. Finally Avani noticed. Waving her hand absently at the blade, she turned back to Tom and smiled. The sword glowed for an instant then sprang from the tree launching the prince backwards, landing him hard on his bottom.

Goban, Chatur and Malak walked over to Kiran and patted him on the back. "Nice speech! Where'd you learn to talk so good?"

Tom placed his hand on Kiran's shoulder. The two stared at each other in silence.

# Chapter 29: Unlikely allies

Bellchar moved a giant mist covered frond aside and peered through the dense ferns at the collapsed bridge. "What we do?" he asked. "Da bridge fall down."

"It no fall down. Idiot! Da alien female cut ropes," replied Dumerre.

Bellchar faced the ogre. Releasing the fern it slapped Dumerre square in the face, drenching him. "Lardas say he let some elven soldiers go. We supposed to follow dem. Follow dem to find magic thingy. But no soldiers cross bridge."

Dumerre frowned. Dew drops flew in all directions as he shook his head. Dumerre paused, wrinkling his brow in concentration. "No soldiers cross bridge. But children do."

"Huh?"

"Children lead us to talisman," replied the ogre, standing up.

This time Bellchar frowned, his eyes darting left and right.

Dumerre walked away. "Come. Children leave."

\* \* \*

King Dakshi turned at the sound of a mighty horn blast. Battle cries rang out. Sanuu charged around the bend leading a hundred elven troops, weapons glinting in the sunlight, banners flapping loudly in the breeze.

The king had to shout over the noise of flapping banners and swords against mace, spears and shields, "Good timing, Sanuu." Sanuu nodded to Tappus.

King Dakshi dodged a spear as it whizzed by his head.

Sanuu grimaced, searching for the spear's source, but couldn't trace it.

The ogres retreated. Sanuu faced the king and bowed. "We discovered spies betrayed you to our enemies."

"The children warned us but they didn't say how they knew." The king watched as his troops drove the ogres back.

"Children?" asked Sanuu, tipping his head sideways.

"Devraj and Tom and their friends. They're on the other side of the bridge."

Sanuu's gaze searched the chasm. "Bridge?"

The king sighed. "It is a long story. But who were these traitors and more importantly, who did they work for?"

"Two elves of no importance. They are safely in the dungeon. But they were lackeys of—" Sanuu paused. "—of Naagesh. I should've discovered their treachery earlier, sire. I take full responsibility." Sanuu lowered his head, his leather battle armor creaking as he sank to one knee.

"Stand up Sanuu. We have a battle to win."

"My lord," said Sanuu, rising once more.

"Naagesh," the king said gravely. "I had hoped him killed by the mist wraiths."

"As did we all, your Majesty."

By now the elven troops had driven the ogres uphill into the deep woods. Zhang followed them but Larraj strode toward the king.

The wizard tipped his head slightly, first to the king then Sanuu. "My lord."

"Larraj," responded King Dakshi.

"It seems your troops have the ogres in full retreat."

"Sanuu here, says a traitor betrayed us, exposing our mission to the ogres."

The wizard absently pulled on his long white beard. "That explains a lot."

"They worked for Naagesh," added Sanuu.

Larraj froze. "I feared as much."

"We must find a way across this chasm," said the king. "We could go overland. There is another bridge above the falls."

Larraj argued, "There's an ogre outpost near that bridge. They will expect us to try to cross there, and have reinforcements waiting for us. Plus, it would take an extra day at least. We don't have an extra day."

"My lord," broke in Sanuu. "Scouts have spotted large numbers of ogres marching toward Elfhaven." Sanuu glanced from Larraj to the king. "Even more than during the last war."

The king lowered his head in thought.

"If that's the case, your highness, you're needed in Elfhaven. You must lead your people in battle," said the wizard.

The king faced Larraj thoughtfully. "But what of our quest? What of the artifact?"

"Leave that to Zhang and me."

The king thought for a moment, then nodded. Turning to Sanuu, he said, "As soon as the ogres are sufficiently driven back, round up our troops. We make for Elfhaven with all haste."

* * *

The cursed tree had wrapped its twigs tightly around Juanita's arms, legs and torso; so strongly in fact, it was getting hard to breathe. Somehow, miraculously, she still held her sword. The crashing sound of the rapids thundered not far below. Water crashed into the canyon wall sending a massive spray upward, drenching her. She spat out water and shivered.

*I wish I had Tom's knife to cut myself loose. It'd be a heck of lot easier than this awkward sword.* Glancing up, the rocky cliff face disappeared into the mists above.

*Once I'm free, I've got a long climb ahead of me.* She exhaled, then raised her sword and began carefully cutting branches.

# Chapter 30: Here crystal, crystal, crystal

After walking through a dense dark forest for an hour, Tom and his friends entered a long narrow meadow. Even though it was fall, with a slight chill to the air, a few wild flowers were still in bloom. Sweet fragrances of Jasmine, cinnamon and licorice drifted past. Tom smiled as he inhaled deeply.

Goban and Devraj wandered to the right side of the meadow. Malak and Chatur explored the left. Kiran charged down the middle. Tom and Avani stood taking it all in.

"Isn't this beautiful?" she said.

Still smiling, Tom walked over to a clump of brilliant azure blue flowers, bent down and inhaled deeply. The heady odor of a sewage treatment plant assailed his nostrils. Springing up, his eyes closed tight and he coughed violently. "They smell like soiled diapers."

Avani chuckled. "They're called *odeur de latrine*, in ancient elvish."

Tom shook his head several times. Slowly his eyes began to open. He backed away quickly from the offending plants.

"Come on, they're getting ahead of us," said Avani.

The two leisurely walked through the meadow. As he sauntered on, Tom noticed Avani absently running her fingers across her satchel. "Is this similar to the place where you found your Magic Crystals?"

"No. I found the crystals in Elfhaven forest, just outside the barrier. They were near a bend in a small stream. Moss covered the ground, the rocks, the tree trunks, everything." she paused. "Actually, I could hear them calling to me, as if in a dream..." Avani stared straight ahead, unblinking.

They were passing through a section of meadow with hundreds of bright golden flowers. Each one had row upon row of diamond shaped petals. Tom bent down to pick one. Avani stopped beside him. Tom's hand froze. He looked up questioningly. She nodded, so he picked it, then carefully sniffed it. Its stem felt prickly to the touch and it smelled of honey, fresh from the hive. He handed the flower to Avani. Inhaling deeply, she smiled at him.

"Ummm, shouldn't you try and find some more crystals? To boost your magic?"

"What?" she said, snapping out of her remembrance.

"Just sayin'" said Tom.

"I didn't really find them. They found me."

She didn't say anything more, so he tried again, "You're The Chosen One. So just—call them or something."

Avani chuckled. "It's not that simple. I can't just *call* them."

"Why not?"

Avani laughed again. Tom watched her expectantly.

"OK, OK." She looked around then gave a half-hearted, "Here crystals, crystals, crystals."

Tom tipped his head sideways. "Seriously?"

She scratched her head then let out a long, slow breath. Tom saw the muscles in her face and shoulders relax. Tipping her head forward, her eyes nearly closed, she called softly, "Come to me crystals. I need your help." Nothing happened at first. Then the ground began to shake. Directly in front of them two clumps of Magic Crystals pushed the rich moist soil up, smelling of freshly tilled farmland. Sprouting from the ground the crystals glistened in vibrant purples, oranges, yellows and greens. Avani's jaw fell as she looked first at Tom then back at the crystals. Tom gave her a wry grin.

Avani, acting a bit stunned, reached down and plucked a handful of crystals, shook off the loose dirt, then placed them in her satchel.

"Guess you had it in you all along," said Tom. "Just click your ruby slippers together three times and say, 'There's no place like home. There's no place like home.'"

"What?"

"It's from the Wizard of Oz. Point is, you've got it now."

"I guess so. Thanks Tom!"

"For what?"

"For urging me to try. For having faith in me." She leaned forward impulsively and kissed him on the cheek. Tom blushed, then glanced around nervously to make sure Devraj hadn't seen.

\* \* \*

Zhang and Larraj watched as the king and his troops headed back down the mist covered road. The items the wizard had requested lay before them: food and supplies, warm clothing, a back pack, a long bow, a sturdy arrow with a razor-sharp tip and a long coil of rope.

Borrowing one of Zhang's throwing knives the wizard cut two short pieces of rope. Each two hands long.

"Tie the main rope firmly to the arrow," instructed Larraj.

Once Zhang had completed the task, Larraj spoke an incantation as he waved his hand above the arrow. The shaft, tip, feathers, and rope, all began to pulse with a warm golden glow.

Larraj pointed his staff at the chasm. The mists swirled then parted revealing the other bank. Their side of the chasm stood slightly higher than the other. Larraj pointed to a spot across the gorge just below them. "Fire the arrow into that large tree trunk on the far bank."

Zhang placed the arrow on the bow's rest and the gut string in the nock. He raised the long bow ten degrees, drew back the string flexing the bow fully to arm's length then smoothly released. The arrow shot across the river, the rope whining as it whipped from its coil and raced to follow. Hitting the tree trunk dead center *'thunk,'* glowing yellow bands of magic leapt out and circled the tree trunk several times. The tree, arrow, and rope all began to glow.

Larraj picked up their end of the rope. "Tie this securely to that tree. Make sure there's no slack."

Once done, the wizard handed Zhang one of the small pieces of rope he'd cut earlier.

Zhang took the piece in hand, tossed the free end over the main rope and grabbed it with his other hand. He squatted, putting his full weight onto the main rope. The rope sagged a bit then sprang up. Without looking back, Zhang leapt off the cliff. Again the main rope sagged slightly. The makeshift zip-line zinged and a small whiff of smoke rose from the friction of rope against rope. Within moments Zhang stood safely on the far side of the gorge.

Larraj grabbed the remaining short rope awkwardly holding it and his staff in his left hand, then flipped the other end over the main rope, just as Zhang had done. But as he reached for the free end he heard a noise, coming from the chasm. He tipped his head sideways then walked over to the edge. A hand reached up and slapped the ground hard, then grasped an exposed root, the knuckles turning white from the strain. The wizard stared in disbelief.

"Well, are you just going to stand there like you've seen a ghost, or are you going to give me a hand?" wheezed Juanita.

* * *

After Avani finished placing the last magic crystal into her satchel, they heard a rustling from the forest behind them. Turning toward the sound, meadow grasses thrashed about as something made a beeline straight for them. Avani and Tom stepped back just as a small furry black creature popped into view directly in front of them. It immediately launched itself into the air straight for Avani. Avani's eyes ballooned as the long eared critter landed in her arms. She took another step back, but didn't drop it. As it smiled up at her, the distinctive white mark on the creature's head shone clearly.

"It's that gremlin," said Tom. "From the Citadel."

"The one that helped us solve the riddle of my father's cube," she added, sounding shocked. Avani smiled at the warm creature in her arms, absently stroking its soft black fur.

At that moment Kiran yelled, "Hey everyone. Come look at this." He stood at the far end of the clearing. A warm gentle breeze sent golden waves rippling across the meadow grasses. Everyone headed toward him.

As Goban and Prince Devraj neared Tom and Avani, surprised looks spread across their faces.

"Where did you find your pet gremlin?" asked Goban.

"He's not my pet, and anyway—he found me," replied Avani. Goban continued staring at the creature as the four of them walked toward Kiran.


"Well, what is it?" said Devraj as he and Goban, Tom and Avani, stopped beside Avani's brother. Malak and Chatur were still a ways behind.

"Look," Kiran said, pointing to a tree completely covered with neon blue flapping wings.

"Butterflies!" cried Tom. They all stared at him.

"On my planet they're called butterflies. Mostly because lots of them are yellow. The color of butter."

No one moved.

"No butter in Elfhaven?"

"Course we have butter," said Kiran. "But it's green."

Tom nodded, then reached out his hand to touch one of the creatures. Goban sprang forward, grabbing Tom's arm.

"What? They're just butterflies."

"Here we call them fire bugs," said Devraj. "During mating season they flock to meadows like this one by the thousands."

"Sure. We've got the same thing back home. There's a place in Mexico where the butterflies go each year. They cover the ground, the shrubs, the trees. I've seen videos of it. When they take off, they turn the sky bright yellow. It's wonderful!"

"It may look wondrous," began Avani, "but when it's mating season the fire bugs legs develop a strong acid that burns anything that's not a fire bug."

"When they leave here in a few days, these trees will be scarred, burned, and pitted," added Kiran.

Malak and Chatur walked up.

"What's all the fuss about," asked Chatur, leaning up against the nearest tree. Instantly thousands of fire bugs swarmed into the air, coloring everything a rich azure blue and making it impossible to see more than a foot around them. The gremlin leapt from Avani's arm and bolted into the forest.

One of the bugs landed on Malak's arm. "Ouch," he said, shaking his arm wildly. The creature flew away. A whiff of smoke rose from Malak's arm. "You idiot!" he yelled at Chatur.

One touched Tom's hand. He jumped a foot in the air. "Youch!"

Goban unslung his battle axe and held it over his head as a shield. "Run," he cried, launching himself into a full sprint toward the deep woods.

# Chapter 31: We're being followed

A twig snapped somewhere behind them. The forest suddenly went silent.

"We are being followed," Devraj whispered to Goban, "and it is not the gremlin."

"Yup," Goban agreed. "I first heard them just after we left the river." Goban looked over his shoulder.

"How many do you think?"

"Two. And one's taller and heavier than the other," Goban replied.

Prince Devraj glanced sidelong at the dwarf. "How do you know?"

"One of their footfalls is louder and less frequent. So that one's heavier and has a longer stride. Could be a troll."

Devraj looked impressed, then caught himself. "Of course." Then a thin smile crossed his face. "We will set a trap."

This section of forest was overgrown with shrubs and vines. Around the next bend, the path led between two large thick-barked trees a couple feet apart and ended at the edge of a small muddy pond. The trees surrounding the pond were densely packed and covered with heavy vines. A large fallen log spanned the pond, providing the only way across. The others joined Goban and Devraj at the water's edge. As usual, Chatur and Malak were arguing.

The prince stared intently at them. They shut up. Once it was quiet Devraj whispered, "We are being followed. We need to set a trap."

Tom spoke up, "Leave that to me." Rummaging through his belt pockets, he pulled out a coil of thin wire and a pair of pliers. Kneeling down he wrapped one end around a tree trunk, twisting the loose end of the wire around the other end until it was tight. Moving on to the second tree he repeated the procedure. Virtually invisible, the wire stretched between the two trees a foot off the ground. Tom plucked the wire which made a satisfying hum. He stood up and smiled at the others. Goban grinned back.

Devraj hurried across the log to the other side, saying nothing to Tom.

Kiran faced Tom. "The prince is just jealous of you." Avani's brother dashed across the log followed quickly by Max then Goban. Tom was next.

The log lay only a couple of feet above the mud but still Tom wobbled a bit, throwing his arms out wildly. Avani grabbed his sides, holding him steady.

"I got ya," she said. Tom slowly swiveled around till he could see her, then gave her a weak smile. Moments later they were across. As usual, Malak and Chatur had not paid attention. They were arguing again.

"What do you think's following us? Demons?" whispered Chatur, his eyes darting all around.

"Don't be ridiculous. We're far from Demon Forest," rebuked Malak. "It's probably just a zhanderbeast or a mist wraith." Chatur froze.

"Just kidding," said Malak, his face breaking into a wide grin.

Chatur slugged him in the stomach. Malak raised his own fist.

"Shush you two!" whispered Devraj from across the pond. The prince motioned for them to follow.

Malak lowered his fist and the two walked toward the log. Almost immediately Chatur tripped over the wire, falling headfirst into the pond. Malak broke up laughing. Devraj bared his teeth at Malak who slapped his hand over his mouth, but they could still hear muted giggling.

Chatur righted himself. Mud and sand fell from his face in thick, gooey clumps. He reached up but slowly began to sink.

"Help!" he gasped, a panicked look crossing his face. Malak continued to snicker. Slowly Chatur's head sank lower and lower. "Help!" he cried again. Then his head dropped below the surface and all that remained was his upraised hand, which slowly descended.

"Quit kidding around," said Malak, still trying to keep a straight face.

A moment later Chatur's hand vanished beneath the mud. A bubble emerged. *'Bloop!'* Then the pond's surface went still.

"Chatur?" said Malak quietly. The smirk dropped from his face. "Chatur?" he repeated, louder this time.

Goban raced back across the log and reached down, but his arm wasn't long enough to reach the surface.

"Come on, help him!" yelled Goban, glaring at Malak. Malak blinked then laid down on the log, thrust his hand beneath the surface and waved his arm around frantically in the thick mud.

"Chatur! Chatur!" screamed Malak, tears streaming down his cheeks. Suddenly his arm went taught. Malak pulled, his arm shaking from the strain. Goban grabbed Malak's arm and helped pull. Their faces turned red as ever-so-slowly, Malak's arm began to rise. A moment later Chatur's hand appeared above the mud. It seemed an eternity but finally Chatur's head broke the surface. He gave a loud gasp. Within moments the two had Chatur draped across the log, clumps of mud dropped off him into the pond below. Everyone else let out their long held breaths. Everyone except Devraj, who just shook his head.

"Stop fooling around and get over here," snapped the prince.

Malak wiped the tears from his face then helped Goban. Together they got Chatur across the log, Chatur spitting and cursing Malak the whole way.

Tom took Chatur's hand and sat him down.

"What happened?" asked Tom.

"It felt like a giant had grabbed my feet and pulled me down. The harder I struggled the faster I sank."

"Quicksand," said Tom. No one said a word.

"I've never actually seen it, but I've read about it. Mud or sand that's so thick and so deep that it takes too much strength to overcome the suction. People go under and are never seen again." Chatur gulped.

"OK, enough fun," said Devraj, then barely above a whisper he added,

"Act as if we are leaving, then we will double back and hide behind those bushes." He shielded his hand and pointed. "If by some miracle our pursuers were not watching you two imbeciles, perhaps we can still salvage our original plan."

Tom and Avani helped Chatur to his feet. He scraped some mud from his eyes, glared once more at Malak, then stomped off after the prince. Chatur's receding form resembled a walking head of celery that had been dipped in chocolate.

* * *

"You take too long," said Bellchar. "Now kids gone."

"Had to wiz," replied Dumerre, pulling up his britches. "Besides, der tracks clear. Dey not get far."

Bellchar stomped ahead fast. So fast, Dumerre had trouble keeping up. As the path curved around a corner a muddy pond came into view directly ahead.

"Don't hear notin'," said Bellchar, glancing over his shoulder at Dumerre. "Where da kids, den?" At that moment Bellchar ran smack into a huge branch that crossed their path. The force of the impact sent him sprawling backwards, right on top of Dumerre.

"Get off me, idiot!" cried the ogre.

"Not Bellchar's fault. Branch hit me."

"Oh, did poor ol' Bellchar get hit by nasty branch? Get off me you oaf!" Dumerre struggled under the bulk of the heavy troll. "Trolls all idiots, but you make others look smart."

Bellchar jumped to his feet, bared his teeth at the ogre then stormed off and immediately tripped on the wire. Flying far out over the pond, his arms flailing wildly, he landed with a 'Plop.'

Dumerre stood up laughing. "I see why you called a rock troll. You dumb as a box of rocks." Tears flowed down the ogres face and he doubled over with laughter.

Reaching up Bellchar grabbed the sides of the log, but his hands slipped free holding only clumps of moss and bark. Struggling, he reached up again but could no longer reach the log.

"Help!" groaned the troll.

Finally containing his mirth, Dumerre took a couple steps forward. Kneeling down, his smile vanished as he studied the tripwire. He plucked the wire with his fat green finger, '*hummmm*.' He looked pointedly at Bellchar. "I tink dey know we following dem."

"Never mind dat," said Bellchar, struggling to break free of the mud. "Help!"

Across the pond, from behind a group of trees, out stepped the prince and his friends. Devraj drew his sword, Goban his axe, Tom his Swiss army knife, making sure to open the main blade instead of the spoon. Max barked. Dumerre stepped back, quickly disappearing into the forest beyond.

"Dumerre, Wait!" cried Bellchar, a panicked look now on his face. He tipped his head back to keep his mouth above the mud.

"Why were you following us?" demanded Devraj.

"We just watch. Bellchar no hurt little ones."

"Why were you watching us then?"

"You help me, if I tell?"

"Sure—we—will," Devraj assured him, smiling broadly as he glanced at his friends.

"Evil wizard tink elves lead us to magic thingy."

"Evil wizard?" said Devraj.

"Naagesh," spat Avani.

"Magic thingy?" said Goban.

"The power source," stated Tom.

Devraj continued, "How many are following us?"

"Just us two."

Devraj twirled around and strode briskly down the path. "Coming?" he called over his shoulder.

"But you said you'd help him," exclaimed Tom.

The others stared at him in disbelief. "He's a troll!" they said in unison. Tom watched as they all disappeared into the dense underbrush. Glancing back Tom recognized Bellchar from the jagged scar above his right eye. In a moment the troll's head would be totally submerged.

Tom hesitated. "You're Bellchar, right?"

The troll nodded.

"If I help you, you promise you won't hurt us?" Again Bellchar nodded. "And you won't turn us in to the ogres, deal?" Bellchar nodded once more.

"You swear?"

"Trolls honor."

Tom snorted out a laugh. "Trolls have honor?"

"Uh-huh. You save me. I owe you."

Tom pondered that for a second then quickly looked around. A stout vine hung nearby. Grabbing it, Tom jumped up and put his full weight on it. He rotated slowly, slightly above the ground. *Seems sturdy enough.*

Running to the edge of the pool he threw the vine as hard as he could. It landed in the mud only a foot away. *Arrgh!* Quickly reeling it back in, he took a deep breath then slowly stepped out onto the log. A few feet from the bank his foot slipped. Holding tight to the vine he swung out over the quicksand. When he drifted back he placed his feet on the log and regained his footing.

*That was close!* Letting out a deep sigh he started moving again. When he arrived at the spot nearest the troll he steadied himself. By now only Bellchar's rock encrusted arm stood above the mud. Tom tossed the vine. It landed to one side of the troll. *Ahhhh!* Tom pulled in the vine and tried again.

This time his throw hit the mark. As it brushed the trolls arm, Bellchar's massive hand clamped down on it. His other muck-encrusted hand slowly rose from the mire and grasped the vine above the first hand. The vine snapped taut and inch-by-inch Bellchar's muscular frame began to rise from the quicksand.

Turning ever so slowly, and with his arms outstretched and waving slightly, Tom tiptoed back across the log, letting out his breath when he finally reached the shore. Glancing back, he saw Bellchar was half-way there. As Tom raced after his friends he decided it best not to tell them what he'd done.

# Chapter 32: The Library of Nalanda

"Stop," said Zhang Wu, his hand flying out to grab the wizard's cloak. The monk pulled Larraj back then knelt on the path. He plucked the trip wire, '*hummmm*.'

"Tom's been here," said Juanita, kneeling beside Zhang.

The wizard scrutinized the pond. "They set a trap. They must've realized they were being followed."

Brushing some dark green leaves from the path Zhang replied, "One troll, and one ogre."

Larraj squinted. "By the look of it, the two tread quietly behind. They weren't trying to overtake the children, they were just following them."

"Why?" asked Zhang.

"To lead them to the artifact."

"But how would they know or care about the power source?" asked Juanita.

The wizard's gaze rose across the pond. "Naagesh."

\* \* \*

Several hours ago, the path left the cover and relative safety of the dark forest and began ascending into the foothills of the rugged Icebain Mountains. Millions of years ago this area had been a tropical sea, but powerful tectonic plates had collided with the shoreline, thrusting the mountains upward as the plates dove down into the magma below. Eons later, dwarves had chiseled a steep narrow stairway into the cliff face. Tom studied the rock. Gold colored flecks sparkled in the day's last rays of sunlight. It appeared similar to granite, except the stone had flakes of a dark blue mineral instead of the black hornblende found on Earth.

The mountains themselves were as rugged as the highest peaks in the

Colorado Rockies, only these jagged mountains stood completely devoid of vegetation. Ribbons of snow lined the deep ravines and the higher passes, but the peaks themselves lay covered in sheets of solid ice and snow. In a day, perhaps two, they would reach that elevation. Tom shivered.

They continued on. The higher they climbed, the steeper the stone stairway became. Making matters worse, the temperature had dropped well below freezing and snow and ice now covered whole sections of the stairway. The wind howled as if it were alive. Tom shivered, hugging the mountain side of the path, staying as far away from the cliff edge as he could. Even with the cold, Tom began to sweat.

"When are we going to break for lunch?" asked Goban, huffing and puffing as he climbed.

"You asked the same question two minutes ago," said the prince. "We'll stop when we reach the ruins of the Library of Nalanda."

Goban took something out of his pocket and unwrapped it. The stench of a slither-toad pastry burned Tom's nose and his eyes began to water. Goban popped it in his mouth. Tom gagged.

"We should reach the ruins before dark," said Avani. "I can sense they're near."

"You can sense ruins?" Tom said.

Avani paused. "The library held the collected knowledge of magic written down through the ages. Even though the books were destroyed during the War of the Wizard's, perhaps a remnant of their magic still exists."

Tom nodded. "The Librarian told me that the library of Nalanda had been destroyed." The banter helped keep Tom's mind off the cold and the sheer cliff that lay only inches from his left foot.

After climbing for several hours, the steps got closer together, then curved sharply right opening onto a plateau covered by a grove of dark, gnarled, stunted trees. They resembled the trees that would reach out and grab him, only these seemed spookier, like fairytale monsters. As Tom approached he realized the trees were made of stone.

*Petrified wood? I've never heard of a whole petrified forest with the trees still standing. I've only seen broken pieces and fallen petrified logs. What could be holding them up? Magic?*

As they left the cliff face the howling of the wind died down. Winding their way through the stone forest, they were careful not to touch any of the trees. At the edge of a steep rise a huge mound of stone rubble stopped them. Some of the stones had runes written on them.

"What do they say?" asked Tom.

Avani squinted at one of the larger ones. "Um, ..brary ..anda."

Devraj quickly surveyed the area. "It is the Library of Nalanda."

Goban examined some of the writings. Reaching out to touch a rune, orange lightning leapt out, striking his hand. The dwarf leapt back.

"Youch!" he said, shaking his arm vigorously. Max licked Goban's hand, covering it with slobber. Malak and Chatur snickered. Goban shot them a menacing look.

Avani beheld the rubble with wonder. "Before the War of the Wizards, kings and dignitaries, scholars and wizards from all the realms came to study here. But the library wasn't just for the elite. It was open to all—dwarves and elves, kings and commoners. Even trolls and ogres were allowed to visit, though not many could read or write, or cared to anyway."

"Trolls are not smart enough to learn magic," said the prince sharply.

Avani surveyed the ruins, visualizing what it must've looked like during its golden period. "There were rumors of gifted trolls—" but Devraj cut her off.

"Bah! Bedtime stories to amuse children," he said dismissively.

Gazing up, Tom's eyes followed the rugged cliff that towered above them into the failing twilight. "How big was the library?"

"I've heard it stretched far back into the mountain, perhaps a kiloter and it extended five levels down into solid rock."

"Wow! Do you think the books were all destroyed?"

Avani pursed her lips. "That's what people believe. One legend states that when the evil wizards realized they were losing the war they made a last stand in the library. During the ensuing battle the library was destroyed.

"Another legend had it that the good wizards burned the magic books to prevent them from falling into the hands of the evil wizards. Then they summoned a massive rock slide, burying the entrance. Lastly, they put a spell on it, so no one could ever enter." She looked at Goban who was still shaking his hand.

"That's a lot of trouble to go to if they already burned the books," said Tom, staring at the ruins. "I don't see any evidence of a fire. Would the good wizards really have burned the books? Maybe they just said they burned them, so nobody'd go looking for them."

"Hmmm," was all she said.

At that moment, a padding, scratching sound came from somewhere within the petrified forest. Devraj and Goban reached for their weapons, but before they could draw them, out stepped their gremlin friend. Avani's eyes sparkled.

"We thought we'd lost you!" She bent down and petted the creature behind its ear. Smiling up at her, it then turned to face Tom. It winked, then shuffled right up to the crumbled stones that marked the library's entrance. Cautiously it stuck out its paw. *'ZAP!'* The creature withdrew its paw quickly, shaking it as Goban had. Squinting at the stones it then shifted over a bit. Slowly, very slowly, it stuck out its paw once more. *'Zap!'* This time the sparks were not as bright and the sound not as loud. The gremlin shifted farther over to a place where two massive stones leaned together precariously. The creature got down on its belly and peered underneath the stones. Reaching out once more a tiny *'zip'* sounded. The gremlin faced Avani and tipped its head, then it blinked, expectantly.

Avani glanced at the others then back to the creature. "What do you want me to do?"

The gremlin waited patiently.

Avani blinked. "Oh. Let me try something." She relaxed her shoulders and tipped her head. "Aperi dicit mihi." The howling of the wind behind them stopped and an eerie silence fell over them. From the satchel, containing her newly found Magic Crystals, several colored tendrils of magical energy reached out and danced together before them. Slowly the tendrils morphed into the ghostly image of a wizard. The wizard faced the ruins and his mouth moved, as if speaking, but they heard nothing. The wizard raised his hand and an orange glow spread across the ruins. Avani watched the wizard's lips move, studying him. A moment later the image dissolved back into brilliant rays of light and flew back into her satchel. Everyone stared at her.

Avani swallowed. "I don't know what just happened. I think we were seeing the past. I believe the wizard put a spell on the stones to prevent entry. And I don't know how I know it, but the spell he used just leapt into my mind."

They all watched her closely.

Shaking slightly, she lowered her head and began chanting. Instantly, light burst from the satchel, spinning in a large circle that quickly shrank tighter and tighter as it spun faster and faster. A multi-colored spinning drill bit, the magic aimed for the weakness in the defenses that the gremlin had found. As the glowing tornado neared the stones, brightly colored sparks arced toward the rubble. Suddenly the whole pile of rocks was covered in brilliantly flickering orange lightning. Then a hole in the protective magic appeared right in front of the gremlin. The creature grinned up at Avani, then leapt through the hole.

# Chapter Thirty-Two

Several minutes passed. Still chanting, Avani shook from the strain of holding the spell, sweat dripping from her forehead.

"Come on," she said, from between clenched teeth. "Please, I can't hold on much longer." The orange lightning danced faster and the hole began to shrink. The muscles in her arms shook savagely. Avani collapsed just as the gremlin leapt through the hole, dragging two large books behind. Brilliant orange sparks flew in all directions, momentarily lighting their faces and the rocks and the trees with an eerie tangerine glow. Then the magical hole collapsed with a loud *"bang,"* sending bits of rocks and sand flying.

Avani lay in a heap. Smoke and the smell of super-heated rock wafted from her satchel. The gremlin sat on his haunches beside her, prodding her side with a tiny finger.

Tom hurried over and shook her gently. "Avani? Avani!"

Prince Devraj stepped up and glared at him. Tom stepped back as Devraj knelt beside her.

The prince spoke softly, "Avani? Wake up. It is Devraj. Your prince."

Avani smiled, "Tom?" Then she opened her eyes. "Oh, it's—it's you." Her smile faltered momentarily, then returned. "I thought—I thought I heard Tom's voice."

The prince clenched his teeth, then turning to the others said, "Let's make camp here. Avani needs rest, and this spot is sheltered from wind and prying eyes."

Goban's face brightened. "Dinner!" At the comment, Chatur's face beamed as well.

Devraj lifted the books causing a small cascade of dust and dirt to spill from them. At the same time tiny yellow sparks of magic danced playfully across their covers before fading. The leather bound books were badly cracked and worn. Their titles were hand written in a language Tom could not read. Glancing over at Goban, Tom noticed he'd been watching, too. The prince stuffed the books into his knapsack.

Casually walking over to his friend, and with his back toward Devraj, Tom whispered, "Goban, could you read those titles?"

Goban glanced at the prince. Then spoke quietly, "They were written in an ancient elvish script, but yes—one title read '*A Master Wizard's guide to the Darkest Magic.*'"

"And the other?"

Goban paused, studying Tom's face. "*The Prophecy of Elfhaven.*"

Tom stared blankly at the prince's knapsack.

# Chapter 33: The hills are alive...


It was the middle of the night. Tom couldn't sleep so he decided to go for a walk. Flames from the small fire they'd built cast a flickering red glow on the rock face of the library. With his arms across his chest, he rubbed his hands up and down the opposite arm, trying to stay warm. High above him the Ring of Turin sparkled like a thousand diamonds set in a giant's necklace. Tom inhaled a cold, crisp breath, then headed into the petrified forest.

Having no leaves on the trees, what little light there was easily made its way to the ground. Tom leaned against the nearest tree, tipped his head up and admired the stars. The tree suddenly shifted back. Tom almost fell. Spinning around he stared in horror at the scene before him. Not only had the tree moved, a raised face frozen in a look of terror stared out at him from the nearest tree. Tom clamored backwards up against another tree. Impossibly, its solid rock limbs began to encircle him. Tom whirled around again, and stepped back. Another face greeted him, even more frightening than the first.

"Help us!" cried the tree.

Tom turned a full circle. The forest had closed in around him. Completely surrounded, he had nowhere to go. Pulling out his Swiss army knife he flipped open the long blade and slammed it against the nearest tree. The blade shattered. Pieces spiraled outward in slow motion.

"Help us!" moaned the whole forest.

"Noooo!" screamed Tom, covering his ears.


"Wake up! Wake up!"

Tom's eyes sprang open. Goban hovered over him, shaking him.

"Goban?" Tom jumped to his feet and faced the petrified forest. It looked the same as when they first arrived, only darker. Turning back to his friend he grabbed Goban's tunic. "It was awful. Like the scariest Doctor Who episode I ever saw. There were stone statues and every time you'd blink or the lights would go out they'd move." His hands opened a pocket on his belt and pulled out his knife. The blades were whole.

Goban gently pulled Tom's hands off himself. "Who?"

"That's right," said Tom. "Only these trees spoke."

"Spoke did they?"

"Yes. It was like spirits had been trapped inside the trees. They asked for help!"

Goban shook his head. "It's OK. It was just a bad dream, that's all. Oh, and by the way, it's your turn to be lookout. Avani's watch just ended."

"Lookout?" said Tom, still in a daze.

"Yup." Goban chuckled as he walked back to the fire.

Tom gulped, staring hard at the petrified forest in the dim light.

\* \* \*

Tom kept watch for several hours. After his nightmare he couldn't sleep anyway. The fire light caused shadows to dance playfully across Avani's face as she bent over and stirred the embers with a stick. Tom strolled over.

As he approached he saw she was reading something. "Can't sleep either?"

Avani quickly hid the book behind her and looked up startled. Seeing Tom, she relaxed. "I was anxious to read the books from the library." Avani replaced the book on her lap.

"The prince let you?"

"Devraj doesn't control me!" she snapped. Then she sighed and gave Tom a sheepish grin. "I didn't ask. Besides, the gremlin gave them to me."

Tom looked around. "Say, where is the gremlin?"

"I don't know. I haven't seen him since I woke up."

"What book are you reading?"

"The one on dark magic. Here." She scooched over next to him and patted the ground. Tom sat down cross-legged beside her.

Sitting next to her felt good, warm and comforting. The sparkling, crackling embers of the fire added to the warmth, and provided enough light to read by.

"What does it say?" he asked.

Avani reached out and touched the page. Yellow swirls of magic twisted around her finger, for an instant, then seemed to evaporate. "It's a spell to call demons to do your bidding."

Tom swallowed hard. "Ahhhh, a perfect scary read for a campfire."

"It's OK. It tells how to control them," she reassured him.

"Read it to me."

She cleared her throat and shifted her weight.

*"To summon a demon army chant the following spell three times. Daemones voco. WARNING: must be done with total concentration. Make sure you say the words evenly yet forcefully. Once the demons materialize, do not look them in the eye. Look instead at your foe, the person you want the demons to attack. Do not show fear or the demons will turn on you."*

Absently Tom began, "Daemons voco, Daemons voco—" Frightening howling noises drifted in from far away. Avani slapped her hand over his mouth, her eyes saucers. The howls died.

She slowly removed her hand.

"Oops," he said.

Avani slammed the book shut.

"Sorry." Tom shifted his weight nervously, "What about the other book?"

"The prophecy? Oh, I guess you would be more interested in that, wouldn't you?" She reached beside her and lifted a large dusty tome. "The Prophecy of Elfhaven by Earstadomous." As she held it, the same yellow light swirled around her hands momentarily, then faded.

Suddenly someone stepped into the firelight. Avani quickly slipped the book behind her.

"Goban," she said. Which sounded more like a squeak than his name. "I—I thought you were— Never mind."

"It's my turn to keep watch." Goban's eyes ratcheted between the two of them. Neither Tom nor Avani spoke.

"OK, what's up? You both look as guilty as Malak and Chatur every time they screw up. You should work on your acting skills."

Tom and Avani glanced at each other, then giggled nervously.

"Just doing some light reading—learning how to conjure up a demon army, and such," said Tom, matter-of-factly. Avani pulled the book from behind her and showed Goban.

"Ah, nothing useful then—like conjuring up some more food."

"We'll leave you to your watch," said Avani, as she and Tom stood and walked off into the darkness.

\* \* \*

By morning clouds had moved in, draping the plateau in a chill fog. Devraj insisted they leave at once, but Goban refused to budge without breakfast. Grudgingly the prince agreed.

They ate a meal of dried fruit, stale bread, and a bitter, tough jerky. Packing up their things, they continued on. The trail led around the ruins and back out onto the windswept cliff staircase, heading higher into the Icebain Mountains.

145

As they disappeared from sight, a shadow emerged from the petrified forest. It materialized into a darkly cloaked figure which floated toward the ruins of the library. Stopping in front of them, emerald colored magic encircled his bony left hand as he reached toward the rubble. Suddenly orange magic from the ruins itself, lashed out. A hissing noise, accompanied by multi-colored smoke rose from where the two energies met. Slowly the figure withdrew his hand. Both magics sparked and fizzled, then stopped. Rotating his hand slowly in front of his face, he began to smile.

The figure gazed up the stairs, in the direction the children had gone. He muttered an incantation. It immediately began to snow, lightly at first, then steadily heavier. A chill wind blew the snow around the clearing.

Naagesh wrapped his cloak tight around his body then strode up the path.

# Chapter 34: The end is nigh!

For several hours Tom and his friends struggled up the narrow stone stairway, now slick with snow and ice. The wind blew savagely and the once gentle snow had become a violent blizzard.

"I can't go on much longer," said Malak, his lips blue from the cold.

"Come on you wimp! It's not that bad," replied Chatur, blowing into his cupped hands, then rubbing them together vigorously.

Malak shivered, took another step and then collapsed on the staircase. He began to slide over the cliff. Chatur grabbed him and pulled hard, but Malak's weight was too much for him.

"Help me!" screamed Chatur. Devraj and Goban ran over and together pulled Malak back to safety.

"Malak. You idiot! What were you thinking? You almost fell to your death!" Chatur shook Malak. Malak didn't move. Chatur slapped Malak's face. He still didn't move.

"Guys? Guys! I think Malak is—is dead." A tear fell from Chatur's eye.

Devraj knelt beside Malak and placed his ear near his mouth. "He's not dead. He just passed out from the cold." Devraj stood up. Chatur gulped, then wiped the tear from his cheek.

Goban whispered to the prince, "We've got to find shelter, and fast. And we need warm clothes or we're all going to die."

"My father's men had all the supplies, the food and warm clothing. We intended to warn them, then head straight back to Elfhaven. I certainly had not planned on venturing into the Realm of the Ogres dressed like this." Devraj pulled on the sleeve of his surprisingly warm looking tunic.

"No one's blaming you. I'm just stating the facts."

Devraj slowly nodded, then scanned the area near them. "There," he said, pointing up the trail. "There is a small ledge up ahead. We will take shelter there."

Goban followed his gaze, squinting to see through the blizzard.

Chatur, Goban and Devraj dragged the limp form of Malak up the stairs. A small rock shelf indeed existed off to the right of the trail. A snow covered gnarly tree hung over the clearing providing a modest shelter from the wind and snow. Kiran and Chatur gathered what few small twigs and branches they could find and stacked them before Avani.

"Avani," said Goban. "Do your thing. Create a fire, like you did in the castle's secret passage."

"I only know how to create magical flames. They give off light, but no heat, remember?"

"Oh, yeah."

Tom's face lit up. "Light bulb!" Tom grinned. "Guys, look behind tree trunks and under fallen logs. See if you can find some dry moss, leaves, and twigs." In a few moments the others laid the requested items beside him. Tom arranged them carefully surrounded by the larger wood pieces. He reached into a pouch and pulled out a rock. "I found this in the cave of dreams, remember?"

"The fire-rock," said Goban.

From another pouch, Tom pulled out his Swiss army knife and opened a blade.

"We did this in boy scouts." Tom held the rock in his left hand, just above the dried moss, then slid the knife briskly across the rock. Nothing happened. He tried it again, hitting it harder this time. A faint spark flew into the moss and fizzled out.

"Close," Tom said. Goban leaned over his shoulder to watch. After his fifth try a small flame flickered. Tom shielded the infant fire from the wind and snow with his cupped hands. Then he blew gently across the flame. Within moments the entire moss pile flared up, igniting the dry leaves surrounding it.

Tom held up his hand. Goban smacked it heartily.

"Now give it some of the smallest twigs." Tom stepped back.

Goban and Kiran carefully fed the fire some stems, leaves, and branches. Within minutes they had a small fire going. Yet the wind still howled. The snow still fell. They all crowded round, eager to feel even the tiniest hint of warmth. Tom pulled the drawstring on his hood as tight as it would go.

"Next time let me try that," said Goban. "I've used fire-rock to light a pitch-covered torch, but never from scratch."

"Sure thing," said Tom.

Chatur dragged Malak's still form close to the fire. "Don't you die on me." Chatur sniffled. Another tear began to form. "If you die, I swear I'll kill you."

Tom glanced uneasily at Goban, then changed the subject. "Say, where's Max? Has anyone seen Max?" Some shook their heads. Others just stared blankly at the fire.

"Max," called Kiran. "Max!" There was no answer.

With his hand over his brow, to shield his eyes from the snow he scanned the surrounding area, but there was no sign of his dog.

Lacking anything else to do, Tom pulled out the bone needle and gut thread that Avani had given him, from his pocket. He twisted around his hoodie and started sewing its torn hood.

Avani held her hands out near the flames. She looked gravely at Tom, leaned toward him and whispered, "I wouldn't have expected Malak to be the first to go."

Tom paused from sewing and studied her face, then shivered. "I don't think I can last much longer, either." Avani met his gaze, then she turned and stared at the fire once more. As if in a dream, a part of Tom's mind heard the howling wind and the crackling fire, saw the flames reflecting in Avani's dark almond eyes.

Kiran scooched up tight beside his sister. Avani put her arm around him, pulling him close.

"We'll all make it. I know we will," she said. Then, as if to herself added, "We've got to…"


An hour later, with no more wood to be found, the fire burned out. Goban and Devraj lay crumpled on the ground. Their cloaks covered with snow. Chatur was curled around Malak, trying to keep his friend warm. Avani had fallen asleep leaning against Tom, her arm still around her sleeping brother.

A lone tear dripped down Tom's cheek. *Josh was right. I'm a loser.* Tom sniffled. *I really thought we could do this. I thought we could find the power source and bring it back to Elfhaven. We'd save the day and everyone would be proud of us. I didn't think—* Tom swallowed hard. *I didn't think it would end like this. Mom's dead. And now we're all going to die. Everyone trusted me. It's all my fault!*

As Tom's eyes started to close he knew it was the end because he began to hallucinate. First he heard a faint fluttering noise as tiny fairy folk flew toward him on impossibly bright, glowing wings. What's more, they were led by his dog Max, vigorously waving a Chicago Cubs banner held between his teeth.

Tom smiled. "Go Cubs!" he said, then passed out.

## Chapter 35: Mom in hot pursuit

It had begun snowing lightly as Zhang knelt beside the charred remains of a fire at the ruins of the Library of Nalanda. Reaching beneath the thin coating of snow he pulled out a piece of charcoal and rubbed it between his fingers. "The coals are yet warm." We are only a few oorts behind them. Half a day at most."

The wizard pointed his staff at the ruins. Orange lightning flickered across the rubble. "The magic yet holds."

"What?" said Juanita.

"Near the end of the great wizards war we collapsed the entryway to the library, then put a spell on it, protecting it from curious intruders."

"But I thought the library had been destroyed."

"That was a rumor, spread to keep Naagesh's followers from trying to break in." The wizard rubbed his cheek, thoughtfully. "Something has disturbed the magic, though. And recently."

Larraj strode to the nearest petrified tree. His hand reached out and reverently stroked its hard, cold surface.

"If we're that close behind them, shouldn't we get going?" asked Juanita, anxiously.

"Soon," said the wizard. "I want to find out who's been tampering with the protection magic."

Juanita looked confused. "What? How?"

Larraj didn't answer. Instead he tapped his staff gently on the side of the tree. Once, twice—then he vanished.

Juanita hurried to the spot, then waved her hands where the wizard had just stood. He wasn't there. She locked eyes with Zhang. The monk shrugged.

Several hours passed before the wizard rematerialized. In the meantime it had gotten colder and the snow and wind had built to blizzard strength. Daylight was fading into twilight.

"Where have you been," asked Juanita anxiously. "We've got to get going or we'll never catch them."

"It's too late to proceed further. It will be dark soon and the snow covered stairs will be treacherous at night."

"But—"

"We will make camp here and leave at dawn." With that the wizard pointed his staff at the ground and a campfire crackled to life.

Larraj faced Juanita. "Sorry, but I had to know the answer."

"And how did disappearing for several hours answer anything?"

"These petrified trees were once wizards. A dark spell, cast upon them, turned them to stone." Larraj gestured at the forest around them. "In this realm they are no longer alive, yet there is another realm, called 'The Void' where a part of them yet dwells. I entered that realm and questioned them."

"What did they tell you? Was the information worth the delay?"

"I believe so. The tree spirits told me that Avani, with the help of a gremlin, opened a small hole in the guarding magic that protects the library. While the hole remained open the gremlin retrieved two books. An impressive feat."

"Was Tom with them?"

"Yes."

Juanita breathed a deep sigh. "Did you learn anything else?"

"The wizard spirits did reveal more."

"Yes?"

"They said the children were being followed."

"By whom?"

"By a troll, and an ogre and—"

"And?"

Larraj paused. "And by Naagesh."

"What? Then we must leave now!" she cried.

"Naagesh might slow them down so that he may catch up to them, but he will not harm them. At least, not until after they've led him to the artifact. And they are still a couple of days away from the crash site. No, we will leave first thing in the morning and we'll overtake them by mid-day. I promise."

"No," said Juanita. "I'm not waiting." She stormed off up the path. Within moments the blizzard had enveloped her.

Zhang bent down and warmed his hands on the fire, peering up at his friend.

Larraj exhaled heavily. "Come on." Waving his staff casually over the fire, the flames extinguished. A last forlorn puff of smoke lazily rose, dodging snowflakes as it went.

Zhang gazed wistfully at the now dead fire, then stood and followed his companion up the stairs.

# Chapter 36: Déjà vu all over again

Tom awoke. It was nighttime, yet warm and humid. Smells of exotic plants and flowers surrounded him.

*Where am I? Am I dead? Is this heaven? I thought heaven would be brighter. Unless—I'm in—*

Tom stretched, then smiled. *I don't remember the last time I felt this good.* But there was something else, a tiny tingling feeling in the back of his mind. A whisper of déjà vu, something he'd experienced before, something that was trying to get his attention, but he couldn't quite grasp the memory.

*Something's wrong. I can feel it. We were doing something important. Something only we could do. There wasn't much time.* He struggled with the memory, but it was far away as if from a dream that when awakened, quickly faded.

Tom shrugged, then pulled out his headlamp, placed the elastic strap around his head and switched it on. Nothing.

*Why's the battery dead? When did that happen? How come I can't remember?* Tom's eyes narrowed. *I guess I'll have to use my night vision goggles instead.* Tom rose to his feet and reached up to remove the headlamp. At the same time he took a tentative step forward in the darkness. Instantly, near his feet, round saucer-shaped plants glowed bright neon blue. He took another step. More of the plants lit up in front and beside him. Tom lowered his hand, the headlamp forgotten.

In the faint light given off by the plants he could see the outline of other vegetation surrounding him. Raising his outstretched hand his fingers casually brushed a tall spiky bush. Instantly, several glowing pink whirligigs launched into the air. Spinning like tops they slowly drifted away, lighting the forest still further.

Continuing on, he reached out to touch a tall orange flower that still glowed brightly. The moment he touched it, the plant gave off a deep croak like a startled toad, then promptly shrunk down into a small hole in the ground. Tom grinned. Using both hands he ran forward and playfully touched several more of the orange flowers. They all produced similar deep pitched tones and all disappeared as before.

Gurgling noises sounded from somewhere ahead. Walking toward the sound, he brushed aside a massive blue-green fern the size of an elephant's ear, and peered at the sound's source. A small brook flowed gently by. Several large flat moss-covered stones stuck up slightly above the water. Tom stepped onto the nearest one. The moss lit up with a deep emerald glow. He hopped from stone to stone, each one lighting up in turn. His grin stretched. As he rounded a sharp bend in the brook, he saw someone lying on the ground. Jumping to the stream's bank he rushed over.

"Avani." She lay on a thick mat of green moss. Tom knelt down beside her and shook her gently. "Wake up. It's me, Tom."

She smiled, but didn't stir. Her eyes, though closed, moved.

*She must be dreaming.* He sat down beside her and leaned back against a tree. Reaching out, he brushed a lock of hair from her face. Suddenly her satchel began to shake with the sound of crystals clanking together. A golden glow flowed out from under the flap. Then a strand of magical energy flew outward, smacking Tom directly on his forehead. It flared brightly for an instant. Memories flooded into his mind.

*We were on some sort of quest. Treachery was involved. We had to find something. There wasn't much time.* The light faded. The tinkling subsided. The magic gone.

*I remember.* "Avani, wake up. We've got to go. We've got to find the power source."

A twittering noise came from the trees above him. It sounded like voices only incredibly fast and high-pitched. Tom scanned the trees. Several brilliant white specks, resembling fireflies, drifted high above him.

"Who's there?" called Tom.

Warbling, squeaky laughter filled the glen. At that same moment, from behind the tree, a yellow, trumpet shaped flower curled around playfully, stopping directly in front of Tom. He thought he heard faint music as the flower's head rotated toward him, stopping right in front of his face.

Tom reached for the somehow familiar flower. A hissing noise sounded, accompanied by a sweet smelling fog. Tom breathed deeply. "Avani, we've got to go—" he called absently, then promptly slid sideways off the tree and collapsed beside her, fast asleep.

When Tom opened his eyes many hours later, sunlight flickered through huge rain-forest trees that towered above him. Exotic birdsong and the happy buzz of insects surrounded him. Where the sunlight touched him, Tom's skin felt hot.

*Where am I? Am I dead? Is this heaven?* Lifting himself to one elbow he inspected his surroundings with awe.

Tom drew in a deep breath and stretched. He smiled.

*I don't remember the last time I felt this good.* But a tiny tingling feeling in the back of his mind, tried to exert itself.

*Like a déjà vu.* Tom narrowed his eyes. *I've forgotten something important. I almost had it, before I fell asleep. Something made me fall asleep. Something made me forget.*

He struggled with the thought a moment longer then shook his head and sat upright. Turning, he noticed Avani lying beside him on the thick moss.

"Avani."

She stretched, arched her back, then opened her eyes and upon seeing him, her face broke into a broad smile.

"Avani. Where are we?"

Sitting up she looked around, then shook her head, sleepily. "I—I don't know. I've never seen anything like this before." She cocked her head. "Yet it somehow feels familiar."

"To me too," said Tom.

"It's beautiful," she added.

Tom shook his head in agreement. "It's hash-tag amazing!"

"What?"

"It's a social media thing. On the web."

Avani regarded him strangely. "A spider web?"

"No—it's a web of wires and fiber-optic cables."

She stared at him.

"The important thing is—you post things with a hash-tag. Things that are fun or interesting."

"Then it is indeed—hash-tag amazing," she agreed. But suddenly her face showed concern. "Why are you wearing that head strap? Do you have a headache?"

Tom reached up and pulled off his headlamp. "Ummm, it's my headlamp." He flicked the switch. Nothing. "That's odd. The battery's dead." Tom paused. "I don't remember putting it on and I can't remember when the battery died. Can you?"

Avani stared blankly at it. "I don't remember ever seeing that device."

Tom glanced from her to his headlamp then rolled it around in his palm, thoughtfully.

"Avani, do you remember what we were doing before we arrived here?"

She squinted, then shook her head.

"I can't remember either. But it was something important. And we had little time."

Avani gazed up at him, but said nothing.

Tom stood and changed the subject. "I wish I'd brought a charger with me from Earth. Course here, there aren't any outlets to plug it into."

"A charger?"

Tom met Avani's gaze. "A battery charger. To charge my headlamp battery."

# Chapter Thirty-Six

"Like when we fed your robit's energy to the Citadel?"

"Robot," corrected Tom. "So you do remember some things?"

She nodded.

Tom addressed her previous question, "Sort of—it's a similar concept. But in that case we jump-started the Citadel from Chloe's battery. Hey, that gives me an idea."

"What?" she asked.

"Do you have lemons on this planet?"

"Lemons?"

"Or any highly acidic fruit or vegetable? You know, something sour that makes your face pucker up and your eyes close when you bite into one?" Tom made the face.

Avani giggled. Suddenly her eyes lit up. She leapt to her feet and dashed around a bend in the stream.

"Hey, wait up!" called Tom, but before he could move the underbrush rustled and out stepped Goban, yawning.

"Goban, No time. We've got to catch Avani." Tom sprinted after her.

"Avani?" said the dwarf.

"Come on," yelled Tom.

A few minutes later Tom caught up with her. Avani stood by a small tree covered with orange fruits. She plucked one and held it out to Tom. The fruit was spiky, lumpy and measured six inches across. Each spike had an eye on the end. The eyes followed Tom as he approached.

"It's called a watcher melon," she said.

"I wonder why." He scrunched up his face as he accepted the creepy fruit, then sat down with its many eyes staring up at him from his lap. Several eyes blinked.

Goban sprinted up, placed his hands on his knees, and took several large breaths. "What are you doing?"

"Hi, Goban." Avani smiled at him.

"I'm gonna build a battery charger, to recharge my headlamp. Watch."

Tom grabbed a tiny screwdriver from a pocket on his adventurer's belt, then unscrewed the back of the light and removed a small flat battery. From other pockets he produced his Swiss army knife, a coil of copper wire, a long nail, and some duct tape.

Avani sat down beside him, watching intently. Goban leaned over her, reached down and picked up one of the screws, then rolled the tiny object around in his palm.

Tom noticed. "It's a screw. See the threads are twisted. Likewise, there're matching threads in the hole. When you rotate the screw into the hole with a screwdriver," Tom held his up, "it tightens the two pieces together."

Goban's eyes shone. "Like glue!"

Tom paused, cocking his head. "Exactly. Good analogy. It's like a mechanical glue. Only—it's removable."

"Wait 'til I show the dwarf master smiths!"

Tom nodded absently, then cut a small slit in one side of the melon and squeezed the fruit until a few drops oozed out. Relieved that the melon didn't seem to mind, he wiped the thick gooey liquid off on his finger, then touched his finger to his lips. Tom's mouth watered and his eyes shut, making that same sour face he'd shown Avani earlier only—unintentionally this time.

Tom choked out the words, "Wow, this is even sourer then a lemon."

Avani hesitated. "Is that bad?"

"No, it's good."

"When Nadda cooks with this fruit he uses a lot of squamberry juice as a sweetener. Should I search for some?"

"No, no. This is perfect."

Using his knife Tom widened the cut in the fruit, then coiled the copper wire around his forefinger four or five times. Carefully pulling the wire off his finger he inserted the coil into the slit in the melon, leaving one end of the wire sticking out.

"There. The copper coil will serve as the battery's anode."

"Anode," repeated Goban, staring intently over Avani's shoulder.

Tom picked up the nail and twisted another piece of wire tightly around it, pulling on it to make sure it was secure. "And this is an anodized steel nail. It's coated with zinc and will act as the battery's cathode." On the side away from the coil of wire, he pushed the nail in until only the head was visible.

Holding the two wires so Avani and Goban could see he said, "Ta-da! We've built a simple battery." Grabbing his headlamp he lined up the wires and touched them to his lamps exposed contacts. The LEDs lit up, although dimly.

"That's amazing," said Avani. "But people may stare at you if you walk around with a watcher melon on your head?"

"People already stare at me. I'm an alien, remember?" Tom chuckled. "No. Actually, I'm going to use this melon battery as a battery charger. Let me show you." Tom removed the wires from the headlamp. Then he carefully laid the anode wire to the positive side of the flat watch battery. Next he placed the cathode wire on the negative side. Lastly, he wrapped the battery with duct tape, making sure the wires still firmly touched the battery.

"This assumes, of course, that this melon battery produces more voltage than my watch battery needs. I didn't bring my voltmeter with me, but the fruit's so sour I bet it's producing plenty of voltage."

Setting the whole contraption on the ground he added, "Now all we have to do is wait!" Tom rubbed his hands together feeling satisfied with his handiwork.

"Now all we have to do is wait," repeated Avani, staring at the science project strewn haphazardly across the forest floor. "Can you teach me this magic?"

"It's not magic."

"I'd like to learn it, too," added Goban.

"I'll bet lots of kids would be interested in learning these wonders," said Avani.

Tom gazed at the two thoughtfully. "I guess I could teach a class in basic electricity, once we're back in Elfhaven, if you think anybody'd wanna learn it."

The two nodded.

Tom studied their faces for a moment. "Come on, while it's charging, let's see if we can find the others."

As if on cue they heard yawns, and exclamations of surprise from somewhere nearby.

"Over here," called Avani. Within moments Kiran and Prince Devraj stood beside them.

"Well, at least we are alive," said the prince, looking up at the tropical forest canopy. "At least—I think we are…"

"It's hash-tag amazing," said Avani, smiling and glancing at Tom. Devraj looked at her like she'd gone mad.

"Your sword's missing." Tom pointed to the empty scabbard hanging from the prince's waist.

"Yes, I noticed." The prince glanced at Goban's shoulder. The dwarf's hand shot up for his axe handle but grasped only air.

Tom stood, then reached down to give Avani his hand. Devraj pushed Tom aside brusquely and offered her his hand instead. She smiled courteously at them both but instead, rose on her own and stood beside them. The prince absently brushed his hands together.

"Five of us. Three to go." Tom looked at the prince. "Shall we find the others?" Devraj nodded.

After walking through dense tropical underbrush for ten minutes, they came to a clearing. Pushing aside huge ferns they stepped into the meadow. Long strands of lush green moss hung from giant trees that towered above the edge of the clearing. At the far side of the glade a herd of large animals grazed. Easily twice the size of a buffalo, they had three long curving horns in a line, one over the other, rising from their heads. Even stranger, they had four eyes, two in front and one behind each ear. They also had slits in the side of their necks that fluttered each time they breathed.

"Those animals have gills. Like a fish," said Tom. The nearest animal raised its head. The eye behind its ear swiveled to regard him.

"They're called *trimastalo*," said Avani, with reverence in her voice. "They're supposed to be extinct. No one's seen one in hundreds of yaras."

"Cool!"

At that moment a noise came from somewhere off to their right. They followed the sound back into the tropical forest then squeezed between two giant trees the size of redwoods, stopping in another smaller clearing.

Goban said, "Say, I've been meaning to ask, where are we anyway?"

Tom stared at the others. "We're not sure."

"Wherever it is, it's paradise!" Avani's eyes sparkled as she gazed up at the trees.

"If it's paradise," said Goban, rubbing his round portly belly, "there must be food here."

Kiran agreed.

A single trail led from the meadow. Following it they rounded a bend and a larger clearing opened directly in front of them. At the far side of the meadow, a long wooden picnic bench stood draped with a bright white tablecloth of fine linen. On the table were platters piled high with steaming food. Kiran got there first and sat down. Goban eagerly sat beside him.

"Took you guys long enough," said Kiran, as he reached for a pink spotted fruit.

"That's odd," said Tom. "Goban mentions food and it suddenly appears."

Goban picked up a huge steaming golden brown bird's leg and raised it cautiously to his lips. He paused, then slowly stuck out his tongue. Touching it, he faced the others and beamed. "It's real!" Turning back he took a gigantic bite of the succulent meat, chewed and heartily swallowed.

"Why wouldn't it be?" asked Tom.

Goban faced Tom and blinked. "I—I'm not sure. I remember something." Goban paused, stared hard at Tom, then shook his head, turned back and started eating again.

Tom frowned.

The others sat down. The moment was interrupted by the sound of two people arguing.

Kiran yelled, "Malak and Chatur. Over here. There's food." Within seconds the two arrived. They hurried over and joined the others.

Malak grabbed a loaf of bread and pulled off a huge hunk, squeezing it tightly into a ball, he stuffed the whole thing into his mouth.

Chatur poured himself a flagon of a bright pink fruit juice.

"So where do we go from here?" asked the prince, spreading green jam on a dark spotted roll. "We do not know where we are and we do not know where we are going."

"If we don't know where we're going, any road will take us there. To quote the Cheshire Cat," said Tom, cautiously sniffing a fragrant tart.

"What?" said Devraj, jelly dripping down his chin. Avani pointed at the glob. The prince dabbed at it with his napkin.

Goban shrugged. "There he goes again with that cat. Must be a philosopher or something."

\* \* \*

Several hours had passed since lunch. By now the group had explored more of the forest, played hide-and-seek, took a nap, ate a fabulous dinner that mysteriously appeared just like lunch. Now they sat contented, their backs against trees, the day nearly past. Shadows lengthened as the daylight hours dwindled. It would soon be dark. They needed to find a good place to spend the night, while there was still light.

Tom got up. "Shall we go?"

Reluctantly the others stood and stretched. They were all smiling.

No one seemed eager to lead, including the prince, so Tom picked a direction and headed off into the forest.

For some reason, Tom thought of his uncle. *I miss Uncle Carlos. Where is he? He's not here, is he? He's somewhere else. Somewhere far away, yet...* Tom knew he had forgotten something important. He shook his head.

After a few minutes Tom, Avani, Goban, and Devraj entered a section of jungle where the trees stood farther apart. Here sunlight penetrated the forest canopy high above and lit up the small clearing surrounding them.

"Where's Kiran, Malak and Chatur?" asked Tom.

"They'll catch up," replied the prince.

Suddenly they all turned as a thrashing noise off to their left grabbed their attention. Ferns and bushes were violently thrown aside. The ground shook.

"What—" began Tom.

"Shush," said Goban and Devraj.

A moment later a ferocious beast stepped up onto a fallen log directly ahead. Razor-sharp claws jutted from its knuckles, elbows and shoulder-blades. Raising its scarlet and blue head, it opened its mouth exposing long glistening teeth. Its nostrils flared as it sniffed the warm moist air of the clearing.

"Is that a zander—" began Tom, barely above a whisper.

"Yes. A zhanderbeast," replied Avani, equally quiet.

"Did you conjure—"

"No. Don't move. They've got terrible eyesight, but their hearing and sense of smell is keen."

As one, Devraj and Goban reached for their weapons. They weren't there.

"Nobody make a sound," whispered Avani.

At that moment Malak, Chatur and Kiran strolled into the clearing from one side.

"What I meant was—" said Chatur.

"I know what you meant," began Malak. Then he noticed the others.

"What's going on?" shouted Malak. "Did someone use a freeze spell on you?"

Chatur snickered. "You look like a bunch of statues."

The zhanderbeast's head whipped around. Malak and Chatur's eyes popped open.

"Run!" yelled the prince.

# Chapter 37: How soon they forget

"Everything ready?" asked Carlos, standing near the detection grid in the brightly lit makeshift control room.

"Power supply, check," said Leroy.

"Detection grid, check," Cheng responded.

"Sensor array, check," said Sashi.

"What about the radio connection to Tom's robot?" Carlos asked.

"Radios are online. However, Tom took the controller with him to the other universe. Even if we successfully create a portal, we've got no way of switching on the robot from this side. If Chloe's not on, or is out of power, we won't be able to communicate with her."

The side of Carlos' lip curled up into a half smile.

"Uh-oh. He's getting that look again," Leroy said.

Cheng glanced nervously at Sashi.

"No, no," said Carlos. "I just remembered. Tom gave one of his walkie-talkies to his friend James. If Tom's in range, maybe we can contact him that way."

"Well, first we've got to open a portal before we can even attempt to contact him," Sashi reminded him.

Carlos studied the blank wall behind the detection grid, as if he could magically see though a portal which did not yet exist.

Carlos nodded. "Right. So let's see what this baby'll do. Give me ten percent power at my mark."

Sashi grabbed a control slider and waited expectantly for Carlos' signal.

"Now," shouted Carlos.

Sashi pushed the slider up. A hum quickly rose in volume. "Power level's at ten—"

Sparks flew in all directions. The lights flickered, then went out entirely. The hum stopped. A final burst of sparks dimly lit the space for a second. Like ghosts, the shocked looks on the faces of the scientists slowly faded into total darkness. Silence.

"Well, that went well," said Carlos.

Nervous laughter echoed in the pitch-blackness.

\* \* \*

Tom bolted into a small clearing and screeched to a halt just inches before a thousand-foot cliff. Water thundered over a massive waterfall fifty yards to his left. Another waterfall cascaded off the precipice to his right. Two rainbows making complete circles glistened in the mists below. Goban and the others popped out of the forest behind him. Everyone stopped but Goban. The stocky dwarf couldn't slow down quick enough and collided squarely with Tom. Tom teetered on the brink, his arms waving wildly. Goban reached out, grabbed his arm and pulled him back.

"Thanks," said Tom.

"For saving your life again?" Goban grinned.

"No, for almost ending it."

The smile abruptly dropped from the dwarf's face.

Devraj glared at Chatur and Malak as they rushed from the forest and stopped. "We are trapped, thanks to you two idiots!"

"Malak is indeed an idiot," said Chatur, soberly.

"I'll show you who's an idiot!" warned Malak.

"Quiet! Listen," commanded the prince. Malak glared at Chatur but said nothing. Branches snapped. The sounds grew louder. Within moments, ferns were thrust aside as the zhanderbeast stomped into the clearing. Malak and Chatur stood closest. The beast headed straight for them. Chatur stepped back, but had nowhere to go. His foot knocked a few of stones over the edge. They clacked against the cliff face below. Chatur teetered precariously, then began to cry out. Malak grabbed his friend with one hand as the other hand slapped across Chatur's mouth. The two shook from fear. Sniffing Chatur, the monster opened its mouth. Chatur closed his eyes. Suddenly, a long pink forked tongue flicked out and licked Chatur's face. Withdrawing his tongue, the zhanderbeast blinked, then turned and calmly walked back into the forest.

Chatur wiped his face, his voice quavering, "Why didn't it eat me?"

"You must've smelled a bit off," said Kiran.

Goban frowned. "Something's not right here."

"Zhanderbeasts always attack," agreed Devraj.

"You sure you didn't conjure it up?" Tom asked Avani. She shook her head.

As the sounds of the monster's passage slowly faded into the distance Tom relaxed and studied the clearing around them.

The sunlight felt especially warm and the clearing was covered with wild flowers, similar to the ones he'd seen before, but many more varieties and in bold pastel colors of mauve, azure blue, and tangerine orange interspersed with multicolored spotted mushrooms. Bees happily buzzed from flower to flower. Tom inhaled deeply. The fragrance of licorice and lemon, mixed with cinnamon and butterscotch, was overwhelming.

Tom turned around. In all the excitement he hadn't noticed that in a corner of the meadow stood several miniature houses, some with mushrooms for tops, others with pine-cone petal shingled roofs. Still others were covered with yellow-green moss. Tiny oval doors and windows adorned the structures, and they weren't just on the ground. Many more stood in crooks of trees or even far out on branches.

Shielding his eyes from the sunlight, Tom peered straight up. Hundreds of bright specs of light drifted leisurely around the clearing. *Insects?* The spots sparkled as if lit from within.

"They're beautiful," said Avani, kneeling beside a tiny house and peering inside. Instantly, a streak of white light shot from the back of the house, then rocketed skyward.

"Good morning, dearies," said a high-pitched voice. "We wondered when you'd join us. You're looking more and more refreshed."

Tom and his friends turned all around, searching for the speaker.

"Over here," said a tiny being the height of Tom's palm. She sat perched on a tree branch ten feet above the meadow floor.

"Who are you?" asked Avani, taking a tentative step toward her.

The sprite smiled down at her. "Ahhhh, Avani Dutta. Keeper of the Light and The Chosen One by the Magic Crystals. Have you forgotten me already?"

Avani shifted her weight uncomfortably.

"My name is Mab. I'm queen of the Ellyllon. But perhaps you'd know us better as Wood Sprites."

Avani asked, "You said '*We wondered.*' Are there more of you?"

"An astute observation!" The sprite winked at Avani then snapped her fingers. Suddenly each of the points of light drifting about the meadow expanded into a fairy the size of Mab. They hovered around the clearing, their voices twittering so fast and high-pitched they sounded like bees buzzing.

Goban blurted out, "Careful, we were chased here by a zhanderbeast. It may be back."

"Ah Goban. It's so fun to host a dwarf after all these yaras."

"You—you know my name?"

"Of course, child. And don't you worry. You are safe here in the Realm of Fairie," several sprites twittered. "No creatures will harm you. Not even a zhanderbeast. You are safer here than in any place in this world."

Tom got that same tingling feeling in the back of his mind. "You said, we're looking more and more refreshed. What did you mean by that?"

"Each day you seem more relaxed," said the fairy, staring intently at

Tom.

"Each day? But we just got here."

The creatures buzzed with what sounded like high-pitched giggles and blown raspberries.

Mab grinned playfully down at Tom. "You've been here two weeks."

"Two weeks!" cried the prince.

"If that's true, why don't we remember?" asked Avani.

"It's so peaceful in our realm, other beings tend to lose themselves here. Oorts feel like myntars, days like oorts. At night, as you sleep, all your cares and troubles are washed away. In the morning you're completely rejuvenated, ready to start your lives anew." Mab tipped her head toward Avani.

"You're stealing our memories," said Tom.

Mab scowled at him. "No, no, child. We relieve you of your cares, your worries. We grant you peace."

"We can't have been here two weeks!" exclaimed Devraj.

"Oh, dear. Did I say you'd been here two weeks? My mistake. When we first rescued you from the blizzard you slept for three days. You actually first woke up two weeks ago."

"Two weeks and three days." Devraj, his back against a tree, sank to the ground looking dumbstruck. "If we had been here that long? I think I would remember it, would I not?" His words sounded hollow though.

"Realize that you are in the domain of faerie here. We are ancient beings, with ancient magic. Our magic is far stronger than elven magic, or what's left of elven magic, that is. Oh, and besides losing your cares, there's one more minor benefit of fairy magic. If you remain here with us, you will live forever…"

Tom and his friends remained silent, taking it all in.

The sprite queen continued. "I assure you that you've enjoyed many feasts and plays, games and music, and treasure hunts."

"Treasure hunts," said Kiran, Chatur and Malak excitedly.

"You mentioned you rescued us from a blizzard," said Tom. "I remember something. We were on a rock ledge with a drop off beside us. It was snowing and cold. We had a fire but it went out." Tom struggled to bring up the memories. "We were trying to get somewhere. To find something—" Tom glanced from Devraj to Goban to Avani. No one spoke. No one moved.

Shifting her attention to Tom, the fairy queen deftly changed the subject, "And how is the famous Thomas Holland today?"

"Ah—you know my name, too?" Tom asked. Mab remained silent. "But of course you do. If we've really been here over two weeks." Something in the back of Tom's mind told him this was true.

The sprite grinned broadly.

Tom stepped toward her. "I can't remember it all, but we need to leave. We've got something important to do and we don't have much time."

"Calm down. Calm down." The fairy glowed brighter as she hovered in front of him. "Time does not work the same here in the Realm of the Wood Sprites. I hope you will all stay with us forever. We so miss having guests to dote over." More happy twittering sounded. "But should you ever decide to leave us, you will have only been gone from your world but an instant."

"*When* we leave, you mean," said Tom. Another memory surfaced.

"You're not the first queen of the wood sprites we've met on our journey. The other queen was trapped in the form of a fountain in the haunted forest. She called herself '*The Oracle of Demon Forest.*'"

The fairies flitted around wildly, flying fast and making sounds like angry electric razors.

Queen Mab raised her hands and the sounds died down. Mab's expression now appeared that of someone who'd just taken a large bite from a watcher melon. "She—or it, I should say, is not, and never was a wood sprite! It's a demon, posing as a fairy, preying on unsuspecting travelers who are stupid enough to pass through Demon Forest." Mab's eyes narrowed. Goban and Avani looked at each other, sheepishly.

"You weren't fool enough to go through the Cave of Dreams, were you?"

"Um—well—yes, actually," replied Tom. "Though, for the record, I voted against it." He charged on. "You've probably told us this before but, how did you find us? How did we get here? You must've been nearby but, if so, why is this a tropical paradise instead of the frozen wasteland where we were?"

Mab snickered. "So many questions. 'Nearby' is somewhat meaningless when you're dealing with fairy magic. But to answer your last question, ancient and powerful magic sustains our warm, sunny climate. Secondly, Maximus, your giant furry friend came to us and asked for our help."

"Maximus?" said Tom. "You mean Max? My dog? Are you saying Max found you and asked for help?" Tom laughed. "For one thing, how could Max have found you? And for another, Max can't talk."

Mab snapped her fingers again. This time the vegetation parted and out stepped Max. He barked. Kiran ran over and hugged him.

"There," said the sprite. "Of course he can speak."

"That was just a bark," replied Tom.

The wood sprites tinkle-giggled again. Mab stared dumb-founded. "You can't understand him? Interesting."

By now the sun had set and the rainbows had ceased playing in the mists below.

"Max—" Tom's eyes narrowed in thought, staring hard at his dog. "Yes. We were somewhere. On a ledge. It was cold. We were freezing." Tom scanned the others faces. They seemed confused, uncertain. "Max came, leading the fairies. We were on a quest for something—"

The fairy queen broke in, "Well, I think that's enough excitement for one day. It's bedtime my dears."

Before anyone could say a word Mab snapped her tiny fingers. Yellow trumpet flowers rose from the ground and encircled each of them. White mists spewed from the flowers, accompanied by a hissing sound.

"No. Don't breathe it!" yelled Tom, but within moments he and his friends lay fast asleep.

## Chapter 38: Avani gets a makeover

The next morning Avani awoke, smiled and stretched. Sunshine sparkled through the trees. Hints of rose and honeysuckle fragrances drifted on a warm gentle breeze. The dark green moss she'd slept on felt thick and soft.

A tinkling, buzzing sound brought her to her feet. A moment later she was surrounded by twenty bobbing, hovering fairies.

"Who are you?" asked Avani.

"I'm Mab, queen of the wood sprites. We've met before."

"Have we?"

High-pitched giggling sounded.

"Yes my dear, we have." The fairy flew down, hovering right in front of Avani's face. Mab tipped her head sideways as she studied Avani. "Hmmm, you look a lot prettier with a few subtle touches."

"Prettier?" Avani looked down at her drab brown cloak. "What's wrong with the way I look?"

A large round mirror instantly appeared in front of her. Mab fluttered to the side, so Avani could see her own reflection.

"I look fine."

"Yes, of course you do, but may I try a little something?"

"Something?" Avani said uneasily.

"A touch of magic, that's all. It won't hurt, I promise."

"Ah—well, all right."

Mab waved her tiny hand and Avani's hair suddenly fluffed out. Mab flicked her wrist and Avani's hair grew lush, full curls. Another flick and her hair sparkled like gold. One last circle with both hands and Avani's eyelashes grew long and dark.

"What do you think, child?" asked Mab. The other sprites flew in close.

Avani leaned hesitantly toward the mirror. "Wow! I look—beautiful."

"But no princess would be complete without a gown,"

"I'm not a princess."

"You're engaged to Prince Devraj, correct?"

"How did you know that?"

"You will one day be queen?"

"Yes, but—"

"That makes you a princess."

Avani laughed. "Not exactly."

"Close enough." Mab waved her hands with a flourish, and a plain pink full-length gown surrounded her.

Mab squinted at her. "Hmmm. It needs—something. Perhaps a dash of color. Fairies, will you assist me?"

High pitched laughter sounded as the rest of the fairies dove to the ground and picked an assortment of multi-colored wild flowers. Next they circled Avani and dropped their bouquets. As the flowers touched the gown, bright light burst forth and her dress was now covered with a dazzling floral print in pinks, lavenders, and golds including matching bows and ribbons at the shoulders and waist.

Mab nodded appreciatively.

Avani stepped back in shock. She twirled around, gazing at her reflection. "I'm—I'm—"

"You look adorable." Mab sounded exceedingly pleased with herself. "Simply adorable."

"Wait till I show the guys." Avani twirled around, hiked up her dress, and dashed into the forest.

Tom said, "Wow, that's cool!" Goban, Devraj, Kiran and Tom huddled around a stump in a small clearing.

Avani rushed into the glen.

"Oh, hi Avani," said Goban, without looking up.

"Um—what are you guys looking at?" Putting her hands behind her, Avani pulled her shoulders back, raised up on her tiptoes and twisted gently side to side.

No one looked up. Goban grabbed a stick and bent closer to the stump.

"Goban found a terrestrial mollusk," said Tom.

"A what?"

"A slug," said Kiran.

"You're fascinated by a slug?" Avani didn't hide her disgust.

"No, this is interesting," said Devraj. "Come watch."

Avani sulked, but peered over the prince's shoulder.

Goban touched the slug with the stick. It shriveled protectively, then glowed bright blue. A brilliant flash then burst from the slug covering the stick in a thick gooey slime.

Avani yawned. "Wow, that is something."

"Yeah, isn't it," said Tom, excitedly.

Avani cleared her throat and strutted around. "Seen anything *unusual* today?" Her head tipped upward slightly, lighting her face in the sunlight.

The guys stood up and stared at her strangely.

"You mean—besides the slug?" said Tom.

She scowled, put her hands on her hips and leaned forward. "Yes! Besides the slug!"

The boys leaned back and glanced at each other nervously.

Avani pivoted around smoothly, tipped her head, placed one hand on her waist and jutted her hip out sideways. "Devraj?" she flashed him a brilliant smile as she fluttered her long dark eyelashes.

"Ah—no." The prince's face twitched. "Should I have noticed something?"

"Ahhhh!" she screamed. Glaring at them all she stormed off into the forest.

"What's up with that?" said Tom.

Goban shook his head. They all watched her retreating form.

"Women," said Kiran.

The guys cracked up.

"Men," said Mab disgustedly, after Avani explained what happened.

Avani scowled so deeply her eyes virtually disappeared.

"There, there, child." Mab brightened. "They were probably just preoccupied. I'm sure they'll notice next time."

"No!" Avani crossed her arms. "I want my old look back. I want it now!"

Twenty high pitched disappointed "Oh's" sounded.

"Are you sure, dearie?"

"Yes! I'm sure."

Mab raised her hand with a flourish, but suddenly her nose rose, her mouth opened and her eyes shut. "A—Choo!" She sneezed so loudly trees shook as a blast of golden magic burst forth.

"Oh dear!" Mab froze staring blanking at Avani.

Avani's hair had exploded into a large ball around her head. Sooty smudge marks covered her face, hands and dress. Smoke lazily rose from the ends of her hair. Avani blinked.

Mab, looking embarrassed glanced at the other fairies, giggled, then leaned toward Avani and frowned. As if holding a giant eraser she moved her hand vigorously back and forth. A moment later Avani was restored to her old self, long straight blond hair, short eye lashes, and drab old clothes.

"That was cool," said Kiran. "Can I try?" Goban handed him the stick and stepped aside.

Kiran bent over the stump and gently nudged the slug.

Avani walked up beside them. "Hi, guys."

# Chapter Thirty-Eight

They all stood up and faced her.

"Hi, Avani," said Tom. "Say, did you do something with your hair?"

"Boys!" she screamed, then stormed off once more.

* * *

The next morning Tom opened his eyes. Lifting himself to one elbow he gazed in wonder at the tropical paradise surrounding him.

*Where am I? Am I dead? Is this heaven?* Tom stood, drew in a deep breath and stretched.

*I don't remember the last time I felt this good.* But a somehow familiar tingling sensation filled the back of his mind. A deep uneasiness washed over him.

*Something's wrong. We were on a mission. A mission to find something. We had to bring it back somewhere, before something awful happened. Why can't I remember?*

Tom shook his head, then got up.

He stood in a small clearing. The others lay scattered about, still sleeping. Sounds of nearby waterfalls thundered and the rich smells of breakfast filled his nostrils. He spun around. Park benches stood mounded high with a fragrant feast.

But that tingling sensation returned, stronger than ever. Tom frowned. *I'm forgetting something. Something important.* He struggled but the memories wouldn't come.

From somewhere ahead, Max barked, then barked again. Tom headed in that direction.

"Quiet Max. You'll wake the others." Walking through the thick jungle undergrowth, Tom brushed aside a tall fern and stepped onto a narrow path. A small stream flowed beside the path. Max barked once more, sounding close.

"I'm coming, Max."

Tom jumped from moss covered stone to stone down the center of the stream. As he rounded a bend, his dog stood beneath a tree on the far bank. Max barked one last time. Tom jumped to the bank and hurried over.

"What is it boy? Why all the fuss?" The tree Max stood under had large orange fruit hanging from it and each fruit had eyes that followed Tom as he moved. Max pawed the ground where one of the fruits lay. Light reflected off something shiny. Tom bent over.

Coils of wire led from the fruit to a small flat round object covered with duct tape.

"What the—" Tom reached down and pulled the wires from the fruit. "It looks like a watch battery." He pulled the tape off. "It is a watch battery." Tom stood there bewildered for a moment, then hurriedly pulled out his headlamp and unscrewed the back. There was no battery in it. Placing the battery he'd just found into the lamp he screwed the back on, turned it over, and flipped the switch. The light shone brightly.

"But—that means…" Tom's eyes shot open, then he sprinted back the way he'd come, yelling, "Guys! Guys!"

# Chapter 39: Play it again, Tom

"Where dey go?" Dummere kicked the coals across the small shelter. "You 'sposed to watch dem!"

Bellchar snorted. "We saw dem go to sleep."

"Dey musta left. Was your turn to watch. It your fault."

The troll shrugged. "I watch. Dey sleep. Bright light come. Dey gone."

"Bright light? You fall asleep. You dream."

"Bellchar no dream."

"You dream!"

Bellchar glared down at the ogre. Steam from his wide nostrils enveloped Dummere's face.

The ogre coughed then asked, "If dey leave, where der tracks?"

Bellchar pointed to a set of tracks heading up the stairs.

"Dat only one. And dey too big."

"Dey not big," said Bellchar, raising his leg. "Dis big." The troll slammed his foot down on the ogre's.

Dummere screamed.

"Oops," said the troll.

\* \* \*

Larraj's staff glowed bright, yet it was still hard to see through the blizzard that pelted the three of them.

"What's this?" Juanita stood over an abandoned campfire. Someone had kicked it across the small plateau.

The wizard took in the scene. An overhanging tree set back from the cliff face provided a slight shelter. There were deep indentations in the snow surrounding the cold remnants of a fire.

Zhang Wu bent down and examined the few still partially visible footprints. "They bedded here for the night."

"It's still night? Where are they?" asked Juanita.

Another, more recent set of footprints, led up to the campsite, circled it, then continued on. Zhang rose to his feet. "It appears they were huddled together by the fire, some sitting, some lying. Only three sets of prints continue up the hill. A large troll, an ogre, and an adult elf."

"The elf is Naagesh," said Larraj, coldly.

"Without the kids?" said Juanita. "They didn't fall off the cliff, did they?"

"No. They didn't fall and Naagesh went on without them."

"Did the troll—or the ogre—" she began.

The wizard shook his head.

Juanita looked confused.

"I sense ancient magic at work here."

* * *

"Guys! Guys, wake up." Tom raced to Goban and shook him. "Goban, we've got to leave."

The dwarf yawned, stretched, then got to his feet and headed straight for the food. Tom stepped in front of him.

"Goban, our quest. Remember our quest. The wood sprites made us forget."

Goban paused, then his bushy brow rose. "Food's getting cold." Stepping around Tom he sauntered toward the table.

Tom hurried over to Avani. "Avani, wake up."

"Did you sleep well?" she asked, as she opened her eyes and smiled up at him.

"Avani, remember the fruit? With the eyes? The—Watcher Melon? I built a battery charger, remember?"

She looked at him with concern. "Are you OK?"

"Yes. No. YES!" He paused. "I—I think I'm more OK now then I've been in a long time. I think, no, I *know* we've done this all before."

Avani yawned as she stretched. "That's nice." She smiled at him then strolled over to join Goban, who sat eagerly wolfing down a stack of squamberry pancakes with steaming chokebutter syrup.

"Avani?" Tom called. But she just sat beside Goban and began eating.

"Arggghhh!" Tom scratched his head. "Why won't anyone listen to me?"

Prince Devraj stood and followed the others. As he passed by, Tom grabbed his arm.

"Devraj. Remember our quest?"

"Our quest?" said the prince, groggily.

"Yes. Remember?" We've got to find the power source and get it back to Elfhaven before the barrier collapses and the ogres destroy your home." Tom's eyes bored into Devraj's, then he glanced at the prince's empty scabbard.

Devraj's eyes were narrowed. "Quest?"

Tom's face went taut. "Draw your sword."

"What?"

Tom slapped the prince hard across his face. "Draw your weapon, you coward!"

Immediately Devraj's hand shot down to grab his sword's hilt but his hand grasped only air. First he looked angry, then perplexed. "I'm not a coward. I—I was too young to help my mother."

"Help your mother?" said Tom. "Was that from the cave of dreams? Hang on to that memory."

Devraj squinted at him.

Tom grabbed the prince with both hands and shook him. "Think!" urged Tom. "You've got to remember. We've got to leave."

"Leave? Our—Quest?" Slowly a fog seemed to lift from the prince's face.

Devraj looked down at Tom's hands then scowled. Tom released his hold on the prince's tunic and scanned his eyes questioningly.

"Tom's right," called Devraj to the others. Everyone slowly turned and regarded the two blankly.

"Remember our mission. We've got to find the magical artifact and save Elfhaven."

The others gawked at each other then slowly, one-by-one they got up from the table. Avani and Goban shook their heads then stepped beside Tom. In their eyes Tom could see clarity return as their memories flooded back.

"It's not a magical artifact," Tom corrected the prince. Devraj scowled at him.

Tom smiled. "The old Devraj is back!" Then he squinted, scanning the forest above "Mab. Mab, we need to leave."

Tom shielded his eyes from a brilliant flash of light. The queen of the wood sprites floated above them. More flashes and pops as the glen quickly filled with fairies.

"We remember everything," said Tom.

"Oh, dear." Mab looked annoyed. She snapped her fingers. Yellow trumpet vines sprouted up. Tom grabbed the nearest one and pulled it up by the roots. The flower wilted. Tom tossed it to the ground. The others did the same.

"I demand you return us at once," said Devraj, angrily. "You've been holding us against our will. We must find the artifact before it's too late."

"You were free to go whenever you wished," said the sprite.

"You made us happy. You made us forget our problems!" bellowed the prince.

The fairy grinned. "You're welcome."

Avani leaned toward Devraj and whispered, "We need their help."

"What? I do not need anyone's help! Least of all a bunch of childish—"

Ignoring him, Avani stepped forward and cleared her throat. "What Prince Devraj means, in his awkward way of asking for it is—we need your help."

"What? I didn't say—" stammered the prince.

Avani continued, "Your magical powers far exceed ours. Will you help us find the artifact and get it back to Elfhaven before the barrier collapses, before our home is destroyed by the troll and ogre armies?"

Mab faced the other sprites. A buzzing occurred, rising and falling in pitch, it lasted several seconds. Tom couldn't tell what they were saying, but it didn't sound good.

Queen Mab inhaled deeply then let out a long sigh. Her eyes slowly scanned Tom and his friends.

"I'm sorry, but long ago, long before you were even born, the wood sprites swore an oath never again to interfere in the lives of elves or dwarves, trolls or ogres. Never."

"You've already interfered, by saving our lives," said Tom. "And again by keeping us here."

"Well—" began the sprite, "—it has been rather dull since we left your world. Truth be told, we miss the excitement and drama that you crazy beings constantly seem to generate."

"Please," begged Avani. "All those people. Those children. You can't just let them die?" Avani leaned forward staring intently at the sprite.

"If you help us *crazy beings*, as you called us," began Tom, "we'll create even more drama for you."

Mab gave him a sly grin. "You've said this before. Wouldn't you rather discuss this tomorrow, after you've had more rest and more fun?"

"No, we wouldn't," said Devraj.

"You've said that before, too."

Devraj fumed. "Then I'm saying it again. But I mean it this time."

"We really do need to leave," pleaded Avani. "But we also need your help."

Mab paused, "Very well, if you're sure this time." Avani and Devraj nodded. Mab turned back and conferred once more with those around her.

Finally the fairy faced them. "We will consider your request further, but why the hurry. As I said, whenever you choose to leave you will have been gone from your world for but a moment. Stay with us for a while longer. Enjoy our hospitality. It's warm here and there's plenty of food," Mab looked pointedly at Goban. "We'd love to hear more of your tales of adventure. News from the outer world has been a bit lacking of late. You could stay and regain your strength. Stay a month or two, perhaps a year."

Chatur glanced excitedly at the others.

"One moment," said Devraj, frowning. He motioned them all to come near. They huddled together.

The prince whispered, "I don't trust them. They are luring us in again, making us feel comfortable, making us soft. Their talk has obviously worked on us before. If we wait too long, we may never leave." The others looked expectantly at Tom. He nodded.

"But they're wood sprites," argued Kiran.

"Yeah, wood sprites," chimed in Malak and Chatur.

Avani nodded. "I agree. Wood sprites have always been friends to the elves."

"And the dwarves," added Goban.

"Yes, but as they said, they are ancient beings, from ancient times. They do not think the way we do," argued the prince. "You heard her, time means little to them. Our concerns mean little to them."

"But if we stay, we will live forever," reasoned Chatur.

"We could stay awhile longer—just 'till we recover fully, I mean," added Malak.

Goban seemed torn. "The food is awfully good."

"No. We need to leave now," said Devraj. "We must not lose focus.

# Chapter Thirty-Nine

We have to get the artifact back to the Citadel, and fast."

"For once, I agree with the prince," said Tom. He and Devraj faced Avani.

She scanned each of their faces. Finally she let out a deep sigh. "OK."

Chatur and Malak looked crest fallen.

Avani stepped forward. "We thank you for your kind hospitality and for the wonderful care you've already given us. But we are refreshed now and wish to be on our way. Everyone in Elfhaven is depending on us. But we still need your help."

The buzz rose in volume. At first it sounded sad, then angry, then sad once more.

Tom noticed Devraj anxiously shifting his weight from foot to foot, his patience growing thin.

Mab paused. "As I said, we wish you'd stay. We enjoyed talking with you. It has been so long—" Her high-pitched voice held a note of sadness, of longing. She sighed, a sound like a far off violin tuning. "But we've decided to hel—"

Devraj cut her off. "As prince of the realm, and heir to the throne of Elfhaven I demand that you—"

"You demand. You demand!" stammered the sprite. "I've had it up to here—" She raised her tiny hand above her head. "—with your self-absorbed snobbery." The fairy turned an ominous shade of red as she flew to within an inch of Devraj's face. "We had decided to help you. But now I'm reminded why we abandoned the world of elves, dwarves and wizards in the first place. Be gone!" Mab raised her hand, preparing to snap her fingers.

"Wait!" cried Avani. "The prince *is* hot headed and obnoxious." Devraj scowled at her. "But we desperately need your help. Please, please help us." Avani's eyes pleaded with the sprite.

Mab's stern gaze moved from Avani to Devraj and back, then she conferred with the fairies one last time. The buzzing sounded furious and lasted several long seconds.

"We will provide you with warm clothes and leave you near the goal you seek. The rest is up to you."

"And food?" piped up Goban, hopefully.

The sprite paused, staring hard at Goban. "That would be your primary concern, would it not, dwarf?" But her face softened as she regarded him. "And food," she promised. Goban grinned. Then Mab added, "I do hope you like pickled toad stools and roasted fire-beetle butter." The other sprites giggled, despite the tense situation.

The grin dropped from Goban's face.

"But—" began Avani.

"No buts." Queen Mab snapped her fingers.

# Chapter 40: Lava, geysers, and ice-worms?

They found themselves standing on the slope of Mt. Ogram, a volcano deep in the heart of the Realm of the Ogres. Several days journey from where they'd nearly frozen to death.

Now dressed in shaggy white fur coats with matching hoods and over-pants that draped down all the way over the tops of their shoes, they looked at each other in shock. Against the snow covered mountain they were virtually invisible. A white backpack lay on the ground beside them. Goban's axe and Devraj's sword had been returned.

Avani reached up and found a necklace around her neck. Suspended from the necklace was an amulet. She lifted the object. It pictured an intricately carved likeness of Mab. As she touched it the fairy queen's voice spoke in Avani's mind.

*Keep this with you always, child.*

*What is it?* Avani thought.

*It's a magical charm, of course. What else would it be?*

*What's it for?*

*When the time comes, you will know.*

Avani frowned. *That's a bit vague.*

"*Of course it is. I am a wood sprite, after all. Good luck on your journey. Good bye Avani.*"

"No, wait!" cried Avani, but the voice had gone.

The others stared at her expectantly.

"I was— Mab said—" Avani decided it best not to mention it. She gave an awkward smile, then turned away and slipped the necklace beneath her tunic.

This high up they were above the storm. Here, only a slight breeze and a few large snowflakes lazily drifted down around them. Massive jagged stones lay ahead along with hundreds of heat hardened mud funnels jutting up ten or twenty feet in the air, resembling African ant hill mounds. Steam rose from several of the funnels, as well as from small cracks in the ground. If Tom needed a reminder he was on an alien world, this was it.

Avani faced Devraj. "Why did you do that? The wood sprites were going to help us, before you *demanded* they do so."

"I was in a hurry. They were taking too long. Anyway, how was I to know they intended to help?"

Avani glared at him.

Suddenly the mountain shook violently. An instant later a geyser erupted fifty feet up the slope sending steam and superheated water vapor high in the air.

"What was that?" asked Chatur nervously.

"We're on a volcano," said Goban. "Volcano's do that."

"We look like a herd of abominable snowmen," said Tom, studying each of them in turn. "Very short abominable snowmen." No one spoke.

Tom faced Goban. "If I remember right, the holo-map in the Citadel showed the crash site to be up ahead, around those boulders just past the steaming geysers, the boiling mud-pots, and the super-heated pools."

As if on cue a mud-pot erupted to their right. Head sized chocolate brown bubbles burst sending brown mud flying accompanied by a loud, deep burp.

Goban nodded, then reached down and picked up the pack. Cautiously peering inside, his eyes lit up as the smell of fresh baked soda bread, tart cheese, and savory meat filled his nostrils. An enormous grin spread across the dwarf's face.

A mile up the trail, Mt. Ogram still towered above them to their right. A massive glacier covered the mountain. The ground shook accompanied by a deep rumbling as a dense cloud of ash billowed from the volcano's peak. Intense heat caused the ash cloud to rise and twist with tremendous force. Continuous bolts of lightning flashed across the face of the dark cloud, far above them.

At the volcano's summit, crimson lava oozed down forming rivers of shimmering molten rock. Where glaciers lay in the lava's path, the solid ice exploded shooting plumes of steam high into the air. Farther down the slope, trees burst into flames as the molten rock neared the forests.

The trail they were on wound between the volcano and the top of a collapsed cinder-cone, a mini volcanic peak on the side of the main volcano. Where the cinder-cone had collapsed, a giant hole, one hundred feet across opened beside them to their left. They stopped on a narrow rock ledge overlooking the crater. A few tough vines grew across the ledge, stubbornly trying to get a foothold in the solid rock shelf.

To their right, a glacier rose up the slope of Mt. Ogram. Tom walked to the crater's edge and cautiously peered into the depths below. The bottom was obscured by fog, but for a moment Tom caught a glimpse of a small lake at the bottom.

Kiran kicked a stone over the edge. Tom counted to ten before he heard a faint 'plunk.' Tom shuddered, then scooted away backwards, but was quickly stopped by something cold and hard against his back. Pivoting around, the glacier towered above him. To his left, Tom noticed a perfectly round hole in the ice five feet off the ground. The hole appeared tall enough to stand in.

Tom pulled on Goban's sleeve and pointed. "Goban, what made that hole?"

"Ice-worms."

"Ice-worms?" whispered Tom.

Goban chuckled. "No. We call them that, but they're really caused by steam and hot water from the geysers. Cracks in the glacier allow the steam in. It bores holes and polishes them smooth. They're fun to play in, only you have to be careful of—the hazards."

Tom studied the hole thoughtfully.

"Come on," said Goban. "They're leaving us behind."

A few minutes later, the trail wound around the side of the volcano and started across a rock-strewn plateau interspersed with more tall, steaming mounds. Above and off in the distance, wisps of smoke from the ogre village of Ogmoonder rose lazily into the late afternoon sky.

The path led between several large volcanic rock outcroppings and at times was so narrow they had to go single file. Jets of super-heated steam launched from chalky-white, hard baked cracks on either side of the narrow trail. They had to time their movements just right to avoid the deadly geysers. After ten harrowing minutes of timing, dashing, and waiting, one last pair of particularly large jets lay directly in their path.

"One, one thousand, two, one thousand." A blast of steam erupted ahead. Tom rotated his head and squinted at his watch. The moment it stopped he yelled, "Go!" Tom sprinted past the last two vents. Avani, Goban and Kiran raced after him. A second later a powerful jet erupted just behind them. At this point the path opened onto a wide mist covered basin. There didn't appear to be any steam vents here.

"Where are the others?" asked Tom.

"They were right behind us," said Avani.

Goban took a step toward the path, "I'll go back and get them." Tom's arm shot out and stopped him as a jet of boiling water and steam erupted right where Goban would have stood. Their eyes met. Goban gasped. "Thanks!"

"I know the path. I timed the eruptions. I'll go." Tom checked his watch. Another jet shot upward just ahead. Tom rocked back, tensing his leg muscles. As soon as the jet stopped Tom sprang forward, but at the same instant Devraj, coming from the other direction, slammed into him knocking Tom over backwards. The prince fell directly on top of him. Chatur and Malak raced by, hopping sideways to avoid ending up on top of the dog pile.

Chatur choked back a laugh. Everyone else cracked up. Everyone except Prince Devraj, who scrambled to his feet and shot the others a murderous look then meticulously dusted himself off.

Tom got up and faced the mist covered basin. A slight gust of wind swirled the fog exposing a glimpse of a pool with unbelievably clear emerald green water. Bright orange algae surrounded the area with chalky white salt beyond that. The mist quickly returned, engulfing the water once more. Tom proceeded cautiously forward. As he approached the pool, intense heat radiated to the exposed skin of his face and hands. Steam rose from the pool making it difficult to see what lay beyond. Tom began to sweat. He unbuttoned his heavy winter coat. The emerald pool was so clear that folds and ridges, at least fifty feet below the surface, were easily visible.

"Hey, look at this," he called. "Careful though, there were hot springs like this in Yellowstone, back on Earth. The water temperature could reach boiling." The others stopped beside him.

"Oh, that smell," said Chatur, scrunching up his face.

"Who sliced the cheese?" chimed in Malak. Kiran and Chatur snickered.

Tom explained, "There's sulfur in the water. Sulfur smells like rotten eggs."

"A whole crate of rotten zapter-chick eggs, I'd say," added Chatur. More chuckling. Devraj's jaw tensed menacingly.

Ignoring them, Tom squinted, trying to see through the steam farther down the trail.

"Guys, come quick!" Tom bolted around the edge of the pool, then stopped, facing straight ahead. "Whoa—"

A few seconds later the others stood beside him. They all shared a moment of silent awe.

"I told you we could do it!" said Kiran, reverently.

A hundred feet ahead, up a slight rise and sitting atop a glacier, lay a circular silver tube with a rounded front end, the bow. It was roughly fifty feet long by twenty feet wide. The crumpled remains of an alien spacecraft lay before them. Large bulbous appendages jutted out from the fuselage at odd angles. Some places were shiny, though most appeared tarnished with pitted burn marks and covered in dirt and grime. One of the bulbs had broken off and lay badly twisted ten yards behind. A deep rut in the ice extended back a hundred yards from where the craft now lay.

They hiked up the glacier to the ship. A large burn mark accompanied by a jagged tear spread from the bow. The tear reached all the way back to mid-ship. A rectangular hatch sat up a couple feet off the ground near the stern.

Kiran walked up to the tear in the hull. He picked up a stick and poked it through the jagged hole in the ship. As he removed the stick a thick, goopy silvery liquid covered its tip. It gave off a hissing sound, then a small flame shot up, accompanied by a puff of smoke. Kiran dropped the branch. The flame quickly engulfed the whole stick. The ice below it hissed and steamed. Within moments the flames went out, leaving only red glowing embers of charred ash, which crackled and sputtered, sinking slowly as it melted the ice beneath it. Kiran gulped.

"I thought it would be bigger," said Goban, gazing up at the ship. Others nodded.

Tom walked to the hatch, which stood partly ajar. "What can we use to pry this open?"

Goban joined him, pulled Aileen off his back and started to wedge it into the hole. But he paused, staring at the hatch. Replacing his axe on his shoulder he reached up and touched a raised red symbol beside the hatch. Immediately the hatch slammed shut, followed by a loud hissing sound.

"Hmm," he said, then he touched another symbol, a green one this time. The hatch disappeared inside the hull with a *'whoosh,'* leaving a wide opening.

Tom beamed proudly at his friend. "I should've been the one to think of that."

"I can't let you and Avani solve all the problems," Goban said with a grin.

"Here, help me in," said Tom. Goban laced his fingers. Tom stepped up onto the dwarf's hands and pulled himself into the hatchway. Carefully he half-walked, half-slid down the inclined floor. At the same time a humming noise sounded, followed a moment later by lights flickering to life all around him. "So far so good," he called.

Goban jumped up and pulled himself in, then slid over and stood beside Tom.

"Are there any dead aliens in there?" asked Chatur nervously.

"Or—live ones?" whispered Malak.

"No aliens. Not yet anyway."

"Tom?" called Avani softly from outside. No response.

"Tom?" she called again, a little louder. A moaning sound emanated from inside the hull. Tom appeared, a horrified look on his face. He reached toward them, then collapsed in the hatchway.

"Tom," cried Avani. The others stepped back.

"Just kidding," said Tom, standing up smiling. "Come on in. The ship must've been on autopilot. We'll need help moving the power source once we find it." Then he added, "But don't touch anything!"

Kiran clamored inside, a huge smile on this face. Malak and Chatur slowly crept in, glancing around nervously.

"Avani and I will keep lookout," yelled the prince into the open hatch. Those inside covered their ears and squinted, waiting for the loud ringing to stop.

The ship had two main bulkheads. One forward. One aft. The forward one was bent slightly from the crash. Alien symbols resembling hieroglyphs were etched above each of three oval bulkhead doors. Tom peered inside the forward opening. Its outer curved walls were covered with more of the unfamiliar symbols. Multi-colored crystals jutted from panels along with hundreds of switches and levers. Some of the panels remained dark while others glowed dimly. Still others intermittently arced sending sparks flying across the cabin. In the center of the room, giant electrodes attached to a massive blue crystal slowly pulsed with light, sometimes dim, sometimes too bright to look at.

"This must be the control room," said Tom, pointing through the forward doorway. "And no seats, so that confirms it was an automated ship." Tom stepped back and faced the other way. "There are two aft doors. Malak, you, Chatur and Kiran take the left one. Goban and I will take the right. Let us know if you find anything." Goban followed Tom through the narrow doorway to the right.

*What is all this stuff?* Multi-colored displays lined the left hand wall with more of those bizarre hieroglyphs beside each one. Several of the instruments appeared dead, but a few still seemed to be functioning. Etched into the front wall was a giant symbol consisting of three squares, forming the points of a triangle, with a small circle in the center. A squiggly line radiated between the circle and each square.

"Look," said Tom excitedly, pointing at the wall. "It's the same symbol! Like the one on Avani's cube."

"Makes sense," said Goban. "This ship was built by the same beings that built the Citadel, right?" Tom nodded.

"Hey, we found something," yelled Kiran.

Goban left the room. Tom started to follow but something caught his eye. A few feet away, an oval shelf jutted from the wall. On the shelf sat a dark black cube, an inch square per side. The object appeared so dark it was hard for Tom to focus on.

*This looks as if it's made of the same material as the key to the Citadel.* Beside the cube, in the center of the shelf was a square indentation, the same size as the cube. Tom lifted the surprisingly heavy object and rolled it around in his hand. It felt warm. Tom placed the cube in the hole. A faint hum sounded as the cube slowly sank into the shelf. When it was flush with the top, light sprang outward and a slowly rotating star map hovered before him. Three of the stars were surrounded by green spheres. Another star shone highlighted in red.

"Tom, come on," called Kiran impatiently. Tom reached out and touched the top of the cube. The hologram shrank back inside and the cube lifted from the platform. Tom scooped it up and shoved it in his pocket.

Malak and Chatur stepped aside as first Goban, then Tom, squeezed into the tight space beside Kiran.

"It's shaped sort a like The Guardian said—only it's got a coat or something on it." Kiran scratched his head.

In the center of the room a four foot long by two foot wide dull gray rectangular box hung suspended in a cradle. Spotlights highlighted the object. One end had several large rings molded into the structure. Two buttons jutted up from the top. One was in the shape of a cross, the other a circle. Tom pressed the circular one. The box gave off a loud hiss, then the container hinged open and a cold mist spewed forth.

As the mist cleared, a shiny metallic cylinder, a few inches smaller in circumference than the outer shell, lay cushioned securely inside its container. Surrounding the device at its center, a row of bright ruby red crystals slowly pulsed with light. These crystal bars were a foot long and spaced parallel to each other at two inches apart. Tom's hair stood on end and he suddenly felt cool, as his body heat radiated to the much colder object. He pressed the other button and the container hissed closed once more, sealing itself. His hair immediately fell back down to its usual jumbled mess. Tom ran his hand through his hair, to little effect.

"Help me lift it," he said, bending down to grab one end. It was all the five of them could do to lift the heavy object and carry it over to the main hatch. Tom climbed outside. Devraj, Avani and Tom pulled while the others pushed from inside the ship. A moment later the unit dropped to the ice. The glacier shook making a deep cracking noise.

"Careful, we don't want to damage it," said Tom. Devraj's eyes narrowed. The others looked guiltily at each other. Goban and Kiran climbed out of the ship and ran over.

"Avani, ah—Kiran, could you do that thing? That thing you did with my robot Chloe? You know, that magic thing that made her float." Tom glanced sidelong at Avani. She nodded.

Kiran focused his mind on the container. Raising his hands over the object he muttered an incantation. Sweat formed on his brow. One end of the container rose a little, then settled back down. Tom's eye caught Avani's. She tipped her head ever-so-slightly and whispered something. The power supply rose to a height of two feet, wobbled a bit, then floated steady.

Winking at Avani Tom said, "Great job Kiran!" Kiran beamed at them all.

Tom stepped over to the container. "Let's tie the rope around it so we can pull it behind us." Goban looped one end of his rope through two of the rings on the end of the container then tied a bowline knot making a secure bridle. He pulled on the rope, testing his handiwork.

"Come on you two, let's go!" called Tom to Chatur and Malak, still inside the ship.

Turning to the others Tom said, "We did it! Great job everyone. We've got the power source. There's not much time, but if we're lucky, we can get it to the Citadel before the barrier collapses." The others looked excited. Even Devraj seemed mildly pleased.

## Chapter 41: And things were going so well...

Suddenly a high pitched alarm shrieked from inside the spaceship. Chatur bounded out of the craft, immediately followed by Malak.

"Chatur did it," cried Malak.

"No I didn't." Chatur took a swing at Malak. Malak ducked just in time.

"Did—what?" said Tom, suspiciously.

"Ahhhh—touched that button. The one surrounded by all those huge red symbols." Chatur looked guiltily at Malak. Malak's look shot daggers at Chatur.

"Then what happened, after you *didn't* press the button?" Tom asked.

"That giant crystal, the one suspended by those thick metal ropes, crashed to the floor, shattering to bits," said Chatur sheepishly.

The noise continued to rise in pitch.

"I think it's going to blow. Everyone, get behind those boulders up ahead. Now!" yelled Tom.

The others dashed toward the rocks, some fifty yards up the glacier, leaving the power source floating beside Tom. "Arrgghh! I meant, take the power source with you!"

Max barked urgently.

"I know, I know." Tom grasped the rope and struggled to pull the heavy box toward the others. Max bit down hard on the dangling end of the rope and helped pull. Or else he was just playing, Tom wasn't sure which.

Even floating, its heavy weight and inertia made it hard to get it moving. If he could just get it going, that same inertia would keep it moving. Struggling with the effort, the crate started to move. Tugging with all he had, it began to pick up speed. The pull on the rope lessened.

*It's working,* he thought. Then the rope went totally slack. *Uh-oh, now it's moving too fast. If I slow down it's gonna bowl me over.* Tom sprinted as fast as he could, frantically hopping over loose rocks like a scared jack-rabbit, while at the same time trying not to slip on the glacier ice. Max, clearly enjoying the game, shook his head vigorously as he continued tugging on the rope.

Up the glacier Tom saw Kiran jump behind a rock slab, the last to reach safety. The high pitched scream was getting unbearable. *Just another thirty yards.*

Tom glanced over his shoulder. The hull began to glow bright yellow. *Twenty yards...* Suddenly the sky lit up with a flash. A brilliant emerald green beam shot skyward as a thunderous boom shook the ground. The glacier cracked underfoot. A deep crevasse opened right in front of Tom.

For several seconds, small pebbles rained down on the area. They shielded their heads with their arms and cloaks. A putrid smoke burned their eyes and noses. When the smoke and dust finally settled, they peeked out from behind the boulders. A few paces away the power source floated toward them, hit a rock and stopped. There was no sign of Tom, or Max.

"Tom? Tom where are you?" called Avani. "Tom?" her voice quavered slightly. "Are you alright?" No answer. "Tom!" she screamed.

A tear ran down her cheek. "Tom?" she whispered. She heard a sound behind her. Avani whipped around excitedly. "Tom—" but she froze mid-sentence. There, standing before them were twenty ogres. One exceptionally large one held a huge club with gnarled, jagged roots sprouting from it. The ogre adjusted a long devilish horn on his leather battle headdress then stepped forward. Around his neck he wore a razor-sharp zhanderbeast claw necklace.

"How nice you come visit," said Lardas, his ear-to-ear grin exposing several brown rotting teeth.

# Chapter Forty-One

*  *  *

It had taken the king's soldiers several oorts to defeat the ogre ambush. Then another two days to make their journey back home without being seen by the thousands of ogre troops that had amassed near Elfhaven.

"What shall we do now?" asked Tappus, holding back a branch to peer through the dense tree cover into the clearing beyond. A thousand ogre troops stood just outside the North gate of Elfhaven's outer shield wall.

"I say we charge them from behind," said one of the king's military advisors. "We've got a company of your finest elven troops and the element of surprise."

King Dakshi looked from his advisor to Tappus to Sanuu. He paused. "What do you think, Sanuu?"

"Sire, the ogres outnumber us a hundred to one. The barrier yet stands. I think we should sneak behind the ogre forces, find a break in their ranks, then run through the barrier and call to one of our sentries on the parapet. Have them open the West gate." Tappus nodded in agreement.

"Sneak around?" snapped the advisor. "We are warriors, not thieves. We should fight!"

The king paused, glancing first at Sanuu, then Tappus, then his advisor. "We shall *sneak*."

*  *  *

Tom awoke to a series of wet slobbery kisses.

"Avani, no! What are you doing? Stop!" Lying on his back, Tom opened his eyes and tried to push her away. Three copies of Avani's face rotated in front of him. The gross thing was, she was drooling. Tom squinted against the bright blue light. Slowly the three faces spiraled into a single face. Then she barked.

# And things were going so well...

"Max?"

Max barked again.

Tom let out a deep sigh, then studied his surroundings. He lay on his back in an ice cave. That explained the blue light which seemed to come from everywhere, as if the ice was lit from within. Ten feet above him was the opening in the crevasse he'd fallen through. The walls of the cavern were polished silver blue with gentle curves, like half-finished ice sculptures. *Quite pretty, actually.* A frigid draft blew in from somewhere. Beneath them lay a large flat sheet of ice.

Tom scanned the walls looking for footholds he could use to climb out. "Goban! Goban throw me down your rope." No response.

"It could be worse," said Tom, as he pushed himself up onto one elbow. Just then an ogre face appeared above him in the opening.

"It's worse," said Tom.

The beast jumped down beside him and smiled.

Tinkly noises sounded as hair-line cracks formed beneath them. Then a loud shot rang out as a huge crack spread across the floor. The ogre looked down, then back at Tom. His smile had disappeared.

"Way worse." Tom grabbed Max tight as the whole floor collapsed with a *'boom.'*

# Chapter 42: Frozen waterslide from Hades

Standing by the smoldering ruins of the crashed space ship, Juanita knelt down and examined the ground. "These are Tom's sneaker prints. And look." She pointed. "Several other small prints. Tom's friends."

"Yes," replied Larraj, "and ogre footprints." He stared at her. Neither spoke.

The wizard raised his staff and moved it slowly back and forth across the area. The staff gave off a bright white light and an eerie hum. Like brush stokes painting a picture, with each pass a portion of a scene revealed itself. A moment later a shimmering image of the original space craft appeared before them.

The wizard's arm stopped moving and the scene faded. "Something happened. Something recent. Something that destroyed this craft."

Juanita swallowed. "Are the kids— Were they—"

"I sense they yet live. And their footprints lead off in that direction, along with those of the ogres."

"What about the power supply? Was it destroyed in the explosion?" she asked.

Larraj regarded her thoughtfully. "I don't know. If dragged behind them, it would have left a trail. There's no such trail. And unfortunately, their path leads up the glacier. It will be hard to track them. Though we know where they're headed."

"The ogre city," she said. The wizard nodded.

At that moment deep raspy voices sounded from over the hill. Whispering an incantation the wizard waved his hands. Wind began to swirl around them. Everything got darker. Their surroundings became distorted, harder to see, as if gazing through a water filled fish bowl.

Two ogres crested the rise.

"Where others go?" asked an ogre, its voice sounding muted, muffled.

"Take young ones to ogre city."

"And magic talisman?"

"Dey take dat too. Da Evil wizard want it."

"He give me da creeps."

His partner snorted in response.

The ogres were headed straight for them.

Juanita grabbed the hilt of her sword as Zhang pulled a glowing magic enhanced throwing star from his belt. The star popped and sizzled. The wizard touched their arms lightly, stopping them.

Larraj leaned forward and whispered, "They cannot see us. They can only hear our voices as ghosts in the wind." When the ogres neared them the wizard snapped his fingers. The beasts stopped.

"What dat sound?" said one, looking around.

"Don know," said the other, raising his club, his eyes darting left and right.

Larraj pointed his staff at the ogres. Abruptly the two changed course, walking off down the path, they were quickly obscured by steam vent eruptions.

The wizard waved his hands. The wind whirred around them once more. Everything looked clear and sound had returned to normal.

"The evil wizard?" spat Zhang.

Larraj paused. "That confirms it. Naagesh seeks the artifact."

"We know the kids are alive and where they've taken them. We also know they have the power source," said Juanita. She drew her sword and strode up the glacier covered mountainside.

"Coming?" she called over her shoulder.

\* \* \*

Tom and Max tumbled down a perfectly round ice tunnel, the ogre tumbling close behind.

Tom's hands and feet flailed around wildly, trying to find something to grip, something that might slow their decent. By pushing on the tunnel walls he eventually stopped tumbling. *This is a frozen waterslide from Hades.*

At that moment the tunnel banked hard left and he and Max slid up the side from the centrifugal force, Max above, Tom right below him. As the tunnel straightened out, they slid back down. Max's tail end was only inches from Tom's face. Tom wrinkled his nose and strained to push his heavy dog away.

"Max, move," pleaded Tom. Max squirmed, trying to turn around but his struggles just started them spinning again. The tunnel banked right and they flew up the other side.

*Or maybe we're like that Olympic bob-sled team—from Jamaica.* Tom smiled despite the dire circumstances.

Somehow the ogre stopped spinning, reached out and grabbed Tom's hood. Tom faced him, swallowing hard. The ogre grinned. At that moment the tunnel straightened then dropped off steeply. They picked up speed.

The ice around them shook followed by a thunderous blast. Small cracks formed around them. The tunnel rose sharply, then suddenly ended, launching the three of them up and out into open air.

They were flying through a large ice cavern carved by a giant geyser. Stalactites and stalagmites of solid ice whipped by on both sides. They slowed slightly as they leveled off.

Tom looked down. Something moved below. Something big. Several somethings. They were coiling around the ice columns. One of the creatures twisted upward, it's front end was nothing but a giant mouth with teeth which spun like a food processor. Its head swiveled back, slamming into the side of the ice cavern. Shards of ice flew as it began boring into the cavern wall.

Tom gulped. "Ice-worms! But—Goban said..." Max pawed him.

Tom faced forward. The geyser's spout made up of super-heated steam and boiling water loomed dead ahead. Tom screamed, his voice echoing throughout the cavern. Just before they hit the scalding water the eruption stopped and the spout abruptly vanished. Flying through a warm fine mist, they picked up speed again as gravity's pull caused them to angle out and down.

Now they were headed straight for the opposite cavern wall. Tom screamed. The ogre screamed. Suddenly the continuation of the tunnel they'd just been in reappeared and they miraculously flew into it.

Immediately the tunnel banked hard left, then right, then left again. Still holding Tom's hood the ogre tightened its grip. Tom and the beast began to spin in a wide arc. First Tom slid up the side of the tunnel, then the ogre. As in a tennis match, Max's head moved from one to the other as the two kept passing him. The next time Tom passed by, Max latched his teeth onto Tom's pant-leg. Now they all spun, though at a slower rate.

The tunnel banked hard right. Dead ahead a huge icicle, at least a foot across, hung in the center of the tunnel. Tom leaned back and closed his eyes. As they slowly rotated, Tom and Max missed the icicle by less than an inch. The ogre's eyes however, blossomed as he slammed into the obstacle. The icicle exploded into a thousand pieces causing the beast to lose his grip on Tom. Shards of ice rocketed past them, some spinning wildly.

When Tom stabilized, he lay beside Max, facing backwards. The ogre appeared dazed. Due to the collision, the beast had slowed down some, but he quickly picked up speed. The monster did not look happy.

Reaching into his adventurer's belt, Tom pulled out a smoke bomb and his lighter. Flicking the lighter, a tall flame shot up.

The tunnel widened. Tom glanced over his shoulder. Up ahead in the distance the tunnel split into three branches. Tom faced the ogre once more. Reaching down, the beast drew a bone handled dagger from his belt. Tom touched the flame to the smoke bombs fuse. The fuse fizzled, then went out.

"No!" cried Tom.

At that moment, a deep rumbling shook the tunnel. An instant later, shards of ice fell on them as a huge ice-worm mouth, teeth spinning wildly, burst through the ice above them. Tom ducked as the creature roared.

Glancing back, the ice-worm exploded from the tunnel ceiling just behind the ogre, missing him by inches. The creature began boring into the tunnel floor.

The ogre's eyes were wide yet the beast recovered quickly and reached for Tom's hood.

Frantically, Tom flicked the lighter several times. It finally lit. Touching the flame to the fuse once more it sparked, sputtered, then finally a column of dense black smoke billowed forth. Tom thrust it in the ogre's face.

Glancing over his shoulder, they were nearing the three tunnel split, heading for the center branch. The beast coughed and tried to kick himself away from the smoke. Unfortunately, he kicked Max. The tunnel split. The force of the kick sent the beast flying into the right tunnel while Max flew into the left. Tom sped down the center branch.

"Max!" he cried. There was a muffled bark.

"I've got to find a way to slow down." Tom pulled out his Swiss army knife.

Part of his nerd brain wondered, *What's the best blade? Should I use the cork screw or the saw blade?* Another—more practical part of his mind cried out, *who cares, you idiot. Just try something!*

Flipping out the saw blade, he slammed it down hard onto the ice behind him. The ice gave off a high pitched scream and his hands shook savagely, then his whole body shook, causing his vision to blur. The tunnel jumped all over the place in his mind.

Tom's strength began to fail. "I can't—last—much longer." The words vibrated loudly in his shaking skull. Just when he thought he couldn't hold on another second, he began to slow down.

The tunnel banked hard right. Tom flew up the side and lost control of his knife. It spun wildly beside him. Frantically reaching for it, his finger brushed the end of the blade sending it spinning even faster. The knife picked up speed, quickly disappearing down the tunnel.

"Well, that's it then. I'm dead." At this point, he was lying on his back, looking over his feet facing downhill. The tunnel began to shake.

"Not again."

Another ice-worm blasted from the ceiling just behind him.

"What next? What else could possibly go wrong?"

A tunnel merged with his from the right. It began to get brighter. The walls regained their brilliant ice blue. The light was brightest up ahead.

Another tunnel merged from the left. Tom squinted, shielding his eyes from the increasingly bright light. Suddenly, the tunnel ended launching him feet first into open air. He landed hard on his back on a flat rock shelf, a few feet down from the tunnel mouth. His speed and inertia kept him sliding forward.

A cliff lay ahead. As he neared the edge, he flipped over onto his stomach, reached out and grasped an exposed root. The root slid through his fingers. Tom tightened his grip. The root burned like a rope. Tom grimaced from the pain, but hung on. His legs and hips slid over the edge. Tom clamped down on the root as hard as he could. He stopped, his body dangling over the cliff.

Tom glanced down and gasped. Far below, wisps of fog drifted across the surface of a small lake. A nearby volcano rumbled angrily. Tom grasped the root even tighter. Hearing a noise, Tom glanced up just as the ogre launched from the tunnel. Things shifted to slow motion. The ogre's arms and legs flailed. The beast had a startled look frozen on his face. Their eyes met. Time paused. They both blinked, then time resumed its normal pace. The ogre flew straight over Tom, missing him by inches, then disappeared into the mists below. Seconds later Tom heard a faint '*plop.*' He shuddered.

As he began to pull himself up, Tom saw something sparkle to his right. There, on a small ledge two feet away, lay his knife, resting half over the edge. Tom began to sweat. He focused on the mists far below him, then slowly let out his breath.

Grasping the root in one hand he stretched out his other hand toward the knife. His fingers barely brushed it. The knife slid closer to the edge. Small pebbles fell, echoing down the cliff face. The knife began to teeter. Tom gasped, reached way out and grabbed the knife. The root he was holding made a cracking sound, then shifted down six inches. More stones fell. Tom dangled in open space, still holding the root by one hand. The root made that cracking sounded again. Tom thrust the knife into a pocket, grabbed the root with both hands and pulled with all his strength. Slowly, hand over hand he slowly rose over the lip. The root snapped. Tom's hand flailed for a second till he grasped hold of another vine.  He glanced over his shoulder. The root he'd been holding twisted as it fell, then disappeared into the mist below.  Tom swallowed, then strained to pull himself up the rest of the way.

For a moment he just lay there. Then he remembered. Max! He jumped up and ran toward the tunnel.

"Max?" he yelled. At that exact instant Max bounded out of the tunnel landing square on top of him, knocking him over.

Lying atop him, Max frantically licked Tom's face.

"Max, I can't breathe." Tom struggled to get free from under his shaggy pet. Standing up, he inhaled a huge gulp of air. Max barked, then pawed Tom's leg.

"No Max, we can't do it again. We've got to find our friends."

Max whined.

Tom arched his back stretching, then slowly dusted himself off.

Looking around more carefully, he noticed that the cliff he'd almost fell from was actually a collapsed cinder-cone. Tom whirled around. The ice tunnel he'd been ejected from was a hole in the side of a glacier that towered above him. A geyser erupted to his left. Tom's face turned ashen.

"Oh, no. We're back where we started. Back where the wood sprites left us." Tom exhaled heavily. "Come on boy. We've got a long walk ahead of us."

\* \* \*

Avani leapt up from the floor of the hut where the ogre had tossed her. Her look shot daggers.

"Wait till the elven army gets here. They're right behind us. You're in big trouble!" she said. Three of their captors stood in their make-shift cell, a shabby hut with a grass roof and cold dirt floor.

One of the ogres yawned. Another one pushed Avani hard, slamming her against the plank wall, causing the Magic Crystals to tinkle together softly.

Yellow light flowed from her satchel as she began to recite an incantation. Before she could finish, an ogre grabbed her glowing pouch and tossed it across the room. Another ogre stuffed a filthy rag in her mouth, then spun her around and tied the ends of the cloth around her head, then tied her hands behind her back.

Avani's pouch lay beside the floating case containing the power source. The light from the satchel slowly faded.

"Der. Dat better," said the beast, pushing her to the floor once more.

Avani glared up at him.

The ogre grunted, then all three ogres left, slamming the massive wooden door behind them. The sound of a large timber being placed into metal brackets filled the room. Heavy footsteps receded into the distance.

# Chapter Forty-Two

"Ahph ag lato!" mumbled Avani, trying futilely to speak through the gag.

"They took your crystals and bound your mouth so you can't cast spells," said Goban. "And they took my axe and Devraj's sword, as well as Chatur and Malak's knives."

"I've got a small dagger, hidden in my boot," said Kiran, hopefully.

"That could be useful," said Goban.

The prince struggled against his bound hands and feet.

Goban surveyed the room for anything that might help them escape. A large wooden bucket lay atop an old rickety crate. A pile of straw lay in one corner. The power source hovered beside Avani's satchel, otherwise the room was bare.

"I wonder why they didn't take the artifact?" Goban said, as if to himself.

"Ogres are stupid," Kiran answered. "They probably don't know what it is."

"Perhaps," said the dwarf.

Chatur interrupted. "We need a plan."

"And who's going to come up with this brilliant plan? You?" scoffed Malak.

Chatur's face turned red with anger. "No, and neither will you, but if Tom was here—"

"We don't need Tom," snapped Devraj. "I've got a plan."

The others waited expectantly.

Devraj scanned their faces. "Ah—first we will free ourselves. Then— we find our weapons—"

"Then what?" asked Malak.

"Ah—I had not strategized beyond that point."

"That's not a plan," laughed Chatur.

"Is so," said Devraj.

"Barely an idea," agreed Malak. Chatur and Malak nodded knowingly.
Devraj fumed.

Kiran chuckled.

Avani mumbled.

Suddenly their attention shifted to a commotion outside. A brilliant green light filtered in through cracks in the hut's timbers. A moment later the door swung open. They squinted at the figure silhouetted in the doorway. As the light faded, the figure stepped in.

"Naagesh!" gasped Kiran.

"Ah, you remember me, do you? Kiran Dutta. But I'd have thought you'd call me Professor Snehal," the wizard said with a sick grin.

Naagesh spotted the prince. "Oh, Prince Devraj, your highness." The wizard gave a curt bow. "I'd ransom you to your father but he's probably dead by now."

Devraj jerked, frantically trying to break free.

Naagesh continued, "And soon there won't be anyone left alive in Elfhaven to pay me, so..."

The wizard scanned the area. His eyes locked first on the power source, then on Avani's satchel. Briskly striding across the room he lifted the satchel.

Naagesh studied Avani's reaction as he asked, "And what do we have here? Your Magic Crystals, perhaps?"

"Yv etta gv dem bk," she shook her head vigorously.

Naagesh raised his brow. "What? Laptar chick got your tongue?" His thin lip curled up into a sneer. Avani glared back at him defiantly.

The wizard snapped his fingers and the gag vanished from her mouth.

"Those crystals are mine! Give them back!"

Naagesh sneered, then reached inside her satchel.

Avani's eyes widened. "No!"

As the wizard pulled them free, the crystals glowed brightly. Tendrils of neon colored magic flowed around his hand. The room grew bright then suddenly there was a flash accompanied by a loud 'bang.' The light faded and the crystals crumbled into dust. The wizard's lip twitched as he casually brushed the dust from his hands.

"Ah, a pity. No matter. I can't use them—but neither can you." Naagesh gestured toward the floating power source. It obediently glided past him and out the door. The wizard followed it, then paused in the doorway.

"Oh, I almost forgot." He snapped his fingers again and Avani's gag reappeared. The wizard sneered a final time, then slammed the door behind him.

# Chapter 43: Ogre hospitality — somewhat lacking . . .

It took Tom an hour to retrace his steps past the geysers, the boiling mud pots, and the superheated emerald pool.

When he got to the remains of the crashed ship, no one was there.

"Goban?" he called softly. "Avani?" Silence.

Tom studied the ground. He spotted a few of his friend's footprints along with many ogre prints, plus three sets of what appeared to be adult elves. Mostly, the wind had blown the snow away, exposing sections of hard rock and solid ice. From the prints he could see, he concluded the ogres had captured his friends. But it was impossible to tell which way they'd gone.

"No sign of the power source. The ogres must've taken that too." Tom searched the area. His gaze fell on his dog.

"Max, can you smell them boy? Where did they go?"

Max put his head down and sniffed, then bounded up the glacier.

* * *

It had started snowing lightly as Larraj, Zhang and Juanita hid behind some scraggly, wind-blown trees near the main gates of the ogre city.

The walls of the fortress were constructed of massive logs angled outward ending in roughly chiseled points. Every so often a chimney towered above the wall. A foul, oily black smoke billowed from each chimney's stack.

A hundred feet ahead two ogres stood guard outside the city's main gates. On either side of the gateway, skulls hung suspended above flaming torches. The skull's eye sockets flickered eerily from the flames below.

A moment later, the gates flew open and out marched two lines of ogre troops. Their leather and bone battle armor creaked and clicked as they strode briskly by. Larraj signaled the others to crouch lower. It took almost an oort before the last troops filed out of the gates and disappeared over the rise.

"At least two thousand," said Zhang.

The wizard nodded. "Headed for Elfhaven."

"And they're just the latest group," added the monk. "There are probably thousands there already."

The three stared in the direction the soldiers had gone.

"What do we do now?" asked Juanita.

Before the wizard could respond, an ogre and a troll crested the same rise the troops had crossed, but they were headed the other way, toward the ogre city. As the two approached, the gates were again thrown open and out walked an ogre patrol.

Their voices were faint but understandable.

"You two late," said an ogre.

"Bellchar fall in mud. I rescue him. But we lose little ones."

"You no rescue me, Dummere! You run when see da little pups weapons," huffed the troll.

The ogre in charge continued, "No matter. Lardas capture kids and magic device. Dey inside."

Bellchar glared at his ogre partner. Dummere returned his steely gaze.

"Naagesh want to question dem, afor we kill dem," added the ogre leader. The group turned and headed back toward the city gates. Bellchar and Dummere followed.

Juanita raised her sword and stepped forward. Larraj lightly grabbed her arm.

She glared at the wizard. "You heard them. They're going to kill Tom and his friends once Naagesh has questioned them."

As answer, Larraj reached into a pouch and threw a sparkling powder over them all. Next he spoke an incantation. Each one's appearance began to change, subtly at first, then quickly becoming more substantial.

They grew bigger, fatter, greener.

She glanced at the three of them, then seemed to relax. "How come I'm the ugliest? And this outfit—it makes my tush look big."

Zhang snorted. Having never heard his friend laugh, Larraj stared at the monk in shock, then fought to keep from laughing himself.

Larraj cleared his throat. "Follow me, quickly now," The three *Ogres* stepped out and hurriedly followed the patrol though the city gates.

* * *

Tom and Max had left the remains of the crashed space ship an hour ago. It was a steep climb over huge expanses of glacier ice, and deep snow drifts. Plus they had to avoid crevasses, like the one they'd fallen into earlier. Sometimes the crevasses were so long they had to detour a great distance to find a safe route. Here and there a stunted tree provided some cover. It had started snowing, lightly at first, but soon grew heavy.

*It's a good thing I've got this shaggy white coat. Keeps me from being seen.* Tom peered down at Max's black nose, black ears and his mottled brown and white coat. He sighed. *So much for not being seen.*

At that moment he heard voices up ahead. Running behind the nearest tree he cautiously peered around the trunk. Though hard to see with the storm, Tom could just make out two ogres, a hundred feet away, standing guard outside the main gates of the ogre city, holding tall, metal tipped pikes.

"Not too welcoming are they Max?" whispered Tom.

Suddenly the gates were thrown open and two lines of ogre troops marched out in full battle gear, carrying clubs and spears. And they were headed straight for them. Tom whipped back behind the tree, then looked around frantically for another place to hide, but there was none. The first ogres were only twenty feet away. Tom scrunched down as low as he could. Suddenly the troops turned and headed downhill. An endless line followed them.

"That was close," whispered Tom. Max just stared at him.

After nearly an hour things got quiet as the last ogres followed their brethren down the mountain.

Tom peeked around the tree. "We've got to find another way in. The gate's too heavily guarded."

As he stood up to leave, an ogre and a troll crested the rise only a few feet away. Tom whipped back out of sight. The pair turned and strode toward the city gates. Tom peeked out. The gates swung open once more and several ogres walked out to greet the new pair. They spoke briefly, then the whole group headed toward the city gates.

"Looks like Bellchar made it," said Tom.

From behind a small grove of trees, fifty feet away, three more ogres stepped out and hurried to catch up with the others.

Tom pointed at the stragglers. "Check out those three at the rear. They're even uglier than the rest." One of the ogres turned his head and looked straight at him. Tom ducked back behind the tree.

*That was weird. No way he could've heard me from that distance.*

Max gazed up at Tom and pawed him.

Tom peered around the tree once more. The last of the ogres entered the city. One glanced back in Tom's direction. The gates closed.

"Let's find another way in."

* * *

"What is it?" asked Zhang Wu, glancing at Larraj curiously.

"I don't know. I sensed something. Just outside the gate." The wizard looked over his shoulder. "Someone. Someone familiar." Larraj furrowed his brow, concentrating. He shook his head. "It's gone."

The three trudged past haphazardly formed rows of arched huts constructed of mud, rock, and bark-covered logs capped with thick grass roofs. Several ogres passed going the other direction. The three slowed and lowered their gaze, letting the patrol move on without them. Up ahead, another group of ogres met the patrol they'd been following. Grunts and growls followed.

"Here." Larraj gestured to his right. They rounded the corner and moved along a row of several large huts. The wizard stopped at one, then tentatively moved aside an animal skin suspended across an oval doorway. They heard the rumblings of ogres arguing. The sounds grew louder. Quickly pulling the skin all the way open, Larraj motioned for his friends to enter. Once inside, the wizard released the door skin. The floor of the hut trembled as several ogres passed by.

After they'd gone, Larraj waved his hands and their disguises slowly faded. His staff began to glow, giving off a soft, white light. Clubs and spears lined the walls and rusty bone handled daggers covered several large crates and littered the floor around them.

"An armory," said Zhang, walking over to inspect a tooth encrusted dagger. "Looks more like a troll ceremonial dagger than an ogre blade." A large red gemstone was embedded in the hilt. Black animal fur surrounded the stone. The monk flicked the knife high in the air. It spun around several times then he caught it. "Well balanced." He slipped the dagger into his belt.

"Why get rid of our disguises?" said Juanita. "They worked pretty well."

"I thought you weren't pleased with your appearance?"

She cocked her head sideways and stared at him.

"If Naagesh is nearby he may sense the use of magic. We mustn't alert him to our presence too soon." Larraj glanced around. "It should be safe enough in here. Let's wait until dark, then search for the children."

"They're in danger. We should find them now," argued Juanita, a determined look on her face. Larraj quickly raised his finger to his lips.

Another group of rowdy ogres stormed past.

The wizard met her gaze steadily. "If they intended to kill the children, they'd already be dead. Once the beasts have had their fill of food and drink, they'll sleep. At that point it will be safer and easier to find the children, and to set them free."

Juanita's eyes darted from Larraj to Zhang and back. "OK, I'll wait. But only until things quiet down."

The wizard nodded, then moved the skin curtain slightly and peered out into the late afternoon gloom.

* * *

Sprinting from tree to tree, Tom and Max reached the city's massive log wall. Hiking along the fortress's edge, away from the main gates, they searched for a way in. Suddenly Max raced ahead.

"Max, no!" whispered Tom, running to catch up. Twenty feet away, hidden behind a snow covered clump of bushes, Tom found Max digging frantically.

"What is it, boy? What'd you find?" Moving closer Tom could see. Something had dug a small hole under the wall.

*An animal must've created a way into the ogre city. For food?* Tom wondered. He turned to avoid the flying dirt as Max eagerly widened the hole.

It took them over half an hour to dig their way in. Once inside, walking between the snow covered huts was slow going. Each time Tom heard deep grunts of ogres nearby, he and Max hid behind barrels or stacks of wood. Some of the huts smelled bad—really bad. Tom's eyes began to water.

They traipsed down a narrow path between buildings. Up ahead, a group of ogres turned into their row, heading his way. Tom whirled around to run, but ogres blocked that way too. Tom threw back the flap on the nearest hut and jumped inside, Max bounding after him. It was nearly pitch black inside. Tom took a step and fell face first into a pile of rotten fish.

He raised himself up onto his arms and Max licked his face. "Not now," whispered Tom. The voices grew louder. Both groups stopped directly outside the hut. Tom turned over quietly.

"Me hungry," said a voice.

"Just ate," said another.

"Not 'nuff," said the first.

Suddenly a large green hand reached through the flap and patted the floor. As the hand neared Tom's leg, he frantically tried to move up the pile of fish but immediately slid back down. Near panic, Tom kicked a fish toward the outstretched palm. The ogre raised his hand directly over Tom's leg. Tom scrambled sideways. The beast's hand slammed down on the fish, grasped hold of it and yanked it back outside.

Tom let out a long sigh. Leaning forward he carefully peered out by the edge of the flap. The beast bit off the head of the fish, spit it out sideways, then swallowed the rest of the fish whole. Tom scrunched up his face and pulled back away from the door flap.

"You always hungry," said an ogre. The others laughed, then slowly moved on.

Tom relaxed. "Well, that could have been worse." A creaking noise came from behind them. Tom looked back just as the whole wall of smelly fish collapsed, burying them both.

"Remind me never to say that again," said Tom, as he slowly climbed out of the pile. Tom pulled a fish from his coat pocket with disgust.

"Ughhh, I smell awful."

Max lay down on the pile of fish and rolled over vigorously several times.

"Oh, Max!" Tom shook his head. Carefully he pulled back the curtain and peered outside. Stepping out, he signaled for his companion to follow.

Max gazed up at him with big eyes, his tongue hanging out to one side.

Tom looked both ways. They were alone. He bent down eye-to-eye with his dog. "OK Max, I'll run to that next row of huts. You stay here. If the coast is clear, I'll whistle for you. Got it?" Max opened his mouth and pawed Tom's leg.

"Good." Tom started to move. So did Max.

"No Max. Stay!" Tom watched his dog intently. Max panted, despite the cold.

Tom took another step. Max followed.

"Max!" whispered Tom, exasperation in his voice. "Stay. Got it? Stay!"

Max sat heavily on his haunches, watched Tom and drooled."

"Good." Tom took a step, then whipped back around. Max sat still. Tom repeated the move. Max stayed put. Tom sprinted to the corner, looked both ways then whistled.

\* \* \*

"What was that sound?" asked Juanita.

"Shush," whispered Larraj. The wizard released the door skin and extinguished the light. "Sounded like a whistle, and nearby."

"And that smell!" said Juanita.

# Chapter 44: Trolls honor?

Tom bent down and patted his dog. "Good boy."

As he stepped out, a troll and an ogre walked around the corner directly ahead. The ogre faced the other way but the troll looked straight at Tom. Bellchar froze, as did Tom.

Tom's finger shot to his lips. "Shush," he mouthed. Bellchar blinked, then turned and tapped Dumerre on the shoulder.

Tom jumped back around the corner and held his breath.

"What?" said Dumerre.

"Someone here. Da boy," said Bellchar. "Come."

Tom heard footsteps approaching. He and Max hurried around the next corner and hid behind a stack of crates. The footsteps grew nearer.

Bellchar's hand slapped down on the crate above Tom. Tom held his breath.

"Der no one here," said Dumerre.

"But I saw—" bellowed Bellchar.

"Ha! You saw," laughed Dumerre. "What you saw? You just dumb troll. Trolls see tings. Come. We supposed to guard prisoners." Tom heard the ogre walk away.

Bellchar lifted the top crate, exposing Tom. Tom froze. But Bellchar was looking the other way at the receding form of Dumerre. The troll closed his hand, effortlessly crushing the crate. Bellchar tossed the broken shards to the ground, then stomped off after the ogre.

Tom ducked down and waited a few seconds for the footsteps to die away. His head slowly rose above the remaining crates. Bellchar and Dumerre were gone. He bolted to the next corner, and cautiously peered around it. Bellchar had caught up with Dumerre and they were now far down the lane. Stepping quietly, Tom and Max followed the two at a safe distance, careful to stay in the shadows.

A few minutes later Bellchar and Dumerre halted before a large hut. Two ogres stood guard outside the entrance. The four spoke, then the two guards left.

"Bellchar and Dumerre must be relieving them," said Tom to Max. Tom spotted a pile of poorly stacked barrels ten feet from the hut. "I can't hear what they're saying. Let's move closer." As Bellchar and Dumerre turned away to watch the departing guards, Tom and Max dashed behind the barrels.

A few minutes later another ogre, rounded a corner and stomped up to the hut. "Dummere. Bellchar. Come wid me. Get food for prisoners," said the new ogre.

Dummere grunted his disapproval. "We spose to guard prisoners. Be in trouble if leave."

Tom got down on his hands and knees and peeked around the barrel, his head sticking out.

"You in trouble wid me if you don't!" The new ogre raised his club, threateningly.

Dummere grumbled, but followed the other around the hut. Bellchar started to leave then looked back and spotted Tom. Standing up, Tom stood up his shook his head at the troll. Bellchar frowned.

"You—owe—me," Tom said quietly. "I saved your life. You gave your word you wouldn't turn us in."

Bellchar snorted, his nostrils flaring, his foul breath visible in the chill air. He paused, then followed the ogres. Tom froze, but heard only the sound of heavy footfalls receding into the distance. He slowly let out a long held breath, then hurried over to the hut and signaled Max to follow him. Max padded over, sniffed the wooden door, then pawed it. Max barked.

Tom's eyes shot open. "Shhhhh."

"Max?" said a faint voice from within.

"Kiran?" whispered Tom.

"Tom!" said Goban.

"Rromppph!" attempted Avani, her gag still in place.

"I'm here. I'll see if I can get you out." Tom scanned his surroundings. A barrel stood on end beside him, and a staff leaned against the wall next to the barrel. The barrel clinked as he rolled it underneath the log that barred the door. Tom inspected the barrel's top. It was loose. Twisting the lid one way, then the other, he pried it open. Peering inside, Devraj's sword, and Goban's axe, stood upright, and a couple of daggers lay on the bottom. Tom replaced the top, then stood on the barrel and pushed up as hard as he could but the log wouldn't budge.

He glanced around again. Just below the plank that locked the door, the end of a log which was part of the wall, jutted out sideways. Tom's eyes fell on the staff leaning against the hut.

Moving the barrel over to the corner of the building, he grabbed the staff and used it as a lever. With the staff on top of the lower log, and one end under the plank that barred the door, Tom applied leverage by pushing down and putting all his weight on the far end. The plank lifted from its iron brace slightly, then fell back down. Tom tried again but with the same result. He desperately searched the area for anything else he could use. At that moment, a troll walked around the hut.

"Bellchar," said Tom, taking a step backwards.

Max growled.

"Max shush." Tom grabbed his collar.

Max whined.

The troll flared his nostrils then blinked dully. Bellchar twisted his body to call out.

"Bellchar. You promised if I saved your life you wouldn't turn us in. You owe me. Trolls honor, remember?"

The troll frowned again.

Tom stared at him. "Help me Bellchar? It's too heavy for me. I can't lift it." Tom moved over and pushed upward on the plank that barred the door, without effect.

The beast's scowl deepened. His gaze landed first on Tom, then on the log, then around the corner he'd just come from.

Bellchar clenched his jaw. "Den we even?"

Tom nodded. "Den we even." Tom shook his head. "Then we're even."

Bellchar paused, then with one finger the troll lifted the heavy log from its iron rungs. The door swung open a few inches, with a creak. Bellchar dropped the log. The ground shook.

Tom released his dog. Max walked over and sniffed the troll's leg. Bellchar bared his teeth.

"Bellchar," called a voice from around the corner. "Bellchar, where you? You spose to help me wid dis food."

Tom's eyes shot open. He grabbed Bellchar by the arm and pulled. "Come on," whispered Tom, struggling to lead Bellchar into the dimly lit hut. Bellchar pulled the door closed behind them. Tom's friends stared in disbelief.

"I'll explain later. Quick Bellchar hide!" Tom pulled Max down behind the crate and hid beside him. Bellchar looked around dully. He picked up the bucket, walked into the corner by the door and put the bucket over his head.

"That won't work," whispered Tom in frustration. At that moment the door swung open and Dummere stomped through balancing several precariously stacked plates of steaming, foul smelling 'food.'

"Who open door?" demanded the ogre.

"Door," said Chatur. "You mean—that door?"

"Yes dat door!" roared the beast. "No other door!"

"I believe—it was—another ogre. That's it, and—ah, he was looking for you." Chatur glanced nervously at Malak.

Malak chimed in, "Chatur's right. He said—you should've been guarding the door better, and—you're in big trouble."

"Exactly!" added Chatur. "You'd better go now and stop him, before he turns you in." Malak and Chatur nodded vigorously in unison.

Dummere threw the plates of food roughly to the ground in front of them. Something on the plates wriggled.

"I be back wid da rest of da food." Dummere started to leave, looked straight at Bellchar, blinked, squinted, paused for a moment, then turned and walked out. The door slammed, followed by the sound of the log being replaced into its rungs. Thudding footsteps receded into the distance.

Tom stood. "You can remove your disguise now."

Bellchar lifted the bucket from his head and tossed it noisily to the ground. The troll walked to the door and pushed. The door flexed slightly, then relaxed.

"How come the ogre didn't see you?"

"Dummere an idiot," said Bellchar. Turning, he threw his shoulder hard against the door and it burst apart, shards of wood flying everywhere. The troll stepped through the splintered doorway.

Tom hurried over to him.

"Oops," said Bellchar, giving Tom a sheepish grin. The troll turned to leave.

Tom grabbed his arm. "You won't tell the ogres, right?"

Jerking his arm free the troll trudged away saying, "Bellchar even."

Tom watched him go. "Yes, but you won't turn us in, right?"

The troll kept walking.

\* \* \*

Tom removed the gag from Avani's mouth, then untied her hands.

She wrinkled up her face and twisted away. "Oh, I thought that stench was the troll, but it's you."

Tom exhaled deeply. "Sorry."

Avani faced him, but leaned back and squinted. "Where'd you go? I called for you after the explosion. You didn't answer. I thought you were—" Avani paused, her eyes tearing up, "dead."

Tom regarded her for a long moment. "The explosion opened a crevasse. Max and I fell in. An ogre jumped down and he was so heavy we broke through. There was this frozen water-slide and a geyser and an icicle and ice-worms. I thought we were goners for sure." They all just stared at him.

"Anyway—Goban, remember that hole in the glacier? The one you called an ice-worm hole?" Goban nodded. "There really are ice-worms by the way. Well, that's where we came out. It was a long walk back." Tom hurried over to untie the prince.

"You asked a troll for help?" Devraj's eyes shot daggers. "Are you crazy?"

Tom's face began to flush. He and Avani rushed to untie the others. As he did, Tom studied each face, searching for support. They all stared at him as if he'd gone mad.

"I saved Bellchar's life. He owed me," stammered Tom.

"Bellchar? You know the troll by name?" said Devraj, turning even redder than before.

"He's the troll who kissed me."

"What?"

"Ah—when Avani turned me into a female troll. When we rescued my robot Chloe, remember?"

Devraj continued to glare at him. "Are you saying, you enlisted the help of a troll—because he kissed you?"

"No! Of course not. That's gross. He smelled of alcohol and slobbered. We were trying to distract him. Avani used her magic. She made my lips—and my chest—" Tom paused, watching the prince. "You don't care. Anyway, it was Bellchar, back at the quicksand. He was the troll that was stuck. So, after you left, I threw him a vine." The prince's jaw dropped.

Tom looked pleadingly at Avani.

She met his gaze for a moment then said, "Trolls killed our father." She put her arm around her brother. A tear rolled down Kiran's cheek.

"Goban?" said Tom, desperately.

The dwarf gave him a sad look. "Trolls are the sworn enemies of the dwarves."

"Come on," said the prince. "We've got to find our weapons. Then the artifact."

"Your weapons are in the barrel just outside the door," Tom responded feebly.

Without saying another word, the prince stepped through the remains of the doorway, opened the barrel, grabbed his sword and strode off. The others followed. As Avani walked past, she stared at Tom as if she didn't know him. Goban glanced at him but said nothing. Neither Malak nor Chatur would even look at him.

"Wait," said Tom feebly. "I'm the one that knows the way out."

## Chapter 45: Find Naagesh, we find...

"Well, where are they then?" asked Juanita, squarely facing Larraj as the three stood just inside the shattered remains of the cell door. "I waited, as you suggested. Now they're gone. Where are they?"

Larraj's eyes quickly scanned the room. "They were being held here. And recently."

"That's obvious. I don't need *magical super-powers* to deduce that." Juanita's face went rigid.

"I sense no harm has befallen them." Larraj walked to the center of the room and knelt. He reached down, picked up some ash and rubbed it between his fingers. Tiny flecks of magical energy sparked. He sniffed the powder. "These were Magic Crystals. Their magic hasn't completely dissipated." The wizard's eyes flicked this way and that, considering. "Naagesh was here and tried to use the crystals. Naagesh has the artifact."

"Fine, but where are the kids?"

The wizard stood and calmly faced Juanita. He paused. "It doesn't take *magical super-powers,* as you put it, to deduce where they've gone."

"Oh? Then where?" she asked.

"Naagesh is the key. They'd follow Naagesh to retrieve the artifact." Larraj paused. "Find Naagesh and we find the children."

\* \* \*

"Find Naagesh and we find the power supply," said Tom, standing on a glacier covered rise a mile downhill from the ogre city. The wind had picked up, causing the light snow to drift in deep mounds. It was the deepest powder Tom had ever seen.

"We failed. Admit it," said the prince, glaring at Tom, "Like the rest of you fools, I was emboldened by Kiran's speech. But once again we failed."

The prince locked eyes with each of them in turn. "Yes, I wanted to believe we could do it, I wanted to believe a bunch of sniveling children, led by me, could save Elfhaven, that we could save it when kings and wizards and the finest elven guard could not." He glared at them all. "I, Prince Devraj, heir to the throne of Elfhaven, was drawn in by the power of Kiran's optimism.

"If I'd returned to Elfhaven, as my father has likely done, perhaps I could have made a difference. Instead, I attempted another of Tom's foolish schemes. Now we have lost everything. The barrier is about to collapse, and thanks to Malak and Chatur who exploded the sky ship and got us captured, Naagesh has the device. What's more, once the ogres realize we have escaped, the whole ogre nation, those who are not already surrounding Elfhaven, will be hunting us."

Devraj stared at the horizon, in the direction of Elfhaven. "Well, I have had enough. I am fed up with following Tom and his hair-brained schemes. Prophecy or not!" The prince paused. "I am leaving. Who is coming with me?" No one spoke. "Come along, Avani."

"You are not—yet—my king. I am not yours to command. Nor will I ever be," Avani said, but the usual fire was lacking from her voice.

Devraj's face went rigid. He pivoted sharply and strode down the mountainside, avoiding the deepest drifts as he went.

Avani walked over to Tom and put her hand on his forearm. She looked sad. "It's not your fault, but Devraj is right. We failed. How could we have thought—" Her eyes misted over. She gave Tom a weak smile, squeezed his arm, then lowered her gaze and followed the prince.

Malak and Chatur peered at Tom sheepishly, then hurried after her.

Goban hiked to the top of the rise and stood beside his best friend. From their position the two watched as Devraj entered the tree-line a hundred yards below and disappeared from sight.

"Wait," cried Kiran. Avani, Malak and Chatur stopped, then turned back. Kiran smiled brightly. "We can call a dragon. Like I read in my book."

"Kiran. Everyone laughed at you the last time you suggested that. In the Citadel, remember?" said his sister. "Come on. Let's go back to Elfhaven and see if there's anything left of it, see if there's anything we can do." She continued walking down the slope.

Kiran raised his arms defiantly. Suddenly his voice boomed out, "Huc draco, draconem, draco." Everyone stood silent. Kiran squinted, putting his hand up to shield his eyes from the late afternoon sun. No one spoke.

"There!" cried Kiran pointing off toward the horizon.

Everyone looked where he pointed. There was something, a faint speck. It slowly grew larger. It had wings. It flew straight toward them. Kiran yelled. "It's a dragon!"

"No. It's a bird," said Chatur.

Squinting, Tom could faintly make out one of those colorful four winged flying creatures with the kangaroo tail, the ones he'd seen in magic class. Tom gave Kiran a sad smile.

Goban and Tom watched their friends, now halfway to the tree line. Tom glanced at Goban. Goban nodded and they headed after them.

* * *

Kiran heard laughter from Chatur and Malak, down the slope. He looked at the distant horizon. A tear rolled down his cheek. Running back over the rise, away from his friends, he sat down heavily behind a large snow covered slab of stone.

*No wonder they laugh at me. I'm a failure. Dad might still be alive if I'd begged him to stay, if I'd begged him like Avani did. Instead, when he said he had to go to war, I yelled at him. I told him I didn't care if he lived or died. I saw Dad's lip quiver. I saw a tear run down his cheek as he turned and slowly walked away. That was the last time I ever saw him. Maybe, 'cause I said those things, he was distracted in battle…*

Kiran wiped the tear from his cheek. Another replaced it.

\* \* \*

"Devraj, wait!" cried Chatur, as he struggled in the deep powder. Malak and Avani were close behind. The tree line was still a ways away. "Devraj!" Chatur toppled head first in a deep drift.

"Are you crazy? Stop yelling. You're going to attract ogres, you idiot!" yelled Malak, a moment before he too, fell in the same drift. Chatur brushed the snow from his face, then threw a snowball at Malak, smacking him on the side of his head.

The prince stepped out from the trees, far below. He drew his sword.

"Look out behind you, you idiots!" called Devraj, charging uphill.

Chatur and Malak slowly turned, another snowball in Chatur's hand. Twenty ogres crested the snow covered rise above them. Spotting the elves, the beasts screamed, raised their clubs, and trudged through the deep snow, right for them.

\* \* \*

"At least it has stopped snowing," said Zhang, sighting down his silver handled sword. In a flash, he flipped the blade around in a wide arc and slid it effortlessly into its scabbard.

Unseen beneath the monk's cloak, the ruby on his new dagger began to glow.

"Yes," agreed Larraj. "That should make it easier to follow them. But the wind is drifting the snow, filling in their footprints."

"They're headed downhill. Do you think that's where Naagesh went?" asked Juanita.

The wizard scanned their surroundings one last time. "I don't see his tracks. Only the children's." Larraj glanced at her. Juanita said nothing.

* * *

In some places, where the wind had blown off the snow, the glacier was solid ice. In other places, waves of snow drifts filled the area, but there was no cover nearby. Avani, Malak, and Chatur huddled close. The ogres were almost there. Prince Devraj trudged up and stopped in front of them. Malak and Chatur drew their daggers and stood nervously beside him.

A loud horn blast sounded. The ogres stopped, confused. Over the crest, from behind the ogres, hundreds of dwarves flew down the slope on snowboards.

"Now that's odd," remarked Malak. Chatur just blinked.

One of the boarders flew off a snow covered rock slab, did an unintentional back flip in midair, his arms waving frantically. Colliding with an ogre, they both went down, disappearing in a deep snow drift. Two other dwarves banked hard and crashed into each other. Their boards flew off. One board struck an ogre in the head, knocking it out cold.

"Those must be the glacier planks Tom gave Goban the plans for," said Chatur, staring at dwarves crashing into ogres, crashing into each other, and just plain crashing.

"Snowboards," corrected Malak.

"I think they need more practice," said Chatur.

* * *

Tom and Goban tried to run and help but the snow was too deep, and their friends were too far away. A squad of dwarfs saw them and veered over, stopping beside them.

"Prince Goban," said one of the warriors, bowing deeply.

"Cut that out," said Goban, glancing at Tom. "I've got an image to keep."

The soldiers looked at each other, then nodded.

"Where's my father?" asked Goban.

One of the soldiers pointed to the tree-line far below. "King Abban is leading a platoon of soldiers behind the ogre forces, while the plank riders distract them. He will attack soon."

"Give us your snowboards," commanded Tom.

The soldiers raised their brows and looked to Prince Goban for guidance.

"Do it," said Goban.

The dwarves quickly unfastened themselves from their boards. Tom sat down and began lashing his sneakers to the nearest board's makeshift bindings. Goban, watching Tom, did the same.

Tom rolled up onto his board, pushing off with his hands. Goban followed him, still paying close attention to Tom.

Tom grinned at his friend. Goban wobbled a bit, then gave Tom a nervous grin.

Tom leaned back, picked up speed and putting the board on edge, he threw up a large cloud of powder as he banked hard.

*A little heavy. A little sluggish. A little stiff, but all-in-all, not bad for a prototype,* he thought, smiling. *Let's see what this baby'll do.*

Tom straightened out, then rotated around, his other foot now forward. A fallen log lay ahead, barely poking out of the snow. Tom jumped up, landed on top of the log sideways, his board hanging over both sides. Tom slowly rotated, then jumped off the end of the log landing easily in the soft snow.

"Cool!" he called out loud.

Tom looked back. Goban was just approaching the log. The dwarf jumped, landed off center, waived his arms frantically, teetered, then did a face plant beside the log. Raising his head, he spit out a mouthful of snow. "I'm OK!" He gave Tom a thumbs up.

*Goban's fine.* Tom faced forward. Ahead, a heated battle between dwarves and ogres was unfolding. *Time to get serious.*

An ogre stood over two dwarves that had crashed together. The beast raised his club. Tom flew off a snow covered boulder and banked the board left in midair. Holding the board's tip he slid across the ogres back then launched off the other side. As the beast twisted around to see what had happened four dwarves tackled him.

Tom landed hard, flying snow momentarily blinding him. A second later he burst out of the snow cloud.

*Just like riding the rails at the terrain park back home.* A hint of a smile crossed his face. *I wish Uncle Carlos could see me, he'd go ape! Though he'd probably be pissed that I'm not wearing a helmet.* Tom grinned at the thought of his uncle, but he had no time to dwell on it.

Thirty yards ahead, three ogres surged forward in a line a few feet apart. They were closing on a handful of dwarf soldiers. Several more dwarves were coming to their aid, but they'd never make it in time. Tom banked hard, lined them up, then carved sharp 'S' turns, using the ogres as poles in a slalom course. Slapping the beast's legs as he flew by for good measure, the startled ogres turned, lost their balance and fell into each other in a tangle of arms and legs.

*Where's my go-pro when I need it? The video'd go viral for sure back home.*

Up ahead, Tom noticed more ogres had surrounded a group of dwarves. *Wait—those aren't dwarves, its Avani, Malak, Chatur, and Devraj.*

The prince valiantly swung his broadsword, keeping the nearest ogres at bay. Avani conjured up the image of a zhanderbeast, its razor sharp claws slashing out. The ogres jumped back. But without her crystals, the image kept shifting and fading. The ogres would not be fooled for long.

Tom scanned the slope around him. Off to his left lay another fallen log braced against a tall pile of stones. He leaned back, veered left hard, throwing up a rooster-tail of snow high into the air.

"Hold on!" he yelled to his friends. It was going to be close. He leaned over farther, steepening his turn. Jumping at the last second, he landed hard on the log, but his weight was too far back. Struggling to keep from falling, he waved his arms wildly. Just before he fell he threw himself forward with all he had. The board slowly tipped upright. Springing off the end of the log, he sailed through the air pivoting slowly. *Did I time it right?*

The zhanderbeast faded. An ogre raised his club and charged straight for Avani.

Tom landed square on top of the ogre's head, knocking it sideways, spoiling its aim. Unfortunately, this sent Tom spinning wildly, causing him to crash into a deep snow drift ten yards away. The ogre screamed. Miraculously, Tom's board was still tied to his feet. Tom looked left. There, mostly hidden by the trees, hundreds of dwarf warriors on foot were headed his way.

Tom climbed out of the drift, then yelled at the ogres surrounding his friends, "Hey you ugly smelly beasts. Can't catch one scrawny kid on a snowboard?" The ogres cursed, raised their clubs, and charged right for him.

Tom gulped, then pushed off with his hands toward the forest and the onrushing dwarfs. In the deep snow the board slowly picked up speed, but not fast enough. The ogres were gaining on him.

Only a hundred feet more. Fifty feet. Tom glanced over his shoulder. An ogre was right behind him, close enough that Tom could smell the stench of his breath. The beast raised his club. Tom ducked, turned around and raced through the line of dwarf soldiers, narrowly missing two of them, but colliding with a third. Tom and the dwarf ended up in a pile.

"Sorry," said Tom, standing up and helping the dwarf to his feet. The soldier didn't look happy. Hurriedly brushing himself off, the dwarf charged toward the battle. The ogres were quickly overwhelmed.

Tom took off his board, then struggled uphill through the deep snow.

When Tom reached his friends, Goban was once again back on his board just uphill from where they stood. The dwarf's arms flew around wildly, but he managed an awkward stop beside them.

"Wow," Goban said to Tom. "You've got some moves. When you spun around in mid-air and landed on that ogre's head, that was great!"

Tom grinned. "Well, I had a bit of luck hitting him, but then I couldn't maintain—" Avani cut him off.

"Where's Kiran?" she asked, a panicked look on her face. "Wasn't he with you?"

"Ahhh," began Tom, glancing at Goban, "I thought he was with you."

Another group of ogres was headed their way.

"Worry about Kiran later," screamed Devraj. "Run for those rocks." The prince pointed to a nearby pile of massive stones. "Now!"

# Chapter 46: Go now, or feel our wrath!

Several ogres raced past their hiding place.

"We can't stay hidden forever," said Chatur. Hearing his voice, two of the ogres stopped and swiveled to face them.

Malak rolled his eyes. "Now you've done it."

Prince Devraj swore beneath his breath. Drawing his sword, he stood in front of the others, his eyes seething with anger at Malak and Chatur.

Goban whipped Aileen off his shoulder.

The ogres screamed and attacked. Devraj swung his sword at the first one, did a somersault under the beast's legs, then leapt to his feet behind him.

Goban slammed the blunt end of his axe down hard on the other ogre's foot. The beast screamed in agony, grabbed his foot and hopped around wildly. When the ogre faced the other way, Goban sprinted up a rock slab and leapt into the air landing on the ogre's back. The dwarf grabbed the beast around the neck and squeezed hard. Goban hooked his fingers inside the monsters nostrils and jerked upward, causing the ogre's head to snap back. The beast screamed once more then violently flung his body around. Goban's legs flew outward but he managed to keep his grip tightly around the ogre's neck and nose.

Meanwhile, the prince fought a desperate battle with the first ogre. Devraj brought his sword around in a wide arc, aiming for the beast's leg but the beast managed to block the prince's sword with its club. Devraj swung valiantly, chips of club flew but he couldn't get to the ogre that wielded it. The monster remained just out of reach.

At that moment, the other ogre twisted around violently. Goban lost his grip and flew off, colliding with the prince. The two tumbled to the ground in a heap. The ogres raised their clubs above them.

"Come on," said Tom, to Chatur and Malak. "We've gotta help."

Tom pulled out his knife and opened the main blade. "Stop!" he yelled. The ogres turned to face him.

"Come on," whispered Tom. "Help me!" Malak looked at Chatur. They gulped in unison, then drew their daggers and stepped beside Tom.

"Leave them alone," yelled Tom, taking a step forward. "Go I say. Go now, or feel our wrath!"

"Yeah, feel our wrath!" said Chatur, shaking slightly.

The ogres looked at the three of them and grinned. But the grins abruptly dropped from their faces as they looked up. Their eyes bulged. The beasts took a step back, then turned and ran.

Devraj stared at Goban's ogre-snot covered hand resting on his chest.

"Sorry," said Goban, sheepishly. As Goban slowly pulled his hand up off the prince, stringy globs of ogre goo stretched between his hand and Devraj's previously spotless tunic. The bond finally broke leaving ogre slime on both of them. Devraj's face reddened.

"Guess we told 'em!" cried Chatur, slapping Malak hard on his back. Malak coughed, but slowly smiled.

Tom gave them both a half-hearted grin, then scanned the battlefield surrounding them. Everywhere dwarves and ogres alike stared upward, shielding their eyes with their hands. Several pointed to the sky. Tom glanced back to see what they were looking at, but his view was blocked by the large boulders they'd hidden behind.

"What's going on?" asked Avani.

"Beats me," said Tom.

Suddenly, all across the battlefield ogres and dwarves hopped, slide, and fell down the mountain as fast as they could in the deep snow.

\* \* \*

Kiran walked to the edge of the knoll and stared dumbfounded at the battle raging far below him.

"How could I not have heard that?"

Kiran drew his dagger, preparing to run and help his friends. But something strange was going on below. All the ogres and dwarfs suddenly stopped fighting. They pointed up at the sky, yelling something, but Kiran couldn't make out what they were saying. Then everyone bolted down the mountain.

A warm breeze began to blow. Squinting upward against the bright sunlight, Kiran tried to see what they'd been staring at.

A thunderous "*whoosh, whoosh*" sounded and the largest dragon Kiran had ever heard tale of dropped from the sky like a rock. Miniature tornadoes of snow, dirt, and small stones spiraled off its beating wingtips. The ground shook as its massive talons slashed deeply into the ice and snow. Kiran raised his hand, shielding his eyes from the flying debris. The creature's wings crackled and creaked, like old leather as the beast folded in its wings by its sides.

Standing only ten paces from Kiran, the dragon cocked its massive armor laden head sideways. Its huge dark eye studied the elf lad intently. The monster flared its nostrils. Steam spewed forth followed by a puff of smoke.

Kiran's eyes began to water. *Wow, it's warm. And that smell— brimstone, onions, and grilled lizard meat.*

The ground shook as the beast roared, "Who dares summon a dragon?"

"Um, it was me, actually. I called you. Hi, my name's Kiran. Kiran Dutta—of Elfhaven." Kiran took a step forward and offered his hand to the beast.

The dragon reared up slightly, its eyes now wide. The beast snorted. Flames leapt out. Kiran dove to the ground, just in time.

"I, Ninosh, mightiest descendant of the dragons of Mount Zaadin, was summoned by a scrawny elf brat?" The beast once again flared its nostrils and moved its head until its massive eye hovered only inches from Kiran's face.

Kiran scooted back on his bottom, then got up and quickly patted several singed and still smoking spots on his cape.

Turning his head slightly Kiran yelled, "Ah—hey, guys. It worked! I called a dragon." Kiran, still eying the creature sidelong, waved his hands wildly, motioning for the others to come.

The dragon blinked, then slithered its monstrous serpentine neck around looking in the direction Kiran waved. Halfway down the slope, from behind several large boulders, Kiran's friends slowly stood. Glancing nervously at one another, they crept cautiously toward the giant winged beast.

Ninosh's left eye scanned those before him, finally stopping at Tom. He sniffed the air.

"You are not of this world." Steam lazily drifted up from the monsters flaring nostrils.

Tom wasn't sure if the beast was actually speaking out loud, or if the words just sprang into his mind. He took a tentative step forward. "Ah, hi. My name's Tom. Tom Holland. I'm from Earth. It's—kind of a complicated story." Tom quickly scanned the other faces. "You see, it all started when I took my robot Chloe to the lab to meet—"

"Stop!" boomed the beast.

Tom leaned back, swallowing hard. Max barked. Tom grabbed his collar. The dragon's eye flicked from Max to Tom.

"A boy and his beast. Thomas Holland. From the prophecy? The destroyer from another world?" Ninosh stared intently at Tom.

"He's here to help us!" said Kiran stepping beside Tom. The winged beast shifted his gaze to Kiran. The dragon snorted. Flames launched over their heads.

As if to himself, Ninosh said, "The Prophecy is unclear. Elves enjoy writing their prophecies as riddles. Perhaps it is no coincidence we meet today."

The creature raised its head, flexing its powerful shoulder muscles. "Why did you summon me, boy from the prophecy? Boy from another world? What is it you desire?"

"Tom didn't summon you. I did!" protested Kiran. Everyone, including the dragon, ignored him.

"Ahhhh—we need your help," began Tom. "Naagesh stole the replacement energy source that powers the Citadel. If we don't get it to Elfhaven before the barrier collapses, the city will be destroyed by Naagesh's minions of trolls and ogres."

Ninosh raised his head and screamed, flames launched high above him. The ground shook as the dragon roared, "Naagesh!" The beast glared at them, his eyes lit from within with a flickering red light.

"In days of old, hundreds of our kind flourished. We inhabited all the lands. When Naagesh arrived, he tried to control us. Those he could not control, he killed and used their parts for his foul magic potions." The dragon raised his right leg and slammed it to the ground. The hillside shook once more. Malak fell over and immediately jumped back up. Chatur snickered, but shut up when Ninosh's eyes focused on him.

"So you were one of the dragons controlled by Naagesh?" said Devraj, the knuckles on his sword hand turned white as he raised his weapon. Goban stepped beside him.

The dragon eyed them both warily.

"I was. Myself, and four other dragons were under the wizard's spell."

Avani lightly touched Devraj's arm, then met his gaze. The prince slowly lowered his sword.

"But you're no longer controlled by Naagesh, right?" she said.

"No."

"How? What happened?"

Ninosh seemed lost in thought, staring off at the horizon. "The evil wizard used the five of us to attack his enemies during the great war.

241

# Chapter Forty-Six

Many wizards died under dragon fire."

"Yes, but how did you escape?"

Ninosh scrutinized Avani, letting out a long, slow breath. Hot, moist, steam surrounded them for a moment, then cleared.

"Another wizard freed us from Naagesh's spell."

"Who freed you?"

"Larraj," said the dragon. "The wizard's name was Larraj."

Avani cleared her throat, then took a step forward.

"We need your help," she began. "As Tom said, Naagesh stole a magical artifact. Without it Elfhaven's barrier will collapse. The troll and ogre nations, puppets of Naagesh, will destroy the elves first and then move on to the dwarves."

"That is of no concern of mine. Besides, why should I help the elves when they did not help us fight Naagesh?"

"We tried, but Naagesh was too powerful. We asked the wizard council for help, but by then Naagesh and his followers controlled the council."

"The results are the same. You did not help us. So I will not help you." The dragon unfurled his massive wings and flexed his powerful leg muscles, preparing to launch.

"Wait," said Tom, stepping beside Avani. "If you won't help the elves, will you help the wizard Larraj instead?"

"Larraj yet lives?" said Ninosh, his outstretched wings lowered slightly.

"Yes, and he's trying to stop Naagesh."

The beast paused, his gaze moving slowly from face to face.

Ninosh drew in his wings once more. "I will fly you to wizard's lair. No further. And I can only fly three of you. Choose wisely."

"I called the dragon, so I'm going." Kiran stepped forward. Avani grabbed her brother's arm, stopping him.

"No, Goban goes, since he's the best fighter. I'm going, since I'm the best at magic. Tom's going 'cause he's..." Avani stared at Tom. "Ah, 'cause he's the one with the plan. You do have a plan, don't you?"

Tom gave a weak grin. "Ah, sure. Course I have a plan. I'd have to have a plan, wouldn't I?"

Prince Devraj studied Tom suspiciously. "Fine. You three follow Tom's—plan. Get the artifact and bring it to Elfhaven, any way you can. The rest of us will make haste for home and meet you there."

"But I summoned the dragon. It's not fair!" said Kiran. "I should be the one—" The dragon regarded him.

"Kiran, you summoned the dragon," began Avani, "and proved us all wrong. That was amazing. But now you've got the most important job of all. You take Max and when you get home, get Nadda and Nanni to the castle before the barrier collapses. I'm depending on you. They're depending on you. Once we arrive, you can help us with the artifact."

Kiran sulked as he glowered at her. Max pawed his pant leg. Bending down he absently scratched Max behind the ears, though he continued to glare at his sister.

## Chapter 47: Dinosaurs and giant serpents

"There're too many prints," began Juanita. "I can't figure out what happened."

Larraj faced downslope. "A battle took place here. No more than an oort ago. Dwarves fought ogres, but I don't recognize some of these tracks. They appear to be made by giant serpents, though no reptiles of this size exist in the Icebain Mountains, other than ice-worms, but they live underground." The wizard bent down and examined an unusual long S shaped groove in the snow. It started above and continued far below them.

"They look like snowboard tracks," Juanita replied absently. "Snowboards? Here?"

"Snowboards?" said Larraj.

Juanita burst into a smile. "Tom must've given Goban the plans."

She knelt down, examining the ground. "These are Tom's sneaker prints, but they seem to end beside what appear to be dinosaur tracks." Her scientist's curiosity kicked in to high gear. "An extremely large dromaeosaurid theropod, commonly known as a raptor, perhaps." She brushed aside some snow and studied the print intently. "Or possibly a T Rex, though the prints are a bit small for a Tyrannosaurus."

Juanita stood up. "Are there dinosaurs on your planet?"

Larraj glanced uneasily at Zhang. The monk nodded.

"Those are dragon prints."

"Dragons? You're kidding, right?" She laughed. Then she noticed they weren't laughing. The smile abruptly dropped from her face. "What are you saying? You think Tom was eaten by a dragon?"

"No, I am not saying that at all."

"Then what are you saying?"

The wizard exhaled sharply then studied the scene around them. He and Zhang exchanged a quick series of whispers. Larraj faced Juanita. "The signs tell us that the dwarf army surprised the ogres. They fought a fierce battle. The dwarves were winning. Then a dragon appeared, frightening away both ogres and dwarves."

Zhang pointed at some tracks that led downhill. "These small prints started below, led to this point, then headed back downslope."

The wizard nodded. "A dragon landed here. Several children walked uphill, toward the beast. They stopped beside the dragon then calmly walked off back downhill following the dwarves, presumably toward Elfhaven."

"And Tom? What of Tom?"

"There's no evidence of a struggle." The wizard got down on one knee and pointed at the nearest dragon footprint. "See, Tom and two other children's prints end here, beside the beast's leg." Larraj faced Juanita calmly.

"Then they disappear," she said, looking at the ground, then at Larraj.

"The only explanation that fits all the clues is—" The wizard paused. "Is that somehow the children enlisted the aid of a dragon. It appears Tom and two friends flew off on the creature."

Juanita gasped. Involuntarily taking a step back she stared dazedly at Larraj and Zhang. "You've got to be joking."

The two just stared at her.

"That's totally ridiculous. For one thing, Tom's deathly afraid of heights. And for another, he promised never to accept a lift from a stranger."

Her mouth abruptly closed. She gasped, paused, then let out a long, slow breath. "So—where did they go? How can we trace a dragon's flight? There won't be any footprints."

The wizard watched as his monk friend meticulously polished his new bone handled dagger. "I still believe they seek the artifact. They would head for Naagesh's lair."

Juanita glared at Larraj. "And where might that be?"

"Knowing Naagesh, it would be somewhere in those rugged peaks off to the North West." The wizard pointed uphill to their left. Juanita studied the long line of jagged spires, like giants teeth, which formed the backbone of the Icebain Mountain range trailing off into the distance.

"Can't you narrow it down a bit? That's way too much area to search. We'll never find them in time."

Neither Larraj nor Zhang spoke.

Juanita flushed, letting out a long, slow breath. "Lead on."

* * *

"Wow, what a view," said Avani. The wind whipped her hair and she wore a huge smile. Tom sat behind her, his legs firmly gripping the dragon's neck and his arms wrapped tightly around Avani's waist. Directly behind him sat Goban, his eyes darting around, looking excitedly at the countryside far below.

Tom's eyes, however, were closed.

Avani twisted around. "Come on, open your eyes. You may never get another view like this."

"I don't want another view like this. I don't even want this view." But Tom opened one eye a tad and peered down cautiously. Then he slowly opened the other eye. They were high above the ground, easily a thousand feet. The volcano was now directly behind them. A tall ash cloud spewed from its peak darkening the lands behind it. Sparkling scarlet ribbons of molten rock streamed down the mountain. From this height, the ogre city of Ogmoonder, off to the left of the volcano, was barely visible. Hundreds of tiny strands of smoke lazily drifting skyward from the ogre huts, were the only things that gave the village's location away.

With each flap of the dragon's powerful wings, they were pushed down hard against Ninosh's muscular neck. Every so often they could relax when the dragon held steady and would just glide. Their legs moved in and out as the creature breathed. The sucking sound from its breath was barely audible over the rush of wind across their bodies, and over the dragon's wings. Avani was right, the view was incredible.

A jagged mountain peak completely covered in snow and ice lay directly ahead. Just below the peak stood a castle in ruins. On three of the four corners of the structure, tall pointed spires reached high into the sky. The fourth corner tower had crumbled to the ground eons ago. Whimsically curving stonework wound around each of the three remaining spires, all the way to the top. Most remarkable were the bright gold and silver banners that flapped in the stiff afternoon breeze. The crisp, colorful pennants flying above the decrepit ruins looked somehow out of place.

"Wow," said Tom, pointing to the rubble. "What's that?" Tom was so taken with the view he forgot to be scared of the heights.

"That's Castle Dunferlan," said Goban. "Once home to my great-grandfather King Zabund, and his father before him. It was destroyed during the great war. Not by wizards, by ogres. No one's lived there in over a hundred yara."

Tom pointed to a puff of smoke, billowing out from the far end. "Looks as if someone's living there now."

Goban narrowed his eyes and touched his axe handle. "So it does."

Tom leaned out around Avani and yelled, "Ninosh, can you take us lower, so we can get a better view of the ruins?"

Ninosh swiveled his head sideways and nodded, then pulled in his wings and dove. The wind howled furiously and threatened to yank Tom off the dragon's back. He tightened his grip around Avani's waist. A moment later the dragon extended its wings and the violent wind subsided.

Though they were still high up, from this elevation the destruction looked complete. The roof had long since collapsed and large, dark and sinister vines twisted around the few remaining columns and windows. Like evil snakes strangling what was left of the building.

"How come the banners survived?" Tom asked, trying to shake the image of giant snakes from his mind.

"The pennants were a gift from the wood sprites. They're infused with fairy magic. They've been flying above the castle ever since it was first constructed three hundred yaras ago. They flap even without a breeze, and they look as nice today as when they were first raised."

At that moment the dragon banked sharply. The G forces from the turn threw Tom violently to the side. He tightened his grip around Avani's waist once again.

"Ouch," she said, squirming to relieve the pressure.

"Sorry," said Tom, without loosening his grip.

Everyone's hair blew wildly as the turn steepened and the wind picked up. Goban pointed at something below. Tom squinted, his eyes watering, trying to see what Goban was pointing at while avoiding Avani's whipping hair. Far below, a figure wearing a long black cloak, strode purposefully toward the ruins. Something sleek and gray floated behind him.

"Naagesh," cried Goban, above the noise of the wind. "And he's got the artifact."

"What?"

"Naagesh," yelled Goban, even louder.

Tom nodded. The wizard entered the ruins through a side archway.

Ninosh pulled out of his turn and leveled off. Tom realized he'd been holding his breath. He let it out, then loosened his death-grip on Avani.

She turned and flashed him a big smile. "Thanks," she said, breathing deeply.

Ninosh's head twisted around. "I'll land on the far side of the peak, where we'll be out of sight."

The dragon flew level for a couple more minutes, then pulled in his wings and dove, spiraling downward toward the back side of the peak. Tom felt weightless and he squinted from the hair whipping around his face as they picked up speed. If he hadn't been holding tight to Avani, he'd have flown off.

*How is Avani staying on?* he wondered. A moment later, the dragon's wings extended and pivoted forward, acting as two giant parachutes as it flared for landing. Now Tom felt heavy as the G forces suddenly increased. Ninosh's powerful wing strokes caused a flurry of snow to fly up, hiding the landscape from view. The dragon reached out with his talon armored feet and stepped down. They rocked forward violently as the air slowly cleared.

Ninosh lowered his neck and the three slid to the ground. Tom moved quickly away, then sat down holding his stomach. *Did the dragon just smile at me?* Tom groaned.

The creature extended its wings, preparing to launch.

"Wait," cried Avani. The beast regarded her calmly.

"We still need your help. After we find the device we have to get it back to Elfhaven before the barrier collapses." Avani's eyes implored the creature.

"I have interfered in events too much already."

"I know. And we thank you. But we need your help one more time?"

"No. I'm finished with the affairs of elves and dwarves. Your path now diverges from mine."

"I can understand if you're afraid of Naagesh." Tom glanced at Goban. "I know I am."

The beast's gaze ratcheted from one to the other, steam wafting from its open mouth.

"After all," added Goban, following Tom's lead, "He did slaughter most of your kinsman. I guess the wizard's just too powerful for you."

The dragon's eyes narrowed and turned a dark crimson.

# Chapter Forty-Seven

"Be back here in exactly one oort. A myntar later and I will be gone."
At that Ninosh leapt into the sky. Shaking the ground with the power of
his launch, snow flew in all directions.

"What about Naagesh?" yelled Goban, brushing snow off his bushy
eyebrows. The beast paused, flapping its massive wings hard to hover.

Flames leapt from the dragon's mouth. "Leave the wizard to me."
Banking sideways, the dragon quickly disappeared into the late afternoon
sky.

# Chapter 48: A Battle of Titans

It took them twenty precious minutes, picking their way carefully over rocks, ice, and snow covered ledges as they wound around the jagged peak where Ninosh had left them. Rounding a final sharp finger of rock, Castle Dunferlan appeared to their right. As they neared the ruins they heard voices.

"Are you afraid, wizard?" boomed the dragon, now perched upon a massive pillar high above the ruins of the castle's north gate. "You should be!"

Quickly hiding behind a massive fallen pillar, Tom and his friends could make out the wizard Naagesh boldly stepping forward and addressing the beast.

"It is you, dragon, who should be afraid. I thought I taught your kind a lesson when I sent you all scurrying to your caves to sulk." Naagesh sneered.

The dragon sprang from the pillar and dove straight for Naagesh. Flames launched toward the wizard. The dragon extended his legs. Sharp talons jutted forward. The dragon's eyes were ablaze. Immediately a magical shield appeared in front of Naagesh. The shield easily deflected the flames, yet the wizard had to dive to one side as the razor sharp talons reached for him.

The moment the dragon flew by, Naagesh stood and raised his fist. His cape fluttered in the breeze, sporting three slash marks across its back.

The winged beast roared as he pulled up hard from the dive, narrowly missing the castle wall he swooshed up and sideways. The wizard fired a magical blast, missing the dragon by mere inches. Ninosh hovered a couple hundred feet away, then dove for a second attack. Flames once again launched forward. This time the wizard raised both hands. Emerald green magical fire raced to meet the dragon's crimson fire. As the wizard fire touched the dragon fire, the dragon's flames immediately froze, then fell. With the sound of a chandelier smashing, the massive block of red and yellow ice shattered as it crashed to the ground. Ninosh's eyes bulged. The wizard leered at the winged giant.

At that, the dragon exhaled a huge cloud of smoke, engulfing the whole area. Naagesh coughed and waved his hands, impatiently waiting for the sky to clear.

A moment later the smoke dissipated. The dragon now sat on a tall tree at the edge of the forest a hundred yards away. The tree sagged, making an ominous cracking noise.

"Well, what are you waiting for, wizard?" asked the winged beast. "Have you conceded defeat, then?" Ninosh chose that moment to spring into the air causing the tree to snap in half. The dragon banked hard then flew off low over the forest, away from the castle ruins. Naagesh ran after him, shouting.

* * *

"Come on, now's our chance." Avani stepped out from behind the fallen pillar and dashed toward the ruins.

Tom and Goban quickly hurried through an arched doorway after her.

"Well, where is it?" she asked, as the two stopped beside her. "We don't know how long Ninosh can keep the wizard distracted."

"It's not in the courtyard. Naagesh must've hidden it away somewhere." Tom frantically scanned their surroundings. Several collapsed rooms lay in various states of decay, but far off to their right stood a massive entryway, perhaps to a once great hall. A wisp of smoke rose from that direction.

"That way," said Goban, pointing toward the smoke. Tom nodded. The two followed the dwarf across the courtyard, careful not to trip on the broken stones, the shards of frozen red dragon fire, or the dark thick vines that covered everything.

"Why's there no snow in here?" asked Tom. The other two looked around uneasily.

"Naagesh must've used a spell." Avani stopped as they reached the massive entryway. Steps led downward into total blackness.

"Avani, some light," whispered Goban.

Swirling her hands in front of her, a warm yellow glow appeared between her palms. She released the light and it slowly floated ahead.

"Come on," Goban unslung Aileen from his shoulder. "Follow me." The dwarf walked cautiously down the stairway into the now slightly illuminated gloom. His footfalls echoed eerily off the walls and ceiling.

Tom glanced at Avani and swallowed hard. She gave him a nod, then followed Goban with Tom close behind.

The stairway quickly leveled out. Another doorway stood directly ahead. As they passed through they entered a massive hall. Light from several windows dimly illuminated sections of the room. Most of the pillars were intact. A large dais stood at the far end. A tall throne made of shiny black stone dominated the dais and though empty, seemed to be staring at them, judging them, willing them to leave.

"This place gives me the creeps," whispered Tom. "Feels like something's watching us." He pulled out his infrared night goggles, slipped them on and flipped the switch. Turning all around everything took on a uniform green.

"I don't see anything. If something was hiding I'd see the heat leaking out from wherever it was hiding." Tom switched off the goggles and put them away.

"I feel it too. Something doesn't want us here," said Goban.

"Naagesh put a warding spell on this place," whispered Avani. "It's making us afraid. Making us question why we're here. Making us want to leave."

"Well, it's working," said Tom. "Maybe the device isn't here. Maybe we should look for it somewhere else." Tom started to turn around.

"Wait!" Goban's voice echoed throughout the hall for several seconds. "Sorry. Didn't mean to shout." Goban pointed to a small alcove to the left of the dais. Something gray floated within. They cautiously crept toward it. Nearing the platform, they passed the black crystal throne. It felt powerful, evil.

Ahead, they could now make out the power source case floating in the room. The closer Tom got, the more the hairs on the back of his neck stood on end.

Tom stopped. "I can't go on. I can't breathe."

"It's just the spell. It's not real. Try to ignore it," said Avani. She grabbed Tom's hand and led him forward. His forehead began to sweat.

"I can't," said Tom.

Goban stopped beside them. "I don't think I can either."

Avani paused, then relaxed. A golden bubble of light appeared at their feet then quickly grew larger until it surrounded the three of them. "How's that?" she asked.

"Better," said Tom, taking a deep breath. Goban nodded.

"What did you do?" Tom asked.

"I created a protection bubble. We've got to hurry, though. I can't hold it for long."

The three cautiously crept through the doorway and up to the floating vessel. Goban's rope lay in a heap, still tied to one of the eyelets. They picked up the rope and pulled the floating case through the doorway. They sprinted across the great hall, but as they approached the stairway, Avani collapsed. Tom grabbed her before she hit the floor. The protection bubble shimmered then dissolved.

"It's OK," said Tom. "We're far enough away from the room. Naagesh must've placed a spell on the room, not on the power source."

Avani nodded then coughed. "I just need a moment."

Tom glanced at Goban nervously.

Presently, Avani stood back up. "Come on, we're late. We've got to get back or Ninosh will leave without us."

As they raced from the inner stairway into the open courtyard, streams of light filtered in through the archways to their left.

Avani shielded her eyes from the sunlight. "Come on, let's go!" she urged. As the others followed, out stepped a dark figure from behind a pillar.

# Chapter 49: Ready, fire, aim

"You three are becoming a nuisance. It was you who summoned the dragon to distract me. Impressive, though ultimately useless." Naagesh took a step closer. Emerald lightning encircled the wizard's hands. The sparks cast a faint glow exposing sharp facial features previously hidden beneath his hood.

Goban grabbed his battle axe. Yanking it off his back he twirled it around in front of him, its handle slapping loudly in his open palm. At the same time Avani's gaze met Tom's. She glanced at his adventures belt. He stared at her for a moment then nodded and stepped behind her, hiding from Naagesh's view. Reaching into a belt pocket Tom pulled out his flare gun and loaded his last shell. Then he tapped Avani on her shoulder.

"That pathetic toy axe of yours, dwarf, worries me not." The wizard glanced at one of the dark vines beside them. Naagesh gave a sickly grin, then muttered an incantation. Off to Goban's right, a giant plant sprang to life. Like octopus-legs, the vines squirmed and coiled at the center of the plant, then raced across the stone floor straight for Goban. The nearest creeper climbed up his leg, encircled the axe handle and yanked it violently from his hands. A moment later more vines wrapped around Goban's arms and legs, then began dragging him toward the center of the plant. Still more creepers coiled around the spot where he was headed. A seething mass of vipers. As he got close the vines uncoiled. A huge mouth opened at the plant's center. Massive teeth glistened.

"Guys," cried Goban. "Guys, think of something. Anything!"

Avani chanted. Yellow magic raced out and encircled the wizard. Naagesh looked horrified. Then he grinned, tipped his head and her magic exploded in a shower of harmless yellow sparks.

"Not too powerful without your crystals, are you?" said the wizard.

Avani met Naagesh's gaze, then smiled. "I was just distracting you." She stepped aside. "Now Tom!"

With the flare gun aimed at Naagesh's head, Tom closed his eyes and pulled the trigger. Things happened in slow motion. As the flare leapt forward red sparks jetted from its tail-end. The tiny rocket swiveled side-to-side awkwardly, slowly picking up speed as it headed straight for the startled wizard. Naagesh leaned back. The flare swerved, missing Naagesh's left cheek by a whiskers breadth.

Time sped back up and the flare continued flying harmlessly through an archway, briefly lighting up the darkening evening sky. The action, however, caused Naagesh to lose focus and the vines dropped to the floor, releasing Goban.

The dwarf ran back over. "Thanks."

"I missed," Tom said disgustedly.

Naagesh blinked. Then sneered. Then laughed. "Ha, ha, ha, ha. A good effort, I'll give you that. Too bad you're such a lousy shot." The smile abruptly dropped from the wizard's face.

"Enough childish games." Green lightning appeared around the wizard's hands, circling faster and faster, getting brighter and brighter.

Avani's eyes met Tom's.

"What?" he asked.

"Naagesh said I'm not powerful without my crystals—" She gazed down at the castle floor and relaxed her shoulders. "I don't know why you chose me, crystals. But you did, and I need your help." The floor began to shake, to rumble. Cracks formed. The cracks widened. Suddenly, a hundred Magic Crystals thrust up between the cracks all around them. In one quick motion she bent down and scooped up two handfuls of the multicolored gems. Instantly beams blasted from the stones just as Naagesh's magic launched toward the three of them.

Tom and Goban hopped around wildly, trying to get off the sharp pointed gems underfoot.

# Chapter Forty-Nine

Avani leaned forward and the crystals multi-hued magic deflected Naagesh's green beam to one side where it struck a fallen column. The column exploded.

A startled look crossed the wizard's face. Then he fired another, stronger blast. This time Avani's magic deflected the beam to the other side, burning a perfectly round hole through a low rock wall. The hole steamed, hissed, and sputtered.

Naagesh raised both hands. Green energy popped and sizzled as it arced from out-stretched finger to finger. Goban and Tom glanced at each other, panic stricken. Goban picked up his axe, preparing to throw. But a deep calm came over Avani.

"Daemones voco, Daemones voco, Daemones voco," she chanted. An eerie wail sounded. Wind whipped their clothes. Pale ghostly images began to form, then faded, only to form again. Naagesh looked around nervously. The images faded once more.

"Help me Tom!" yelled Avani. Tom blinked, a puzzled look on his face.

"The book, Tom. From the Library of Nalanda," she said desperately.

Understanding slowly dawned on him. Tom swallowed hard, then nodded.

Together they faced the wizard.

"DAEMONES VOCO, DAEMONES VOCO, DAEMONES VOCO," boomed Tom and Avani in unison. The wailing sounds resumed. The sounds grew louder. Brilliant beams of magic arced from the crystals, multicolored strands of lightning snaked around attaching themselves first to the floor, then to the walls, then to the columns. The wind whipped Tom's hoodie savagely, causing him to squint. Suddenly hundreds of creatures—demons—rose from the castle floor. A moment later a demon army stood staring blankly at Tom and Avani, awaiting their general's command. The two stared at each other in surprise, then slowly pointed at Naagesh. The demon army advanced on the wizard.

"That's impossible," cried Naagesh, taking a step backwards he came up against a wall. The demon hordes closed in.

"No!" he yelled, firing a blast. It missed the creatures and instead slammed into a tower on the far side of the courtyard. The tower shook violently, causing the turret above to collapse thunderously into a pile of rubble. Dust, dirt and debris flew everywhere. Tendrils of orange fairy magic rippled across the turrets lone banner as it slowly drifted back and forth on its way to the ground. Coming to rest, it sparked once, then lay still.

Magic flared again from Naagesh. This time several demons dissolved into dust. But more followed, surrounding the wizard, some crawling, some floating, some lurching.

They all pounced at once. For a moment everything went silent, then an explosion rocked the area and debris flew everywhere. When the dust cloud settled, all that remained was Naagesh.

Casually brushing himself off, he glared at Avani and the others. His arms shook as he raised them palms up. Green lightning once again raced around his fingers, growing steadily brighter.

"My turn," hissed the evil wizard.

"No, I believe it's my turn," said a deep clear voice from off to the side. "Through playing with children?" said the wizard Larraj, stepping from the shadows. "Perhaps you'd care to challenge an adult for a change? Although, the children seemed to be doing quite well without me." He gave Tom and Avani a strange look. Wonder, mixed with respect and—concern?

Larraj nodded at Tom. "That was brilliant, summoning me with your sky beacon."

"My sky beacon? Oh—my flare," began Tom, turning a bit red. "Ah—I didn't actually intend to summon—"

Zhang Wu leapt from an arch beside Naagesh, his sword '*whooshing*' as it swung through a wide arc. Naagesh seemed to disappear, then reappeared ten feet away. Zhang charged again.

At that moment, Juanita stepped from another archway right behind Tom.

"Mom!" yelled Tom, his voice cracking as he hugged her tight. "I thought you—you were dead." Tears streamed down his cheeks.

The two hugged for a long moment. Finally Juanita held her son at arm's length. "Dead? I have far too much left to do in this life." But a tear trickled down her cheek, as well. "Go! You three wait for us outside. We'll take care of Naagesh, then come get you."

Goban grabbed the rope and pulled the floating artifact outside.

"But—we've got a dragon—" began Tom.

"That's nice," said his mom, as she drew her sword and dashed back to the fight.

Tom blinked at her receding form, then wiped the tears from his face.

"Come on." Avani grabbed Tom's hand. "We've got to hurry. Maybe Ninosh is still there."

"But, Mom told me to wait."

Avani hissed with frustration, then pulled Tom forcefully after her.

* * *

The three watched as Ninosh's outline slowly receded into the darkening northern sky.

"We're too late," said Goban, stating the obvious.

Tom faced Avani. "Call him back."

"How?"

"Kiran called him. If your little brother can call a dragon, so can you."

Avani watched the retreating speck in the distance. She exhaled sharply. Raising the crystals she still held in her hands, she said, "Huc draco, draconem, draco." The crystals began to glow. She repeated the incantation, "Huc draco, draconem, draco." The glow brightened, spreading up her arm.

Impulsively, Tom placed his hand on hers, his thumb resting directly on a crystal. The gem began to vibrate, as if responding to his touch. "Ninosh. Come back. We need your help!" The crystals flared brilliantly and a beam of magical energy shot skyward.

Avani stared at Tom in disbelief. He swiftly removed his hand from hers and the light faded. Even Goban looked stunned.

Tom gulped loudly. "Ah, actually—I don't know why I did that."

"You touched the crystals—and they weren't destroyed," whispered Avani. "In fact, the crystals responded—"

"So?" said Tom.

"The crystals choose only one person per lifetime."

"Yeah, you're The Chosen One," Tom assured her, glancing nervously at Goban.

Goban clapped them both on the back. "I guess you're the chosen couple."

Tom and Avani stared at each other in horror.

## Chapter 50: Wisdom in silence

For over an oort the elven guard trod quietly around the shield wall. The West gate lay dead ahead. At this location, only a few dozen ogres stood between them and the barrier.

"Sanuu," whispered the king. "You and Tappus *sneak* past the ogres and through the barrier then head down the shield wall." King Dakshi glanced at his military advisor. The elf's face went rigid, but he said nothing.

The king again spoke to Sanuu. "Once there, make some noise to create a diversion. Stay behind the barrier where it will protect you. The ogres will go investigate. Then get the attention of an elven sentry. Tell him to unlock the West gate and rouse the army. Once the ogres have gone, I'll lead our troops through the gate."

"Yes sire." Sanuu bowed, then he and Tappus drew their swords and slipped silently between the trees.

A few moments later, a disturbance came from some distance away. The ogres headed in that direction.

"Follow me," whispered King Dakshi to his troops.

As they stepped into the clearing, another group of ogres walked into the same area. Both forces froze. Then the ogres screamed, raised their clubs and attacked.

Drawing his sword, the king locked eyes with his advisor. King Dakshi gave him a slight nod, acknowledging that his advisor had been correct. The advisor drew his own sword but wisely remained silent.

* * *

A deep pitched scream sounded high above them. Looking up, a faint speck formed in the sky. The speck grew larger. Within moments Ninosh flared his wings and landed beside them. The beast scowled at Tom, Avani and Goban.

"Twice in one day I've been summoned by a child! This never happened in the olden days." He snorted. Goban leapt sideways, flames narrowly missing him.

"You came back," said Tom.

"Before, you used my ego and hatred of Naagesh to trick me into aiding you. Yet on reflection your words rang true. Naagesh once killed most of my kind. If he now conquers this world, he will try to enslave or kill the rest of us."

The dragon seemed lost in thought. "And they were aided by a king among dragons. Perhaps the dragon The Prophecy refers to, is me—"

The beast observed them thoughtfully for one last second then lowered his neck. "Well, what are you waiting for?"

\* \* \*

"Why Naagesh?" said Larraj. "When last we met, you said it wasn't just about your father's death."

"That's right. It's really about you."

"Me? You're not still sore about me feeding you to that zhanderbeast during the War of the Wizards, are you?"

"No. This started long before the war." Naagesh's face went rigid. "When we were in school, it was always about you. Everyone talked about you. 'Larraj shows great promise.' 'Larraj is head of his class.' 'Larraj this, Larraj that.' Nobody ever noticed me, and I *by far* the more gifted wizard!"

Larraj's eyes narrowed. "I can't believe this is all about some petty childhood rivalry."

"No!" screamed Naagesh. "You left me to die."

"What?"

"That day, on the hike. You dared me. I accepted your dare. You and I set out to view a dragon's nest. We found one. The dragon mother lay sleeping. You were afraid. I was not. I snuck up to the nest and touched the dragon egg. It felt bumpy and warm, and smelled of spoiled milk."

Larraj listened impatiently.

"The dragon mother awoke. She whipped her head sideways, flinging me into a deep crevasse. I broke my arm. You ran away and left me to die! If it wasn't for the headmaster happening along—"

"I went for help. I was the one who roused the headmaster."

"Liar!" yelled the evil wizard. Bands of brilliant emerald magical fire burst from Naagesh's hands. Larraj dropped to the ground, the blast narrowly passing over him.

Larraj raised his staff, firing his own blast of blinding blue energy. This one landed on target. Naagesh flew backwards from the power of Larraj's magic. The evil wizard struck the far wall hard, blue magical lightning surrounded him. Naagesh's body shook violently for a moment, then the blue magic faded. Naagesh slowly slid to the ground unmoving. Smoke drifted up from the crumpled form of the evil wizard. Larraj walked over and nudged the still form with his staff. Naagesh didn't move. He knelt and felt for a pulse.

"He's just unconscious." Larraj stood and stared down at his long-time foe, then he rejoined his friends.

At that instant a thunderous flapping sounded. The commotion caught Juanita, Zhang and Larraj off guard. Turning quickly, a bizarre spectacle unfolded before them. A colossal dragon lifted off. What's more, the three children rode atop its back and a tethered gray box floated along behind.

"That's a sight you don't see every day," said Larraj. Zhang nodded absently.

"Tom said they had a dragon." Juanita recalled as she focused on their receding form. "I wasn't really paying attention."

"Naagesh!" cried Larraj. The three whirled around. They now faced three Naageshes. No five. No Ten! It was an evil wizard's convention.

\* \* \*

A wall of ogres separated Tappus and Sanuu from the rest of their platoon.

"Open the gates!" yelled Sanuu to an elven sentry standing on the rampart above them.

"And summon the army!" added Tappus. The guard stared first at Tappus, then Sanuu, and finally down the wall where the king and his men fought desperately as more and more ogres rushed to surround them.

"NOW!" yelled Sanuu. The guard took off running. A moment later a horn sounded. Torch light burst to life above them, all down the wall.

Tappus drew his sword. "We've got to help."

Sanuu stepped in front of him, blocking his way. "No, I'll help the king. You lead the elven army when they arrive. They need a leader to break through the ogre ranks."

Behind them chains rattled, the wooden gate creaked as it began to rise.

Sanuu continued. "You'll serve King Dakshi best by leading the army to his rescue." He met Tappus's gaze straight on.

Tappus solemnly nodded.

"Go!" yelled Sanuu, drawing his own sword. Tappus sprinted through the gate. Sanuu turned, pointed his weapon at the nearest ogre, and charged.

# Chapter 51: Open the gates!

It was now after dark, yet the view from the dragon's back was incredible. Being this high up the wind was frigid. Tom squinted, his hair whipping about his face. He'd managed to keep his eyes open for most of the trip, and even loosened his death grip around Avani's waist, somewhat. Tom stole a backwards glance. The case still floated behind them at the end of Goban's tether, buffeted only slightly by the wind.

As they neared Elfhaven, the outer defensive wall became visible. Hundreds of torches outlined the parapet at the top of the shield wall. The torchlight revealed dark flickering images of thousands of Ogres attacking the main defenses. Brilliant blue flashes highlighted ogres who'd foolishly slammed their clubs into the barrier and were rewarded for their folly by being hurled back violently.

"The barrier's still holding, at least in places," Tom said. Goban surveyed the grim scene below.

"But look at the elven troops," said Avani. "What are they doing? They're fighting outside the shield wall. The barrier must be failing."

As they neared the wall Ninosh banked sharply. "Dragon-kind cannot pass through the barrier. I will land near the East gate. You'll be on your own from there." Steepening his turn still further, Ninosh pulled in his wings halfway and dove. The dragon began to shake violently from the speed, and the increased wind threatened to rip Tom off Ninosh's back. He tightened his grip around Avani and somehow, through sheer force of will, kept his eyes open.

Just before they plowed into the ground, Ninosh flared his wings and flapped down and forward, slowing their decent. Even so, when the beast's powerful legs met the ground it nearly threw the three of them from the creature's back.

"Run for the gate," ordered Ninosh. They slid to the ground, Goban pulling the floating device behind him.

Several ogres had seen the dragon land and inched backward in fear. But when they saw Tom and his friends dashing toward the gate, the ogres regained their courage and stormed to intercept them. Ninosh reared up onto his hind legs beating his massive wings at the charging horde, causing many to fall backwards from the blast of wind. The dragon roared. Flames shot out sweeping the area between the kids and the ogres, forcing the beasts back.

As the three neared the shield wall, the familiar blue lightning of the barrier highlighted their bodies, though much dimmer than usual.

"The barrier's failing," cried Avani.

"The Guardian said he'd keep it up only where it was most needed," Tom reminded her.

Avani grabbed the gate's handle and pushed.

"It's locked," she screamed. "Open the gate!" Avani slammed her palms against the massive wooden door.

Ninosh swiveled his long neck toward them and roared. "Move aside. Now!" They jumped away just as dragon flames engulfed the gate. Avani stepped further back, squinting and twisting her head away from the intense heat. Sparks and tangy smoke filled the air. Tom covered his ears from the deafening roar of a blast furnace. Within moments, the charred remains of the door fell inward. What was left of the gate crackled and popped, sending smoke drifting up from where it lay.

Ninosh reared back, tipping his head skyward. The dragon let out a high-pitched, haunting cry that lasted several long seconds. Elves and ogres alike stopped fighting momentarily to look in the dragon's direction. Suddenly, the beast's powerful legs catapulted him into the air, his wings flapping hard as he quickly gained altitude.

"What was that call?" asked Tom.

Avani shook her head.

Faint torchlight reflected off the scales of Ninosh's retreating form, as he quickly disappeared into the dark Northern sky.

Goban stared at the smoldering remains of the East gate. By now several elven sentries, on the rampart, gazed down at the same charred wreckage. "Hope they don't expect us to pay for that," said Goban.

Tom ignored him. "If the barrier fails the ogres will have an easy way in."

"Then we'd better make sure the barrier doesn't fail," Avani yelled, as she dashed across the still smoldering gate. "Come on boys, last one there's a rotten zaptor-lizard egg!"

\* \* \*

Zhang Wu leapt into the air once more, his swords a blur of flashing silver. As a blade met the nearest Naagesh it passed right through him without slowing down. The evil wizard didn't even flinch. Sparks flew as Zhang's sword glanced off the ruins. The monk landed in a crouch then leapt toward the next Naagesh.

"Watch out," warned Larraj. "Most are illusions. Only one is real."

Out of the corner of her eye Juanita noticed a swirling shadow pass under an arch. Careful to avoid the nearby Naagesh clones she crept to the archway. Squinting against the wind-driven snow, she cautiously peered outside.

Faint light from the Ring of Turin, reflected off the snow covered rubble beyond.

She sensed movement to her right. Instinctively she stepped left and swung her sword. Her blade met only empty space.

Then a haunting sound of other-worldly voices began, accompanied by a chill wind. The wind built. Looking in the direction of the sound she saw nothing. *No, wait! There was something.* A section of the rock strewn snow field seemed to twist, to distort, as if the stones were made of rubber and being swept toward a drain.

# Open the gates!

*Something is warping space-time. It's making the objects behind it appear distorted.*

Sand and small pebbles suddenly launched toward the rift, thirty feet away. When they reached the vortex they just disappeared. Larger stones shook for a moment then seemed to elongate before being sucked into the rift as well.

The wind whipped Juanita's hair about her face so hard it stung. Sounds of the tormented voices grew louder. She squinted.

The distortion quickly increased, both in size and intensity, warping the scene behind the rift still further. A few feet in front of her a massive rock stretched, then seemed to turn to liquid as it was pulled into the vortex.

"Something's happening," she yelled over her shoulder while still keeping her gaze fixed on the steadily building rift. Her right foot began sliding toward the vortex. Throwing out her hands she tried desperately to grab hold of something, anything, but nothing was there. Then her other foot began to slide. The rift loomed ahead. She felt a strong pull, as if her body was being stretched like taffy.

"A little help," she cried.

Suddenly a hand grabbed her arm. It was Larraj. A moment later Zhang Wu appeared beside him. Then Zhang began to slide too. Larraj's other arm grabbed hold of the monk.

The wind continued to build, and the voices threatened to drive Juanita mad. She felt the pull increase and saw the strain in the wizard's face as he held them both back. Yet even as Zhang and her robes flapped about them wildly, Larraj's cloak barely moved, somehow unaffected by the torrent.

Zhang reached inside his violently flapping cloak, pulled out a glowing magic infused throwing star and hurled the weapon straight for the heart of the rift.

"No!" cried Larraj, but it was too late. The moment the magical weapon entered the maelstrom there was an explosion of blinding green light. The three were thrown back violently where they landed hard on the snow covered ground. The rift slammed shut, shaking their surroundings.

Larraj slowly rose to his feet and brushed himself off, the whole time glowering at Zhang Wu.

"What?" said the monk. "It was worth a try."

The wizard continued to glare at him.

"It closed the rift, didn't it?"

"What was that thing?" asked Juanita.

The wizard faced her. "Naagesh opened a rift to the netherworld. The voices you heard were poor tortured souls. Had you touched the vortex or even gotten close—" The wizard let the unfinished statement linger.

Larraj glowered once more at Zhang. "If my impatient friend here had given me a chance, I could've done a counter spell, closing the rift and at the same time locating Naagesh. To open a rift of this magnitude, he had to be nearby."

"So where is he?" asked Juanita. "Where's Naagesh now?"

"Gone," replied the wizard. "Long gone."

As Larraj's keen eyes scanned the bleak snow covered mountains surrounding them, his gaze froze on a tattered banner lying on the snow. A spark of orange fairy magic raced across its surface. The wizard stepped forward and held his hand over the banner. It rose slightly off the ground, then settled back down. Larraj gazed at it thoughtfully.

\* \* \*

"We've got to break through the ogre lines and get past the barrier before more reinforcements arrive," said the king's aide.

King Dakshi raised his voice, "Why hasn't Sanuu and Tappus returned with the army? We have the advantage of numbers, for the moment, but we'll soon be overwhelmed."

"The ogres are smarter than trolls," said his aide. "They're concentrating their forces between us and the barrier. If we could just get beyond the barrier we—"

"I'm well aware of the protection the barrier affords," snapped the king.

His advisor took a step back and lowered his gaze. "Of course, your highness."

The king let out a long breath through clenched teeth, then noticed a disturbance ahead. Sanuu was trying to fight his way to them.

"Help Sanuu!" cried King Dakshi. "You there, give Sanuu some relief." Several elven guards split from the others and dashed to where Sanuu stood fighting. He had the element of surprise, but that wasn't advantage enough.

The sounds of swords, mace, and clubs striking each other grew deafening.

Sanuu ducked one ogre's club then immediately parried another. As he did so he dipped down, picked up a handful of dirt and threw it in the ogre's face. Temporarily blinded, the ogre staggered backwards. Sanuu seized the opportunity by somersaulting beneath the ogres legs. Springing up behind the beast he rushed onward. Within moments he stood beside King Dakshi.

"Took you long enough," said the king.

Sanuu's brow rose slightly. "I was—preoccupied."

"So where is my army?"

"The sentry sounded the alarm. Tappus went to lead them. They should be here any moment."

The king nodded. "They had better be. Each myntar they are delayed means a hundred more ogres we will have to fight."

"They'll be here, sire," assured Sanuu.

As if on cue, Tappus burst through the gate leading a thousand elven guard.

"Have our men form a wedge," said the king. "Start moving through the ogre line straight for the barrier. Tappus will see what we are doing and focus his forces there."

Sanuu nodded, then rushed off to relay the king's orders.

King Dakshi could see Tappus weaving and attacking. Ducking and slashing. *Shades of the sword master monk, Zhang,* thought the king, proudly.

Within myntars, Sanuu's guards met Tappus's troops in the middle. They formed a small pathway through the ogre forces.

"Sire," yelled Sanuu. "Go through now."

"Not until the last of my men are safe."

Sanuu winced, then hurried back to fight beside his liege. Soon the troops had made it through and Sanuu and the king hurried after them, now within the safety of the barrier.

The ogres screamed. Several swung their clubs at the barrier. Blue sparks leapt outward, throwing their clubs back but with less force than usual. Others hit the barrier with their fists and were thrown backwards into the woods. But each time the barrier was hit it flickered ominously.

"Back to Elfhaven castle. Now!" yelled the king to his troops. To Sanuu he whispered, "I sense the barrier is about to collapse."

## Chapter 52: Home, home, yet lost

"Come on, hurry," said Goban, as he struggled to pull the long gray case.

At that moment a loud hum sounded, then dropped in pitch, so low in fact that they could no longer hear it, but they felt it shaking them. A few blue sparks danced playfully around their feet, then vanished.

"Was that—" began Goban.

"Yes. The barrier's down," said Tom.

A second later he had to cover his ears from the roar of a thousand excited ogres just outside the outer shield wall. Tom stole a hurried look over his shoulder as he ran. Hundreds of ogres stormed through the charred remains of the East gate. A moment later the West gate splintered, then blew apart as hundreds more ogres forced their way through. The elven troops dropped formation and sprinted full out toward the castle. The main gate's portcullis began to lower.

"They're closing the gate," yelled Avani.

"Forget the gate," cried Tom. "We've got to get the power source to the Citadel."

Tom glanced back. "Here they come. Run!"

* * *

As they neared Elfhaven castle, the battle noise grew intense. Above the roar Tom could just make out the sound of grinding gears, chains and pulleys coming from the mechanisms that lowered the portcullis. Running past the main gate they turned up a narrow lane that led to the Citadel. As soon as they entered the street, they were engulfed by a sea of people desperately running the other way toward the safety of the castle. Mothers held small children tight to their sides and the panicked look in their eyes was haunting. Tom had to slow to a walk.

"Excuse me," he called. "We've got to get to the Citadel. It's urgent!" In their haste to save themselves and their loved ones, nobody moved aside.

Searching for a way through, Tom realized he was alone.

"Goban? Avani?" he yelled. No answer.

To his left he spotted a narrow side street with only a few people on it. Tom began working his way over to it.

"Excuse me," said Avani. "Please, I must get through." She was having no luck swimming upstream in this mad rush for the castle. Shouts and screams almost drowned out the clanking of the chains as the castle's gate lowered. *Where's Tom?* she thought, realizing he was gone.

"Avani!" cried a voice.

"Tom?" she said, searching for the voice. But the tone of relief in her voice, changed to that of bewilderment. "Nadda? Nanni? Why aren't you in the castle? Didn't Kiran take you there?"

"We haven't seen Kiran," said Nadda, looking concerned. "We thought he was with you."

"Come child," said Nanni, taking her hand. "We must get you to the castle. They're lowering the gates."

"No, I can't," said Avani, looking from one to the other. "I've got to find Tom and Goban."

"Please, Avani," urged Nadda. "We've only sectars."

Avani glanced at the gate. It stood fifty paces away and hundreds of frantic townsfolk crowded the space pushing and shoving and screaming, trying desperately to get to safety.

The gates suddenly stopped lowering, just five feet above the ground. Still, a mob of people blocked their path.

Avani froze, her eyes closed tight.

"Avani dear?" Nanni reached out and gently touched her arm.

Avani's eyes sprang open. "Do you trust me?" She studied their faces, intently. Her grandparents looked at each other uncertainly, then slowly nodded.

"Good." Avani grabbed their hands and pulled them hurriedly across the pushing, throbbing masses, making her way slowly toward the shops on the far side of the street. Once there, she hugged the edge of the buildings, pulling her grandparents after her, away from the castle gates. Nanni stared at Nadda with fear in her eyes.

"It'll be OK," he reassured her. "We've got to trust our Avani."

A tear rolled down Avani's cheek. "This way," she said, pulling them onward.

Goban struggled, but being short, no one saw him. People kept running into him, tripping over the rope or bumping into the floating case. He'd actually lost ground.

"Tom? Avani? Help!" No one answered.

Leaning forward he struggled against the crowd once more. Just then a plump older woman with a huge wart on the side of her large double chin, slammed into Goban head on. Both fell over backwards.

"Beggin' my lord's pardon," she said, scrunching up her face as she stood up awkwardly. She swayed a moment, looking as if she might throw up. With a horrified look on his face Goban tried to scoot back, but the crowds prevented him from moving.

She belched, then grinned. "That's better, dearie." She hiked up her skirts then trudged off into the crowd. Glancing back she winked at him.

Goban stood up, blinked, then shuddered. "Glad to hear it," he said, watching her go. Turning, Goban tried to move forward once more, but someone ran between him and the floating case. The fellow tripped over the rope and got his leg tangled up in it.

"Great!" said Goban. Sighing he reached down and fumbled for the rope, but before he could find it, two tiny dark hands reached out and with lightning speed untied the elves foot.

"AAAAHHHH!" screamed a woman. "It's a gremlin!"

Goban looked down and smiled. "Our gremlin friend."

Another person screamed. People started moving away. Goban's face lit up.

"I need to get to the Citadel," he told the gremlin. "They're blocking my way. Can you help?"

The critter winked, then galloped off into the crowd.

"Look out," cried Goban, his hands cupped around his mouth. "It's a mad gremlin. Run for your lives!" The sea of elves parted.


Several long minutes and a couple of wrong turns later, the smooth outline of the Citadel came into view. Its distinctive oval shape set it apart from all other buildings in Elfhaven. Tom hurried around the side to the entryway.

"Nadda? Nanni?" said Tom, caught off guard seeing Avani's grandparents here.

"Where've you been?" cried Avani, her eyes swiftly scanning Tom's face.

"I got stuck in the crowd. I found another way. Where's Goban and the case?"

"I thought he was with you?"

Tom gasped involuntarily. "We're dead without the power source." Tom and Avani froze. The sounds of fighting grew nearer.

"I'm sure you two are concerned about your friend," said Nadda, breaking the awkward silence, "but shouldn't we find a safe place to hide?"

Avani reached inside her cloak and pulled out a blacker-than-black star-shaped object then placed it in its matching indentation in the Citadel's entryway. A loud hum emanated from the wall behind them, then the wall simply vanished. Her grandparent's mouths fell open.

"Wait for us inside." Avani pointed into the Citadel.

"What? Aren't you coming with us?" asked Nanni.

"We'll be in as soon as Goban gets here."

Tom craned his neck around the corner. Twenty or so ogres were headed this way. A handful of elven guards fought valiantly to hold them back, but the ogres steadily gained ground.

"They'll be here any moment," Tom said.

"Hurry," urged Avani, pushing her grandparents into the dark Citadel entranceway. "We'll be right behind you."

"But..." began Nadda.

"And don't wander about," added Tom. "There's this bottomless pit thingy."

Nadda and Nanni stared at each other in horror. Avani pushed them the rest of the way in and removed the key. The wall reappeared.

Grunts of ogres sounded from just down the block. The elven guards scattered, unable to hold back the beasts any longer.

"We've got to go inside," said Avani. Tom slowly nodded. Avani raised the key.

Suddenly they heard a noise of fingernails scraping on stone, coming from behind them. Turning they saw their Gremlin friend scamper around the corner and stop in front of them.

"What are you doing here?" she asked. The critter looked up at Tom and grinned.

At that instant Goban rounded the same corner. He bent over, his hands on his knees, gasping for breath. Tom noticed with relief the power source floating behind him. It glided up, bumped into Goban's backside then stopped.

"What happened? Where've you been?" Avani asked anxiously.

"No time. The ogre—" Goban took a deep breath then stood up. "Let's go!"

Avani shoved the key into its socket.

# Chapter 53: A turn for the worse

From a turret high up on Elfhaven Castle, King Dakshi stared in disbelief at the chaotic battle beneath him. Just moments ago the barrier had collapsed completely, causing the ogre forces to roar in glee. Ogres streamed through the charred remains of the East gate. The elven army had rushed to stop them. The enemy, however, used giant logs as battering rams and the North gate in the outer defensive wall exploded inward, followed quickly by the West gate.

From the top of the outer curtain wall elven archers frantically fired longbows and crossbows with little effect. The enemy forces were quickly driving back the hopelessly out-numbered elven troops.

"Did you ask King Bharat of the lake elves, for help?" asked Tappus.

"No," replied King Dakshi.

"Shall I send a messenger now, sire?"

"It is too late. This war will be won or lost long before my cousin could assemble his army and reach Elfhaven. I failed to anticipate the possibility of the barrier collapsing this soon. I should have contacted him long ago."

"Has anyone seen my son?" asked King Dakshi.

Tappus scanned the faces of the king's advisors. They all shook their heads.

"No, sire," Tappus replied. "I could speak with General Kanak?"

The king sighed. "The General has no time to be nurse-maiding Devraj."

An advisor cleared his throat. "We must lower the portcullis the rest of the way before the castle's main gate is overrun, your highness."

"Are all the townsfolk safely inside the castle?" asked the king.

The aid nodded. "The last are entering now, sire."

"Why weren't they brought in sooner?" The king's face took on a deep shade of red.

"Ah—you were gone, my lord. Things happened so fast—"

"In any case," broke in Tappus, "Our troops are still out there. We've got to bring them back first."

The king glanced from Tappus to his advisor. They both waited expectantly.

King Dakshi paused. "All right. We wait for the troops."

"But sire," began the same advisor. "We may not be able to stop the enemy from following them in."

The king spoke slowly through clenched teeth. "The gate—remains—open."

King Dakshi grabbed the walkie-talkie that Tom had lent him. "General Kanak? General Kanak, are you there?"

Static blared from the device for a moment. "Kanak here. Yes, your Majesty?"

"Bring the troops inside the castle. At once."

"But sire—"

"No buts. Do it now! That's a royal order."

"Yes, your highness."

"Oh, and General?" A pause.

"Yes, sire?"

King Dakshi glanced at Tappus. "Have you seen Prince Devraj?" Faint voices discussed something on the other end of the line.

"No, your highness."

"Bring the troops home."

"Yes, sire." More static, then the line went dead.

* * *

"More power!" cried Carlos. "We need more power." He stood before the detection grid holding the walkie-talkie Tom had given his friend

279

# Chapter Fifty-Three

James.

"We're already at ten times the level from when the first portal opened," said Sashi, her hand shook as it hovered above the power control slider.

It had taken them a day to figure out what went wrong during their last attempt. And two more days to fix the damage their mistake had caused.

A tremor passed through the underground structure. Dust fell from several new cracks in the nuclear accelerator's tunnel ceiling.

"The director's not going to be happy when he sees what we've done to his multi-billion dollar lab," said Sashi.

Carlos ignored her. "Full power. Give it to me now!"

"The detection grid wasn't designed for that much power," warned Cheng.

"You reinforced it, right?"

"Yes, but not for this much—"

"Just do it." The others froze under Carlos' fierce scrutiny.

Sashi glanced anxiously at her fellow scientists, took a deep breath, then grabbed the slider with both hands and slammed it all the way up.

Alarms blared. Red lights flashed. The building shook violently.

A tiny green dot appeared in the center of the detection grid.

# Chapter 54: All for nothing!

Tom pulled on his LED headlamp. Light burst ahead of him as he sprinted on. At the same time Avani conjured up her own magical glowing orbs and cast them forth.

"The Citadel's lights are out." Avani called nervously, as she bolted down the mostly dark hallway. Goban followed still pulling the floating crate.

"The Citadel is out of energy in its primary power unit," Tom replied, breathing hard. "I hope there's enough reserve power to keep the Guardian functioning." Tom faced Avani. "He's got to tell me how to install the new power source."

She nodded solemnly.

"Do you think Nadda and Nanni will wait for us up at the entrance?" Tom asked.

"They said they would—"

Tom glanced back. "At least the traps are down. The bottomless pit thingy must've required a lot of power." Tom could hear Goban's labored breath behind them. Tom slowed, grabbed the rope and helped pull.

*I bet Goban never ran this much in his life!* Tom grinned at the thought. *And they don't have health clubs where he's from.*

As they entered the Citadel's main chamber a few dim emergency lights flickered to life, faintly illuminating the central console. The lights flickered once more then failed completely.

"Not a good sign," said Tom.

The 3-D holographic displays weren't lit, and none of the usual lights that dotted the control console were on either.

Even this far inside the Citadel, Tom could hear the muffled sound of fighting from somewhere outside.

"Guardian!" called Tom. "Guardian! We're back. We've got the new power source."

"Guardian? Can you hear me? Are you still with us?" Tom felt panic well up inside him. An uneasy look spread across their faces.

"What do we do now?" asked Goban.

Tom's shoulders slumped. "I can't install the power source without the Guardian."

"Why not?" asked Avani. "You healed the device once before, with your robit, remember?"

"Robot," Tom sighed heavily. "I didn't heal it, I just transferred Chloe's power to the unit, that's all. Besides, the Guardian told me what to do."

"Still," she said, glancing at Goban for support. "Is it that different? Anyway, you've got to try."

Tom faced her. He could see the trust in her eyes. He glanced at Goban. Goban attempted a half-hearted smile.

Tom took a deep breath, then let it out slowly. "OK, what've we got to lose, right?" *Except maybe blowing up the Citadel if I screw up.* Walking over to the side of the main console, he opened the same access panel he'd used the last time.

*I wish Chloe were here. Not that my robot could help, of course. I just miss her, I guess.* Tom adjusted the beam on his headlamp so it focused on the panel. The square and triangular indents he'd used to connect his jumper cables to Chloe's battery were right in front of him. Below that was a circular indent a foot across. Beside the indent, two alien hieroglyphic symbols stood out. The one above was red and resembled a cat throwing up a hairball. The one below was blue and looked more like a snake swallowing its tail.

Tom scratched his head. "Bring me the unit."

Goban pulled the rope until the case floated beside them. Tom got up, flipped the latches and opened the container. A cold mist poured out. As the mist cleared, the familiar shiny metal cylinder with its pulsing red crystals lay before him. Tom reached out and placed his hand on the right side of the device. It felt warm and amazingly smooth to the touch.

"Help me, Goban." Tom bent down and wrapped his arms around the cylinder. Goban did the same on the other end.

"OK, on my mark," said Tom. Goban glanced uncertainly at Avani.

"One, two, three—" The two strained to lift it. Their eyes scrunched shut and their faces turned red, but the device didn't move. They relaxed.

"Oh, right. It took five of us to lift it from the space ship," said Tom. "What do we do now?"

Avani groaned, "Boys. Can't you see the solution is *floating* right before your eyes?"

The two remained silent.

"You need girl power. Leave it to me." Rolling her eyes she stepped forward, gently pushing them aside.

Reciting the same incantation she'd used before to levitate the case, she waived her hands over the unit. The device immediately floated free from its container.

Tom smacked his forehead with his palm. "Dah!"

Avani nodded, knowingly.

Goban pulled the case away.

Tom knelt beside the round opening in front of the unfamiliar symbols. His hand shook as he slowly reached out.

"Um. I think—perhaps, it's the snake one." His finger hovered over the lower blue snake, getting closer and closer. As his finger descended, he suddenly reached up and pressed the red barfing cat. Immediately the circular indent moved aside with a loud hiss. An icy fog drifted out, then the old power source shot from the opening missing Tom and the new device by a hair. The unit flew across the room, slammed into the wall and fell to the floor with a loud *thump*. The floor shook for a second.

"Oops. That was close," Tom said. Goban and Avani stared blankly at the ejected unit.

"Goban, help me line up the new one." Tom stood and grabbed one end the floating power source. Goban grasp the other end. The unit floated a few inches too high so they had to lie on top of it to get it to sink to the correct level. For some reason, Goban's end sank lower. Goban tried standing with part of his weight on the floor and some of it on the device. After a couple of tries they positioned the cylinder directly in front of the hole in the panel.

"Avani, my hands are full. Press the symbol of the snake biting its tail."

"Me?" she said, swallowing hard. "Ah, what's a snake?"

"A serpent," Tom gasped, sweat dripping from his brow. "Just press the lower blue button."

Avani stepped forward timidly. Glancing at Tom she slowly reached out and touched the hungry blue snake. Immediately the unit shot from beneath Tom and Goban into the hole. A sound like a giant slurping in a mouthful of spaghetti filled the chamber. More mist drifted out then the circular panel closed with a "whoosh."

The mist cleared.

They all held their breath. Nothing happened.

"Now what?" asked Avani and Goban in unison.

"Ah—I kind of hoped it would just—restart," said Tom. The three stared at each other.

"So—what do we try next?" Avani asked.

Tom paused, glancing from one to the other of them, a defeated look on his face.

"I don't know. I'm out of ideas." His shoulders sank.

Just then a shudder shook the building. The lights blinked, then blinked again. Sounds of static accompanied by the hazy outline of a person appeared before them. The outline flickered, disappeared then reappeared. The image grew brighter, then solidified into that of a fat kindly wizard, complete with a bent pointy hat and a gnarled wooden wand.

"Guardian," began Tom, smiling broadly. "That's a new look for you, isn't it?"

"This is my default persona. At this point I can't switch avatars until the Citadel has completely rebooted."

"It's a bit stereotypical, but on you it works."

Looking miffed, the Guardian said, "It took you long enough. I thought you'd never get the new power supply installed. And when you almost pressed the wrong button—"

"You were conscious? Why didn't you help me?"

"I ran too low on power to speak, let alone create an image. It was quite amazing I was able to function at all. I shut down all unnecessary subroutines, brilliant really. I sometimes amaze even myself. I am sure I could not have held out even a sectar longer. Who knows what catastrophe might have befallen Elfhaven had I lost consciousness complete—"

"That's great. I'm sure they'll erect a statue in your honor, but we're in a bit of a hurry here. Is the barrier back up?"

The Guardian glanced skyward. "No. Quiet. Listen."

In Tom's haste he'd tuned everything else out. He stopped, and listened. Faintly, but recognizably, he heard muffled cries and shouts, even the faint clinks of sword against club. The war still raged outside. The barrier was still down.

"Do you have to reboot again?" Tom asked.

"Yes."

"Arrggghhh! How long will it take this time?"

The Guardian paused. "I began the reboot sequence when we first started speaking. At this point it will take exactly five more myntars, ah— approximately six Earth minutes."

Tom glanced at his watch. "Come on, maybe we can help." Goban and Avani hurried off up the still dimly lit passageway.

As Tom turned to follow, the Guardian called to him, "Thomas. There is one more thing."

"Yes?"

"Someone's trying to open a portal, a portal from Earth."

"Uncle Carlos!"

"The barrier will not come up until the system has been fully rebooted. However, I could divert a small amount of energy now to aid your uncle's efforts. Shall I?"

"Of course!" Tom grinned as he ran after his friends.

# Chapter 55: Shades of Aladdin

For over an hour Juanita had held on tight to the wildly flapping pennant, the one Larraj had magically converted into a flying carpet. *I wish he'd created one with a smoother ride. And perhaps a railing to hold onto.* Juanita's skirt mimicked the pennant, flapping wildly about her legs. *I feel like I'm in a Marilyn Monroe publicity stunt.*

As they approached Elfhaven, it became clear they were too late. Up ahead in the distance, she could just make out a horrible scene. The gates of Elfhaven's outer shield wall lay shattered in ruins. Thousands of ogres surged through the broken gates, with thousands more behind them. Even with the formidable powers of the wizard, and Zhang's martial arts mastery, and her own meager martial skills, they were still only three. Three against thousands.

Larraj uttered an incantation, coaxing the flying banner to pick up speed. It hurled them forward faster and faster. Tree tops whizzed by only inches beneath their feet. Every now and then a spark of orange fairy magic raced across the pennant beneath them, the thin sheet of magic infused fabric which kept them from plummeting to their deaths.

Zhang's arm sprang out, pointing urgently at a flock of colorful four-winged flying creatures that suddenly appeared from behind a grove of trees to their left. The birds flew directly in front of them. The avians squawked, flapped, dove, and zigzagged wildly. With only minor course corrections Larraj somehow managed to miss them all, though a couple of feathers clung to Juanita's hair and face. She spit out a feather. Angry bird cries scolded them from a distance.

Glancing sideways, she noticed Larraj and Zhang stood atop the possessed tablecloth as if out for a simple jaunt in the park. In fact, though her hair whipped about violently, the wizard's hood barely flapped.

"Look!" Releasing her right hand's death-grip on the banner, Juanita pointed down at a small clearing ahead. Four figures dressed in over-sized white coats followed by a large dog, raced toward the outer shield wall.

Larraj waved his hand. The banner sparkled then tipped, banking sharply to the right then back to the left then right once more. With each turn they lost altitude. Pulling the makeshift craft up at the last moment it skidded to a stop right beside the startled four. Stunned, Devraj, Kiran, Malak and Chatur froze speechless. Max panted heavily.

"We were just passing by," said the wizard. "Care for a lift?"

* * *

A few myntars later, Larraj and the others jumped and ran as their flying banner collapsed in a heap of dirty laundry behind the frantically retreating elven army, just outside Elfhaven Castle's main gate.

"Kiran," said the prince. "Take Max. Go find your grandparents. If they are not already in the castle, get them to safety." Kiran took off running, Max loping behind.

"We'll go help the king," said Malak. Chatur nodded agreement. The two sprinted toward the castle.

Devraj frowned as he watched them go, then turned his gaze to General Kanak's troops struggling to reach the safety of the castle. The prince faced the wizard.

Larraj understood. "Go aid your troops."

Devraj nodded, pulled his sword from its scabbard, and sprinted toward the elven forces.

Without a word, Zhang Wu drew his own silver handled swords and dashed off after the prince.

Larraj was about to follow when he saw a huge troll and a small group of ogres break through the elven line. But instead of heading for the castle they stormed past the entrance.

"They must be headed for the Citadel," said the wizard.

Juanita gasped. "That's where Tom and his friends will be."

\* \* \*

King Dakshi's dark elven eyes smoldered as he watched the continuing disaster unfold below. The battle field stood eerily lit by flickering torchlights on the outer shield wall, adding to the faint light from the Ring of Turin, high above. What remained of the elven army was trapped just outside the castle gate.

"General Kanak? Come in—" The king released the talk button and waited. "Can you hear me General?" Static blared for a second more.

"Kanak here. Sire, your son. He's headed this way."

The king let out a long breath. "General, what is going on? Why have your men not entered the castle as I commanded?"

"It's my fault, your highness. It's too late. If we turn and enter the castle now, the ogre army will pour in behind us. Elfhaven will be lost." Only static for a long moment. "Sire, you must lower the gate."

King Dakshi cursed beneath his breath. Glancing at the courtyard below, hundreds of elven citizens stood huddled in fear in the inner courtyard. One woman knelt beside her daughter and held her tightly to her bosom. The king recognized the woman. He knew she was desperately searching the sea of faces on the other side of the castle gate. Searching for any sign of her husband, the girl's father, one of his elven warriors.

The king clenched his teeth.

"Lower the gate," he said, barely above a whisper.

"But your son," stammered Sanuu. "Prince Devraj is still out there."

King Dakshi paused, his voice cracking slightly as he said, "Lower the gate, now."

# Chapter Fifty-Five

\* \* \*

"What about your grandparents?" Tom asked Avani.

"They'll be safe in the Citadel."

Tom, Goban and Avani charged around the last corner before the castle's main gates and stopped. A few hundred elven soldiers stood fast, defending the gate from thousands of angry ogres. The sound of chains lowering the castle gate could barely be heard over the deafening volume of the beasts' battle cries.

Out of the sea of ogres a lone troll spotted them, raised his club and charged. Goban drew his axe and stepped toward him. Tom grabbed the dwarfs arm.

"Bellchar, it's me. Tom."

The troll halted directly in front of them, several ogres crowded behind.

"Trolls honor, remember?" said Tom, his eyes showing as much courage as he could muster.

\* \* \*

Kiran sprinted up the dimly lit main street, but it was blocked by heavy fighting. Glancing around he spotted a dark alley and ducked into it. The alley was deserted and though dark, he picked up speed.

Two alleys later he rushed up the steps to his grandparent's house and burst in the front door. Max right behind.

"Nadda, Nanni?" he called. No one answered. After a quick search of the house he stopped just inside the door.

*What should I do now? They aren't here. They must've made it to the castle. Tom, Goban and Avani will be at the Citadel. They'll need my help.*

"Max, you wait here. I'll be back soon."

Max peered up at him and tipped his head, inquisitively.

Kiran closed the door and took off running.

He hadn't gotten far when, as he neared an intersection, he heard deep raspy voices. Stopping, he peered cautiously around the corner. Two ogres were headed his way. Looking around frantically, he spotted an empty barrel lying on its side nearby. Jumping behind it he lay on his stomach, held his breath, and closed his eyes. The voices grew nearer.

"Where da troll army?"

"Only a few trolls so far. Naagesh supposed to lead dem. He not here neither, dey all cowards."

"We no need stinking trolls. We no need wizard. After ogres destroy elves and dwarves, we go for da trolls." The ogre spat.

As they approached, their footfalls shook the ground and the barrel rolled away loudly. Kiran opened one eye. The barrel was gone.

The ogres turned at the sound. They froze at the sight of Kiran.

Kiran smiled sheepishly. "Ah—I was just looking for my rock. Oh, here it is." Kiran picked up a stone, jumped to his feet and threw it as hard as he could at the nearest ogre. The rock bounced harmlessly off its fat belly.

"Kill da brat," yelled the beast.

Spotting the barrel beside him, Kiran kicked it toward the ogres. The two tripped over the rolling cask and landed in a heap.

\* \* \*

Devraj raced toward General Kanak's troops, now surrounded by ogres.

*There's a space, over to the right, without too many of the beasts. If I time it right, I can get past the ogres before they even know I'm there.*

"Kill da pup," yelled a deep voice right behind him. Instinctively, Devraj jumped sideways and whirled around. The ogre's club just missed his head but slammed into his sword arm, causing the prince to drop his weapon. Pain radiated down his arm as he reached for his sword.

"Argh," he cried as he grasped his swords hilt, his right arm badly injured from the blow.

Devraj sneered at the beast, then grabbed the sword's handle with his left hand. At the same moment the ogre stomped down on the blade, putting his full weight on it. The prince struggled but couldn't pull the sword free. Letting go, he whipped around to run. Two more ogres stepped up, surrounding him.

As one, the beasts raised their clubs.

# Chapter 56: Out of time

Bellchar blinked dully. Tom's expression pleaded with the troll. The ogres behind Bellchar were getting restless.

"I saved your life. You owe me," said Tom.

"Bellchar even."

"Without me you would've drowned. Imagine what it would be like to drown in quicksand."

Bellchar regarded him for a long moment.

"And he," continued Tom, pointing at Dummere, "ran away and left you to die."

Bellchar slowly turned. Several ogres stood behind him, Dummere stood first in line.

Bellchar raised his club. The ogres stepped back, nervously facing the huge troll.

"Bellchar?" said Dummere, displaying a broad, phony smile. "It me. Your friend Dummere."

"Friend? You left me to drown." Bellchar pulled back his club, winding up as if he was standing at home plate in Wrigley Field on opening night.

Hearing an odd sound Tom gazed upward into the darkened sky then stepped beside the troll.

Bellchar paused, then followed Tom's gaze. The ogres' heads rose in unison.

Up in the sky, highlighted by the dim light from the Ring of Turin, a faint dot appeared. The dot split into five dots. The dots grew. The dots sprouted wings. The dots roared.

"Dragons!" screamed an ogre.

\* \* \*

"It's Tom and his friends," cried Juanita, pointing down the dim torch lit street. "They're surrounded by ogres." She drew her sword preparing to run, but stopped when she noticed Larraj's staff had begun to glow.

The wizard raised his arm. Brighter and brighter the staff flared as it prepared to unleash its magical fury. Juanita squinted and turned away from the blinding light. One of the ogres, surrounding Tom and his friends, suddenly pointed to the sky. The other ogres glanced up, howled, then bolted away.

Larraj lowered his staff. The light slowly faded. He and Juanita turned, then stared upward in awe.

* * *

Kiran dashed from the alley onto the main battlefield. A moment later the two ogres appeared and were gaining on him. To his right the castle gate lay closed, with what remained of the elven army valiantly standing their ground, awaiting the main wave of the ogre forces which were almost upon them.

Kiran thought he might be able to make it to the elven army before the ogres got there. Rushing toward them he could feel the thundering footfalls of the ogres that chased him. Even so, he suddenly stopped and his jaw fell open.

Just ahead, ogres leapt aside as five dragons landed in their midst. The winged beasts' mighty talons scored the ground, leaving deep trenches behind them, as they skidded to a stop.

Ninosh, the largest of the five, landed directly in front of Kiran. The dragon's eyes latched first onto Kiran, then onto the two ogres which chased him.

"Down!" boomed Ninosh. Kiran dove to the ground just as the ogres reached for him. Flames flooded directly over Kiran's head. His cloak began to smoke. The two startled ogres leapt away from the blast, then bolted off in terror!

The dragon lowered himself as he faced Kiran. "Well, come on then."

Kiran grinned. Scrambling to his feet he patted his smoldering cloak then quickly clamored up Ninosh's leg and onto his neck. Ninosh rose up tall and stomped toward the battle.

The five giant lizards formed a line in front of the startled elven warriors. Ninosh raised his head and roared. The other four dragons did likewise. Their combined cries shook the ground. Ninosh surveyed the ogres frozen in shock. Wisps of smoke and steam rose from his flared nostrils. As one, the five dragons spewed a wall of flame toward the now panicked ogres.

Ninosh turned to the frightened elven guard saying, "What? Never fought beside a dragon before?"

Sanuu blinked, then raised his sword and charged. Racing beneath Ninosh's outstretched wing he met the ogre forces head on. The elven army cheered and raced after him, swords held high.

Wingtip to wingtip the dragons strode slowly forward. With each step the ground thundered. Ogre spears bounced harmlessly off their armored hides. As they marched, they swept their heads left and right sending a wall of flames over the elves heads, lighting up the dark battlefield and causing the ogres to flee wildly in all directions.

As if a general leading the dragon army himself, Kiran rode proudly upon Ninosh's neck.

# Chapter 57: Never too late

In the dim light, with the battle raging near the castle's main gate, no one seemed to notice when a tiny green dot appeared near the outer shield wall. The dot pulsed and danced, weaved and shuddered. It appeared timid, at first, as if it shouldn't be there, as if its very existence violated the laws of physics. Which indeed many Earth scientists might have said it did.

The dot seemed to struggle to exert its will over nature. After all, what did nature know of what was possible, or impossible, for that matter?

"*Whoomp!*" Suddenly the dot expanded into a large green square, its edges pulsing and seething with brilliant green sparks, all the while making a loud crackling sound. Something had torn a hole between universes and seemed to dare anyone to say it had no right.

In the center of the green portal a hazy outline of a figure appeared. Though moving in slow motion, the figure grew steadily larger as it approached. Detail resolved into sharp focus—a wide brimmed hat, a weathered leather aviator's jacket, and an antique hand gun raised high.

A moment later the figure stepped through the portal just as the breech collapsed '*Boom.*' The battle field shook. Green sparks flew in all directions.

Carlos was thrown to the ground from the power of the portal closing. Jumping to his feet, he whirled around, shielding his eyes from the remaining sparks. "Now what? The portal was supposed to stay open."

Turning around his jaw dropped as hundreds of fat green monsters, carrying clubs and spears, charged straight for him. He blinked. "Ogres? You've got to be kidding." He took a step back. The beasts kept running toward him. He raised his gun, pointing it at the nearest one. Cocking his head sideways he scrunched up his face and pulled the trigger "*click.*" He pulled the trigger again "*click,*" "*click.*"

The nearest ogre lifted its club above him. Carlos threw his gun at the monster then raised his arms in front of his face, trying to protect himself. But the beast froze.

*Huh?* Carlos blinked. *I must've scared him.* He lowered his arms.

"What? Ya chicken?" yelled Carlos. But the beast wasn't looking at him, Carlos realized. The ogre looked past him. Carlos slowly turned. The ground shook as five huge pterodactyl-like creatures, wings outstretched, thundered straight for him. A blast of fire erupted from two of the monsters.

Carlos stared up at them dumbfounded. "Dragons? First ogres, now dragons? What next?"

He looked down. Hundreds of thin long-eared aliens, swords drawn, dashed between the dragon's upraised wings and charged toward him.

*And I suppose those are elves, right? What else would they be?* He started to laugh hysterically till he realized he was about to be run over by the mob. He dove behind the massive body of a fallen ogre and covered his head as the elven warriors charged past, intent on reaching their foes, apparently the ogres.

Remembering the radio still held in his hand he twisted the knob and spoke, "Tom, are you there? This is Carlos, over." A pause.

"General Kanak here. Yes, your highness?" Carlos tipped his head sideways and stared at the radio.

As the first wave of aliens passed Carlos timidly rose up to peer over the fallen creature. "General who? Ah—I'm looking for Tom—" But before he could continue, a huge reptilian foot slammed to the ground beside him. Carlos rolled away. The beast's other foot crashed down, mere millimeters from his outstretched hand. Looking up, the dragon's scale-covered underbelly passed directly overhead. Carlos wrinkled up his face and twisted away. "Oh—that smell."

The winged beast stopped, swiveled its long neck, steam wafting from its nostrils as it glared down at him. A voice suddenly sprang into Carlos' head "That smell?"

Carlos' eyes bulged as the dragon flared its nostrils, then sniffed him.

"It is you, human, who smells bad." The creature uncoiled its long neck, then continued on.

Carlos shakily rose to his feet staring dumbfounded at the retreating form of a talking dragon. Then a second wave of elves began rushing past. Before he could dive to the ground, one of the soldiers collided with him. The two collapsed in a heap. Carlos used his elbows to scramble backwards.

The warrior raised his sword, then stopped. "Another Earthling? How? They're multiplying like zapter-flies!"

"Are you really—an elf?" asked Carlos.

"Of course I'm an elf! What else would I be?" The warrior whipped around and sprinted toward the battle.

"No Wait!" cried Carlos, reaching for him in vain. "If you recognize I'm from Earth. You must've seen my sister and my nephew." But the soldier was gone.

*I was right. He's an elf.* Carlos chuckled. *Of course he's an elf. Ogres and dragons and elves, oh my.* He started laughing uncontrollably. *What's next? Trolls and dwarves?* His merriment was cut short, however, as hundreds more elves rushed past. This time, there was no fallen ogre to hide behind, so he just dove to the ground. Some of the warriors were nice enough to run around him, while others jumped over him, but some just ran right across him.

\* \* \*

At the blare of a mighty horn, King Dakshi squinted, scanning the forest beyond the shield wall for the source of the disturbance. Slowly cresting the far rise, row upon row of tall banners flapped in the breeze. Soon the holders of the banners marched close enough to be visible in the shield wall torchlight. Dwarves carried the banners. King Abban, Goban's father and king of the dwarves, strode boldly out front. Behind the standard bearers marched row upon row of dwarf soldiers carrying battle axes, crossbows, and a few mostly broken boards slung over their shoulders.

"My dear friend Abban. He's always late to the party," said King Dakshi with a wry grin.

Tappus snorted involuntarily, then quickly regained his composure.

"You won't tell his Majesty I said that, will you?"

Tappus grinned and shook his head.

* * *

"Have you ever seen such a sight?" Tom asked, as he watched the elves and dragons fighting side-by-side.

Avani shook her head.

Suddenly the hairs on the back of Tom's neck began to stand on end. He glanced at his watch. A familiar sound dropped lower and lower in pitch until it could no longer be heard.

By now the nearby ogres had all run away, leaving only Bellchar. The ground shook beneath their feet, accompanied by a rumbling noise. Blades of grass began to twitch, highlighted with blue sparks.

Bellchar faced Tom, his dark hollow eyes looked sad. Tom raised his arm by his side, palm outward toward the troll. More blue lightning raced across the ground beneath their feet. Slowly Bellchar raised his own leathery hand, in the same manner.

"Thank you," said Tom.

"Bellchar even," said the troll.

"More than even," replied Tom. Impulsively, Tom reached out to hug the troll's leg, but before he could, Bellchar was launched high into the sky as the barrier sprang up. In fact, as far as Tom could see, thousands of ogres were catapulted into the air, topping out at some point then falling back to hit the barrier, then being launched skyward once more, eventually flying off into the forest beyond.

"Bye Bellchar," said Tom, looking up into the dark sky. He could no longer see his friend.

Tom did, however, spot Ninosh. For even the dragons had been launched skyward, though they just spread their wings and flew.

Ninosh flapped strongly, hovering nearby.

Tom waved to the dragon. Ninosh appeared to see him. *Did he nod?*

"Thanks," whispered Tom.

A voice immediately sprang into his head saying, "'Twas an honor, Thomas Holland. Apparently I, too, am part of the Prophecy. We shall be remembered together in legend."

"I'm glad you came back," said Tom, a tear trickling down his cheek. "Thanks!"

Tom squinted. A tiny figure rode the dragon. He pulled Avani's sleeve. "Is that Kiran?" Tom pointed at Ninosh.

Avani's mouth fell open.

At that, Ninosh flared his nostrils, let out a fierce piercing cry, then banked hard and flew off northward. The other dragons followed, for a time, then they each split off, heading their own separate ways.

"Well, Kiran's gonna have a story to tell," said Tom, watching the retreating form of the pair as they disappeared into the darkness.

Avani only nodded.

\* \* \*

"General Kanak, are you there?" King Dakshi held his breath. "General Kanak. Respond!" Only static for a time, then finally the line crackled to life.

"General Kanak here. Is this King Dakshi?"

"Who else would it be?" The king sighed. "My son—Prince Devraj…" The king glanced at Sanuu.

A pause seemed to draw on forever. "The prince took a hit to his sword arm, but he'll live," blared the general's voice from the device.

A look of deep relief spread across the king's face. He let out a long held breath, then resumed in a more dignified tone, "I'll send a healer for my son. Have your troops aid King Abban and the dwarf army in any way you can."

"Yes sire," replied the general. "It will be my pleasure."

# Chapter 58: A universe apart

"Where are the others, Prince Goban and The Keeper of the Light?" asked The Guardian, in the Citadel's now well-lit main chamber. The central control panel's crystals glowed bright and columns of continuously changing numbers filled the 3-D holographic displays nearby. This time The Guardian had chosen the guise of a humble monk.

Tom answered, "We slept in late. Goban's off at the castle, with his dad. Probably eating. Avani's with her grandparents. She lent me the key to the Citadel."

"For a thousand years the secret society of the 'Keepers of the Light' have guarded that key with their very lives. Only senior members of the ancient society were allowed inside this sacred shrine." The monk frowned. "Now it has become a mere tourist attraction with people traipsing in and out at their leisure."

"Whatever," said Tom, as he pulled a dark black cube from his pocket. He rolled the heavy object around in his palm, then placed it on the control panel. "By the way, I found this in the crashed space ship. It contains a sort of star map." Instantly laser beams shot from the ceiling and scanned the object. A moment later the lasers stopped and a green flashing square appeared a few feet away on the control panel.

Tom reached for the cube, assuming The Guardian wanted him to place it on the green square, but before his hand touched it, several small holes opened across the control panel's surface. Up from the holes sprang hundreds of tiny ant-sized robots, making clicking noises as they rushed to the cube. Once there, the miniature bots lifted the cube, moved it to the glowing square and set it down. Then the bots rushed back to where they came from and the holes closed.

With a deep hum the cube receded into the surface of the control panel. When it was flush with the top, a 3-D hologram of the same star map Tom had seen in the space ship appeared before them.

"Wow, that was cool," said Tom. "But you could've just asked me to move it, instead of using your micro-bot minions."

The monk-clothed Guardian ignored Tom's remark. "You are somewhat correct in calling it a star map. It is, however, far more than that. It is actually a map of parallel universes. See that green sphere around the object to your left?"

Tom nodded.

"That dot represents your universe. Touch it."

Leaning over the control panel Tom stood on his tip toes and reached up. As his finger approached the green sphere the area expanded until a new star map filled the room.

"This is your universe," said The Guardian. Thousands of multi-shaped objects floated above them. "Those are your galaxies. Touch the one on the far right surrounded by the green triangle." Tom did. The view expanded again until the Milky Way filled the room. "See that green cube in the spiral arm? That is your solar system."

Tom reached up and the view expanded once more. "That's Earth!" Tom pointed excitedly at the map. "And there's the Sun and Mars and Venus." He pointed at the Earth and the scene expanded yet again. "And look. There's the moon. And on the Earth I can see the continents. There's even clouds, and the clouds are moving. Whoa! Is this in real-time?"

The Guardian nodded. "Yes, it is happening in your universe as we speak."

Tom stepped back and the scene shrunk to its original view of the universes.

"So, if the left green sphere represents my universe, what do the other green spheres represent?"

"The second sphere is a map of this universe. The one that contains Elfhaven's solar system."

"And the third green sphere?" Tom reached up and touched the last green sphere. Another universe expanded into a beautiful collage of wholly different galaxies.

The Guardian said, "That is the universe where my creators live."

Tom pointed to a green square that expanded into a beautiful multi-fingered galaxy, the fingers of which each curved off gracefully at the ends. "They live there?"

"Yes," said the monk.

Tom lowered his hand and once again the map shrank to the original view.

"Wow," said Tom. "Each one of those points of light are actually a separate parallel universe?"

The Guardian nodded.

"Cool! Mom will go ape over this." Tom scratched his neck. "So what's that red sphere around the fourth object."

"That universe is off limits."

"Off limits?" said Tom.

"Long ago, back when the race that first created and installed me here were exploring the nearby universes, as part of that exploration, they opened a portal to several unremarkable universes, but when they opened a portal to that one—" The Guardian's transparent hand reached up and the universe surrounded by the red sphere expanded several times until it showed a close-up of a planet. Bright crimson ribbons of lava flowed freely across its dark surface. Lightning flashed constantly all over the globe and near the poles an eerie orange glow pulsed and seethed in an ocean of light.

The Guardian continued, "several beings came through. The locals, here in Elfhaven mistakenly called them demons, but they were nothing like the demons that inhabit this world. These were powerful creatures of pure evil that fed on people's life force."

"Like vampires, only they drink life force instead of blood?" asked

Tom, in horror.

The Guardian monk nodded. "Quaintly put, but yes."

"What happened? What did they do?"

"Many lives were lost. It took years, but finally my creators, aided by hundreds of Elfhaven wizards, captured the vile beings and sent them back to their own universe, to their own planet. I closed the portal and they've been trapped there ever since."

Tom gulped. The universe map shrank back inside the cube and the cube slowly rose up from the control panel.

"Thanks for all you've done," said Tom, still in a bit of shock. "Mom will let you know when we're ready, so you can open a portal to Earth." Tom picked up the cube and started to leave.

"Thank you Tom Holland. Without your help I would no longer exist. Oh, and I have a special goodbye gift for you." Once more a hum sounded and a small black orb, an inch and a half across, rose from the control panel.

Tom walked over and picked up the object. "What's this?" It felt warm and like the cube, was remarkably heavy for its small size.

"It is an upgrade for your robot Chloe. When you rebuild her, just place the unit on top of Chloe's CPU. The device will do the rest."

"Chloe was destroyed. I can't rebuild her. Without her memories, stored on her hard-drive, she wouldn't be the same—"

The Guardian regarded Tom with a knowing look, but remained silent.

# Chapter 59: The Prophecy's over?

"Tom," Avani waved as she sat on the front steps of her grandparent's house.

Tom walked over and sat beside her.

"I want to read you something."

"Ah—sure. OK. What is it?"

Avani reached behind her and withdrew one of the books they'd rescued from the Library of Nalanda. "It's the Prophecy of Elfhaven."

"Wow. I forgot all about it," said Tom.

Avani opened the ancient tome to a page near the beginning. She cleared her throat.

> *"In the year of the serpent, space folds;*
> *Creature and boy, odd companions—"*

"Larraj already told me that," Tom said, interrupting her.

"He did? When?"

"In the Citadel. After we saved Elfhaven the first time."

Avani nodded. "I'll bet he didn't tell you this part." She rifled through several more pages, then stopped.

> *"Their mechanical pet,*
> *sacrifices her spirit to save Elfhaven,*
> *sacrifices her body to save the boy."*

"It's talking about Chloe. By spirit it means her power. Remember? We used the juice from her battery to get the barrier temporarily back up. That bought us enough time to go get the replacement power supply, well nearly enough time."

"Of course I remember," said Avani, frowning. "I was there, you know."

"And the second reference," began Tom, ignoring her remark, "is when she attacked the troll and saved my life."

"With the gremlin's help," Avani reminded him.

"True."

"Shall I go on?" she asked.

"Sure."

Avani cleared her throat once more.

> *"Aided by a king among dragons,*
> *Creature and boy retrieve the magic talisman;*
> *Restoring The Citadel to its past glory."*

"And that," said Tom, excitedly, "means Ninosh. Creature and boy, hmmm, that's odd. It must mean Max and me. I guess you and Goban don't get any credit." Tom smiled sheepishly, then continued. "Anyway, then it refers to us finding the new power source and installing it."

Avani nodded and began again,

> *"The third time—"*

"Wait. What?" said Tom. "But it only happened twice!"

Avani just stared at him.

He stared back.

"Shall I continue?" she asked, placing her hand lightly on his.

Tom paused. Then slowly nodded. She removed her hand and turned the page.

Avani fidgeted, then, with her head still down over the book, she glanced up at Tom. The silence lengthened.

"OK, so read it already."

# Chapter Fifty-Nine

Avani let out a long slow breath.

> "The boy and The Chosen One stand at a precipice;
> The two must decide;
> One shall live;
> One must die;
> Elfhaven hangs in the balance;
> The boy chooses—poorly."

"What? No!" cried Tom. Inside the house Max whined, then pawed at the door. "Just a minute, Max."

"That can't be right! It's gotta be wrong." Beads of sweat formed on his forehead. "For one thing, I won't even be here. I'm going home—to Earth."

Avani's eyes rapidly scanned his face. Closing the book she thrust it toward Tom.

"What?" he said.

"I want you to have it."

"But—I can't read elvish."

"Doesn't matter. It's about you. You should keep it."

Max whined again.

"Hold on Max."

Tom took the book and turned it over in his hands. It was heavy and felt dry, rough, and smelled of old leather. He nodded. "Thanks."

Avani squirmed nervously. "Do you think The Chosen One means me?"

"Probably. The Magic Crystals chose you." Now Tom squirmed.

"I think they've chosen both of us."

Tom stood and opened the door. Max burst outside, nearly knocking Avani off the steps. Running back and forth in the street he barked at them. Tom walked down to him.

"Shush," he said, petting his dog absently. "This still doesn't make any sense. We've already saved Elfhaven. There's no need for anything more. The Citadel is at full power. The power will last a thousand years. Larraj will catch Naagesh, I'm sure. The trolls and ogres are a bit dim, but they must've learned their lesson by now, don't you think?"

"I'm sure you're right," she said, standing up. "The Prophecy is more of a guideline than a law."

Tom laughed.

"What's funny?"

"That's a line from '*Pirates of the Caribbean*.'" Tom stood up tall and spoke in a deep voice, "The code is more what you'd call '*guidelines*' than actual rules."

"Pirates of the Ka—ra—bee—an?" she said, slowly.

"It's a movie. Oh right. I never explained movies..." Tom walked around in a circle, thinking. Max followed him, looking up at him, wagging his tail.

"A movie is a story you watch and listen to, but it isn't real."

"Not real?" she said, tipping her head sideways.

Tom frowned and stopped walking. "Actor's play roles." Tom's eyes lit up. "Like in plays. You must have plays here, right?"

"Sure, we have many great playwrights: Chekhon, Wildest, Softarplees, Shakeclub."

"Shakeclub?" said Tom. He blinked a couple times then continued, "A movie just records the play so you can watch it whenever you want."

Avani's eyes lit up and she hurried down the steps and stood beside him. "It's magic."

Tom snorted. "Close enough."

"Oh Tom. So there is magic in your world. I knew it! I'd love to see Earth."

Tom looked dumb-founded. "Ah—I thought you weren't interested in seeing my world."

"That was before, when you said there wasn't magic on your planet. But now you've proved there is."

Tom studied her face. "Technology, ah—Earth magic is different than your magic. Though it's no less amazing, if you think about it."

"I wish you'd stay here in Elfhaven," she said, then hastily added. "Stay here with Goban and me. With Malak and Chatur, with the ghost of the library and the Guardian." Impulsively she leaned over and kissed him on the cheek. Tom swallowed.

Avani stepped back then pulled nervously on her tunic. "It's just that I—er—we are going to miss you." She looked away. Tom stepped forward, reached up and slowly turned her face back toward him. A tear cascaded down her cheek. He wiped the tear away.

"I'll miss you, too. You and Goban I mean. You two are my best friends. I've got a friend back home. He's my next door neighbor, James. But he's nothing like you and Goban. James is my best friend on Earth because he's my only friend. At school, I'm always the last one chosen for team sports, and in the lunch room kids won't sit beside me. I guess they're afraid my unpopularity will rub off on them." Tom gave a hollow laugh. "Plus I'm a favorite target for bullies. They're always beating up on me."

"Then why don't you stay here? You're famous. A hero. Everybody likes you here."

"Everybody?" said Tom, with a wry grin.

Avani laughed. She looked down at her feet and kicked a small stone hard. A creature down the street gave a high-pitched squeal.

"Devraj is a special case," she said.

Tom faced her. "As Goban once said, 'Devraj is special, alright,'"

Avani smiled. "He's just jealous of you, that's all." Tom's eyes bore deep into hers for a moment, then he took her hand.

"Come on," he said. I need to say a few goodbyes before I leave.

# Chapter 60: A few goodbyes

As they headed for the Elfhaven Library, Larraj strode up beside Tom and Avani.

"Good meeting, Larraj," said Tom, in the traditional elven greeting.

"Well met," responded the wizard, nodding first to Avani, then Tom.

"On your way to the Library?" Larraj asked Tom.

"Yup."

"Tell The Librarian we may soon be adding a new wing to his library."

Tom tipped his head sideways, inquisitively.

"Thanks to your discovery at the Library of Nalanda, the books are no longer safe there. I will soon lead an expedition to recover the books on magic. They must not fall into Naagesh's hands. I shudder to think what might happen if he had access to all that knowledge, to all that power."

Tom glanced at Avani uneasily.

Larraj stopped, as did the other two. The wizard cleared his throat. "Speaking of books from the Library of Nalanda, and using dark magic in particular." Larraj adopted a stern look. "You should not have read from the book on dark magic, let alone used a spell from it."

"But," began Tom. "If we hadn't—"

The wizard raised his hand, interrupting him. "Naagesh might've killed you, I know. Yet the end does not always justify the means. What if you couldn't control the demon hordes? What if the demons had turned on you? What if they then turned on the elves and the dwarves? Did you consider that?"

"I—" began Tom.

Avani broke in, "It was my fault. I used the spell—but, I wasn't strong enough by myself. I needed Tom's help."

The wizard regarded them both for a long moment. "Well, you succeeded this time. Just don't try any more spells from that book in the near future. I'd like to hold onto the book for you, for a time. I will keep it safe, I promise. When, and if, you are ready I will teach you how to use its magic safely." Avani nodded.

"In fact," Larraj continued. "I'm reopening the magic school. I expect you two to attend class tomorrow."

"Ah—I think I'll be out of town," said Tom. "Mom wants to head back to Earth today."

"I was afraid you might say that. I will be sorry to see you go. You show great magical promise. Plus you've done more than you know for Elfhaven. I, and the people of Elfhaven, are forever in your debt, Tom Holland." Larraj bowed low.

Tom blushed.

"Take care, I'll see you again before you leave." The wizard headed off toward the castle.

The two watched as the wizard walked away, his staff dragging in the dirt. The trail the staff drew on the dry dusty ground, twisted and wriggled, and then seemed to sparkle. Suddenly the wriggling trail turned into a snake. The serpent roared then spread six tiny wings and flew straight for them. Taking a step backwards, their hands flew up to protect themselves. Just before the creature slammed into them, it dissolved in a shower of multi-colored sparks. They stared at each other, then at the wizard's retreating form. Larraj glanced over his shoulder, grinned, then continued casually on his way.

Tom and Avani laughed uneasily.

"Come on," she said. Grabbing Tom's hand, Avani pulled him after her, forcing him to run.

They found Kiran and Goban sitting on the Library steps waiting for them.

"Thought you'd show up here eventually," said Goban.

"Kiran," said his sister, running over to him. "You survived your dragon ride, I see. Tell us all about it."

"It was amazing!" began Kiran. "Ninosh flew me clear around Elfhaven valley up past Icebain Falls, to the Library of Nalanda. It was dark, but the Ring of Turin's light was enough to make out some stuff. I could see lights from the dwarf city of Deltar, sparkling in the distance. Then we flew south over the edge of the Deathly Bog and I saw torch lights reflecting off the water from the lake elves floating city. Finally, we circled back and Ninosh dropped me off near the south gate. By then the elf and dwarf armies had defeated the last of the ogres—those who hadn't already run away, that is. The dwarves kept their distance, until they saw me waving at them. It was great!"

Avani grinned proudly at her brother. "Wow. That was quite an adventure!"

"You deserved it," said Tom. "If you hadn't called Ninosh in the first place, not only would we have failed to get the power source here in time, there'd have been no dragons to help defeat the ogre army. It was really you who saved Elfhaven."

Kiran beamed.

Avani hugged her little brother tight. "Come on, Tom wants to say goodbye to The Librarian." The four raced up the library steps, pulled open the massive door and walked briskly to The Librarian's desk. The ghost sat there attempting to polish a crystal paperweight but of course, his hand passed right through it.

Without looking up, The Librarian frowned at the paperweight and asked, "May I help you?" Then his gaze rose. "Oh—it's you, is it?" The ghost floated out of his seat. "Back so soon from your quest? Made it through Demon Forest alive, did you?" The Librarian twitched when he mentioned the name of the dreaded forest.

Kiran leaned forward and narrowed his eyes. "We were tricked by a demon into going through the cave of—"

"That's OK, Kiran." Tom interrupted him.

"Not my fault." The Ghost glared at Kiran. "I agreed to lead you to—" he paused. "To the entrance of Demon Forest. Any, ah—poor choices you made afterwards were not my fault."

Tom stepped forward. "Nobody's blaming you. In fact, I want to thank you. We were too late to warn the king, but if we hadn't taken that route we probably wouldn't have found the power source.

"Without your help Elfhaven might've been lost. In fact, I'll bet they write songs about your bravery." At that, the ghost drew himself up to his full height. He actually smiled, the first time Tom had ever seen the grumpy old ghost do so.

"His bravery?" spat Kiran, but his sister elbowed him hard in his side. The Librarian leaned forward, glaring at the boy.

"Anyway," said Tom. "I just wanted to say thanks and goodbye."

The spirit raised an eyebrow. "Goodbye?"

"Yes. Mom wants to head back to Earth today. There's nothing more for us to do here."

The ghost pursed his lips, drew in a mock breath, then leaned forward solemnly and stuck out his hand to Tom.

Tom reached up to shake the spirit's hand, but his hand passed right through the ghost's.

"Got you!" laughed the spirit.

Tom shook his head. Waving goodbye, he took a step toward the door then stopped. "Oh, and Larraj says you'll need a new wing for your library."

"A new wing?" said the ghost, looking perplexed.

"Yes. On the way to the crash site, we found an entrance to the Library of Nalanda. The books are all intact. The wizard's going to bring them here, for you to keep safe."

The ghost froze. "Here? Thousands of books on magic? In my charge?" The Librarian puffed up with pride like a blow fish.

\* \* \*

"Oh, there you are," said Juanita.

Avani closed the book she was reading and stood up from her seat on the library steps. "Hello."

"Avani, is there somewhere us girls can have a little heart-to-heart?"

Avani looked inquisitively at her. "How about Bandipur Park?"

Juanita motioned to Avani. "Lead the way."

As they walked Juanita said, "I want to thank you for what you've done for Tom."

"What I've done?"

"Yes, before Tom arrived in Elfhaven, he was—well, how do I put this—a little shy and insecure. He's bright, so other kids made fun of him. Called him names."

Avani cringed. "Yes, he mentioned being called a wimp."

"He was also deathly afraid of heights. Now he's flying dragons, for heaven sakes. Mostly with his eyes open."

Avani met Juanita's gaze. They both laughed.

"You think I helped Tom get over his fear of heights?"

"That, and a lot more. He's really blossomed here. He's learned strengths he didn't know he had. Mostly because of you."

Avani blushed. "Here we are. Bandipur Park." She gestured toward a bench. They sat down.

"Can I ask you something," began Avani. "Something personal?"

"Of course, hon. You're the closest thing to a daughter I've ever had."

Avani's eyes twinkled as she smiled at Juanita. "It's just that I don't really have any females I can talk to. I never knew my mom. Nanni's great, but she's way too old."

"And I'm not?"

Avani blushed again. "Well, not nearly as old as she."

Juanita chuckled. "Go on."

Avani took a deep breath then slowly exhaled. "It's just that—well, I've been engaged since birth to Devraj. I've always known we'd someday be married. But now that it's getting close, and—and—"

"And you're not sure you want to marry him. Is that it?"

"I—I don't know." Avani winced.

"Do you love him?"

Avani sighed, paused, then finally answered, "I—I'm not sure. What does love feel like?"

"Love is made up of several stages. The first, and strongest, is the infatuation phase. That's where you're happy when you're with the person and sad when you're not. You're constantly thinking about them. You don't feel hungry much and you can't concentrate on what you need to be doing."

Juanita put her arm around Avani's shoulders. "Is that how you feel about Devraj?"

"Definitely not!" Avani paused. "Is being in love important?"

Juanita drew in a long breath. "That's a tough one. In most cultures back on Earth, people choose a mate that they're in love with. However, some cultures have arranged marriages, like yours."

"Is one way better than the other?"

"My culture believes being in love before marriage is critical."

"But what do you think?"

Juanita regarded Avani thoughtfully. "I've seen people that were in love when they married and spent a long and happy lifetime together. I've seen others who were madly in love at first, but their marriage was a disaster."

"And what about arranged marriages?"

Juanita stared deep into Avani's eyes. "I've less experience with those. One of the scientists on my team back home is from India. They have arranged marriages there. I've spoken with her a little on the subject." Juanita paused. "A deeper phase of love is when people love each other out of long shared experiences. They know each other so well they can often finish each other's sentences, and know each other's thoughts. I think that can happen in time, in either arranged, or marriages that began with infatuation."

Avani lowered her head in thought.

Juanita watched her closely. "Do you love someone else?"

"No!" Avani blurted. Then she giggled. "At least, I don't think so."

Juanita scanned Avani face intently. "Tom and I are leaving for home today."

Avani didn't respond.

Juanita stared at her for a long moment, then put her arm around Avani and squeezed her tight. "Speaking of leaving. We have some goodbyes to say. Come on." They both stood up.

"Thanks!" said Avani.

Juanita smiled. "My pleasure, honey."

# Chapter 61: Time's a wasting!

"Can't you at least stay for the ceremony? You're sure to get another medal," pleaded Avani, standing beside her brother in Elfhaven castle's central courtyard.

Tom sighed. "I've got enough medals. I've eaten enough bizarre food, and I still don't want to learn to dance." He gazed deep into Avani's sparkling eyes. "I'll miss you. And Goban, of course."

"What about me?" said Kiran.

"I'll miss you, too."

Kiran smiled so large, Tom thought his face might split.

"How about Devraj?" A wry grin crossed Avani's face.

Tom laughed. "I guess. Even the prince. And I'll miss the wizard Larraj."

"Speaking of the wizard, wouldn't you enjoy going back to magic school?"

"That would be fun. I was just getting the hang of it."

Avani snorted.

"Well, sort of," he replied, sheepishly.

Their gremlin friend stood beside Max staring up at him.  '

Kiran knelt down and petted Max. Tom knew it would be hard for Kiran to say goodbye to Max. And he knew Max would miss Kiran too. Tom gazed at them both thoughtfully.

A moment later Tom's mom walked up. Juanita led someone whose arm hung in a sling and whose head was partly wrapped in bandages.

"Uncle Carlos?" Tom bolted to his uncle, threw his arms around him and hugged him tight. "Carlos! Oh, in all the excitement, I forgot. The Guardian said you were trying to open a portal."

"Ouch," winced his uncle. "Yeah, it's me. I came to rescue you two." Tom let go, reluctantly.

"He opened a portal right as the dragons arrived," said his mother.

"I know," said Tom. "The Guardian asked me if he should help you. I said, 'Of course.'"

Carlos' shoulders sank a little. "I thought we opened the portal all by ourselves this time." He paused, then changed the subject. "I tried to shoot one of the ogres but my gun jammed."

"You're lucky it did," said his sister. "We're in another universe. The physics are different here, remember? You of all people should know that. Lucky you didn't blow your darn fool head off." Then she smiled at her brother.

Carlos returned a sheepish grin.

"So, other than talking dragons and the battle with the ogres, nothin' much happened since you two left Earth, huh?" said Carlos.

Juanita glanced at Tom. They both burst out laughing.

"I'll tell you the whole story later, once we're back on Earth." Juanita faced Tom. "Ready to go?" she said, ruffling his hair.

"Oh, Mom," complained Tom, but he looked her in the eye and slowly smiled. "I guess so."

Juanita raised her arm and glanced at her watch. "The Guardian said he'd open a portal to Earth in about—"

A single bright green dot appeared in the courtyard some twenty yards away. The dot quickly expanded into a green square accompanied by a loud "*whoosh!*" Not as dramatic as the last portal opening, yet the edges of the square pulsed and shifted as the unnatural breach between universes strained to close itself.

Juanita lowered her arm. "Just about now."

"Take care," Tom said to Avani, placing his hand on hers.

Tom noticed King Abban standing back a ways, near his son, Goban. The dwarf king's stout arms were wrapped around two plump smiling elven women. The king tipped his head toward Tom.

Tom smiled and nodded back.

Goban sauntered over and offered his fist. Tom extended his hand. The two bumped fists then immediately their hands flew up and apart. They each made gurgling noises as their fingers, like water droplets, drifted downward. Tom laughed then hugged his friend. Goban hugged him back.

"I brought you something to sustain you on your trip home." Goban reached into a pouch on his cloak and pulled out a wrapped bundle. "It's a slither-toad pastry. I know they're your favorite." A horrified look crossed Tom's face. Then Goban, Avani and Kiran all broke up. Tom winced.

"Oh, that reminds me." Tom pulled a roll of parchments from his hoodie. "Here. I drew up some plans for a simple submarine, in case the lake elves are ever in trouble. And also plans for a hang glider, just for fun." Tom handed Goban some sketches covered with tons of arrows and scribbled comments.

"Avani helped me translate written English into Dwarvish. The key to the hang glider is getting the CG, ah—Center of Gravity, right. Too far forward and you'll dive smack into the ground. Too far back and you'll stall, then dive smack into the ground."

Goban's eyes lit up as he eagerly scanned the documents. "This hand glider—"

"Hang glider," corrected Tom. "You *hang* from it—in a harness of sorts."

"This—hang glider—will allow dwarves to fly?"

"Just like those four winged monkey birds."

Tom's best friend hurriedly stuffed the plans in his tunic.

Tom shook Goban's hand, then as he, his mom, and his uncle headed toward the portal, up walked Larraj, Zhang Wu, and King Dakshi. Tom nodded to the wizard.

Larraj tipped his head in response. "Thank you Tom. For all that you've done. The Prophecy choose wisely in you."

Tom bumped his fist to his chest then extended his bent arm out sideways, his two middle fingers spread wide apart in the traditional Vulcan farewell. The wizard raised his brow, glancing sidelong at Juanita.

"It's a long story," she said.

The wizard tried awkwardly to match Tom's gesture.

Next Zhang stepped forward and threw back his cloak. From his belt he pulled the bone handled tooth encrusted dagger he'd picked up in the ogre armory. The monk spun the knife around and offered the handle to Tom. The bright morning sunlight reflected off the gemstone sending ruby-red light dancing across the courtyard.

"Here. You've proved yourself. You've earned a real knife."

"For me?" said Tom. He looked expectantly at his mom. "Can I keep it?"

She shook her head, but Carlos touched her arm lightly and said, "Of course you can. It's not a toy, though. You'll have to have your mom teach you how to handle it safely." Carlos grinned at his sister sidelong. Juanita glowered at her brother, but remained silent.

"Thanks!" said Tom to Zhang. Impulsively, Tom hugged the monk. Zhang froze, looking petrified. The wizard snorted as Tom released Zhang Wu. All the adults laughed, everyone except Zhang, who stepped back, whipped down his cloak and glared at them all.

Prince Devraj chose that moment to make his entrance. The prince's arm was also in a sling. He walked up to Tom holding a large gold medal hanging from a wide red sash.

"I know you're not staying for the ceremony," began Devraj. He cleared his throat. "But you earned this." The prince thrust the medal into Tom's hands. "You saved Elfhaven. With my help of course." Devraj paused, staring deeply into Tom's eyes. "I should have trusted you."

Tom grasped the object. "Ah—thanks. Is it my birthday or something?"

There was an awkward pause as Tom scanned the prince's face. "We don't always get to choose our friends." Tom stuck out his right hand toward Devraj, thumb up.

Devraj returned Tom's gaze for a moment, then grasped Tom's hand in his and shook it. A thin smile slowly spread across both their faces.

Avani stepped beside Devraj. The prince put his arm around her and squeezed. The two smiled at Tom.

Seeing Devraj and Avani not only getting along, but affectionate for one another caused Tom to falter. He couldn't speak. He just stared at them.


Juanita's eyes fell upon King Dakshi. "It was an honor meeting you, your highness." She curtsied.

"Surely, after all we've been through, there's no need for such formality," replied the king.

Juanita stepped forward and gave him a giant bear hug. The king appeared startled for an instant then smiled and hugged her back. The moment froze with a strained silence, then everyone cheered. Once the two released each other, Juanita extended one hand to Carlos and the other to Tom. Taking her hands, they all turned and walked briskly toward the portal.

"Wait!" cried Avani. The three glanced back as Avani hurried over to a wooden barrel, reached inside and lifted out an old leather pouch, then sprinted over to Tom.

"Here, I almost forgot." She thrust the pouch toward him. "I saved these for you." Taking it gingerly, Tom opened the drawstring and cautiously peered inside.

Tom gasped. "Chloe's parts!" Reaching in, he pulled out a large rectangular device. "Do you know what this is?"

Avani glanced at Goban. "Ah—no."

"It's Chloe's—my robot's hard drive."

Avani didn't respond.

"It's her memory. All her memories, in fact. From the moment I first flipped on her power switch right up till the moment she—" Tom paused. His eyes began to water. "—the moment she saved my life. Just before the troll—stomped on her."

Tom swallowed hard then reached into the bag and pulled out a square chip.

"And this is Chloe's CPU. Her brain. With these I can rebuild her. She'll be as good as new!" Impulsively, Tom pulled Avani close and hugged her tight. Avani glanced at the prince. Devraj's face went rigid.

"Ahhh—that's great," she said, blushing slightly as she awkwardly pushed him away.

Tom stepped back and wiped an unexpected tear from his cheek. Avani straightened her skirt.

"It's not my birthday, it's Christmas," said Tom, totally missing the awkward exchange. "Oh, and I just remembered." Still holding Chloe's CPU, Tom reached into a pouch on his belt and pulled out a small black sphere. "The Guardian gave me this. He said to place it on Chloe's CPU."

Tom reached to place the object, as The Guardian had instructed, but when the black sphere neared the chip it sprang from his palm and latched onto the top of Chloe's CPU. Immediately, tiny spindly silver legs extended from the sphere and attached themselves to the chip's metal leads. The orb hummed, vibrating Tom's hand as multicolored lights circled around the sphere. After a few seconds a clicking sounded and the device flared brightly. Then it went dark. Slowly Tom reached over and flicked the unit. Nothing happened. Grabbing the orb he tried to pull it off, but it appeared to be welded solid to the chip.

"That was weird." Tom shook it, studied it from all sides, then placed it back in the pouch.

"Come on Max," called Tom. Avani carefully lifted the gremlin off the dog's head.

Before Max could move, Kiran ran over and hugged him. "Bye Max. I'm gonna to miss you."

Max licked Kiran's face, then raised a paw. The young elf smiled and vigorously shook Max's paw. Kiran stood up and stepped back, a tear trickling down his cheek. Max trotted over to Tom as Kiran wiped the tear and dog slobber from his face.

Tom once again turned to the portal.

"No wait!" cried Avani, running up to him. Tom slowly turned back.

"There's more?" he said.

She leaned forward impulsively and kissed him on the cheek. Then she whispered in his ear, "You are hash-tag amazing. And don't forget it, or me!" She flashed him a huge smile, her eyes misting over slightly, then she hurried back to stand beside a frowning Prince Devraj.

Tom blinked a couple times, inhaled deeply, then grabbed his mom's hand. Together Tom, Juanita, Carlos, and Max walked to the portal.

"Oh, by the way," Tom said to his mom. "I almost forgot. What did you think of the—"

# Epilogue: Library books, long overdue...

The Ring of Turin cast its dim light on a skeletal hand. A dark figure twisted his distorted fingers in a well-practiced pattern. Green sparks raced around the hand arcing from one finger to the next. Launching from the hand, five separate beams of energy arced and twisted, then moved steadily forward, testing their surroundings. As the beams neared the rubble, strong magic that had guarded the Library of Nalanda for a hundred years responded to the challenge with orange lightning leaping outward from the rubble to meet the green magical onslaught. The orange magic took on the guise of a master warrior wielding a staff. The green magic morphed into a masterful sword bearing warrior.

Like a puppet master, the figure subtly moved his fingers. The arcing lines shifted causing the sword wielding warrior to dodge, parry and thrust. But the orange magic matched the green move for move. For several tense moments the two warriors, the two magics, seemed equally matched. Then a second bony hand rose to join its partner. Five more emerald energies leapt forth. Instantly, the green warrior drew a second sword and both swords sped up, redoubling the attack. Slowly the orange warrior retreated, farther and farther back, until finally he reached the ruins where his image exploded in a brilliant orange flare lighting up the petrified forest beyond with the brightness of midday. Yet even that power proved no match for the green and the protective magic collapsed in a soundless explosion of orange sparks. Deep shadows engulfed the vale once more.

The hooded figure floated forward. As the being approached the rubble, he once again raised his hand, this time with his index finger up. At his command, stones and rubble flew from his path. Likewise, his other hand rose and still more rocks flew. A moment later the way lay clear. Ancient runes above a partly collapsed doorway glowed white hot for an instant, then darkened as they cooled. The inscription read "Welcome to the Library of Nalanda. May you find the knowledge you seek. May you use it for the good of all."

The figure stepped through the doorway and opened his palm as he recited an incantation. Hundreds of magical light spheres raced ahead, illuminating the way forward into the far distance. Aisle after aisle of books spread out before him. An aisle ahead and off to his left had a crimson inscription that read: DANGER! Blackest of Magic. Only authorized wizards allowed!

A thin smile spread across Naagesh's face, then the wizard laughed. A playful laugh at first, it echoed joyfully down hallways that had not heard laughter in a hundred years. Then the sound turned into something entirely different; something sinister; something evil…